**Sheri WhiteFeather** is a
author. She writes a va
Mills & Boon and is kn
American elements into her stories. She has two grown
children, who are tribally enrolled members of the
Muscogee Creek Nation. She lives in California and
enjoys shopping in vintage stores and visiting art galleries
and museums. Sheri loves to hear from her readers
at www.sheriwhitefeather.com.

A former job-hopper, **Jessica Lemmon** resides in Ohio
with her husband and rescue dog. She holds a degree in
graphic design currently gathering dust in an impressive
frame. When she's not writing supersexy heroes, she can
be found cooking, drawing, drinking coffee (okay, wine)
and eating potato chips. She firmly believes God gifts us
with talents for a purpose, and with His help, you can
create the life you want.

Jessica is a social media junkie who loves to hear from
readers. You can learn more at www.jessicalemmon.com.

# A CONVENIENT TEXAS WEDDING

## SHERI WHITEFEATHER

# LONE STAR LOVERS

## JESSICA LEMMON

# MILLS & BOON

First Published in Great Britain 2018
by Mills & Boon, an imprint of HarperCollinsPublishers,
1 London Bridge Street, London, SE1 9GF

*A Convenient Texas Wedding* © 2018 Harlequin Books S.A.
*Lone Star Lovers* © 2018 Jessica Lemmon

Special thanks and acknowledgement are given to Sheri WhiteFeather for her contribution to the Texas Cattleman's Club: The Impostor series.

ISBN: 978-0-263-93594-3

51-0318

MIX
Paper from
responsible sources
FSC® C007454

This book is produced from independently certified FSC™ paper to ensure responsible forest management.

For more information visit: www.harpercollins.co.uk/green

Printed and bound in Spain
by CPI, Barcelona

# A CONVENIENT
# TEXAS WEDDING

## SHERI WHITEFEATHER

# One

Allison Cartwright was in a pickle. The dill of all dills, she thought. The big, fat sour kind sold in American delicatessens, known for making one's face pucker. She might as well be making that expression right now.

Her temporary visa would be expiring soon, and she didn't want to return to her family's sheep farm in Kenmare, Ireland, bleating like a lost lamb.

Presently, she sat in the passenger seat of an Uber car. The driver had picked her up at her apartment in Dallas, Texas, and was taking her to the exclusive Bellamy resort in Royal, Texas.

On this hot summer afternoon, she'd donned a sleeveless blouse and a long, pleated skirt with side pockets. Her deep red hair was smooth and straight, and her fair skin was scrubbed clean. Although she'd gotten used to thinking of herself as more plain than pretty, she sometimes wondered what being the sophisticated type would be like. But she had plenty of other things, besides her lack of glamour, to occupy her mind.

As the vehicle advanced on the interstate highway that led to Royal, she glanced down at her cowgirl-style boots with their brown leather, blue stitching and pointed toes. She'd purchased them when she first arrived in Texas, and this was where she wanted to stay. Even as a child, she'd been consumed with America, most specifically Texas, studying about it every chance she got. She'd always dreamed of living here.

During her teenage years, she helped out on her family's farm and took online writing courses. Once she became an adult, she sold magazine articles to a variety of publications. But she also had a regular job, waiting tables in a popular tourist spot. She worked her tail off, saving practically everything she earned so she could visit the States one day and write an epic novel with a dashing Texas hero.

Then, just this year, she'd had an affair with the worst person imaginable, a handsome rancher and businessman who'd charmed her from the first moment he'd come into the restaurant. She'd followed him here to Texas with romantic notions and had spent three months growing closer to the man she'd known as Will Sanders. But that wasn't who he was. About a month ago, she'd learned that his real name was Rich Lowell. By then, he was gone, completely out of her life. But that was a complex situation, too. When they were still together, she'd been informed that he'd been killed in a plane crash.

The funeral had been horrific. But the kicker? The *real* Will Sanders had shown up, walking straight into the service and stunning everyone in attendance. Allison had been shocked beyond belief, particularly when she'd discovered the truth. At the time, she'd thought the man who'd died, the man with whom she'd had an affair, *was* Will Sanders.

The impostor had even stolen Will's face, altering his appearance to look just like him. Allison wasn't privy to the details of where Will had been during the nearly two years that Rich had taken over his life. But she'd been supplied with enough information to know that Will had been recovering from injuries Rich had inflicted upon him.

At this point, Rich was presumed dead. But while the case was still under investigation, the people who'd attended the funeral had been warned to keep what they knew among themselves. For however long it took to fit the pieces altogether, the authorities wanted Will to stay out of sight and "play" dead, as if there had only ever been one Will Sanders all along.

In some ways, Allison felt like a ghost, too, floating around with her pain. Fool that she was, she'd given the impostor her life savings, right along with a piece of her naive heart.

But she was venturing forward, one cautious step at a time. She'd received an anonymous note to meet with someone at 2:00 p.m. today at the statue of Diana in the gardens of The Bellamy. In part the note read: *I heard that your visa is set to expire. Do you want a green card? If you do, I have an interesting proposal for you. Yours, Mr. X.*

She had no idea who this Mr. X was or where he'd heard about her visa or what made him assume that she might want a green card. He could have come to her home since he obviously knew her address, having sent her the note. But he'd invited her to meet in a public place instead. She hoped that meant he wasn't a raving lunatic.

However, just in case, she was armed with a can of

pepper spray in her right skirt pocket. Also, she figured that in an establishment like The Bellamy with security on staff, she could scream if he tried to accost her. Allison intended to be extra careful. Still, this was a risk, meeting a stranger and making herself vulnerable to him.

But damn it, she wanted a green card more than ever, especially after everything she'd been through. Forging ahead was a means of gaining her independence and restoring her self-worth, of not letting the man who'd broken her heart and stolen her money destroy what was left of her already fractured spirit.

Determined to stay strong, she glanced out the window, preparing for her meeting with Mr. X.

When she arrived at the hotel, she thanked the driver and exited the car. Making haste, she entered the lobby and checked her smartphone for the time. She had twenty minutes to spare.

She went over to the concierge and retrieved a map of the resort so she could make her way to the statue. The Bellamy sat on fifty-plus acres of lavish gardens. She wasn't going to wander the grounds without direction.

Thankfully, the marble statue was easy to find. As Allison crossed the lawn, she spotted it in the distance. Diana, the Roman goddess of the hunt, the moon, and nature, proved strong and beautiful, reaching for an arrow from her quiver.

But it wasn't only Diana that Allison saw. As she moved closer, she noticed a tall, striking man. He stood in front of the statue, with his stylishly messy black hair shining in the sun, and he was dressed in a button-down shirt and business tie. His shirtsleeves were rolled up, and with how powerful his aura was, he could've been daring the goddess to hand over one of her prized arrows to him.

Allison's breaths grew labored. He wasn't looking her way. His head was turned, his profile thrillingly familiar. Even from this range, she recognized him as Rand Gibson. He was closely associated with the real Will Sanders, and like Allison, he'd been at the funeral when all hell had broken loose.

Rand turned, all too suddenly, and appeared to catch sight of her from across the grass that separated them. She hoped that she didn't lose her footing and fall flat on her bum. Rand was a local celebrity of sorts, a much-talked-about millionaire playboy with a huge social media following. In her mind, he would make the quintessential book hero, the wild type who made women swoon. Even she had the maddest crush on him, and considering her latest ordeal, she shouldn't be having crushes on anyone.

In the real world, she barely knew Rand. Over the past month, since Will's funeral, they'd crossed paths a few times at the Texas Cattleman's Club here in Royal. Allison wasn't a member of the club. She'd been invited to go there by Megan Phillips, one of the other women who'd been hurt by Rich Lowell. But for now Allison was immersed in the mystery of Mr. X and how that was going to play out.

Rand couldn't be Mr. X, could he? No, she thought. It wasn't even two o'clock yet. Mr. X simply wasn't there yet. Besides, why would Rand offer to help her get a green card? And why would he send her an anonymous note? It didn't add up.

Yet, he seemed as if he were waiting for someone. Most likely he was there to rendezvous with one of his many lovers. Any moment now, a pleasure-seeking beauty was going to emerge from the other side of the garden and catwalk straight into his arms.

So what should Allison do? Keep heading toward the

statue to wait for Mr. X? It was too late to hide behind a tree until Rand was gone. He'd already seen her.

If he knew she was there to meet a stranger, with a can of pepper spray in her skirt pocket, would he shake his head and tell her to go home? Not to Dallas, but back to Kenmare, where she belonged?

With the stubbornness associated with redheads, Allison lifted her chin and flicked back her hair. She wasn't going anywhere, except straight over to that damnable statue. When Mr. X arrived, she would have to lead him away from Rand, if Rand was still milling about. Of course Mr. X might stand her up altogether. She could very well be the butt of a joke. But that was a chance she was willing to take.

As she cut a determined path toward the marble goddess, Rand set out, too, striding, it seemed, in Allison's direction.

He moved at an easy pace, a flicker of a smile forming on his lips. Allison tossed a quick glance over her shoulder, making certain there wasn't another woman behind her that Rand was smiling at. Nope. She was the only female there. Saints preserve her, but maybe he *was* Mr. X.

They came face-to-face, and her heart stuttered in her chest. His electric-green eyes bore into hers. She had green eyes, too, the same noticeably bright shade as his. But on him, she thought the color looked far more intense. Everything about him was supernaturally gorgeous. He stood broad-shouldered and regal, with features consisting of darkly arched eyebrows, a straight, strongly formed nose and a prominent jaw peppered with perfectly defined, expertly trimmed beard stubble. But the final dream factor was his supremely kissable mouth. Insane as it was, she actually imagined taking long, luscious, forbidden tastes of him.

He said, "You're early."

She replied, "So are you." And now she knew, without a shadow of a doubt, that he was the person who'd sent her the note.

He pulled a hand through his already ruffled hair. "I can tell you're surprised it was me."

She was still trying to comprehend it. She was also trying to stop from fixating on his mouth. She even had the weirdly carnal urge to run her tongue along the chiseled edge of his jawline.

"Why did you call yourself Mr. X?" she asked, wishing she wasn't having such bizarre thoughts about him.

"I heard that you're a writer, and I thought you might enjoy a bit of intrigue."

Allison only nodded. Besides being drawn to intrigue, being a freelance writer meant that she could travel and write from anywhere. Working in the States wasn't a problem for her.

Rand gestured to a small, ornately designed bench adjacent to the statue. "We can sit, if you'd like. Or we can walk through the garden and talk. I'm good either way, as long as we keep our conversation private."

"Let's sit." She didn't know if she could walk and talk and breathe at the same time, not while she was in his company, anyway.

They made their way to the bench and sat side by side. His big, muscular arm was just centimeters from hers. But with how cozy the bench was, it couldn't be helped. She should have chosen to stroll along the grounds instead, but she wasn't going to suggest that they pop up and start walking now.

"Before we get to the green card business, I want to say that I'm sorry for what Rich Lowell did to you," he began. "He fooled so many of us. Me included. But I didn't see Rich all that much when he was impersonating Will. He spent more time in Dallas and abroad than he did in Royal."

She had to ask, "Do you think Rich is really dead? Or do you think there could be more to this than meets the eye?"

"I don't have all the facts, but I do know that the body was identified by a reliable source who assumed it was Will. So it sure seems as if he should be dead." He paused for a second and added, "Will told me that the FBI sent the ashes from the urn out for DNA testing. The results aren't in yet, but it's probably just routine. Or I hope it is."

Allison hoped so, too. "I hate that Rich used me the way he did. My heart still hurts from his betrayal, but giving him my life savings makes me feel like a total eejit." When Rand gave her a perplexed look, she quickly clarified, "Sorry. Irish slang. It means idiot."

He turned more fully toward her, angling his body on the bench. "I like the way you talk. Your brogue and whatnot." He playfully added, "Did you know that Irish accents were voted as one of the sexiest in the world?"

Her heart scurried inside her chest. He'd just spun their conversation on its axis, taking it to a flirtatious level. "Who would vote on such a thing?"

"Folks on the internet. I can't say I disagree. It is rather sexy."

So was the slightly Southern way in which he talked. Not everyone in Texas sounded that way. He had a naughty twang that sent erotic ripples down her spine. Struggling to maintain her composure, she politely said, "I like your voice, too."

"That's good to know." He furrowed his brow, squinting in the sun. "With what I have in mind, we need to like things about each other."

Wondering what he meant, she waited for him to expound.

But instead, he asked, "Are you familiar with my position at Spark Energy Solutions?"

"I know that you were the second in command, and that Will was the CEO." She also knew that it was a highly successful oil and energy company owned by Will's family. "Initially, you worked under Will's direction, but you also worked for Rich when you thought he was Will. Then, just recently, you took over as CEO when Will supposedly died. And now you'll continue being the CEO until he can resume his life." She tilted her head. "But what does any of that have to do with me getting a green card?"

"I need a wife, Allison. Someone who can help me combat my image and provide what people think is a sense of stability. In the past, the board of directors let my reputation slide. But now that I'm heading up the company, the chairmen are pressuring me to get my act together. They're even threatening to fire me over it." He paused for a beat. "There's already enough uncertainty at work surrounding Will's stolen identity and how long it'll be before that gets resolved. The board can't afford any issues with me."

Allison could do no more than blink at him. Her mind had gone numb. "Are you suggesting that we marry?"

He nodded. "With the time constraints involved, we should do it as quickly as we can."

Again, she blinked at him. Rand Gibson was as far from husband material as a man could get. Not only was he a social media sensation, with tons of female followers hanging on his every word and sharing his pictures, his photos were sometimes made into sexy memes, garnering him even more attention.

Allison didn't follow him on social media because she didn't want him or anyone else to know that she found him so interesting. But she'd been poking around on his pages for longer than she cared to admit.

He continued, "At first people will be speculating as to whether a country girl like you can keep a playboy like me in line. But we'll make lots of public appearances and show them that you can."

She had no idea what keeping a playboy in line was like. She was already paying the price for dallying with a con man, and now she was being propositioned by a drop-dead gorgeous, modern-day Don Juan. The idea of getting close to Rand scared her senseless. He was everything she should be trying to avoid. Hot and seductive, she thought, and oozing with wealth and charm. Just like Rich when she'd first gotten to know him.

"How long would this marriage last?" she asked.

"It takes about three months to get the immigration interview. I have a friend who works for the USCIS, so I can try to pull some strings and get it moved up. He can definitely get your security clearance done faster."

She wasn't surprised that someone as well-off and socially connected as Rand would know someone at the United States Citizenship and Immigration Services.

"We'll have to work out a prenup that's comfortable for both of us," he said. "I don't want things to get sticky later. But either way, after you get your green card and after I prove myself to the board, we can decide when we should split up. We'll part amicably. Then after the divorce, we can go our separate ways and no one will be the wiser."

"I'm not interested in a financial settlement, so a prenup wouldn't be a problem." Being dependent on Rand to replace what Rich had stolen wasn't the answer to restoring her self-worth. She would rather make her own way, even if she struggled to do it.

"So what do you think of my idea?" he asked.

She tried not to frown. "Of marrying you? What you're proposing is considered fraud. If immigration found out that we faked a marriage, there would be penalties involved. I suspect that your friend at the USCIS wouldn't appreciate you dragging him into a situation like that, either."

"I know, and that's why we couldn't tell anyone the truth, not even our friends or families. In order to make something like this work, we'd have to live the lie." Rand's expression turned dark. "The pressure the board of directors is putting on me isn't just to clean up my act. There's a company here in Royal that they expect me to bring in as a new client. And if I don't secure that account, I'll be ousted for sure. I've been trying to set up meetings with the other company, but their CEO hasn't responded to my calls. From what I've been told, he has concerns about my reputation, too."

"And you think having a wife will help?"

"It's the only solution I can think of that will improve my image in a quick and noticeable way." His expression grew even stormier. "You know what makes it worse? My father was always telling me that I was too much of a party animal to be taken seriously, that someday my behavior would come back to bite me in the butt. He criticized me every chance he got, even when I was a kid."

Allison considered how much information Rand was sharing. Rich used to confide in her, too. But all of his confessions were lies. She hoped Rand wasn't embellishing his tales to create a false sense of intimacy. Although she didn't doubt that he needed a wife, just how far would he go to get one?

"Where is your father now?" she asked.

"He died last year, but I've been feeling the brunt of his words more than ever now. I swear I can just hear him saying, 'I told you so,' along with everyone else who's convinced I'm not worthy of my job."

She couldn't hear anything but the frustration in his voice. "Are you sure that people will even believe that we're a true couple?"

"Granted, we'll be an unlikely match, but you know what they say about opposites attracting." He winked at her. "Especially if we show everyone how desperate we are for each other."

Allison's thoughts scrambled. Was their desperate union supposed to include sharing the same bed? Was that part of the plan of them seeming like a genuinely married couple? Just thinking about it was sending her into a tailspin.

She wanted to remain in the States, to defy the odds, to get her green card. But could she marry Rand? A man she didn't even know if she could trust?

# Two

"Are you interested?" Rand asked. "Will you consider marrying me?"

Allison fidgeted in her seat. A Texas heartthrob, a man she'd been crushing on, was offering to make her his wife and help her get the green card she so urgently wanted. To some women, this would be a no-brainer. But it wasn't that simple. Not to her, anyway. And especially not if he tried to lure her into bed.

She said, "If I agree to do this, there isn't going to be any intimacy. We can't…"

He turned more fully toward her, one of his legs nearly bumping hers. "Sleep together?"

Her pulse jumped. "Yes."

He roamed his gaze over her. "I didn't think it would be an option."

"You didn't?" This was the most uncomfortable conversation she'd ever had. And the way he was checking her out with those wild green eyes was only making it worse. "I assumed that maybe you would…"

"I would what? Try to seduce you? I'm used to having affairs, so, yeah, it crossed my mind. But you're different from anyone else I've ever been with. You just seem so—" he brought his hand to her face, skimming his knuckles along her cheek "—innocent, somehow."

*My goodness, my Guinness.* For someone who wasn't supposed to be seducing her, he was doing a dandy job of it now. She couldn't think clearly, with the way he was touching her.

She forced herself to say, "You shouldn't be doing that."

He lowered his hand. "I shouldn't?"

"No." She didn't want her attraction to him distorting her common sense. "I still need to decide if I'm going to marry you."

"Well, are you?"

"It scares me, doing something so fraudulent." Trusting him scared her, too. But was she making too much of that? He wasn't a sociopath like Rich. He was just a man who needed to reform his image. His womanizing image, she reminded herself. He wasn't exactly an angel.

She didn't know what to do. If she married him for her green card, she would be committing a crime. If she didn't, she would be dragging her sorry arse back to Kenmare.

"I'd rather have an answer sooner than later," he said, "but you can sleep on it, if you think that'll help."

"It won't." She didn't want to think about sleeping on anything—or with anyone, for that matter.

"Then what's your decision?"

She considered her choices. Stay and regain her confidence? Or retreat and return to Ireland? Given her plight thus far, marrying him was beginning to seem like her only option. And at this point, she would rather take her chances with Rand than go home, lost and bleating, like the poor little lamb she kept comparing herself to.

She squeezed her eyes closed. A second later, she reopened them, just to say that she'd gone into this with her eyes wide-open. "I'll do it."

"You will?" He doubled-checked. "For sure?"

"Yes." She was going to take the plunge and become his newly minted bride, fulfilling her dream of living in the States, of working toward her independent future, of being her own woman. Starting now, she thought. Determined to show him that she wasn't a pushover, she reiterated, "I meant what I said before. The no-sex clause still applies."

"I understand. But we're still going to have to be affectionate with each other. We can't behave like strangers out there."

"Don't worry…" She paused, giving herself a moment to breathe a little deeper. "I'll play my part to the best of my ability." She would do what she had to do, short of tumbling into bed with him.

He smiled a bit too sexily. "At least there's no denying that we have chemistry."

In lieu of a response, she fought the warm, slippery feeling that came over her. But who *wouldn't* be magnetically drawn to Rand? Forbidden as he was, she could only imagine what climbing under the covers with him would be like. Hot and thrilling nights, she surmised, where she could let her inner sex kitten out.

Oh, sure. As if she actually had one of those. Even with as deeply as she'd fallen for Rich and his fake persona, she'd been a bit too restrained in his bed. She'd never thoroughly let loose with anyone, and this wasn't the time to start. She was absolutely, positively *not* sleeping with Rand.

"Allison?"

She started at the sound of his voice. "Yes?"

"We need to come up with a cover story about how we fell in love so quickly. But I have an idea about that."

"You do?" She cleared the erotic thoughts from her mind. "What is it?"

He waited until a passerby was out of earshot before he replied, "I thought we could say that we've been seeing each other behind closed doors. That I approached you privately after Will's funeral and we started to get to know each other then. With everything that's been going on this past month, I've been trying to keep a low profile and stay out of the limelight, so it's actually the perfect time for me to say that I've been in a secret relationship."

"That should work." Clearly Rand had a gift for storytelling. So did Allison, of course. Fiction was her forte. "But for the people who know that Will is still alive and that Rich swindled me, we'll have to tell a more detailed tale. We can still use the secret-dating ruse, but we'll also have to say that you helped me overcome the pain of what he did to me. Only that I didn't want to tell anyone that we were together for fear that they would judge me."

"That sounds believable to me. I can more or less say the same thing, but in reverse. I was worried that if people knew we got together so quickly, they might accuse me of taking advantage of you. But now that we're bursting at the seams and eager to marry before you're forced to leave the country, we can't keep it a secret any longer."

She marveled at their savvy. "I'm impressed with how easily we came up with an explanation." Within no time, they'd concocted a believable romantic backstory. "You want to hear something funny? When I was a teenager going to school dances and meeting local boys, I had daydreams about stealing away from Ireland and marrying an American man. I've been consumed with your country since I was a girl. I used to write poems to my fantasy husband, spilling my heart out to him."

He touched her hand, ever so lightly. "Maybe you can incorporate that into the green card interview. The more we reveal about ourselves, the more authenticity it will lend to our case."

Suddenly she was getting nervous again, overwhelmed that she'd actually agreed to marry him. "You don't think it will make me sound foolish?"

"No. Not at all. And I'm glad that you're already sharing personal information about yourself with me. We're both going to have to do a lot of that. We'll need to know each other from the inside out before we meet with Immigration and tackle that interview."

She anxiously admitted, "The most challenging part for me will be lying to my family, calling and telling them that I met the man of my dreams. But the truth would be worse. They would never approve of a ploy like this."

"My brother is going to be my biggest obstacle. It's going to take a miracle for him to believe I've given up my bachelor ways and am capable of being a loyal husband."

"I remember seeing him at Will's funeral." Although Rand and his brother didn't look that much alike, they had the same mesmerizing mouth and sculpted jaw, coming from the same handsome genes. "His name is Trey, isn't it?"

"Yeah, that's him. Aside from our maternal grandmother, he's the only family I have left. Our mother died a long time ago."

"I'm sorry." He seemed genuinely hurt that his ma was gone. She noticed the pain in his eyes. Had she misjudged him earlier when she suspected he'd been embellishing his confessions?

"How many immediate family members do you have?" he asked.

She concentrated on his question. "I've got my parents, one set of grandparents and a brother who owns a media company that's headquartered in London. He divides his time between England and Ireland. Farming will always be in his blood. The Cartwrights have been in Kenmare for six generations."

"Is your father a traditional man?"

"Yes, he is. Angus is his name, and he adores me like no other. He fusses over Ma, too. As much as I hate to say this, he's going to be disappointed if you don't call him and ask for my hand in marriage. But I would never expect you to actually do it."

"Maybe I should, if it'll make things easier."

She nearly gaped at him. "Really, you'd appease my da?"

He glanced at a giant oak towering nearby. "I'd rather appease him than have him think that you're marrying a guy who doesn't respect his values."

"That's a good point." She followed his line of sight to the tree, becoming aware of the tangled shoots creeping up its massive trunk. "He and Ma have specific ideas about marriage. They have opinions about *everything*. I love them dearly, of course, but sometimes they still treat me like a child. Ma is especially good at meddling."

"My family rarely sticks their nose in my business. My dad did, but I wouldn't call what he did meddling. With him, it was more like bullying."

She felt badly for what he'd endured. Her parents

wouldn't dream of bullying her. Everything they did was out of tenderness and care.

"Does your father Skype?" he asked. "Maybe I can video chat with him to ask for his blessing to marry you."

"Yes, he uses Skype. Ma does, too. So she will probably nose in on your talk with him and want to meet you, too. But before you contact them, I'll have to call them and pave the way. They're going to be stunned by my hasty marriage plans."

"We're going to shock everyone." He paused, seeming reflective for a moment. "Do you still have the poems you wrote to your fantasy husband? Did you keep them?"

"No." She was feeling reflective, too. "But sometimes I wish I would have. I've always been a fanciful girl. Too fanciful, I suppose."

He searched her gaze, as if he was looking for something in her character that he'd missed, something he hadn't seen before. Then, in a near whisper, he said, "I think we should kiss."

She started. "I'm sorry. What?"

"Kiss." He repeated, his tone a little huskier, a little more seductive. "We're going to have to get used to kissing. We'll be expected to do it at the wedding, at the very least."

He was right. But with the penetrating look he was giving her, she was getting downright dizzy. She even gripped the underside of the bench, latching on to it with all her might. "You want to do it right now?"

He moved closer. "Now is as good a time as any."

She filled her lungs with as much oxygen as she could get, preparing herself, trying to stay calm. He leaned into her, and her heart boomeranged to her throat, before it zoomed back to her chest.

Staying calm wasn't possible.

As soon as his lips touched hers, she closed her eyes and asked the heavens to protect her. He invoked a carnal yearning in her, a spell he obviously knew how to cast.

He was good at this.

So very good.

An expert in every way.

The tip of his tongue teased hers, and she moaned like the sinner, the soon-to-be fake bride she'd agreed to become.

He cupped the back of her head and drew her even closer. He played with her hair, splaying his big masculine fingers through it, and she imagined making down and dirty love with him. The sex she refused to have.

Allison knew she was in for a rocky awakening, being tied to this wickedly delicious man. She tightened her hold on the bench. Only now she was using it to stop herself from putting her hands where they didn't belong. If one little kiss could affect her this way, she was going to have to fight to keep from mauling him—every desperate day that she was his wife.

Rand wanted to push his tongue deeper into her mouth, to nibble, to bite, gobble Allison right up, but he was holding back, trying to keep their arrangement in perspective. She tasted wholesomely, sensuously sweet, like honey straight from the jar. In his hungry mind, it could've been oozing down their bodies in warm, sticky rivulets.

Before his zipper turned tight and he got unbearably hard, he opened his eyes and eased away from her. It was going to be hell restraining his libido around her. But she'd implemented that no-sex clause, and he had no choice except to abide by it. Rand needed a wife to clean up his image and try to save his job, but he knew better than to take advantage of Allison. He probably could've gotten one of his high-society lovers to agree to marry him, but he'd chosen Allison instead. And not just because he assumed that she might want a green card. Her sweet nature was part of it, too. He thought that marrying a good girl would help his cause.

Her eyes fluttered open, and he stared at her. Even with the way she'd moaned, with the soft murmurs she'd made, she still struck him as innocent. One tantalizing lip-lock wasn't going to change his opinion of her.

She was still the same woman who'd been hurt by Rich Lowell, who'd been heartlessly used by him. He didn't know what that bastard had said or done to con her out of her life savings. To Rand, those circumstances weren't clear. But this wasn't the time to ask.

She peeled her fingers away from the underside of the bench, and he realized that she'd been holding on to it the entire time their mouths had been fused together.

"We did it," he said. "Our first kiss." He figured that talking about it was better than sitting there in awkward silence.

She seemed to agree. She quickly replied, "Where I come from, kissing is sometimes called shifting. We also say 'the shift' or 'to get the shift.'"

"So I just got the shift?" he quipped, without really expecting her to answer. His gaze was still locked on to hers. He knew other green-eyed people, but he'd never met anyone whose eyes mirrored his in the way hers did. He sometimes got accused of wearing colored contact lenses to enhance his appearance. He doubted anyone would accuse her of that. Everything about her seemed genuine.

She blushed. "In some countries getting the shift refers to sex, but that's not how we Irish use it. To us, it's open-mouthed kissing, sort of like getting to first base."

"Where'd you learn about getting to first base?" Surely, Irish boys didn't say that when they scored with a girl.

"I picked up most of your slang from watching American movies. The romantic ones are my favorite."

"Chick flicks." He should have guessed as much. "You definitely seem like that type."

She studied him with those matching green eyes. "What inspired you to hatch this plan of yours? When did it occur to you that I might agree to marry you?"

"It was during the last Cattleman's Club event. I was standing off by myself, stewing about my job. You were there, too, and I overheard you talking to some friends of mine, saying that your visa was getting ready to expire. So later, I looked up your address online and sent you the Mr. X note."

"I was terribly nervous coming here to meet you," she confessed, reaching into her skirt pocket and removing a small black object.

He took a closer look and saw that it was a can of pepper spray with a key chain attached. "Was that to use on me?"

She nodded. "In case Mr. X was a nutcase, and he tried to accost me."

"Maybe I *am* a nutcase." Who else, besides a crazy man, would get married to reinvent himself?

"I think I'm one, too." She returned the pepper spray to her skirt. "So I guess we can be daft together." She referenced her other pocket, the one that didn't have the Mace. "I've got my ID, my money and a few other essentials tucked away in here. I didn't bring a purse because I wanted to keep my hands free to fight off Mr. X. I was prepared to scream, too, and alert security if need be."

"I'm sorry." He should have known better than to put

her in a position that sparked fear. "I should have considered how meeting a stranger might affect you."

"Thank you. I appreciate you acknowledging that." She dug into her essentials pocket and produced a small tube, which turned out to be lip balm.

When she uncapped it and ran it across her lips, she did it so quickly and efficiently, he suspected that adding moisture to her mouth was a habit. Much too mesmerized, he watched her.

"This is probably going to sound strange," he said, "but is that honey flavored, by any chance?"

She snapped the cap back on, suddenly aware, it seemed, that his gaze was riveted to her newly waxed lips. "Yes, it is. But why do you ask?"

"Because I tasted it when we were kissing."

Her skin flushed, her rosy cheeks going rosier. "Should I stop using it?"

"Absolutely not. Use it as much as you want." He enjoyed knowing where the flavor had come from. "I liked it." Probably too much, he thought.

She put the lip balm away. "It's going to be difficult for me to kiss you in front of other people. I don't normally do things like that."

"I do it all the time. And if I don't get romantic with my wife when we're out and about, the gossipmongers are going to say that I'm not as passionate about you as I've been about my other women. And we need to show them that I'm totally enamored with you."

She looked undecidedly at him. Clearly she didn't understand him any more than he understood her. They couldn't be more different from each other.

"Why have you been so public with your private life?" she asked.

"It started as a rebellion, my way of toying with society and thumbing my nose at my dad. And then, later, I just got used to doing socially unacceptable things and giving people something to gossip about. Of course, once social media hit the scene, I used that as my outlet. But at least I never made a sex tape or anything like that."

She all but blinked at him. "I should hope not."

With how primly she reacted, he got the sudden urge to tease her, to make things sound bawdier than they were. "Actually, it's possible I made a tape. There are a few blank periods of my life that I can't remember. But as far as I know, no tapes have surfaced. You haven't seen one with me in it, have you?"

"Goodness, no! I don't watch those." She crossed her arms over her ample breasts.

If she was trying to hide the fullness of her figure, it wasn't working. It only made him notice her delectable curves even more. Even in her loose-fitting outfit, a guy could tell what she had going on under there.

He continued his charade. "Are you sure you're not a sex tape connoisseur?"

"Yes, I—" She stopped and leveled him with an admonishing glare. "Are you mocking me? Is this a prank?"

He nearly cringed at the look she was giving him. "Sorry. I couldn't resist. With all the sordid stuff on the internet about me, I thought a sex tape seemed believable. But I guess I better not tick you off like this when we're married."

She sized him up again. "As long as you don't start talking like a cereal-box leprechaun or spout 'top of the morning' to me, I might be able to tolerate you."

Was she making a joke? He couldn't tell. Playing it safe, he said, "I'd never do anything that stupid." A second later, he saw her smile, and he knew he'd been had. He smiled, too, and they both laughed. He enjoyed the rapport they were building, strange as it was. Curious about her creative side, he asked, "What sorts of things do you write?"

"Magazine articles, lifestyle pieces, mostly for women's publications. But I've also been plotting a novel. It's about an Irish woman who goes to Texas and falls in love. I used to think that it should be a historical tale with the flavor of the Old West. But now that I'm here, seeing everything firsthand, I think a contemporary story might be the way to go. But no matter what time period I use, I want the hero to be the sort of fellow the heroine has to tame."

The way she was supposed to be taming him in this phony marriage? "That would never work on me, not for real."

"I know, but I think it does on some men, if they fall truly, madly in love. I'm a firm believer in destiny. I've always been a hopeless romantic." She rocked in her seat. "And I'm still trying to be. I don't want to lose that part of myself. Or miss the opportunity if the right man comes along."

Even after everything she'd been through with Rich, she still believed in love? He couldn't fathom it. Nonetheless, he said, "That's good, because I need a wife who projects that kind of image." Even if he didn't understand her propensity for love, he was glad it was going to play out in their favor. "Are you working on any projects now? Besides plotting the novel?"

"One of the publications I write for asked me to do a series of featured articles for them. I'm just waiting for the contracts to come through." Her expression turned taut. "I had to borrow from my parents to cover my expenses this month because of what Rich took from me."

He thought about the prenup she'd readily agreed to

sign. "You made it clear that you're not interested in a financial settlement when this is over, but if you change your mind, we can still implement that."

"I won't change my mind. Being independent is important to me. It's everything, in fact. I don't want to be beholden to you, Rand. Not for money or anything else."

"Okay, but I'd still like to set you up with some credit cards while we're married. You can use them to shop or have lunch with other Texas Cattleman's Club wives or whatever society women typically do. But mostly you'll be with me. We'll need to be seen together as much as possible." He glanced down at her hands and how simply manicured her nails were. "I'll be getting you a big-ass diamond to wear, too."

She widened her eyes. "A big-arse diamond? I've never heard it put quite like that before."

"What can I say? I'm new at this fiancé stuff. But I think you should come home with me." Clarifying his intention, he added, "For us to get better acquainted and figure out the details of the wedding. If you're getting hungry, I can order some takeout and have it delivered."

"Thank you. That's a nice offer. I'm famished actually. I was too nervous to eat before I came here."

"Do you need a ride to my place? Or do you have a rental car with you?"

"I need a ride. I haven't driven in America yet. Being on the other side of the road confuses me. I've been taking Uber."

He stood and offered her his hand. "Ready to go?"

She allowed him to help her up. "Yes, thank you."

"You're welcome." He escorted her to valet parking so he could pick up his shiny red Porsche. To keep things fresh, Rand leased a different sports car every couple years. He went through women in a lot less time. In fact, he'd never stayed with anyone longer than a few restless months.

He glanced over at Allison. She seemed so foreign standing next to him. Not just the country she was from, but the knowledge, the hard-hitting reality of making her his wife. But if it worked out like it was supposed to, she would be reforming him in the public eye and on social media, too.

Of course he still had to be careful not to corrupt her with his man-whore ways. Even with the no-sex clause, he was pretty damned sure he could seduce her. Not that he was going to. As tantalizing as she was, he needed to keep his head on straight, to follow the rules. Trouble was, Rand was a rule breaker by nature. Restricting himself from the lust-driven pleasure of a woman's company wasn't something he'd ever had to do until now.

A young valet brought the car around, and Rand slipped the kid a generous tip. Once he and Allison were settled into their seats, he put the Porsche in gear and peeled out of the driveway.

As he headed for Pine Valley, the area where he lived, he asked her, "What should we order? What sort of food do you like?"

"I'm partial to the deep-dish pepperoni pizza you have here. I'm a hearty eater, just so you know. A bit of a pig, actually. I don't mess around where my meals are concerned."

Her candor amused him. She had a knack for admitting what some people would consider faults. "Your enthusiasm for food is refreshing."

"I'm glad you think so. Because it's something you're going to have to get used to."

He stole a glance at her lusciously curved body. "You can eat as much as you want around me." Trying to keep his errant thoughts off her voluptuous figure, he focused on the road.

A moment later, they engaged in chitchat. They revealed how old they were and when they were born. She was thirty-one, and he was thirty-seven. Interestingly enough, their birthdays were only a few days apart. They were both Aries. Normally he didn't follow that stuff. But she did, apparently, referring to their astrological sign as "hard-headed rams." He supposed that part was true, with as determined as they were to make this marriage situation work.

When he reached the entrance of Pine Valley, he stopped at the gate. He had a key code, but a live guard was on duty, too.

Once he moved forward, Allison glanced out her window. "Wow! This is a grand area. Look at all the mansions. You live in one of these all by yourself?"

"Yep. Just me." Pine Valley was a private, upscale community with million-dollar homes, an 18-hole golf course, a fancy clubhouse and other exclusive amenities.

"You don't have a household staff?"

"I use a chef delivery service that comes by a few times a week and leaves my meals in the fridge or the freezer, based on the menus I choose. I use a cleaning service, too. I'd never have anyone live with me. I don't like having people under foot." He turned down his street and approached his home. The Tudor-style architecture featured heavy brick chimneys, decorative stonework, casement windows and a steeply pitched roof. An immaculate lawn dressed out the yard, with summer flowers garnishing the walkway.

He pulled the Porsche into his garage. His other car was a luxury sedan, another leased vehicle. Nothing was ever permanent in Rand's mind.

He gestured to the pearly white sedan. "You can drive that one when we're married."

"Thank you, but I'd rather not."

"Because of your discomfort about being on the opposite side of the road?" He didn't see why that should hold her back. "You plan on driving in the States eventually, don't you?"

"Yes, but I can wait until I'm ready."

Had she waited to have sex the first time, too? He suspected that she'd most likely lost her virginity when she was well into her twenties. He doubted that she'd given it up when she was a doe-eyed teen, writing poetry to her make-believe husband.

He escorted her into his house by way of the garage. They entered through the laundry room, with its high-efficiency washer and dryer, bright white counters and stainless steel sink.

Going from one spacious room to the next, he gave her a tour of the first floor, familiarizing her with the custom-built layout.

"Everything about your home is magnificent," she said.

"Thanks." He'd chosen furnishings that reflected his eclectic taste, mixing the old with the new, traditional with modern. "Let me get the pizza ordered, then I'll show you the rest of it." He called in the food and notified the guard at the gate, too.

While they waited for the delivery, he took her upstairs to where the bedrooms were.

They entered a room with an impressive view of the backyard. "When you move in, you can use this suite. It's the one my lovers use when they stay over. There's an adjoining bathroom with a shower and a claw-foot tub. Women seem to like that."

"It's all very elegant." She studied a gold-leafed dresser, tracing her hand along the wood. She turned and said, "But I hope you don't mind me asking, why do you have a separate suite for your lovers?"

He motioned to a set of ornate wooden doors. "This suite connects to mine, so when I have a woman over, we can open those doors and share both spaces. But we can close them when we want privacy, too. In the old days, ladies had their own boudoirs, and I wanted to create that effect here, too. I think it's sexy, waiting on the other side for my lovers to be ready for me." He walked over to the canopy bed that would become hers. "Sometimes they come to my suite, and sometimes they invite me to sleep in this one with them."

She glanced at the pale beige material that draped the top and sides of the bed, then took a breath-stealing moment to look at him. He returned her gaze, steeped in his odd fascination with her. By now, she was standing in front of a Queen Anne–style vanity table, with her back to the beveled mirror. The wood was a deep, dark cherry, and the seat was upholstered in a light floral print.

Rand imagined her using the vanity on their wedding day. "Do you want to get married here?"

She widened her eyes. "In this suite?"

"No. In the house itself."

"Oh, yes, of course." She seemed embarrassed by her blunder. "That was silly of me."

"That's okay." He liked how unpretentious she was, how she didn't always behave accordingly. "Since we need to do this quickly, I think we should have a small, private civil ceremony. But it can still be traditional, if that's your preference."

"Something customary would be nice. I wish my family could be here, but they'd never be able to leave the farm on such short notice. Of course, they'll probably want us to have a second ceremony in Kenmare, in the church where I was baptized." She spoke softly, shakily, her voice hitching. "The second one would be called a convalidation, where our vows would be blessed and recognized by the church. But our marriage isn't going to last long enough for that. I would never do it, anyway. It be would be too sacred for a deception like ours."

"I know what a convalidation is. But to be honest, I haven't been to church in a really long time." It reminded him too much of his mother's funeral and how painful it had been to lose her. But he didn't want to talk about that. "I totally agree with you that a second ceremony is never going to happen. We just need to get through the first one."

"Yes, but don't be surprised if Da mentions us getting remarried in Ireland when you video chat with him."

"How about if I just go along with whatever he says for now?" Rand didn't want to upset her father. He'd been through enough turmoil with his own dad.

She remained with her back to the mirror. "That'll work. Just pretend you're on board with all of his ideas."

"How do you think your mother is going to react?"

"She cries easily, and me marrying my dream man is going to make her weepy."

"Right. The dream man thing." Never in a million years did he expect to be cast in that role. But here he was, trying to wear that mantle. "So I should prepare for tears when I meet her on Skype?"

"Most definitely. She's going to cry on the phone to me, too, when I first tell her about you. She's also going to offer to alter her wedding dress and send it to me. She always wanted me to get married in the same dress she wore when she married Da, and since she's a seamstress, she'll be able to do it right quick."

Rand winced. He didn't know anything about the process of handing down a dress, but it was obvious how important all this was going to be to her parents. "If you want, I can arrange to have your family attend the ceremony on Skype. We might as well make the most of that medium. Not just for me to meet them and ask for your hand in marriage, but for them to watch you become a bride."

"That would be wonderful. They would love that." She rewarded him with a wobbly smile. "Thank you for suggesting it."

"No problem." As he met her gaze, a stream of silence ensued. A soft, sweet, quiet heat, he thought, with his heady vibes mingling with hers. "We better go back downstairs for now. The food should be here soon. We can figure out the rest of the details while we eat."

She left her post at the vanity. "Yes, we should go."

When he moved away from the bed and turned to leave, she quickly followed. She even shut the door behind her a little too soundly, as if she was eager to close off the room.

And everything that went with it.

# Three

Allison ate more than her fair share of the pizza. She drank the soda Rand had ordered, too. But in the center of her bride-to-be mind, her thoughts were racing.

She couldn't stop thinking about the boudoir Rand had built for his lovers—the sexy, dreamy, lavish suite where she would be staying. How she was going to survive sleeping there, she didn't know. Her crush on Rand was elevating to dangerous levels. Ever since she'd met him at The Bellamy, since he'd proposed this arrangement, since he'd kissed her with that scrumptious mouth of his, her pulse hadn't quit pounding. And now she was going to have to contend with his bedroom being intimately connected to hers, with two big, easy-to-open, elaborately carved doors between them.

"When are you going to call your parents?" he asked.

She glanced up from her plate, her arteries still thumping. "First thing tomorrow." She certainly couldn't call them today. It was later in Ireland than in Texas.

"I'll get your ring tomorrow, too. Maybe one of those sets where the engagement ring and the wedding band are designed to go together. I know someone who deals in antique jewelry, if older pieces are okay with you."

"Yes, of course." She wasn't going to interfere with his choices. "You can get whatever you think is best."

"The dealer works exclusively with a private clientele. She's a longtime friend of my grandmother's. I'll be inviting Grandma Lottie to the wedding, so you'll get to meet her. She's ninety years old and has a condo in a senior community here in Royal. It's a great place, as luxurious as it gets." He hesitated, reached for his soda, took a swig. A second later, he said, "But just so you know, her short-term memory is failing her. She has what's called mild cognitive impairment or MCI. Sometimes she forgets portions of conversations or repeats things we already talked about. I've gotten used to it now, but it was strange at first, trying to get a handle on it."

Allison couldn't imagine her granny going through something like that. Both of her grandparents were fit as fiddles. "Does MCI lead to Alzheimer's or other forms of dementia?"

"In some cases, it does. But her doctor doesn't think that will happen to her. She has a caregiver who lives with her, so it helps to know she has someone with her all the time. Grandma Lottie was my rock when I was growing up. She stepped in when our mother got sick and raised us kids after Mom passed. I was ten at the time, and Trey was only four. He barely even remembers our mom."

"How sad for him. How sad for both of you." She didn't know what to say, except to express the grief she knew he was feeling. "But I'm glad your grandmother was there for you."

"Me, too. Without her, I don't know what we would

have done. Our parents weren't even together when Mom died. They were already divorced. So by then, our father was used to being a weekend dad, to seeing us when it was convenient for him." Rand shook his head in obvious displeasure. "He never tried to take us away from Grandma Lottie, but he butted heads with her about what he called the 'indulgent' way she was rearing us. He didn't think she disciplined us enough."

"My parents coddled me. But maybe if I hadn't been so sheltered, I would have been more streetwise when it came to someone like Rich."

He narrowed his eyes. "I've been wondering about your relationship with him and how it unfolded."

"It's foolish, the way I let it happen." She picked at a piece of crust leftover on her plate, even if she'd been taught not to play with her food.

"Will you tell me about it?"

She winced. "Right now?"

He nodded. "Sorry, yes. But I'd really like to know."

She expelled an uneasy breath, preparing for the shameful truth. She'd already discussed this with the authorities and answered all of their probing questions, but repeating it to Rand seemed different somehow. "I met him at a restaurant where I was waitressing. I'd been working there for years, in addition to my freelance writing, so I could save extra money. Kenmare is a tourist destination, and we have lots of pubs and eateries." She picked at the crust again, tearing it into little pieces. "He said that he was on a much-needed holiday in Ireland, taking a break from his busy life. He explained that he was the CEO of an oil and energy company and how demanding his job was. He mentioned his family's cattle ranch, too, and his devotion to it. He was certainly my idea of a handsome Texan." She remembered how easily they'd talked and how forthcoming he seemed. "I thought he was as charming and interesting as a fellow could be. He took an immediate fancy to me, too. Or so I thought. But now I realize that he just saw me as an easy mark."

"Did you know he was married?"

"Yes. But he told me that he and Megan were getting divorced. That she'd met someone else and was in a secret relationship with that person. He also said that Megan was an emotionally fragile woman. According to him, she wasn't ready to talk to family and friends about the divorce or tell them that she was seeing someone else. She needed more time to get a handle on her new relationship."

"So Rich and Megan were keeping everything hush-hush? Gee, how convenient for him."

Her shame went bone-deep. Her foolishness. Her naïveté. "I shouldn't have fallen for a story like that. But he seemed so kind and sensitive, and I believed that he had Megan's best interest at heart. I didn't have a clue how often he'd been cheating on her or what a lovely and centered person she actually is." She released a sigh. "Of everyone I've met in Royal so far, she's been the most gracious to me. I feel so badly for her, marrying a man who wasn't even who he claimed to be."

After a long and silent pause, Rand asked, "When did your affair with him start?"

"Our romance budded right away, while he was still in Ireland. But I didn't tell my family about him. I knew they wouldn't approve of me seeing a married man, even if he was in the process of a divorce." She shook her head. "Or supposedly getting divorced or whatever." She continued her wretched story. "After he went home, we emailed and texted. He said that when I was ready to come to the States, he would help me get a visa."

"So you took him up on his offer?"

She nodded. "But he also said that he would try to help me get a green card, too, so I could move here for real."

"And make all of your Texas dreams come true?" He squinted at her. "Did he offer to marry you?"

"No." So far, Rand was the only man who'd ever proposed to her. "But his 'supposed' divorce from Megan wasn't finalized, so that wasn't an option. Besides, our relationship was still really new. We wouldn't have been talking marriage, anyway."

"Then how was he going to help you get a green card?"

"He said that he knew some government officials who could probably make it happen." She paused, thinking back on what a tall tale it was. "It's strange because you're the one who actually knows someone who works for Immigration."

"Yeah, but my friend isn't going to just magically get you a green card. It doesn't work that way." Rand watched her with a curious expression. "How long were you together with him in Texas?"

"Overall? Before the plane crash? It was three months." Ninety days in Dallas, she thought, of being duped. "After what he did to me, after being conned by him, it makes me want my green card even more. I don't want him to be the cause of me losing my dream of living in the States."

He continued to watch her. Or scrutinize her. Or whatever he was doing. She glanced away, needing a reprieve.

He asked, "Did Rich know you had a savings account? Did you share that information with him?"

She returned her gaze to his. "Yes, I told him. But it never occurred to me that he was going to swindle me out of it. As far as I knew, he was a wealthy man." After a chop of silence, she added, "When I first got to Dallas,

I rented the apartment I have now, and he would stay with me when he was in town. He took me out from time to time, but he never introduced me to any of his friends or family. He said that he couldn't, not while he and Megan were still keeping a lid on their divorce. I didn't know anyone in Texas besides him, so there was no one for him to meet, either."

"Sounds like your life with him was isolated."

"It was. But at the time, I didn't mind." She winced, hating the stomach-clenching ache that repeating this story gave her. "It seemed romantic, just the two of us. But then he started to seem troubled. Only he refused to tell me what was wrong. He kept saying that he didn't want to burden me with it. It was obviously part of his ploy, pretending to protect me from his problems. But finally, he told me that he was under financial duress. That his personal accounts had been frozen because of something Megan had done, and he wasn't able to make withdrawals or use his credit cards. He also said that he couldn't withdraw money from his business accounts, either, because he didn't want to involve his family, and they were tied to those accounts. He was trying to solve it without them knowing what was going on."

Rand shook his head. "It sounds like he had it all worked out, blaming his wife while trying to get money from his girlfriend."

"I loaned him little bits at a time, until the amounts started getting bigger and bigger. But even so, he never gave me cause to think that he couldn't be trusted. He promised that he would pay me back, and I believed him. The last time I saw him, he said that he was getting close to sorting it out and should have access to his accounts again." She took a long sip of soda to quench her suddenly dry throat, then went on. "Shortly after that, I received a letter from an attorney saying that he was dead, and I was named as one of the heirs to his estate."

When she hesitated, Rand motioned for her to continue. She took one more sip of her drink before she said, "I was devastated by his loss. Then later, of course, things took a different turn. I discovered that he wasn't even Will Sanders. I also learned that four other women had received the same letter, also making them heirs to an estate that didn't even belong to him. It made me feel as if he'd stolen from me twice, first by taking my money. Then by making me part of an inheritance I wasn't able to claim."

Rand nodded, a bit too solemnly. "Did you ever tell your family about him? Do they know he's the reason you had to borrow money from them?"

"I told them a condensed version of the truth. I admitted that I came to America to be with a man and that he'd taken advantage of me and hurt some other women, too. I couldn't reveal the entire story since we're not allowed to discuss the case with anyone who isn't involved in it, but they're still concerned about my emotional well-being. They could tell how badly this affected me."

"And now you're going to tell them that I helped you through it and you fell in love with me."

"Yes." She would be deceiving them about what should be the most important events of her life. Falling in love. Finding her true soul mate. Accepting his marriage proposal.

"It'll be okay," he said, much too softly.

Was he comforting her for the lie she was going to tell her family? Or was he consoling her for Rich's treachery?

Whatever he was doing, it made her feel warm and protected. When she was a girl, eating Ma's bread-and-butter pudding used to make her feel the same way.

Sometimes she used to sit by the fireplace on cold nights and devour the entire pan.

"Do you have a preference for the type of engagement ring I get?" he asked. "The cut of the diamond? Or the kind of setting?"

She cleared her mind. She wasn't supposed to be feeling warm and protected by Rand. She hadn't even decided how trustworthy he was. "I thought you were going to get an antique one?"

"I am, but this will be the first time I'll be buying jewelry for someone other than my grandmother. And I want to do it right."

"I'm sure you'll do splendidly with whatever you choose. But I'll be returning it to you after the marriage ends, so you should get something that has a good resell value so you can get your investment back."

He frowned. "I don't want it back. It's going to be your ring. I'm buying it for you."

"I know, but it wouldn't be proper for me to keep it."

"Then you should be the one to sell it and recoup what you lost."

"That isn't necessary," she insisted. "Besides, I already told you earlier that I don't want to be beholden to you."

"Come on, Allison. You should at least get a diamond out of this deal."

She wasn't comfortable getting anything out of it except her green card. "Maybe we should discuss this another time. I don't want to argue on our very first day."

"All right, we'll figure it out later." He paused before he asked, "Do you know your ring size?"

She shook her head. She'd never worn a ring before, on any of her fingers. She didn't own much in the way of jewelry, aside from the costume stuff that she kept in a small wooden box, all tangled up together.

He said, "There must be a way to measure it. I'll look it up online." He checked his phone. "Oh, here we go. There's a paper method that should work. I'll print this and we can try it." He got up from his seat. "I'll be back in a minute."

While he was gone, she stayed at the dining table, reminding herself to breathe. Within no time, she would be Rand's wife. She would be sleeping upstairs in that scandalous boudoir, with her hot-as-sin husband on the other side.

He returned with the paper chart and a pair of scissors, striding back into the room and catching her eye.

As he stood next to her chair and cut out the ring sizer, she asked, "When are you going to announce our engagement?"

"You mean publicly? I'd rather wait to make a splash until after we're married. We've got too much to do, trying to plan the ceremony this quickly. If we get bombarded with media attention beforehand, we'll never get everything done."

As he took hold of her left hand to size her finger, his touch sent an electric current through her. She nearly jolted from the feeling. Thankfully he didn't seem to notice.

"You're a six." He set the chart aside. "I'm going to have to wear a ring, too. I need to look as husbandly as I can, to flash my status as much as possible. But I'll find myself a plain gold band. Not an antique. Just something simple and modern."

"Yes, plain bands seem to be what most men prefer." Or so she assumed. "Would you mind if I took an Uber back to Dallas tonight, instead of you taking me?" She needed some time alone, to sit quietly in her apartment and try to quell her anxiety. "But you can come over to-morrow, if you want."

"That's fine. I can stop by after I get your ring. We should probably go to the county clerk's office tomorrow, too, to apply for our marriage license. You'll need to have your birth certificate and passport handy for that."

"I will." She thought about his social media followers. "I hope your hordes of female admirers don't hate me for taking you off the market."

"There isn't a person in their right mind who could hate you, Allison. You're just too damn sweet." When she bit down on her bottom lip, he stared at her. She stared back at him, until he said, "Now give me your phone, and I'll give you mine so we can program our numbers into them."

Once that was done, she arranged for her car.

He waited outside with her, with the sun getting lower in the sky. He didn't kiss her goodbye; he didn't put his wickedly delicious mouth against hers. They didn't hug, either. They didn't do anything that rang of affection.

Then, right before she left, he reached out and smoothed a strand of her hair away from her face with the merest skim of his fingers. A barely there touch that gave her that warm, snug, bread-and-butter pudding feeling again.

Even long after she got home.

The following day Allison bustled around her apartment, sweeping the floors, vacuuming the area rug beneath the coffee table and fluffing the decorative pillows on the sofa. True to his word, Rand was on his way over to give her the engagement ring he'd purchased and then take her to the county clerk's office with him.

After she finished tidying up, she smoothed her simple

cotton dress and combed her hair, checking her reflection in the bathroom mirror. She looked as ordinary as she always did, except maybe a tad more flushed.

About ten minutes later the doorbell rang. She answered the summons and greeted Rand. He was as dapper as ever, dressed in casual clothes, his broad-shouldered body filling up the tiny space on her stoop.

She invited him inside, and he glanced around and said, "This is a cute place, a nice little studio."

"Thank you." She'd tried to make it seem more like a one-bedroom by dividing the sleeping area from the living area, but she wasn't able to block her bed completely. A portion of it was still visible, on the other side of a bookcase.

Thankfully, he didn't mention it. But why would he say something about her bed?

"It's bright and sunny," he said.

Allison nodded. Was he getting the small talk over with before he presented her with the ring? "I like bright spaces." But so did he, she realized. He had lots of windows in his house. Most of her light was coming from a sliding glass door that led to her patio.

He asked, "Are you keeping this apartment for after the divorce or are you planning on getting a different one?"

"I was going to come back here." She couldn't afford to start over somewhere else. "Why? Do you think me keeping it is going to be a red flag with Immigration?"

He appeared to be contemplating a solution. "We can say that we're going to use it as our Dallas residence, for those times when I have meetings in this area. Since Spark Energy has an office not far from here, Immigration shouldn't take issue with that."

"Initially, I chose this apartment because Rich suggested that I acquire one near the office where he primarily worked." The same Dallas office Rand had just referred to. "And now this location is factoring into my arrangement with you."

"Everything is going to factor into our arrangement."

That was certainly true. She gestured to the kitchenette. "Would you like a beverage? I should have offered you something before now." She was normally a better hostess than this. But being in such tight quarters with this hot, sexy man was distracting her, especially with her bed being so doggone close. It just seemed so intimate somehow. "I've got iced tea in the fridge."

"No, thanks. I'm fine." He reached into his front jeans pocket and removed a small cloth pouch. "Here's your ring." He opened the pouch and dropped the ring into her hand, treating it like a free-falling gumdrop. "It's an Edwardian piece with a European-cut diamond. But it's not part of a set, like I thought it would be."

"Oh my stars." She gazed at the object glittering in her palm. "It's exquisite." The center stone was mounted in an ornate platinum setting with lacy scrolls and brilliant emerald accents.

"The dealer told me that in the Edwardian era, women usually wore their engagement rings on a different hand than their wedding rings because both rings were so intricate they didn't always match up too well. That's why this isn't part of a set. But I got a small platinum-and-diamond band that will complement it, so you can wear them together. I didn't bring that one with me. I figured I'd save it for the wedding day."

"Should I put this one on now?"

"Sure. Let's see if I sized you correctly."

She slipped it on her left hand. It fit perfectly. "It's exactly as it should be."

"I chose it because of the emeralds. I figured that a green-eyed girl marrying a green-eyed boy should have some emeralds."

"That's a lovely sentiment." But the bridelike feeling it gave her was making her head spin.

He tucked the empty pouch back into his pocket. "Promise me that you'll keep it after we split up. I don't want the first ring I gave someone to be meaningless. I really want you to have it."

Mercy, she thought. Now how was she supposed to refuse? To even the playing field, she said, "All right, but this will have to work both ways. I'll buy your wedding band instead of you getting it for yourself. And you'll have to keep it afterward, too."

He smiled, shrugged. "I don't have a problem with that."

She glanced at the dazzling diamond on her hand, wondering what she'd gotten herself into, making a pact with him to keep their rings.

"Did you talk to your family?" he asked. "Did you tell them about us?"

She redirected her focus. "Yes, I did." She gestured for him to sit, and they proceeded to the sofa. "I spoke to them first thing this morning. Ma cried, just as I knew she would, and offered to remake her dress for me. She said that she could tell how in love I was, just by the sound of my voice. But I did lay it on pretty thick." Allison was still suppressing the guilt that caused. "Now Da, he didn't react as well. He wanted to be sure that I wasn't jumping into anything too soon. Or that I wouldn't end up getting hurt again."

"Given the circumstances of your last relationship, I can understand his concern."

"I told him that you're a good man and you'd never

hurt me." Something she hoped and prayed was true. With her track record, she wasn't the best judge of character. "I had to warn him about your reputation, though. I didn't want him Googling you and finding out on his own."

He made a tight face. "I hope you convinced him that I changed my ways."

"I certainly tried. But I think he'll feel better after you video chat with him."

Rand gentled his expression. "I'll do what I can to help put him at ease. By the way, I was thinking that you should probably pack up some things and start staying with me."

"You want me to move in this soon?"

"Why not? We need to get used to being around each other. It'll be easier to arrange the wedding if we're already living together, too."

He was right. It didn't make sense for her to keep going back and forth from Dallas to Royal. "I can move in tomorrow." Since she wasn't giving up her apartment altogether, all she had to do was pack her essentials. "Will that be soon enough?"

"That's fine."

"Is it all right if I bring my plants to your house? I have some fairy gardens on my patio, and I don't want to leave them behind. They'll die if I don't keep watering them."

"You can bring whatever you want," he reassured her. "I'll help you haul your things over. But truthfully, I don't even know what fairy gardens are."

"Come on, I'll show you." She took him through the sliding glass door and onto her patio, where her creations were. "See, each one is a miniature garden, with living plants, designed as a place for fairies to frolic." She'd used clay pots for the containers, some of them purposely broken or chipped, so the tiny structures inside of them were more visible. "I wrote an article a while back about how popular fairy gardening has become around the world, particularly in the States, and I got so fascinated with it, I decided to build my own once I came here."

He knelt to observe the work she'd done. She watched as he examined the glitter-speckled stones, the moss-covered cottages, the glass mushrooms and wooden bridges. He studied the wee-bit fairies themselves, too.

She said, "In Ireland, some of our fairies can be dark and sinister. But these fairies aren't like that. They have goodness in their hearts."

He was still looking at them, squinting at how small they were.

She continued her tale, "But just because they're kind, doesn't mean that they aren't without mischief. If we're not careful, they might capture us on our wedding day and whisk us off to the Land of the Young." She turned dreamy, imagining how it would be. "It's an enchanting place, a supernatural realm of everlasting youth and beauty. But once we're there, we wouldn't be able to come back, at least not at the risk of turning old right away."

He stood to his full height. "Is that part of your folklore or did you just make that up?"

"It's real." She sent him a silly smile. "Are you sure you still want to marry me?"

He smiled, too, and laughed a little. "I'll take my chances." With a more serious tone, he added, "But for now, I think we should go to The Bellamy on our wedding night. I can book one of their honeymoon packages, so it'll seem as romantic as it's supposed to be. Come to think of it, I should Instagram some pictures of us while we're there. I think that'll be the most effective way to let the masses know we're married, straight from the honeymoon."

She hadn't considered where they would be spending their wedding night. But now that he'd brought it up, her traitorous body had gone much too warm, her blood surging through her veins in short silky bursts.

"We can do a newspaper announcement, too, with a traditional wedding photo," he told her. "But we can do that after our hotel stint. I'd rather reach out on social media first."

She had to ask, "What kinds of honeymoon pictures are you talking about?"

He pushed his typically tousled hair away from his forehead. "Just some cozy shots that make us look like a blissfully happy new couple. 'Cause what the heck, right? That's got to be safer than being whisked away to a supernatural realm."

Allison nodded, even if she didn't agree. Getting cozy in a honeymoon suite with him didn't sound safe at all.

# Four

Rand poured himself an orange juice from the wet bar in his bedroom. With the way he was feeling he was tempted to add vodka to it, but he refrained. It was too early for a cocktail, so he drank it the way it was.

His video chat with Allison's parents had just ended, and it had gone exceptionally well. But it was an uncomfortable reminder, too, of how important he was already becoming to her family.

He glanced at the double doors between their rooms. Allison was on the other side of them, putting her belongings away. He'd helped her bring her stuff over this morning, including the fairy gardens. They were in his backyard now, on the patio near some other potted plants, where Allison could see them from her window. She'd chosen the spot herself.

He left his empty glass on the bar, strode over to the doors and rapped on one of them, giving it a musical rat-a-tat-tat.

She called out, "Come in!" No hesitation whatsoever, but she was expecting a full report from him on how the chat went with her folks.

He opened both doors, leaving them wide-open, and entered her suite. This was the first time anyone had ever occupied it who wasn't going to straddle his lap or purr like a kitten in his ear, and it gave him a strange sensation to see her there. With her casually ponytailed hair and makeup-free complexion, she looked as cute and fresh and off-limits as she was.

He glanced at the bed, where she stood, and where some of her clothes were piled. The rest of them were already hanging in the walk-in closet, which was nearly the same size as her entire apartment. He'd built the closet for his fashionista lovers. Allison certainly didn't need one that big. Her wardrobe was modest, at best.

He moved toward her, without getting too close to the bed. She would be climbing under those very covers tonight. Whether she slept buttoned up, scantily clothed or full-on naked, he couldn't say. But thinking about it sent a carnal shiver through his blood.

"How'd it go?" she eagerly asked.

He cleared the heat from his mind and got straight to the heart of it, the stuff that had been hard for him to swallow. "You were right about how much your dad adores you. He made me promise to protect you with my life."

She made a pained face. "Da can be over the top sometimes."

"It made me feel like a medieval swordsman or something, vowing to safeguard his maiden. I've never been in a position like that before. But I handled it okay." By making a commitment he wasn't going to keep, by pretending to be far more honorable than he could ever be. "He gave me his blessing to marry you."

"Well, thank goodness for that." She sat on the edge of the bed, near her clothes.

"I could tell that he liked me. I liked him, too." Angus Cartwright was a good-natured man, a hardworking sheep farmer, with thinning gray hair, a booming smile and wire-rimmed glasses. By comparison, Rand's father had been the head of a financial institution—a tall, trim, tight-ass CEO who rarely smiled. "Your grandfather jumped in to meet me, but I barely understood a word he was saying. His accent is really thick, and I think he was tossing in some Gaelic words to trip me up."

She laughed. "Granda has a wicked sense of humor."

He managed a laugh, too. "So I gathered." He went serious again. "You were right about your family wanting us to get remarried in Ireland. Your dad mentioned that to me."

She sighed. "How did you respond?"

"I told him that maybe we could do it next year sometime. I was just trying to buy us some time, and then he suggested our first-year anniversary. So I went ahead and agreed to that."

"You did the best you could under the circumstances."

He'd certainly tried. "When your dad introduced me to your mom, she kept staring at me, marveling at how handsome she thought I was. She went a little nutty over my eyes and how similar the color is to yours. She said that we were going to have the most beautiful green-eyed babies ever born."

"How embarrassing." Allison covered her face with her hands, peering at him through her fingers. When she lowered them, she said, "But I told you she was meddlesome."

"Yes, you did." Sheila Cartwright was as sweetly intrusive as a parent could be. "I didn't mind that she thought I was handsome, but the kid thing kind of freaked me out. I didn't know what to say, so I told her that I gave you a ring with emeralds because of how alike our eyes are. She started crying after that and praised me for being handsome *and* romantic."

"At least you made a good impression on her."

He nodded. At this stage of the lie, they had to fool their families before fooling anyone else. "Your mom told me that I'm not allowed to see you in your dress before the ceremony. She also said she was sending you a little silver horseshoe to put in your bouquet for some extra-special luck. She explained that in the old Celtic way, women carried around real horseshoes on their wedding days, but now they do it with small symbols of them."

"Ma has always been superstitious, in all sorts of ways."

"That's what I figured. But she's also one of the kindest people I've ever met. She treated me as nicely as anyone ever has, and it's obvious how much she loves you." Sheila's maternal nature made Rand miss his own mother and a pang of longing went through him. "You're lucky to have her in your life."

Allison smiled with pride. "Thank you."

He studied her from where he stood. "You resemble her." Their glossy red hair, their fair skin. "It makes sense that she would want you to wear her dress." And now that he was prohibited from seeing his bride before the ceremony, he was even more interested in how she was going to look.

"Did you happen to meet my granny? Or my brother?"

"Your grandmother was waving in the background when your mom was talking to me. Your brother wasn't there. I guess he was in London. But I let your mom know they could all attend the ceremony on Skype, and that made her cry all over again."

"You've had quite a morning, with Ma bawling at you."

"You warned me ahead of time that she was going to cry." He thought about how quickly the divorce was going to roll around. "What are you going to tell your parents when we split up? How are you going to explain it?"

"I'll probably just say neither of us was as ready for marriage as we thought we were. That Da was right when he was first worried about us rushing into it."

"We can use that story with everyone. But people will probably think I'm the one who screwed up. You're too sweet to get blamed."

"No one should be blaming anyone, not if we part as friends. I'll tell everyone that you tried to be the best husband you could be."

"I appreciate that." But the promises he'd made to her dad were still weighing on him. "Your family is going to be disappointed in me when it ends."

"They'll be disappointed in me, too. They won't understand why I'm giving up on my marriage so easily. But I'm never going to tell them the truth."

He pressed his lips into a grim line. "I've still got a lot more lies to tell. I'm going to head over to my brother's place to talk to him today."

"Is he expecting you?"

"Yes." And Rand just wanted to get it over with. "I didn't tell him why I needed to see him, but I said it was important. I haven't told my grandmother yet, but I'll do that later today, too. But as befuddled as her short-term memory is, I'm not going to wear her down with an in-person visit. I'm just going to call her." He exhaled roughly. "She'll probably forget bits and pieces of what

I tell her, and I'll have to repeat it before the wedding, anyway. And with how rushed everything is, I might not get the chance to introduce you to her until that day. But we can spend some quality time with her after we're married."

She walked over to the other side of the room, settling on a spot near a window, where the sun illuminated her. "How do you think she's going to feel about you getting married in such a rush? Or getting married at all?"

"She'll be fine with it." He took a moment to observe Allison, to appreciate how natural she looked in the light. She wasn't what most people would consider beautiful, but now that he was getting to know her, he thought she was getting prettier and prettier. Was it any wonder he was eager to see her in her wedding dress? "Nothing I do bothers my grandmother."

She tilted her head. "Your reputation never bothered her?"

"No. She always encouraged me to do whatever felt right. To be impulsive if that suited me. To live life in whatever manner made me happy." And for now, he wished that he could be the playboy he'd always been and seduce the hell out of Allison before their marriage ended. But he didn't have the right to prey on her innocence. Rich had already done enough damage in that regard, and Rand didn't want to fall into the same category as that conniving bastard.

"Your grandmother must be an open-minded woman."

"For not trying to rein me in? She shook things up in her day, too. She had her one and only child, my mother, out of wedlock. Things like that were scandalous back then, especially in her high-society world. But it was her choice to be a single parent. She didn't even tell the father about the baby."

Allison's eyes widened. "Really? How come?"

"He wasn't someone she was going to stay with, so she didn't think it was necessary for him to know. She never talked about him to anyone, either. She kept his identity hidden." Rand cleared his throat. "She met him on a trip to Europe, so no one from her inner circle saw them together. But in his country, he was really famous. Everyone knew who he was there."

Allison's all-too-curious gaze locked on to his, right before she asked, "Do you know who he is?"

"Yes." Rand's grandfather was one of the most notorious Spanish matadors who'd ever lived. "She told me when I was heading off to college. She told Trey when he was an adult, too. But we promised her that we would keep it between us."

"I understand respecting your grandmother's privacy." She frowned, tiny lines forming between her eyebrows. "But I hope he didn't take advantage of her. I hope that isn't the reason she didn't stay with him or tell him about the baby."

He sensed that Allison was thinking about Rich and all of the women he'd used. "It wasn't like that. He wasn't a bad person. But he wasn't the settle-down type, either."

"What happened to him? Is he still around?"

"No. He died a long time ago, so it's water under the bridge, anyway." Nonetheless, Rand felt a kinship toward his grandfather because his grandmother had told him how similar their personalities were. They even looked remarkably alike. He changed the subject, moving on to a more pressing issue. "I should head out to see my brother before he wonders what's taking me so long. I wish it wasn't going to be so difficult, though."

She moved away from the window. "Do you want me to go with you?"

"Thanks, but I need to do this alone." To face whatever Trey threw at him, without subjecting Allison to it.

"Is this a joke?" Trey asked with an incredulous expression.

"No, no joke." Rand had driven straight to his brother's bachelor's pad in Houston to deliver the marriage news. But as expected, his younger sibling refused to accept it.

Trey leaned against the kitchen counter, attired in his running clothes, his face unshaven, his brown eyes narrowed. As a youth, he'd been a star athlete, excelling at every sport he played. He could've gone pro, but he'd decided to enlist in the United States military instead, intent on saving the world.

Typically, Rand and his brother got along well. They'd always been close, often banding together when their dad bullied them. But their dad's influence had made them scrappy at times, too, and if they didn't see eye-to-eye on something, it could get tense between them. Like now, Rand thought.

"Come on." Trey goaded him. "What's really going on?"

"I just told you, I'm in love and I'm getting married."

"To who?" His brother all but scoffed. "Some spoiled rich party girl?"

Rand held his ground, as tightly as he could. "I'm marrying Allison Cartwright."

"The Irish woman who was at Will's funeral? Are you serious?" Trey grabbed his water and took a swig. War hero that he was, he had a sharp mind and a cautious nature, keenly aware of the people and places around him.

In this case, his suspicions were justified, but Rand

wasn't letting up. "I got close to her after the funeral. She was in a bad way, and I helped her through it."

Trey wiped the back of his hand across his mouth. "Since when have you ever helped anyone?"

"You make me sound like a prick." Rand was already feeling like one, after all the romantic jargon he'd heaped on Allison's family today. "I donate time and money to charitable causes all the time."

"That's not the same as being there for a woman who needs you. All you ever do is jump from one lover to the next, and now you're marrying someone who isn't even your type."

He clenched his jaw. "You don't know anything about Allison."

"I know that she sat there at Will's funeral looking like a broken bird. She seemed devastated by everything that went down."

"And I just told you that I helped her through it," Rand said. "That she needs me. That I need her. That we've been having a secret relationship."

"I wouldn't put it past you to sleep with her, but to fall in love, to marry her? I just can't believe it."

"Well, you better start believing it because we're in the process of planning our wedding." Rand battled a tightness in his gut. His brother was wrong about him sleeping with Allison. But he couldn't say anything about that. "Just accept that I've changed. That she changed me. That we're in love and eager to have a life together."

"I wish I could, but something just doesn't feel right about this. Are you sure you're telling me the whole story? That you're not up to no good?"

Well, shit. Rand tried another tactic. "Do you remember when we were kids and I used to dress up as Batman, and you would trail along as Robin? Well, this is sort of like that, only so much bigger, so much more important. So just stick by me, okay? I came here to ask you to be my best man." At least he wasn't lying about that. "I need your support."

"Oh, wow." Trey staggered a little. "You really are serious about getting married."

"I absolutely am." If he failed to pull this off, if he didn't repair his reputation, he would probably fail to bring in the new client at work and lose his job, too. But damn it, Rand had paid his dues at Spark Energy Solutions. He'd worked his way up the corporate ranks, becoming Will's right-hand man, and now he needed to prove to the board of directors that he was every bit the CEO that Will believed he could be. That Rand wanted to be. That his critical father would never have given him credit for. "We're going to get married as soon as we can, right after the Fourth of July."

"Then of course I'll support you. I'll be your best man. But I still have my concerns. Even if your heart is in the right place now, how long will it be before you panic and want to go back to being single?"

Rand hated this conversation, despised it, in fact. It wasn't easy having his brother see through him. Robin was supposed to be Batman's sidekick, not his analyst. "That's a terrible thing to say to a groom."

"I'm sorry. I was thinking about Allison. She seems like a nice person, and I just don't want to see her get hurt."

Rand's gut went tight again. He was getting the same warning from Trey that he'd gotten from Allison's dad. "I'm not going to do anything that will hurt my wife."

"So you're going to love, honor and protect her, the way a husband is supposed to do, for the rest of your life?

That's a hell of a commitment for anyone to make, but for a guy like you, it's major."

"I know, but I'm going to do it." Rand pushed the boundaries of his lie for the second time that day, making lifelong promises he knew deep down he wasn't capable of keeping.

Allison awakened with a cluttered mind. She hadn't slept well. She'd spent most of the night thinking about Rand and how he was on the other side of those big fancy doors. Somewhere in the wee hours, she'd even fantasized about entering his suite, via those doors, and slipping into bed with him. Even now, she wondered what it would be like to explore the depth of her sexuality and have a head-spinning, smoking-hot affair with the man she was going to marry. But as fun and naughty as that sounded, becoming his lover would be even more complicated than becoming his wife. Because the sex would be real, even if the marriage wasn't.

Allison would do well to keep her knickers on. She'd already gotten herself into a painful mess over her affair with Rich, and she needed to learn from her mistakes and comply with the no-sex clause that *she herself* had come up with. She just wished that she wasn't so physically attracted to Rand. That was a complication she could do without.

Preparing to face the day, she entered the bathroom, soaking in the big, glorious tub her suite provided.

A short while later, she donned a carefully considered outfit—a neatly ironed blouse and capri pants—and headed downstairs.

She found Rand in the kitchen, brewing coffee, and as quick as that, she nearly swallowed her tongue. Was this how it was going to be every morning? The man wasn't even properly dressed. The hem of his shirt hung loose, the buttons completely undone. His chest and stomach were casually exposed with impressive pecs, a nifty navel and irresistible abs. Intensifying his appeal was that messy midnight hair, still damp from the shower.

She honestly didn't know where to look. Every part of him was making her warm and foolishly aroused, reigniting her forbidden fantasies. Her nipples were even peaking beneath her bra, rubbing abrasively against the fabric. But thankfully, they weren't showing through her top. She actually glanced down at her chest to be sure.

After that, she settled her gaze onto the floor and noticed that Rand's feet were bare.

"I made enough coffee for two," he said.

"Thank you, but I drink tea." Difficult as it was, she spoke as normally as she could. "I sometimes drink up to six cups a day."

"That's good to know. We're supposed to be learning each other's habits. But for now, I don't have any tea."

"I brought some with me." She darted past him and opened a cabinet to the left of him. "I put it in here."

"Really, when did you do that?"

"When you were at your brother's yesterday."

He grimaced. "What an ordeal that was. But at least he's lending his support, even if he thinks I'm going to be a crappy husband."

Allison didn't reply. Just thinking of Rand as her husband, crappy or otherwise, was enough to make her knees weak. Standing beside him now, she prepared her morning beverage while he poured his.

He said, "I've got ham-and-cheese frittatas in the freezer, with roasted red potatoes and sautéed mushrooms on the side. There's fresh-cut tropical fruit ready to go, too. Will that do for our first breakfast together?"

"That sounds yummy. I guess it's safe to assume all of that came from the chef delivery service you use?"

Rand nodded. "It's convenient, especially for a bachelor like me."

"I can cook for us while we're married."

"Are you sure you wouldn't mind doing that?"

"I'm positive. I like to cook as much as I like to eat. But for the record, I like to keep active, too." She wanted him to know that she was more than just a foodie. "I grew up playing rugby. I was in a league, right up until I came to Texas."

"Really? Well, you're just full of surprises." He went to the freezer and opened it. "I played college ball. I was a linebacker."

He certainly appeared to have the size for it, with that big strong body of his. When he rummaged through the freezer, she ogled his butt. He turned back around, and she glanced away, even though she wanted to run her greedy gaze along his abs.

While he placed their meals in the microwave, she sipped her tea as nonchalantly as she could. He drank his coffee, as well.

The buzzer dinged, catching his attention. After he transferred their food onto plates, he put the fruit in a large glass serving bowl.

They dined at a long marble island, which served as a kitchen table, leather-and-wood barstools already in place. She wished that he would button his shirt while they ate. But he didn't. She was still subjected to his half nakedness.

"We'll have to challenge each other to a match sometime," he said.

"A match?"

"Rugby. Football."

Oh, right. The sports they played. "Yes, we can do that." As long as he kept his shirt on, she thought. Otherwise, how was she supposed to get into a game without drooling all over him?

They both kept eating, until he said, "So what sort of stuff do you normally cook?"

"All sorts. But I can make some traditional Irish meals you can reference during our immigration interview, if they ask you any questions that pertain to my culinary skills."

"It's impossible to know what they're going to ask. But if they ask you about mine, you can always tell them that I don't cook." He rose to refill his half-empty coffee. "I've never had a traditional Irish meal. I like to vacation abroad, though. I have a private jet at my disposal, with a pilot standing by when I need him. But I've never been to Ireland."

"Why not?" She would've pegged him for someone who'd traveled just about everywhere.

He resumed his seat with the steaming beverage in hand. "Because I've never dated anyone from your country and typically I only go where the women are."

She shook her head, letting him know how odd his statement sounded. "The last time I checked there were women in Ireland."

He shrugged, smiled. "You know what I mean."

Yes, she understood. He was referring to his international string of lovers. "So I'm going to be your first Irish woman?"

"That's certainly how it's going to seem. But technically, you aren't really mine."

If she gave into temptation and slept with him, would she become his? Definitely not, she told herself. He didn't commit to his lovers. Besides, she shouldn't even be thinking about things like that. "None of your women belong to you, at least not for very long."

"Yeah, me and my lothario ways. I'm a bad boy cliché in this town." He leaned back in his seat. "So, what's your favorite color? If I had to guess, I'd say it was pink. I noticed a lot of pink clothes in your closet yesterday."

"I definitely like pink. But for the sake of us being together, I would choose green." For the color of their eyes, for the emeralds he'd given her. She lifted her ring to specify, making her reason clear. Then she asked, "What about you?"

"I've never had a favorite color, so if that's a question in our interview, you can say I don't have very many favorite things. I do have a favorite word." He waggled his eyebrows. "But it's a dirty one."

Instead of being coy, she brazenly asked, "Is it the F-word? Because if it is, I've never heard you say it."

"Yes, that's it." He slipped into a mock whisper. "But mostly I only say it when I'm...*you know*..."

When he was what, doing the act itself? Or telling his lovers that was what he wanted to do to them? She tried to brush it off, even if she'd gotten dizzily aroused. Now she wanted to hear him say it, for his spicy Texas twang to slide straight into her. "That isn't something we'll be discussing during the interview."

"No, I don't suppose it is. But can you imagine if it was, if the immigration officer asked us a bunch of questions about our sex life?"

"I'd rather not picture a scenario like that." And especially not after she'd awakened this morning consumed with wild urges about him.

"Yeah, I guess not. But they might ask if we use contraceptives and what type we use. I heard they sometimes ask things like that."

To unmask couples, like them, who aren't sleeping together? "What should we say if that comes up?"

"I use condoms. But if you're on the Pill or something, then we should probably say that since it'll coincide with your medical records."

"I'm not on anything. Condoms would be my choice, too." She thought of a related topic. "What about children? What if they want to know if we plan on having kids?"

He angled his head. "Do you want them?"

"Yes, someday. Two would be nice. Maybe three."

"Then that'll be our story. Two, maybe three little ones. And with green eyes, no doubt, like your mother said."

Envisioning having bright-eyed babies with him was getting her flustered. She took a second helping of fruit and nearly spilled it onto the table, before it reached her plate.

"So what's yours?" he asked.

"My what?" His question confused her.

"Oh, sorry. Favorite word. Or don't wordsmiths have favorites?"

"We do. Or I do, anyway." She struggled to relax, to get the sex and baby subjects off her mind. "It changes, depending on what I'm writing. When I was plotting my book to be a historical, I was rather fond of rake."

He chuckled. "Like the gardening tool?"

She rolled her eyes, but she laughed a little, too. She was glad he'd made a joke. It helped lessen the tension. "I was talking about the other kind, the one that's used to describe a hell-raising man. Rake is short for rakehell."

"I didn't know that's where it was derived from. But raising hell can sure be fun." He winked mischievously. "Of course I can't do that anymore."

"You definitely need to behave yourself." Husbands shouldn't be rakes, and fake wives shouldn't be lusting after them. "We have a marriage to concentrate on."

"Speaking of which…since Trey is going to be my best man, you should have a maid of honor, too."

Allison sighed. If she was in Kenmare, she would have a slew of childhood friends and chatty cousins vying for that spot. But here in Texas, she was just getting to know people. "Maybe I can ask Megan since she's the woman I feel closest to in this town. I first met her at the funeral, and we started to bond after that. A strange bond, I suppose, over being betrayed by the same man, but it's been nice having her as a new friend."

"I think she's a great choice. Let's keep the guest list to a minimum to make things simpler."

She nodded. "Should the guests be allowed to bring a plus-one?"

"Sure. If they want to. But no more than that." He set his fork down and swallowed the last of his coffee. "I'm going to head upstairs to finish getting dressed." He stood and carried his plate over to the sink. "I have to go into the office today. I have a few meetings, but I'll try to be back early."

"That's fine. I should go upstairs, too, and call Megan. My cell phone is in my room." Since she was also done eating, she got up and loaded her plate and flatware into the dishwasher, along with his. She didn't like leaving dishes in the sink.

He thanked her, and as they went upstairs together, he said, "We should use this for the wedding."

"Use what?"

*"This."* He gestured to their current whereabouts. "The stairwell. You could come down it in your dress, and I could wait for you at the bottom. I've seen wed-

dings like that on TV, where they incorporate the stairs as part of the bridal walk."

"That's lovely. I like that idea." She was impressed that he'd thought of it. "But if we do that, the rest of the ceremony should take place inside the house, too."

"That makes sense. But I'd rather have the reception in the backyard. Is that okay with you?"

"Yes. An outdoor reception sounds nice. We're going to need a color scheme. How about the colors that are in my ring?"

"That works for me. We can figure out the rest of the details and order the flowers and decorations and whatnot after I get home today. We'll have to decide on a menu and what type of food to serve, too. I have a great caterer we can use."

She furrowed her brow. "Will they be able to accommodate us so quickly?"

"I hope so. If not, we'll have to find someone else."

Suddenly Allison was getting overwhelmed with everything they had to do to prepare for the wedding. "When I was a young girl dreaming of getting married, I never imagined it happening like this."

"Just think of how I feel," he said, as they turned simultaneously in the direction of their rooms. "And how I never planned on getting married at all."

# Five

While Rand was at the office, Allison tried to make good use of her time. She ran some errands, then met with Megan for a late lunch. They dined together at the Royal Diner, an informal eatery with a decidedly retro vibe. The red vinyl booths and checkerboard floors reminded Allison of the old American malt shops depicted in movies. In keeping with the atmosphere, she ordered a cheeseburger, French fries and a chocolate shake. Megan chose a soup-and-salad combo.

They sat in a corner booth with no one else around. Overall, the diner was quiet. The lunch crowd was gone, and it was too early for the dinner folks.

Gazing across the table at her friend, Allison couldn't help being enthralled with Megan. She was just about the most beautiful woman Allison had ever seen, a glamorous brunette with long wavy brown hair and big blue eyes. Megan was a socialite who owned a designer shoe company, a strong, intelligent, highly capable woman, so different from the way Rich had described her.

If Allison could be honest, she would gladly tell Megan that she was marrying Rand for her green card. Megan, of all people, would understand that after the way Rich had brought Allison to the States and humiliated her, she needed to restore her self-worth and remain in Texas on her own. But this girl-talk meeting wasn't about the truth; it was about pretending that her marriage to Rand was the real deal.

"Thank you for agreeing to be my maid of honor," Allison said. "It means a lot to me."

Megan smiled. "I wouldn't miss it for the world."

"I'm sorry for not giving you much notice."

"Don't worry about the timeline. I can handle it." Megan skewed a forkful of lettuce. "However, to be perfectly honest, I am rather stunned that you and Rand got together. I never would've envisioned you two as a couple. But I think it's wonderful, too."

"We knew that we were going to shock people. But we're very much in love." Playing her part, Allison made a dreamy expression. She was supposed to be a blissful bride, after all. And sometime in the future she would be, just not with Rand.

Gorgeous, tempting, sinfully sexy Rand, she thought wistfully. If only her forbidden fantasies about him would go away.

"What colors are you using for the wedding?" Megan asked.

Trying to clear him from her mind, Allison hastily replied, "I decided on green and silver, or platinum, to be specific, to complement my ring." The diamond flashed as she turned her hand. The emeralds glittered, too.

"It's a gorgeous piece, absolutely dazzling on you."

Megan admired the Edwardian setting with what appeared to be a well-trained eye. No doubt she had plenty of fine jewelry of her own.

"Thank you." Allison was still getting used to the luxurious weight of it, mindful not to snag the ring on her clothes or leave telltale threads wrapped around the prongs. "You can wear any style of dress you want in either or both of the colors."

"Should it be formal or something in between?"

"Semiformal will do. I'm wearing a traditional gown, but it's not a designer dress or anything like that. It's the same one my ma married my da in. We decided on a small, private ceremony at Rand's house, but you're welcome to bring a guest." Allison drank more of her milk shake. "With how we're hurrying to get everything done, we're trying to figure things out as quickly as we can."

"It sounds beautiful. I'm pleased to be part of it." Megan abandoned her salad and crumbled crackers into her soup without taking a bite. "Weddings should be joyous occasions."

Suddenly Allison wondered what Megan's wedding to Rich had been like. When she'd married him, she'd believed that he was Will, and now the real Will was back. Allison couldn't fathom how Megan was handling that. Megan's brother, Jason Phillips, was a childhood friend of Will's. Presumably, Megan had grown up around Will, too. Was it awkward between them now? Or had they become closer, bound by the impostor case? Did Megan have feelings for Will? And how did he feel about her?

Whatever was happening between them, Allison decided not to ask. Prying into her friend's personal business while lying about her own just didn't seem right.

For now, Allison needed to get a grip on her own emotions and figure out how to make her short-lived marriage to Rand work.

On the night before the wedding, Rand couldn't sleep. He had a million thoughts running through his mind and most of them concerned Allison.

He glanced at the double doors that separated their rooms. He assumed his bride-to-be was still awake. A bright amber light glowed beneath the doors. He took a chance and knocked.

A click sounded, and she opened one side.

She immediately asked, "Rand? What's going on?"

"I just wanted to have a last-minute talk."

"Come in." She stepped away from the open door.

Rand entered her room, the suite he'd built for his lovers. But of course Allison didn't resemble anyone he'd ever shared a bed with before. She was attired in a modest pajama top and matching bottoms, a strong indication that she wore clothes to bed. Rand sure as fire slept naked. His lovers did, too, particularly when they crawled under the covers with him.

"How are you holding up?" he asked, pushing past his wayward thoughts.

"I've got the jitters." She held out her hands to show him how unsteady they were.

In addition to her shakiness, he noticed the sparkling white polish on her fingernails. He glanced down. Her toenails glittered, as well. He assumed it was her mani/pedi in preparation for tomorrow.

"I'm nervous, too," he said. But he was trying to keep his anxiety inside, where it didn't show. "I keep hoping that we didn't forget anything." Planning a wedding this quickly was like entering a cake-and-flowers war zone.

They'd even worked through the Fourth of July holiday, missing local picnics and fireworks displays. But they would be attending a Stars and Stripes fund-raiser after the honeymoon, giving them time for a patriotic gathering later. "You seemed emotional this morning when your dress arrived, but I didn't say anything about it." He wasn't even sure if he should be mentioning it now.

"When I opened the box and saw Ma's gown, it made me sad to think I'll be wearing it for a marriage that isn't going to last." She twisted her ring, turning it halfway on her finger. "But that's my fault. I should have come up with an excuse to not wear it."

"I'm looking forward to seeing you in it."

She quit toying with the diamond. "You are?"

He nodded. "I like that it's special to your family. That it has a unique history. I also like that you and I are becoming friends." To him, there was no other way to describe the anxious bond they'd begun to share—the whirlwind that had become their wedding.

In the next bout of silence, the acknowledgment of their friendship turned a little awkward. But that didn't stop him roaming his gaze over her, from thinking how tempting she looked in her plain and simple pajamas. It made him want to touch her, to hold her, to pull her close to him. But most of all, he wanted to kiss her.

"You know what might help us relax?" he asked.

She blinked. "No, what?"

"We should kiss. Shift," he clarified, using the phrase she'd taught him. He needed an excuse to taste her, all the way to his harried-groom soul.

Her voice quavered when she said, "We've only kissed that one time, on that very first day."

"That's why I think we should do it now." On the eve of their wedding, he thought, looking into the familiar greenness of each other's eyes. "Only we should do it longer and deeper than before." He moved forward. "Do you want to try it and see if it helps?"

"Yes." She agreed with anticipation in her voice.

He reached for her, taking her in his arms. "How's this for starters?"

"It's nice, so very nice." She went breathy. "I like how close you are to me."

He trailed his hands down her spine. "And I like how curvy you are. Like one of those old-fashioned pinups." Even in her proper pajamas, her body was lush and full.

"No one has ever compared me to a calendar girl."

"You have the figure for it." He inched lower, cupping her rear and giving her a good, stiff jolt with his zipper.

"Now you're just being a rake." She smiled, laughing a little.

A rake. A rakehell. A hell-raiser. With those words spinning in his mind, he took her mouth, hard and fast, making her gasp. He felt her sharp intake of breath. But he'd warned her how long and deep this was going to be.

He sparred with her tongue, creating a shock of heat and wetness. She clung to him, digging her nails into the back of his shirt. He manhandled her ass, gripping it tighter, keeping her roughly bound.

When they came up for air, it was only for a second, just enough time to dive under again, open-mouthed and carnal.

He rubbed against her, and she reacted with a moan. He liked how easily affected she was, how everything he did triggered a response. Her honey sweetness exploded inside him, and he kissed her over and over, making the most of her reactions, of his all-consuming need.

If they were lovers, he would be yanking off her pajamas by now. But she wasn't his lover, and he needed to end this before he got carried away. He pulled his mouth from hers, and they stared mindlessly at each other.

She stumbled a few steps back. Neither of them spoke, until she bit down on her bottom lip and said, "I hope this isn't going to sound strange, but I took an interest in you when I was still dating Rich, when I thought he was Will."

He stumbled now, too. "How did that come about? You hadn't even met me until the funeral."

"I know, but since he never introduced me to anyone, I Googled some of his friends and coworkers to see who they were. And you fascinated me like no other," she confessed. "You fit the bill for my book hero, so I started checking out your Instagram pictures and reading gossip tidbits about you online. I developed a bit of a crush on you, but I didn't tell Rich about it. I get crushes on actors and singers, too, so I didn't think it mattered."

It sure as hell mattered now, Rand thought. Her sweet little crush gave him a big hard thrill. But he downplayed his reaction. "I don't mind you modeling your book hero after me, except for the part where your heroine tames him." He'd already told her that would never work on a guy like him, but he decided it bore repeating.

"My book is going to be fiction," she reminded him. "Like our wedding."

He nodded. "I should probably go now." His hunger for her had already reached its limits. If he didn't leave, all hell might break loose.

"Yes, you should leave." She fidgeted with her ring again. "We both need to get some sleep."

"I'll see you tomorrow." The ceremony was scheduled for early in the day, accommodating the time difference across the sea. "Dream well, Allison."

"You, too, Rand."

With a quick nod, he walked away. Just as he crossed the threshold into his own room, he glanced back and saw that she was watching him, like the uneasy bride she was about to become.

This was it, Rand thought. He and Allison were getting married. He stood at the bottom of the stairs garbed in a black tuxedo, a white rose boutonniere pinned to his lapel.

To keep from hyperventilating, he took a deep breath, preparing to become a husband and show the rest of the world how much he'd supposedly changed. A husband who couldn't make love with his wife, he thought. Even with as much as he wanted Allison, he was honor bound to keep his hands to himself.

Rand couldn't see the guests, as his back was to them. All of them, including Allison's family on Skype, had a view of the staircase. Grandma Lottie brought her caregiver to keep her company, and Trey brought a date. Megan had chosen to come alone. But nonetheless, Rand had asked everyone to surrender their phones upon entering the wedding. He didn't want anyone taking pictures or videos and posting them publicly before he was ready to announce it on his social media pages. Instead, he'd hired a photographer who was already snapping away, getting images that Rand could use as he saw fit. A professional videographer was filming the festivities, too.

Once the music started, Rand's heart thudded in his chest. He'd hired a harpist to play the Celtic song Allison had chosen for the wedding music. The same harpist would be entertaining them at the outdoor reception, immediately following the ceremony.

But for now, he was fixated on his bride. She glided down the stairs in a delicate, white-lace gown. The collar was high and ruffled and the sleeves were long and sheer. She looked as fresh and lovely as a country maiden, a crown of wildflowers adorning her red hair. She wore it pinned up, with loose tendrils framing her face. He suspected that her mother was crying about now, seeing how beautiful her daughter looked.

Rand smiled at Allison, hoping to ease both of their nerves. She returned his smile and finished her descent. He took her arm and they made the turn, both of them now facing their guests. With the Celtic song still playing, they approached the justice of the peace, who waited in front of a floor-to-ceiling window, sunlight spilling in from the yard.

After the music stopped and Rand and Allison were in position, Allison handed Megan her white-rose bouquet. Nestled within the flowers was the horseshoe ornament that had been included for luck.

The vows were simple and quick to recite. Trey was in charge of the rings, and he had them readily available. Rand placed the diamond-studded band on Allison's finger that complemented the engagement ring he'd given her. She slipped a thick gold band on him, and he noticed that it wasn't as plain as he'd assumed it would be. A leafy design was engraved on it. He didn't understand the symbolism. He would ask her later when they had time alone to talk.

Soon they were prompted to kiss. After the way they'd kissed last night, slanting his mouth over hers felt as warm and natural as he'd hoped it would be. She reacted with a girlish sigh, as if their feelings for each other were real.

The kiss ended, and they faced their guests. Allison waved to her family on Skype. Her mother was definitely crying. So was her grandmother. Rand noticed that Grandma Lottie had tears in her eyes, too, and she barely knew Allison. They'd met briefly this morning, while Allison was getting ready for the ceremony. But Lottie seemed impressed with Rand's bride, nonetheless. She'd already told Rand how "sweet" Allison was.

A knot formed in the center of his chest, knowing how downhearted all of these loving, caring people were going to be when he and Allison got divorced. Even Trey would be disappointed, and he wasn't expecting the marriage to last.

But Rand and Allison were putting on a damned fine show.

At the reception, they smiled happily and accepted well-wishes and toasts.

During the meal, Rand took the liberty of kissing his wife in between bites. She returned his kisses, then fed him tasty morsels from her plate. He liked this part of being married. Cutting the cake was fun, too, as was licking the icing off each other's fingers. No one could deny how hot and hungry the bride and groom were for each other.

Later, while they moved on the makeshift dance floor, swaying the way couples in love were supposed to, Rand said, "Thank you for the engraving on my ring. That was a nice surprise. But what is it and what does it mean?"

Allison nuzzled closer to him. "It's a branch from a heather plant. Since we incorporated some Irish themes into the wedding, I thought a Celtic engraving on your ring would jazz it up. Heather stands for dreams, romance and attraction." She pressed her lips to his ear. "I know none of this is real, but it's going to make my dream of staying in the States come true. And with the book-hero crush I have on you, the romance and attraction part seemed fitting, too."

Her explanation deepened his desire for her, making him wish that he could consummate their marriage tonight. But they weren't even going to be sharing a bed. He would be sleeping on the sofa in their honeymoon suite.

He whispered to her. "Have I told you how wholesome I think you look in your dress? So soft and pure."

"You make me sound like a virgin." She spoke in a hushed tone, too, keeping their conversation private. "I suppose it is a virginal dress. But the designer nightgown Megan gave me isn't. It's sleek and sexy. Of course, there's no way I'll be slipping that on."

"She gave you a sexy nightgown?" Damn, now that was all he was going to think about. "Will you at least bring it to the hotel and show it to me?"

She nodded. "I'll toss it in my suitcase and let you see it."

"Can I touch it, too? Maybe press it against myself or something?" He glanced down, making her aware of the part of himself he was referring to.

*"Rand."* She gasped. "I can't believe you just said that."

Neither could he, but if getting off on her nightgown was the extent of his pleasure, he just might do it. "What color is it?"

"It's a bright shade of emerald. She got it to match the wedding colors."

"Remind me to thank her later." Rand spun Allison around on the dance floor and kissed her one more time, long and slow, with forbidden thoughts encased in his mind. Even if nothing was going to happen, he could at least pretend that he was going to make love with his wife tonight.

# Six

The Bellamy was inspired by George Vanderbilt's iconic French Renaissance chateau, and the luxurious decor in Allison and Rand's suite reflected that theme, but on a newer, trendier scale. The custom-made furniture, constructed from deep rich woods, shimmered with metallic accents and contemporary engravings. All of the latest gadgets and high-speed technology was provided, as well.

This was definitely a modern honeymoon, Allison thought. Soon after they arrived, they started taking pictures for Rand's social media pages. He orchestrated the selfies, and she followed his lead. He suggested they wear hotel-monogrammed robes with their swimsuits underneath. Hers was a classic one-piece. She had too much breast and hip and butt for those little stringy things. But thankfully she was covered in the photos, her robe securely fastened. Being in her bathing suit in front of

Rand was difficult enough. She didn't want strangers seeing her, too.

At the moment, she sat next to him on the sofa in the living room area, going through the images.

"This is a great shot," he said, holding his phone closer to her. "It's my favorite."

She leaned over to check it out. "It is nice." They definitely looked like romantic honeymooners, bundled in their thick white robes, with a bottle of Dom Pérignon between them.

He tapped on another picture, opening it to its full frame. "I like this one, too." A close-up he'd taken of their hands, their rings beautifully showcased.

She agreed it was effective. "How many are you going to post?"

"Just these two. That should be enough to get the ball rolling. I'll keep the hashtags simple. I'll write something uplifting, too, about how incredibly special my new bride is and how she turned me into a one-woman man."

"I'll post something tomorrow." Allison's social media pages were private. Only close friends and family would be able to see whatever she chose to put out there. "But you can post whatever you want tonight."

"I'll take care of it right now. Why don't you relax in the hot tub and I'll join you when I'm done?"

"Okay." The hot tub was located on a private deck attached to their room. Their accommodations were exceptional, but Rand obviously had his choice of suites. He knew the billionaire owners of the hotel. His world was so different from Allison's.

She grabbed a couple of towels, proceeded to the deck, fired up the jets, removed her robe and sank into the water.

She closed her eyes and lost track of time, unsure of

how many minutes had passed or how much longer it would be before Rand came outside.

Allison just hoped the internet trolls didn't pick her apart. She feared that Rand's followers wouldn't think she was glamorous enough for him. While she understood that he thought of her as innocent and was promoting her as his hopelessly romantic, Irish-country-girl wife, she wished she was comparable to his other women. Just once, she wanted to turn heads.

"I brought the Dom."

She opened her eyes. There stood Rand holding a tray that contained two long-stemmed flutes and the champagne chilling in a silver ice bucket.

He placed the tray beside the hot tub and said, "I figured we should partake in this instead of just using it as a prop."

She nodded and asked, "How did the posts go?"

"They're already starting to get reactions, especially the picture of the two of us. In any event, we'll probably be trending in the top posts by morning. It should get picked up by the gossip blogs following me, too." He sat on the deck. "Ready for some bubbly?"

"Yes. Absolutely." She'd only had a few sips of champagne at the wedding. Besides, she wanted to relax and stop worrying about how Rand's followers were going to react to her.

He popped the cork with a heart-thumping bang, filled both flutes and handed her one.

She tasted it and moaned. He smiled and ditched his robe, exposing his godlike body, his swim trunks as stylish as everything else he wore. He settled into the water, right next to her, and she nearly squeezed her thighs together. He was so close she could smell the lingering cologne on his moonlit skin.

"I should have brought you a snack," he said. "I put the chocolate-covered strawberries the hotel sent up in the fridge, but I can go get them."

"I'm fine." The only thing she was hungry for was her wild-spirited husband. But he wasn't on the menu.

"Oh, wow." He teased her. "You're turning down food?"

"Not just food, but chocolate."

"You must be losing your mind."

She most definitely was, with how badly she wanted him. But sleeping with him wasn't a prudent thing to do. She'd known it when she'd first agreed to marry him, and she knew it now, as rationally as before.

Using the champagne as her consolation prize, she drained her flute and grabbed the bottle for a refill.

About fifteen minutes later, she was on her fourth glass and appreciating the giddy sensation.

"You better slow down," Rand warned.

"I'm just a tad tipsy." Enough to act like an eejit and crawl onto his lap.

He looped his arms around her waist. "I shouldn't be letting you do this."

She ignored his concern and kissed him, snaring his tongue, giving him the kind of shift good girls shouldn't give.

Was she grinding his crotch? Was she making him hard? Yes, indeed, and it felt damned good. Water swirled around them, the jets shooting extra heat in their direction.

So much heat, so much lust. He got harder and harder, devouring her mouth and treating her like his guilty pleasure. But it didn't last.

After a slew of scrumptious kisses, he pulled back. "We need to stop."

"And I think we should keep going." She grinded against him some more and thought about the expletive he favored. "You can whisper your favorite word in my ear, all hot and dirty, before you do it to me."

He groaned in agony and nuzzled the damp ends of her hair. "I'm not doing anything to you that you're going to regret later."

In what was left of the rational side of her brain, she knew he was right to refuse her advances. She was in no condition to make sound decisions. But with the fantasies she'd been having about him, she could hardly blame herself for her behavior. Of course that just might be the champagne talking.

She said, "Fizzy alcohol makes a person drunk faster. I read a scientific study about it."

Rand kept his hands wrapped around her waist. Whether he was trying to stop her from moving around on his lap or savoring the bump-and-grind before he let her go, she couldn't be sure.

"I heard that, too," he replied. "But there's an old saying that the bubbles go straight to your head."

"I think it has more to do with the stomach than the head. But my brain does feel fuzzy." Allison kissed him one last daring time and felt him shudder, his aroused state making her smile.

She climbed off his lap and settled back down in her seat. When she reached for the champagne, he snatched the bottle away from her.

"Oh, no you don't." He poured it out, right onto the deck, where it pooled. She thought it looked like a puddle of pee.

She giggled at her goofy little metaphor. "That's a waste."

"The only thing wasted is you. Come on, sweet girl, let me get you up and ready for bed."

"I'm not even slurring my speech." Even if she was light-headed, she wasn't sloshing her words. Soon she might be. But for now, she was holding her sentences together.

"I'll give you credit for that." He eased her out of the water, and they stood on the deck.

She frowned; she swayed on her feet. Steadying herself, she reached out and traced a tingling hand down his abs, following the muscular ripple.

"It's not fair that you're so hot," she said.

"Yeah, I know. I'm your hottie book hero. Now let's get you dry." He cloaked her with a towel, using it to pat her down.

He was still wet. She watched watery rivulets run down his gorgeous body and drip into the spilled champagne. He was standing in the puddle. So was she.

After he finished drying her, he hastily toweled himself off. Next, he helped her into her robe, the way an old-fashioned suitor might aid a lady with her coat. He even knotted the belt for her. He left his robe on the deck and she was secretly glad he was still bare. She didn't want him to cover up.

They entered the suite, and he led her to the bedroom. "Where are your pajamas?"

"Still in my suitcase. I'll go get them." She dug through her luggage, flinging items to and fro. He shadowed her like a watchdog.

She found the nightgown Megan had given her and tossed it to him. "This is for you."

"Cripes." He caught the long, silky, see-through garment. "This isn't a good time for sexy lingerie."

She glanced up and grinned. Rand clutched the fabric as if it might scorch him. She imagined it setting his big, hard body on fire. "It's okay if you press it against yourself like you said you were going to do."

A muscle jerked in his jaw. "Just get your PJs, Allison."

"Maybe I'll wear that." She tried to tug the night-gown away from him, but he held tight, banning her from having it.

"Spoilsport." She searched for the conservative paja-mas she'd brought, plucking them from the pile of clothes she'd dumped on the floor. "I hardly ever drink, but I have to admit I'm enjoying myself." She motioned to the lingerie in his hands. "And don't forget, you're free to enjoy that."

The nightgown fluttered from his fingertips as he dropped it back into her suitcase. "I'm going to strangle you when you're sober."

She shrugged, and he guided her toward the bathroom.

"I'll wait here for you," he said, letting her know he would remain outside the door.

Before he nudged her inside, she glanced back and sent him a starry-eyed look. "You're a protective husband."

"I ought to be, with all the pledges I made."

She smiled and closed the door. She liked how protec-tive he was. It made her feel warm and melty inside. She removed her robe, fighting the knot Rand had tied, and peeled off her swimsuit. She didn't feel steady enough to shower, so she climbed into her pajamas just the way she was and left her bathing suit and robe balled up to-gether on the floor. However, she managed to brush her teeth. She never went to bed without proper oral hygiene.

She returned to Rand and said, "I forgot to get my underwear out of my suitcase. I don't have anything on under these." She flapped her baggy pin-striped bottoms. "Normally I wear knickers. Sometimes I even wear a sleeping bra. I don't want my breasts dangling to my knees by the time I'm an old lady."

He dropped his gaze. "They look plenty perky to me."

"They're too big." She straightened her spine, jutting out her chest, letting him take his fill. "I always hated being busty." But not tonight, she didn't. Tonight, she appreciated what God had given her. And much to her drunk-and-flirty satisfaction, her nipples had come out to play, creating noticeable peaks under her top.

He continued to stare.

She went delightfully smug. "My eyes are up here, mister." She pointed for effect.

He lifted his gaze, his voice going warm and soft. "I know where those green eyes of yours are."

Now she really felt as if she were floating. He sounded beautifully romantic. When he tucked her into bed, she decided that he was the best husband a bride could have. He kissed her forehead and turned out the light, leaving her alone, steeped in bubbly dreams on their wedding night.

In the morning, Rand cursed himself for being a gentleman, especially when Allison stumbled out to the breakfast table. He could have made love with his wife last night. He could have done wild, wicked things to her. Yeah, he told himself. He could have taken advantage of her while she was drunk, and that would have made him the worst kind of jerk.

She was no longer in her pajamas. She'd changed into a plain T-shirt and lightweight sweatpants. He could tell that she was wearing a bra, her breasts curvaceously bound. He assumed she had panties on, too. But her cautious attire only heightened his desire for her.

"I took a chance and ordered for you," he said. "Eggs,

pancakes, the works, in case you're the type who eats her way out of a hangover." With her appetite, he assumed she might be. He gestured to the aspirin he'd left on her napkin. "That's for you, too."

"The food looks fab. I do have a bit of a headache, but I'm not feeling as bad as I thought I would be. I think breakfast will help." With a sheepish smile, she ducked her head. "I feel stupid about the way I acted last night. I'm embarrassed about it now. I should have known better than to drink like that."

"It was fun seeing you so uninhibited." Of course the raging hard-on she'd given him hadn't been particularly fun, not when he'd restricted himself from doing anything about it.

"You're not going to strangle me now that I'm sober?"

He winced. "You remember me saying that?"

"I remember everything."

So did Rand. Every pelvis-grinding rub, every tongue-tangling kiss, every loopy, sexy thing she'd said to him. The nightgown Megan had given her was burned into his brain, too.

Allison swallowed the aspirin with her juice and placed the napkin on her lap, settling in to eat. "How did you know when to order?"

"I heard the bath running." He'd showered earlier when she was still crashed out. He'd stood under the spray and let the water pummel him.

She glanced at the individual-size teapot in front of her. "Thank you for taking such good care of me."

"No problem." He watched her fix her tea, pouring milk into her cup before she added the steeping brew.

"How are the Instagram posts doing? Is the photo of us trending today like you thought it would be?"

"Yep." He drank his coffee while she sipped her tea.

"The gossip blogs grabbed hold of it, too. They featured it with headings like 'Instafamous American playboy takes proper Irish bride.' One site is calling us AliRan."

She smothered her pancakes in syrup. "Oh, my goodness. They gave us a celebrity-couple nickname?"

"It was paired with a question asking people how long they thought it was going to take for you to realize you'd made a mistake and run for the hills. Get it? AliRan. They even made a meme of it. But I expected stuff like that to happen." He'd been in the public eye long enough to know how the media worked. "I shared the meme on my page with a caption that says AliRan represents you running toward me, not away from me."

"That was a good way to twist it in our favor." She seemed impressed with his marketing savvy. "What types of comments are people making?"

"Overall, my followers are being kind and congratulatory. I blocked a few of them who posted snide things. Unfortunately, I can't do anything about the comments on the gossip sites."

She made a troubled face. "What are they saying?"

"Some people think that you're going to get your heart broken by a womanizer like me. That a seemingly nice girl like you deserves better. And others think I should have married someone who was—"

"Prettier? More glamorous?" she asked.

"Yes, but that's a bunch of bull. You're perfect the way you are." With her dazzling green eyes and shiny red hair, killer body and quirky sense of humor, she was absolutely radiant. "I like everything about you. Besides, no one knows the real us."

She frowned at her tea. "The real us is a lie."

He went after his eggs, eating a forkful before he replied, "We're still real people with real feelings."

"If the public knew that I married you for my green card, they wouldn't think I was so nice. And if they knew about my affair with Rich, they'd probably think I was a bitch for sleeping with a married man."

"As far as you knew, he was getting divorced. And after what that bastard did to you and everyone else, you'd still come off as nice." He didn't have an answer about the green card situation. They would both be crucified for that. But no one was going to find out. They would protect that lie to their dying days.

She heaved a heavy sigh. "Were there any positive comments on the gossip sites? Or did everyone trash us?"

"Lots of people jumped in to defend us, saying that we make a fascinating couple. They're anxious to see our wedding photos. I'm going to post one later today, so it'll start circulating. The photographer emailed the images to me this morning. We can go through them after breakfast."

"Are you still going to do a formal announcement in the newspaper?"

"Definitely." He intended to make a splash in the Royal and Dallas society pages. "We have to strike while the iron is hot. Our honeymoon picture is only going to be trending for a day or so. I'm not the kind of 'celebrity' who stays at the top." He wasn't an entertainer or reality star or athlete. And hadn't acquired a following for being an entrepreneur or visionary or business trendsetter, either. He'd gotten noticed for being a Texas millionaire who took flashy selfies and played around. "AliRan isn't going to become a household name."

She flashed a grin. "You mean we're not going to turn into Kimye or Brangelina?"

"Nope." He laughed a little. "But we can milk Ali-Ran for what's it worth and show everyone what a loyal husband I am while it still matters." His first step to becoming a respected CEO was to clean up his image, and by God he was trying.

"When are we going to fill out the green card marriage application?" she asked.

"If you're up for it, we could do it online today."

"Sure. The sooner the better." She dipped her eggs into the leftover pancake syrup pooling on her plate and took a bite. Damn, he thought. Last night she was kissing and rubbing and making him hard, and this morning he was getting turned on by watching her eat. She glanced up, and they stared at each other, caught in a sexually charged moment. Their marriage was a business arrangement, where temptation wasn't supposed to apply, so he'd better get ahold of himself.

And fast.

Rand had no idea what he was going to do after the divorce or how soon he would start dating other women again. But for now, he wished that he didn't crave his wife as badly as he did.

His only comfort was that she appeared to be trapped in the same dilemma, wanting him as much as he wanted her.

After Allison and Rand came home from The Bellamy, they were inundated with cards, boxes of candy and gift baskets, mostly from Rand's coworkers and business associates, congratulating them on their nuptials.

Although Allison helped him sort through them, her mind was elsewhere. She was nervous about an upcoming fund-raiser at the Texas Cattleman's Club, especially since the club catered to such an elite crowd. Rand was a well-known TCC member, and this would be her first public appearance with him. She didn't want people at the fund-raiser to judge her the way she'd been judged online. She wanted to look pretty, as glamorous as any other woman there.

Maybe she should call Megan and talk to her about it. She could ask her friend to help her shop for a dress and to get ready that night. It was certainly worth a try and better than fretting about it on her own.

Rand checked the card on an elegantly arranged fruit-and-gourmet-cheese basket and said, "Oh, wow. This is from Brisbane Enterprises."

She didn't know who that was, but she took an educated guess. "Is that the company the board of directors wants you to bring in as a new client?"

He nodded. "The CEO's name is Ted Marks. He's the guy who hasn't been returning my calls." He waved the card. "And now he's saying that he and his wife will be attending the Stars and Stripes fund-raiser at the club and are hoping to see us there."

The black-tie event she was so nervous about. "That sounds like a good sign."

"Definitely. I used to run across them at other functions in the past, and they never gave me more than a passing nod. Of course it hadn't mattered to me then. I'll bet his wife is curious about you. From what I heard, she has a strong influence over him."

The thought of Ted Marks's wife taking a curious interest in Allison only intensified her pressure. "What are Ted and his wife like?"

"They're both older, midfifties, proper, the conservative-society types."

She studied the fruit basket. "I'll do my best to make a good impression on them." Which meant looking and feeling her best that night. She was definitely going to call Megan for help. "What's the wife's name?"

He rechecked the card. "Sharon."

"Ted and Sharon Marks. I'll look them up online so I'll recognize them when I see them."

"That's a good idea. There are probably pictures of them together at other fund-raisers." He sent her an appreciative smile. "Thanks for offering to do what you can to make a good impression."

"It's the least I can do." She understood how important the Brisbane account was to him. It factored significantly into why he'd married her. "But I could really use a bit of unwinding now."

"With what?" His smile morphed into a wicked grin. "A bottle of champagne?"

"Ha-ha. Very funny." She was never going to live that down. Nor would she ever forget the desperate heat of straddling his lap. "I was thinking more along the lines of our one-on-one football-rugby match."

"You want to play right now? Sure. Let's do it. But with me being so much bigger and stronger than you, I think I should give you a lead."

"No way. We're playing fair and square. I don't want you going easy on me." She stood tough. "No gender bias."

He roamed his gaze over her. "You'll probably knock me out with those boobs."

She rolled her eyes. Along with her champagne fiasco, she was never going to live down her complaint about her breasts being too big. "You better be prepared to get your arse kicked."

"By a girl?" He looked her over again, teasingly, brutishly. "You're dreaming, sweetheart."

"Did you seriously just call me sweetheart?" Now he'd gone and done it. "For your information, I played in one of the most successful leagues in Ireland."

"One of the most successful *women's* leagues. Look at me, Allison." He made a badass gesture to himself. "There's no way you're going to beat me."

"Oh, really? Well, how about this? If you win, I'll be your maid tonight. I'll do whatever chores you require. And the same applies if I win. I'll get to use you as my houseboy."

"Your houseboy?" He laughed, ridiculing her suggestion. "As in me doing domestic chores for you? Good luck with that."

His chauvinistic confidence was going to be his downfall, of that she was certain. "Shake on it?"

"Hell, yes." He gripped her outstretched hand. "But we're going to have to use an American football. I don't have a rugby ball."

"That's fine." She took her hand back. "There's not enough of a difference to matter. You can set the rules, too."

"Are you sure you don't want me to give you a lead?"

"I'm positive." She wasn't taking charity for a sport she'd triumphed in since childhood. "We both need to change. Then we can meet in the backyard."

"It's your funeral. But don't say that I didn't warn you."

"Likewise." She tore off up the stairs before him.

In no time, he shot up behind her with his heavy male footsteps pounding the wood. He was already breathing down her neck, behaving as if he wanted to tackle her right then and there. Allison only smiled, eager for the match to begin. She wanted nothing more than to knock her big, strong, arrogant husband down to size.

# Seven

*Whoop! Whoop!*

Allison did the happy dance. She jumped and gyrated and wiggled her hips. She clapped and rejoiced in her victory. She'd won the match!

It hadn't been easy; she would probably have bruises on her bottom, given how many times she'd hit the ground. She'd never played a more challenging game. But she'd scored more points than Rand. She'd managed to tackle him, too, to knock him tail over teakettle.

In fact, he sat on the grass at this very instant, glaring up at her as she danced.

"Don't be such a sore loser," she said, still whirling about.

He grabbed her ankle, sending her off-kilter. She stumbled and fell, landing next to him with a thud. He laughed and rolled on top of her, pinning her beneath his linebacker's body.

"Who's in charge now?" he asked.

"This doesn't count. I already won." But by goodness, he was heavy. She couldn't get away if she tried.

He stared down at her. "You won because I let you."

"That's hogwash." She was certain that he'd played his best game. "I'm faster than you, and you know it." She'd outrun him when it mattered. "You underestimated me, and it cost you the game."

"All right, so you took me by surprise. But now I've got you, and you can't escape."

"You're still going to be my houseboy." She frowned. "Unless I gave you a concussion. You have a cut on your forehead." She gently touched the area around the wound. "It's bleeding."

"That's no big deal. I'm totally clearheaded. I'm even aware of how damn sexy you look right now."

"You're flirting with me, after I just kicked your arse? Now I know you're concussed." She tried not to swoon. Being called sexy by him was making her heart pound. She skimmed his hair away from his eyes. "Let's go inside and I'll clean that cut and put a bandage on it."

"Okay. But I'm only agreeing because I like it when you touch me." He lifted his body from hers, like a panther releasing its prey.

Allison stood and dusted herself off. "I've got first-aid supplies in my bathroom." She gestured for him to follow her.

They went upstairs together, and Rand sat on the closed lid of the commode while Allison dampened a washcloth at the sink.

She wiped away the blood on his forehead. "The cut's not as deep as I thought it was."

"I knew it wasn't anything to be concerned about."

He watched as she doctored him. "But it feels nice to be cared for."

After dabbing an antiseptic ointment on the cut, she fumbled with the paper wrapping on the bandage.

"I don't think I need that," he said.

"And I say you do." She fitted the flexible material to his skin. "You're all set now."

His gaze locked on to hers. "I like it here."

Did he mean *here* in her bathroom with her standing between his legs? If that was his implication, she liked it, too. His primal scent mingled with hers. They were both sticky with sweat and had grass stains on their clothes, too.

"You're supposed to be fulfilling your duty as my houseboy," she reminded him.

"So give me a chore, and I'll do it."

A crazy, wonderful, dangerously erotic task came to mind. Full-on lovemaking, she thought.

Allison couldn't deny how desperately she wanted her husband. He was all she thought about, dreamed about, fantasized about. But if she went through with it, she would have to be prepared for the consequences. But not all consequences resulted in adverse effects. Feel-good rewards were possible, too.

So was she going to do it? Was she going to give up the fight and have an affair with her husband?

Yes, by God, she was. If she didn't, she would never quit lusting after him. Yet it wasn't just the thrill of sex that drove her. Little by little, she'd begun to trust Rand and stop comparing him to Rich. Rand hadn't done anything to hurt her. He'd been kind and honorable all along. Just thinking about how gently he'd tucked her into bed on their wedding night made her want him even more. He could've taken advantage of her inebriated state, but he'd protected her instead. And now, on this post-honeymoon day, she craved every gorgeous part of him. But she wasn't going to regret her actions later. No remorse, she told herself, no self-condemnation.

Only heat. Only pleasure.

Instead of telling him what she had in mind, she said, "You can draw my bath."

"That's my chore?" His voice turned sandpapery. He even cleared his throat. "I wasn't expecting it to be something so personal. But if that's what you want, I'll do it."

She wanted a whole lot more. But for now, she was taking it slow. "You can pour some of my body gel into the water, too. To make it foamy." She walked over to a freestanding caddy. "It's this one." She lifted the blue-and-white bottle from the top shelf.

He approached the claw-foot tub. "How warm do you like the water?"

"However warm you think it should be." She stepped back, giving him carte blanche.

He turned on the faucet and let the water run. He tested the temperature a few times, adjusting it to a level that seemed to satisfy him. Then he asked, "Do you want to check to make sure?"

"I trust you." But trusting herself was another story. She was breaking all of her own rules.

He took the body gel from her, removed the cap and sniffed the contents. "It's nice. It smells like coconut."

"It's a Polynesian blend." Or that was how the product was advertised.

"How much of it should I add?"

"As much as you think it needs."

"You're making this hard on me."

He had no idea how *hard* she intended for things to

get. But soon he would. "You lost the game. This isn't supposed to be easy."

He poured a capful of the gel into the water. When it didn't foam to his liking, he added more. "How's that?"

"It's perfect. I couldn't have done it better myself."

After the tub was full, he turned off the faucet. "There you go. Your bath is ready." He made a gentlemanly bow, exaggerating his duty to her. "I'll leave you alone now." He turned to leave. "I need to get cleaned up, too."

"You're not going anywhere."

He spun around, stopping in midstride. "What?"

She removed a fresh washcloth from a nearby towel rack and tossed it into the water. "You're going to scrub my back."

He shook his head, backing himself against the sink. "That's not a good idea."

"It's part of your chore."

"Oh, yeah? Well, the minute you take off your clothes and climb into that tub, I'm going to want to do a lot more than scrub your back."

She shot him her best naughty-girl smile. She wasn't skilled at seduction, but she was giving it a heart-hammering try. "So who's stopping you?"

The ruggedness in his voice returned. "You're giving me permission to take what I want?"

"Yes." She most definitely was. But before she lost her nerve, she lifted her top over her head and tossed it aside. She removed her shoes and sweatpants, too. All that was left was her undergarments: plain white knickers and a shock-absorbing sports bra. Not exactly the type of lingerie designed for foreplay. But they'd served her well during the match.

Rand watched every move she made, his gaze darting from her ponytailed head to the wedding-white polish on her toenails.

He said, "This is pretty damned amazing, because after the hot tub incident on our honeymoon night, I've been having water fantasies about you."

"At least I'm sober this time." She was in control of her faculties. Or she was supposed to be, anyway. Her pulse roared in her ears.

He gestured for her to finish. "Go on."

Allison shed her bra, releasing her breasts. Her nipples peaked the second they hit the air. Her knickers came next. She peeled them all the way down, with her husband as her audience.

She sank into the bath. Surrounded by suds, she swished the water and said, "It's your turn."

He didn't waste a coconut-infused second. He got undressed and joined her, facing her, with his legs parted and his knees slightly bent. The tub was big enough for both of them, and she suspected that some of his other lovers had invited him to share it with them, too. She doubted this was new to him. But no one else could claim to be his wife. That was her title, at least for now, and it felt wonderful.

Beautiful.

Erotic.

Exciting.

Rand leaned forward and kissed her, his mouth hot and thrilling against hers. She wrapped her arms around him, dissolving into his fervid touch.

Once they separated, he bathed her. He ran the cloth over her naked body, washing her everywhere, spending extra time on her breasts and between her thighs. Her eyes drifted closed. She was so enraptured she could've been floating out to sea.

"Stand up, Allison."

She started and opened her eyes. "What? Why?"

"Why do you think?"

He smiled suggestively, deliberately, and his intention became clear. Oral sex: his mouth between her legs. She'd never allowed anyone to do that to her. She always thought it was too intimate, too private, too embarrassing. But she wasn't going to refuse him. This was her awakening, her chance to be free. Being repressed wasn't part of the plan.

Still, she hesitated, taking a moment to grasp her newfound abandonment.

"Do you need help?" he asked. "Is the tub too slippery?"

"No. I've got it." As nervous as she was, she was excited, too. She proceeded to stand, offering herself to the man she married.

Rand gazed up at Allison, puzzling over her complexity. She seemed timid, yet anxious to be dominated. Or maybe in her own shyly sexual way, she was dominating him. This was her seduction, after all, her idea to bathe together.

"This is a first for me," she said.

He moved closer. "A first what?"

*"You know."* She gestured to him, down on his knees in front of her.

Holy hot-blooded hell. His pulse nearly jumped out of his skin. "No other man has ever…?"

"I've never been comfortable letting anyone touch me that way. And now here I am standing completely naked in a brightly lit bathroom, in an old-fashioned tub, with my husband…"

He liked that she narrated the scene, even if he was

smack-dab in the middle of it. The verbal picture she painted was wildly arousing. So was the sudsy water snaking down her stomach and heading for the V between her thighs.

He wiped it away in one fell swoop. Then, eager to take what he wanted, he spread her with his fingers and tasted her with his tongue. She shivered on contact, and he repeated the sweet, slick process.

He glanced up to see if her eyes were closed. But they were wide-open. Little Miss Innocent was watching.

He licked and swirled, and she reached for his shoulders, using him as an anchor. He planted his hands on her butt, one on each cheek, prompting her to widen her stance.

She moaned, and he went no-holds-barred. He enjoyed turning on his lovers. But being the first to give Allison this kind of pleasure was exhilarating. She pitched forward, tugging her hands through his hair.

Everything she did, every reaction, encouraged him to take her to the next level, to ramp up the heat, pushing her further and further. He created sensations that he could see in her eyes. She was still watching him.

Rand pulled her closer, treating her to more of the same, and she came in a series of sticky-wet convulsions, pulsating against his mouth.

Upon her completion, she swayed on her feet. Sinking back into the tub, she smiled dizzily at him. Neither of them spoke. There wasn't anything to say. Allison looked as if she might melt and swirl, right along with the leftover foam in the water.

Rand wasn't done with her yet, but with her as loopy as she was, he gave her time to recover.

He continued their bath. He even released her ponytail and washed her hair, using a handheld shower attachment.

She sighed. "Everything you've been doing to me feels so good."

He nuzzled her nape. Presently, she was nestled between his thighs, her back to his front. "If I'd known how seductive losing a football match could be, I would have hurried up and lost it sooner."

She sighed again. "I haven't even done anything to you yet."

"You let me be the first guy to put his mouth on you. That's a major deal." It made him feel more important than any of her other lovers.

She leaned against him. "Do you want to finish this now?"

"Here, in the tub? I'd rather take you to bed." As tempting as her invitation was, he would prefer to roll around in the sheets, where there was more room to play.

"That sounds good to me, too."

"Then let's go."

They exited the bath, and once they were warm and dry, Rand carried his wife straight to her canopy-draped bed.

The crush Allison had on Rand before was nothing compared to how she felt now. This was turning out to be the most compelling day of her life.

While she waited to be ravished by him, he went to his suite to get protection.

He returned with a box of condoms, removed one and put the rest of them in the nightstand drawer. "These are for future use. I still have extras in my room, too."

"You're such a responsible playboy." The Band-Aid on

his forehead made him seem boyish. But his big, strong body was all muscle. "You deserve a merit badge."

He settled into bed with her. "You can give me one."

She reached between his legs. "Maybe this should be your reward instead." As she stroked him, the intensity of touching him rippled through her: the hardness, the silkiness, the power that radiated from him.

He smiled, and she glanced down. He was leaking at the tip. She circled him with her thumb, and he kissed her.

With lust shimmering between them, they closed their eyes and kissed some more, steeped in romantic rapture.

He lifted his mouth from hers, and she opened her eyes. His were open, too, and focused on her.

He roamed his hands along both sides of her body, following her shape, her curves. "Now I have to decide how to take you."

A hungry shiver slid down her spine. She assumed he was talking about sexual positions. "You can do it however you want." She just wanted him inside her, thrusting hard and deep. After what he'd done to her in the tub, she was more than ready for him.

He grabbed her, full-force, and they tumbled over the bed, messing up the covers. "I want it every way imaginable. I think I'm getting consumed with you. But no one has been forbidden to me before."

"I'm not forbidden to you anymore." She arched her hips, savoring the feeling. By now, he was braced above her, his chest upright, his pelvis pinned to hers.

"I know, but it still seems as if you are." He took the condom from the nightstand and tore into the wrapper. "There's just something about us being together..."

She bit down on her bottom lip. "Maybe it's the no-sex clause we're breaking."

"Yeah, that's probably it. This taboo thing we've

got going on, with you seeming so innocent to me." He sheathed himself. "I've been trying all of this time not to corrupt you, and now here you are, being bad with me."

Allison keened out a moan. There was no time to formulate a reply. Not with how quickly he slid between her thighs and pushed inside.

He set a potent rhythm, and soon they were rocking back and forth, moving together, hot and slick and desperate. He caught his breath, and she wondered if his heart was machine gunning his chest. Hers thumped like mad.

He whispered something distinctly dirty in her ear, using his favorite word. She repeated it to him, and a sound akin to a growl rumbled from his throat. His feral behavior thrilled her, but she was being animalistic, too. She dug her nails into his back, probably leaving half-moon marks on his skin.

From his growl of approval, he obviously liked it. So she clawed him with even more force, making the sex rougher.

A few breathless beats later, he rolled over, putting her on top. She straddled his lap, impaling herself and taking him all the way inside. He circled her waist, lifting her up and down. She leaned forward to kiss him, to devour his deliciously sinful mouth.

Nothing was ever going to be the same, Allison thought. Not after having Rand Gibson as her lover. She wanted to eat him alive.

Within no time, he maneuvered their positions again, reclaiming his place on top. Admiring his godlike presence, she thought about that very first day at the statue of Diana and how far they'd progressed since then.

He used his fingers to enhance her pleasure, driving

her toward a release. Thrashing beneath him, her vision blurred and her brain went fuzzy.

She came in a flurry, making orgasmic sounds, lost in the forbidden sensation. She'd never been noisy in bed, but Rand made everything feel so wild and new.

While she morphed into a pool of mush, he spiraled toward his own core-shocking release. When it happened, he tossed back his head, the cords in his neck straining.

In the aftermath, or the afterglow or whatever it was supposed to be, his arms buckled, his body assailing hers with a masculine jounce.

She buried her face in his neck. "I think I just got tackled."

He laughed, his breathing labored. "Am I crushing you?"

"No." She enjoyed holding him this way, his naked-ness warm against hers. She skimmed a hand down his spine, following each and every vertebra. "You can stay a while."

He didn't stay as long as she would've liked. He made his way to the bathroom to dispose of the condom. He returned and got back into bed with her. But he didn't lie down. He propped a pillow and sat up. Alison followed his lead and braced herself with a pillow, too.

He said, "If we smoked, this is where we would break out a pack of cigarettes and light up."

"Have you ever smoked?" There was still so much they didn't know about each other, so much left to learn.

"I tried it when I was a kid, but I didn't like it, so I never did it again. I assume you never have." He reached over to smooth her hair. "You don't seem like the type."

"Your assumption is correct." She appreciated the way he touched her, the gentle dusting of his fingers in her hair. He'd already done a splendid job of shampooing it.

He lowered his hand. "You're not going to go all wifely now that we did this, are you?"

She furrowed her brow. "Are you asking if sex is going to make me feel more attached to you?"

He nodded. "This could never turn real, Allison. No matter how good it is between us, I don't have it in me to be anything more than a fake husband."

Something inside her went tight. Her chest? Her lungs? Her pride? All of the above? Shielding herself from the discomfort it caused, she said, "I can handle having an affair with you. Otherwise, I wouldn't have done it."

"I'm sorry. I shouldn't have doubted you. I guess I just got a sudden fear of how starry-eyed you are."

"I might be a hopeless romantic, but the last thing I want is to fall in love with the wrong man." She wouldn't—*couldn't*—lose her heart to Rand. "Being around you is helping me learn to trust again. But I'm not going to turn it into something more than friendship. Or desire," she added, letting him know how important the sex was. "It's just my cure for lusting after you."

He smiled and invaded her space, lifting her off her pillow and into his arms. "I don't know how I'm ever going to get enough of you."

"We're just going to have to learn to pace ourselves." She trailed a finger down the center of his chest, heading toward his abs and making his stomach muscles jump. "Maybe after this, we should wait a day or so to do it again."

"Are you suggesting that we deprive ourselves of what we want most?"

"Why not?" She liked the idea of rebuilding the tension, of putting each other under a torturous spell. "It'll make the next time even more exciting."

"Maybe so, but I'm not even done this time."

She pondered over him, this man who inspired her to play flirtatious games. "I'm not sure if that makes you incorrigible or insatiable."

"I'm both, especially now that I'm with you. But sex has always been my outlet."

"I think it's becoming mine now, too." She trailed lower. He was getting hard again. "And it's all because of you."

He watched her, his gaze following the movement of her hand. "So I really am corrupting you."

She gave him credit where it was due. "It feels amazing to be this free, this wild, and especially with you." Plus it was a whole lot safer than getting attached to him, she thought.

"Then I'm glad I could be of service." With a tongue-tangling kiss, he stole her breath.

A moment later, he went after another condom and nudged her legs apart, getting both of them ready for another hot, steamy, wickedly depraved round.

# Eight

On the day of the fund-raiser, Allison went to Pure, the spa at The Bellamy, the same fabulous five-star resort where Allison and Rand had spent their wedding night. Megan arranged the entire thing, making sure Allison got everything the luxurious salon had to offer.

Nevertheless, Allison still fretted. Her package included a full makeover, but would it be enough to make her as glamorous as the other women attending the fund-raiser? Would it make the internet trolls sit up and take notice? Of course it wasn't just about them. She wanted to impress Rand, too.

Along with Allison, Megan was getting pampered, as well. And so was Selena Jacobs. Selena was a feisty little thing, graced with sultry features and glossy black hair. She was also Will Sanders's ex-wife—the *real* Will, not Rich Lowell.

From what Allison gathered, Selena and Will had been

too young and incompatible to make their marriage work and had gotten divorced years ago. These days, she was engaged to rancher and business tycoon Knox McCoy. Although Selena and Knox had known each other since college, their friendship had just recently blossomed into love. They were even expecting a child. But the early stages of pregnancy hadn't slowed Selena down. She remained focused on her career as the creator and CEO of Clarity, a locally sourced, cruelty-free line of skin care products and cosmetics. She'd secured an exclusive deal with Pure, and today her products were being used to transform Allison.

Or so Allison hoped. For now, she was getting her hair done. She'd already had a facial, and she had to admit, the deep cleansing mask they'd applied had left her skin feeling smooth and dewy.

Rand didn't know she was at the salon. She hadn't told him that she was getting a new hairdo and having her makeup completely redone. Allison barely wore cosmetics so aside from her wholesome look at their wedding, with just traces of mascara, lip gloss and blush, Rand had never seen her glammed up.

As far as he knew, she was having lunch with Megan and Selena. But Rand was busy this afternoon, too. He was joining forces with Will to discuss the impostor case. Later, he and Allison would meet up at home and leave for the fund-raiser together.

With Megan's help, Allison had already shopped for a gown. She'd chosen a long, flowing, gold-sequined number. She hadn't shown it to Rand. She wanted to surprise him with her makeover, including the dress. This was an important night for both of them. It marked their first public appearance as husband and wife, with lots of photo opportunities. Then there was the friendly conversation they hoped to have with Ted and Sharon Marks, an exchange that could ultimately help Rand land the Brisbane deal and save his career.

Talk about pressure. Allison could barely breathe.

Struggling to relax, she gazed at herself in the mirror. A male stylist stood nearby, mixing a concoction for her hair. Megan and Selena were on either side of her, also getting their hair clipped and swooped and swirled. But they were used to preparing for glamorous parties.

Allison glanced over at Megan. She actually seemed a bit out of sorts today, quieter than usual, as if she had a lot on her mind, too.

As for Allison, she was just trying to fit into Rand's high society world without feeling like a fish out of water. She was also trying to get a grip on her relationship with him. By no means did she regret the marathon sex they'd had. If anything, she craved him more and more. More than she should. More than was natural.

It had been her idea to wait to do it again, and he'd honored her wishes. So yesterday, they hadn't touched each other at all. They hadn't even slept in the same bed. And now she wanted Rand in the worst way.

In the future, there would be no more waiting, no more hungry days or tortuous nights. The next time they made love, they would keep doing it, at least until the divorce. Regardless of how intimate they'd become, their marriage was still going to end. There was no reason to stay together. Allison would be a fool to fall in love with an untamable man.

She might be a hopeless romantic, but she wasn't going to put herself through the wringer.

When Allison fell in love, it would be with someone who wanted her to be attached to him, who wanted to be married forever. The type of guy who valued commitment, needing it as much as she did. Rand had helped her trust again, but he'd warned her time and again that he wasn't meant to be her dream man. All Rand could give her was the affair they'd embarked on.

With lots of glorious hot sex.

Rand met Will on the outskirts of town, with their vehicles parked on the side of an unpaved road. They considered getting together at the Texas Cattleman's Club in one of the private conference rooms, but they changed their minds. On this fund-raiser day, the club was besieged with activity, with caterers and florists and organizers preparing for the event, and Will couldn't take the chance of being seen by anyone who wasn't involved in the case or didn't know he wasn't dead. Since Will was lying low, he never came into the office anymore, either. So, now, whenever the two men consulted about business, it was done behind the scenes. But today they would be talking about the impostor.

Will claimed that he had lots of news to share, and Rand was eager to hear it. They stood outside of their cars, a dry summer breeze stirring the air.

Between the isolated setting and Will's dark glasses and low-brimmed hat, Rand felt as if he was in the throes of a movie with a mysterious plot. Only all of this was real.

Rand studied his friend in the harsh glare of the sun. Will had always been Royal's wonder boy, the envy of many a man and the fantasy of scores of women. Along with his family's connection to Spark Energy Solutions, he was rich and handsome and lived in the main house at the Ace in the Hole, one of the biggest and most impressive ranches in Royal. Success oozed from his blood. At thirty, he was younger than Rand by about seven years.

Today Will looked more like a ranch hand than a wealthy guy. Not only was he dressed like a cowboy, he was driving one of his ranch's work trucks. Rand was driving the luxury sedan he'd offered to Allison for the duration of their marriage. But she was still taking Uber around town.

Will said, "The DNA results from the ashes still aren't in yet. But I'll let you know as soon as they are."

Rand frowned. They had no choice but to wait for the outcome, but he wished it would come sooner than later.

"The authorities have been following the money trail Rich left behind," Will went on to say. "There were plenty of withdrawals and transfers from before, but nothing that indicates whether he's alive or dead now. Also, I've been tracking everything he took from my personal and business accounts, but I haven't come across any purchases or investments that pin him down."

"So where did he stash all that money?" Rand thought about what Rich had stolen from Allison, as well.

"I don't know. But he ripped off the TCC, too. Since I served as treasurer and he was posing as me, he had full access to the club's accounts."

"Son of a bitch." Rand kicked a small stone beneath his shoe. "What else is going on? I can tell there's more." Will's distress seemed evident.

"It's Jason. Megan's brother." His friend blew out a hard breath. "I'm worried that he might be involved. Or he might have been victimized somehow, too. But at this point, I'm just grasping at straws."

Rand shook his head in confusion. "I don't understand. Isn't he overseas finishing up an international deal?" Jason worked for Spark Energy Solutions, too. Rand didn't know him very well on a personal level, but he certainly knew that Jason was a valuable asset to the company.

"Yes, that's where he's supposed to be. But he appears to be keeping his distance, and that isn't like him. He has a little daughter, Savannah, and he always communicates with her when he's on the road. She received some sporadic emails from him, saying that he's been off the grid and can't FaceTime with her. But that's the only explanation he gave."

"That is weird. But maybe it's the truth. Maybe he's off the beaten path and doesn't have reliable Wi-Fi. Didn't he take some extra time away from his assignment to be alone and mourn your death? That could explain why he's in a remote location. People do strange things when they're grieving."

"That's what I thought at first, too. But I've been trying to reach him with emergency calls to let him know what's going on and that I'm still alive, and he hasn't responded to me."

"Are the authorities okay with you calling him?"

Will nodded. "They agreed that I should reach out to him and see what kind of response I get. But I haven't heard from him at all."

"Have you talked to Megan about this?" Rand knew that when Megan first received the urn with Will's supposed ashes, Jason had sent her a handwritten note saying that he'd seen the body. He was the one who identified the person who died in that crash as being Will. Of course later the assumption was that he'd seen Rich's body.

"Yes, I spoke to Megan, and she's worried, too."

Rand thought about the fact that Jason hadn't come back for the funeral. Was that a bad sign? Or was he really just taking time away to mourn Will? "If Rich is still alive, then Jason sending home the ashes makes no sense.

But until the results are back, there isn't much you can do but keep trying to reach Jason and hope for the best."

"I don't intend to give up. One way or another, I'm going to find out what's going on." Will lowered his sunglasses a fraction, giving Rand an intense look. "So I heard you got married." He smiled a little. "*You*. The wilding of Royal."

"What can I say? I fell in love." Rand smiled, too, even if he felt heavy inside. Will never criticized him for his lifestyle. He'd always accepted Rand for who he was, and now if there was anyone Rand hated lying to, it was Will. But he didn't have a choice. "Allison and I bonded after your funeral."

"I'm glad something good came of it," he said. "Congratulations for finding the right woman. I'm happy for you."

"Thanks. That means a lot coming from you." Even if his marriage wasn't what it seemed, he appreciated Will's support.

"You're the last guy anyone expected to settle down. But here you are, with a loyal wife by your side."

"Allison is amazing." Rand couldn't be cleaning up his image without her. She was amazing in other ways, too. He couldn't wait to get down and dirty with her again, to continue the affair they'd started. He couldn't recall wanting anyone so badly. Nor was he going to worry about how he'd "corrupted" her in bed. It wasn't as if she was going to go off the rails and become a wanton woman because of it. Allison was still the same sweet girl she'd been before they'd married. She would always have an innocence about her, as far as he was concerned. "I better go. I've got that fund-raiser later."

"I'll get back in touch when I have more news."

"I hope you hear from Jason soon."

"Me, too." Will paused. "Good luck to you and Allison."

"Thanks." They shook hands and climbed into their respective vehicles. Rand headed home, wondering if Allison was back from her lunch date yet.

When he arrived, she was in her room with the door closed. He knew enough about women not to disturb her. If she was getting ready for the fund-raiser, she probably needed time alone.

Rand got ready, too. He showered and shaved, keeping his beard stubble trimmed the way he always did. His hair was easy enough, cut in a deliberately tousled style that required minimal care.

He checked the time. He had an hour or so to spare, so he sat around in a towel and played on the internet.

Finally, he got dressed. Rand had a collection of designer formal wear to choose from.

Rather than check on Allison or knock on the doors that separated their suites, he went downstairs to wait for her. He sat in the living room like a teenager on his way to the prom.

Rand was anxious about the fund-raiser, with how many different purposes it would be serving. He wanted to get to the club a little early, if possible. Normally he was "fashionably late" to these types of events. But that was the old Rand. The new one was supposed to follow proper protocol and show up on time.

As soon as he heard Allison's footsteps coming down the stairs, he stood and smoothed his jacket. Only the moment he saw her, he couldn't speak. He just stared at her, with his mouth dumbly agape.

Who was this stunning sequined creature gliding toward him? Her hair cascaded in thick waves, with one unusually bright red streak framing the right side of her face. Her eyes were dark and smoky, and her lips were the color of Rand's favorite burgundy wine. She looked airbrushed, flawless…unreal.

A vision in gold.

He blinked to be sure he wasn't dreaming. Her gown fit her to perfection, its long, sweeping lines accentuating her curves.

She smiled. "I wanted to surprise you."

"Well, you did. You totally did. You're so damned gorgeous I don't know what to say." Everything about her was revamped, right down to her femme fatale heels and matching clutch. "I thought you were at lunch today."

"I was at Pure, the salon at The Bellamy. I asked Megan to help me prepare for the fund-raiser, and she arranged for my makeover. She also got Selena involved. The salon gave me a facial and did my makeup with her Clarity products. Selena prepared a care package for me, too, with skin care and cosmetics I can use at home. There's even a honey lip balm, softer and smoother than the one I usually wear." She touched the streak in her hair. "Both Selena and Megan suggested that I get something dramatic done with my hair."

"What about the dress?" He couldn't get over how different she looked.

"Megan helped me shop for it. I trusted her to steer me in the right direction."

Rand wanted to steer Allison back up the stairs and straight into his big brass bed. He removed his cell phone from his pocket to take her picture. "You're going to be the talk of the town. Of the internet, too. The gossip bloggers are going to go crazy for this new look of yours. So are my followers."

She posed prettily for him. "I was hoping to get their attention. But I wanted to look good for you, too. And for myself. I always wondered what being glamorous would feel like."

"And how does it feel?" He took more pictures. She was as glamorous as a woman could be. He'd dated models and actresses and socialites who didn't compare to how breathtaking she looked right now.

"It's a bit like being Cinderella, I suppose. Except without the missing slipper or the happily-ever-after, marrying-the-prince thing." She gestured to him. "I'm already married to a hot guy." She moved closer, just inches from him. "Albeit temporarily."

He put his phone away, and suddenly he felt strange about sharing her pictures on social media. Not because he wasn't proud to show her off. But because he got the uncharacteristic urge of wanting to keep her to himself. Of course that made no sense. He'd married Allison to change his image, and posting pictures of her was an important part of his being-tamed-by-his-wife campaign.

"Are you all right?" she asked. "You zoned out there for a minute."

"I'm fine." It wasn't as if he was actually being tamed by her. He reached around to feel for the zipper on her dress, pulling her close. "I'm stripping you bare after we get back." He already intended to make love with her tonight. He even had something special planned. "I'm peeling this right off you."

"Promise?" She slipped her arms around his waist.

"Oh, yeah." He considered kissing her, but he didn't want to mess up her lipstick. For now, he behaved like the gentleman he was supposed to be. Later, he would mess her up plenty. "I better let you go." Rand released his hold on her. He'd already taken a chance by manhandling her zipper. He knew how fragile ball gowns could be, especially the sequined variety.

"How did your meeting with Will go?" she asked.

"He filled me in on some financial stuff. But there's still no word on the DNA results."

Allison heaved a sigh. "That test seems like it's taking forever. But I guess it's just my impatience."

"Yeah, mine, too. I hate not knowing."

"Megan seemed distracted at the salon today. I figured she might be thinking about the case. But if there isn't anything new, maybe that wasn't what was on her mind."

Rand made a tight face. "She could have been thinking about her brother, Jason." He repeated what Will had told him. "It's probably nothing to worry about. But until someone hears from Jason, there's always the possibility that something went wrong."

"Oh, how awful. I hope it turns out to be nothing."

Rand sure as hell hoped so, too. "We should get going. We have a big evening ahead of us."

"Yes, we do." Her racy red lips curved into a sensual smile. "In all sorts of ways."

Well, hot damn. Now he was back to wanting to strip her bare. "You're a tease, Mrs. Gibson."

She tossed her trendy new hair over her shoulder. "Likewise, Mr. Gibson." She walked ahead of him, en route to the garage, her stilettos clicking on the hard-wood floors.

As soon as he was able, he was going to make her purr like the sex kitten she'd become. But first, they had to make an appearance at the fund-raiser.

Allison was having a grand time. The Texas Cattle-man's Club was known for raising money for organizations throughout the globe, but since the Stars and Stripes fund-raiser was a patriotic celebration on the heels of an American holiday, the proceeds would be divided among

United States charities that included children's hospitals and disaster relief funds.

The ballroom was decorated in red, white and blue, and a majestic bald eagle ice sculpture, representing the United States emblem, embellished the buffet. A fireworks display was scheduled for later, and she suspected it would be nothing short of spectacular.

When Allison and Rand first arrived, they sampled the food, enjoying an array of appetizers. They slow danced, too, showing everyone how blissfully in love they looked, swaying in each other's arms. But now they were mingling on their own. He was having a drink with Ted Marks, and it appeared to be going well. Allison had already socialized separately with Sharon Marks, too. In fact, they'd hit it off splendidly. As it turned out, Ted and Sharon had spent their thirtieth wedding anniversary in Ireland, where they toured the medieval castles that Sharon had been anxious to see. The Marks had also spent a few days in Kenmare, which they both adored. To Allison, that seemed like a marvelous twist of fate.

So far, this entire night had been wondrous. When she spotted Megan and Selena coming her way, she smiled. She couldn't thank them enough for her makeover.

Selena spoke first. "Well, look at you." She checked Allison out with a low whistle. "You're the belle of the ball. I'll bet your husband was drooling all over himself when he first saw you."

Allison laughed. "I did make quite an impression on him. He can't wait to get his hands on me later." She leaned in close. "And I just might let him."

Selena laughed, too. "I'll bet."

Megan stepped up and said, "The dress totally works with the hair and the makeup. It's stunning on you."

"Thank you. I couldn't have done any of this without

you and Selena. You're like my fairy godmothers." She toasted them with her club soda. She decided to skip the champagne tonight. "And speaking of beauties, you're both as gorgeous as ever." Selena wore a blazing scarlet gown, and Megan's long black silk sheath boasted jeweled accents.

After a moment's pause, Allison studied Megan a bit deeper. Did she have thoughts of her hard-to-reach brother on her mind? Allison softly said to her, "I noticed how distracted you seemed earlier, and when I mentioned it to Rand, he told me about what's going on. I hope everything turns out okay. That there's nothing to worry about."

"Thank you. You must be really astute because I was trying not to let my feelings show. I hope I didn't put a damper on your time at the salon."

"Not at all. But I was still concerned about you."

"That's so nice of you, but I'll be fine. Instead of sitting around and worrying, I decided that I'm going to be proactive and take some self-defense classes. I always wanted to learn to kick some butt, and this seems like the perfect time to do it."

Allison couldn't agree more. "Women need to empower themselves."

"Yes, we most certainly do." Megan offered a confident smile. "We need show the world what we're made of."

"Hear, hear." Selena grinned, too, and twirled the straw in her soda.

Allison found both women fascinating. Selena had always been friendly but before their trip to Pure she'd been more aloof than warm. Since Selena had fallen in love with Knox, she was opening up to more people, including Megan and Allison.

Megan and Selena certainly shared interesting backgrounds, Allison thought, with how oddly connected to Will they were. Of course, Selena was happy with Knox now, her past with Will Sanders a distant memory.

Megan was still knee-deep in Will's impostor situation. And so was Allison. Not with Will, per se, but with her marriage to Rand. In that regard, they were impostors themselves.

"I should get back to my husband," Allison said. She noticed that his chat with Ted Marks had ended, and now Rand was looking her way.

"Enjoy the rest of your evening." Megan gave Allison a sisterly hug, and she and Selena drifted into the crowd.

Allison turned toward Rand, and as they approached each other, she disposed of her empty glass. He no longer had a drink in his hand, either. As soon as they were close enough to touch, he swept her in his arms and kissed her. She sighed like a schoolgirl, immersed in the taste of him.

Afterward, he said, "I wanted to do that the moment I saw you coming down the stairs at home, but I didn't want to mess up your lipstick."

She hadn't considered her makeup, but she wasn't used to fussing over it. "Is it messed up now?"

"No. It still looks good. Did I get any of it on me?"

"A little. But I can take care of that for you." She wiped the pale red smear off him, and in that cozy moment, one of the photographers who'd been hired to cover the event took their picture. Allison didn't doubt how tender the image probably looked. But her affection for Rand had been genuine. His kiss had been real, too. They weren't being complete impostors tonight.

Once the photographer set his sights on someone else, Rand said to Allison, "Guess what I discovered about

Ted?" He answered his own question. "His mother lives in the same retirement community as my grandmother."

"Really? Do you think your granny and his ma know each other?"

"We're not sure. But we plan to ask them." He reached for her hand and held it. "We should have Ted and Sharon over for a barbecue at the house. I think they would accept the invitation, and I definitely think it would be good for business."

"Then we'll do that for sure, maybe even this weekend if they're available. We can invite his ma and your granny, too. We can make it a family affair." She beamed. "I can make some traditional Irish food to go along with whatever you want to barbecue. I suspect that Sharon will want to help me. She mentioned being part of a cooking club and likes to try new recipes."

"Thanks for supporting me on this, Allison."

"You're welcome." She squeezed his hand. "It's fun being your wife." She was enjoying her role as his new socialite bride.

"You're doing a stupendous job."

"So are you. We certainly have everyone here fooled."

He glanced around the ballroom. "So who do you think are the most interesting people here, besides us?"

As Allison searched the crowd, her gaze landed on Abigail Stewart, a pretty brunette with long hair in delicately woven braids. Abigail was an accomplished artist who'd donated a critical piece to the fund-raisers for auction. She was also one of the women—along with Allison, Megan, Selena and Jillian Norris—who'd been named as an heir in the impostor's phony will.

In addition to that, Abigail had a noticeable little baby bump. With the way Rich had spread himself around, was it possible that she'd had an affair with him? That the baby was his? Jillian had already given birth to a child Rich had abandoned, so why not Abigail, too? Thankfully, Jillian was engaged to a wonderful man now, Will's stepbrother, Jesse Navarro, who was helping her raise her daughter. But Abigail appeared to be all alone.

Allison said, "I nominate Abigail Stewart as the most interesting woman here."

Rand followed her line of sight to the pregnant artist. But he didn't comment on Abigail or her condition. Instead, he asked, "What man would get your vote?"

Allison scanned the crowd again. This time, she laughed. "How about Dr. Chambers?" Vaughn Chambers was a respected trauma surgeon at Royal Memorial, as well as the heir to an oil fortune. But even with as young and handsome as he was, his social graces were sorely lacking. He looked as if he'd been dragged to the fundraiser by his peers. "Could he be any more miserable?"

Rand chuckled. "Is he grumbling under his breath?"

"It certainly seems that way to me."

"Then he gets my vote, too." A second later, Rand went serious. "Royal is a fascinating place, isn't it?"

"Yes, it is." Allison would be returning to Dallas when their marriage was over, but Royal was definitely making a heartfelt impression on her. She was going to be sorry to leave it behind. Leaving Rand behind was going to be even more painful. She would miss everything about him. To keep from becoming sad, she said, "I forgot to tell you that I'm officially employed again. I received the contracts for the featured articles I told you about. The publisher emailed them to me yesterday, and I signed them this morning and sent them off."

"Congratulations." He straightened his tie in a businesslike manner, behaving like the CEO that he was. "I know how much your work means to you."

"As much as yours means to you."

He moved closer to her. "We're quite the pair."

She thought about the promise he'd made to strip her bare tonight. She stepped into his arms, pressing her body close to his. "I'm looking forward to being with you again."

"Me, too." He grazed her cheek with his chin. "But I think the fireworks are about to start."

She turned to see people shuffling outside. "Then I guess we better join them."

Hand in hand, they proceeded to the courtyard, the night air filled with scents of summer, fragrant flowers blooming on the club's well-tended grounds.

Still holding hands, they watched the sky explode with pops of sound and color. As magnificent as the display was, the only thing Allison could think about was going home—where she and Rand could create their own brand of fireworks.

# Nine

Finally, they were home, Allison thought. Together in Rand's room, with the lights turned low and a candle burning. He claimed the candle held special powers and served a sensual purpose. The strawberries-and-cream scent did seem like an aphrodisiac. But she was already steeped in desire.

He worked her zipper and peeled off her gown, just as he'd promised to do.

"Step back so I can look at you," he commanded.

She followed his instruction, and he sat on the edge of the bed, holding her sequined garment on his lap. Aside from his jacket and shoes, he was still fully clothed.

All that remained on Allison's body was the skimpy lingerie she'd bought to go with her gown.

Rand roughly said, "Turn around. Let me see all of you."

She made a complete circle, turning slowly, and coming back to face him once again. She refused to be shy.

If he wanted to look at her, then she was going to let him take his fill.

While he roamed his gaze over her, she waited for him to give her another command. She would never forget this moment, this feeling—as if she belonged to him. But she knew she couldn't let herself feel this way forever. Once their marriage ended, so would this crazy, wild affair.

"Take those off." He used his chin to motion to her undergarments.

She did his bidding. She unhooked her bra and freed her breasts. She stepped out of her pale pink thong, too.

"You're so damned beautiful," he said.

For once in her life, she felt beautiful. "This is a magical night for me." Like being in the midst of an erotic fairy tale, she thought.

He kept staring at her. "I'm letting the candle heat up. I need to be sure it's warm enough."

She glanced in the direction of Rand's mahogany bureau, where the candle sat, burning inside of a tin container. "It already smells glorious."

"I'm going to use the candle on you. I bought it for tonight to surprise you, just like you got your makeover to surprise me."

She gulped her next breath. "What do you mean you're going to *use* it on me?"

"Don't worry. It's nothing kinky. Once the wax melts, it becomes massage oil."

She gazed longingly at him, with a romantic quaver in her body, in her soul. "So you're going to pour it on me and rub it into my skin?"

"That's exactly what I'm going to do." He placed her dress on a nearby chair, then headed over to the bureau and checked the temperature of the wax, drizzling some of it onto the back of his hand.

She stood back, so wildly aroused, she could hardly breathe. The feeling of belonging to him was getting stronger. But it was just part of their affair, she reminded herself. Part of the thrill.

He extinguished the flame. "It's ready."

So was Allison, ready and willing to try a new kind of foreplay. "Should I get in bed?"

"Yes, but I need to unmake it first."

As he got rid of everything except the bottom sheet, her pulse throbbed in unmentionable places.

"Excited?" he asked.

"Yes." Just thinking about what came next was almost more than she could bear.

"I'm glad you're into it. But I figured you would be." He pointed to the bed. "Okay. Get in."

Swallowing hard, she climbed into his bed, realizing how cage-like it seemed with its brass headboard and footboard.

He came over to her with the candle. "It's the edible kind, so I can taste it, too."

She inhaled the sweet scent, inundating her senses with it. "I should have known there was a method to your madness."

He knelt beside her, his lips curving into a randy smile. *Rand*. His name filled her head. He dripped the oil onto her breasts, and she gasped in immediate pleasure, the sensation warm and sensual. He put his hands everywhere, all over her. Kneading her muscles, he gave her a luxurious massage. She moaned, and he lowered his head to flick his tongue, taking an ice cream cone–type lick right from her navel.

"Is it good?" she asked, on another moan.

"It's better than good. And now I'm going taste you where it counts, like I did before."

Except this time she would be covered in flavored oil instead of sudsy water, making it even more carnal. He lifted her legs onto his shoulders, putting her in a highly intimate position.

He used his mouth, skillful in his ministrations. Her husband, her lover, her friend; she was definitely his for the taking. She reached back, gripping the rails on the headboard.

He buried his mouth deeper, and she held the rails even tighter. He was making her wet, so incredibly wet.

By now, her entire world was centered on the heat, the pressure, the passion that overtook her. She arched her hips and rubbed against his face, participating in her orgasm.

He encouraged her to enjoy every tingle, every shiver, every arousing tremor, and Allison came in a stream of liquid ecstasy.

He kissed her, down there, one last time and removed his clothes, a wicked expression alight in his eyes.

She sat up and stretched, feeling delightfully wicked, too. She could've come a thousand times for him.

He kissed her again, on the lips, giving her a musky taste of herself. Such a bad boy, she thought, such a libidinous man. She slipped away from him and got out of bed.

"What are you doing, Allison?"

"It's my turn to seduce you." She wanted to do to him what he'd done to her. She stood at the foot of the bed and gestured for him to sit in front of her.

He did as he was told, even if he said, "I think I'm in trouble."

"Yes, you are." She was going to make him beg for mercy. She gestured to the small silver tin beside him. "I need the candle." She noticed that the wax was still pooling into oil.

He handed it to her, and she made a slick mess, dripping it onto his chest in circular motions. She poured a straight, thin line down his abs, too, where it moved in a slow and stirring trail. Pushing his legs apart, and being as aggressive as a determined woman could be, she dropped to her knees in front of him.

"Holy hell," he groaned.

Hell wasn't a holy place, but she knew what he meant. Allison roved her hands over the front of his body, rubbing the massage oil into his skin. His erection strained, growing bigger and harder, but she didn't touch it. Not yet.

"Are you going to put your mouth on me?" he asked.

"Yes." She was going to take him all the way to the back of her throat.

He toyed with her hair, the newly highlighted strands flowing through his fingers. "Have you ever done it before?"

"Yes," she said again.

His body tensed in arousal, his hands tightening in her hair. "You never let any of your lovers do it to you, but you were doing it to them?"

"It was easier for me to give than receive." But she'd never been as brazen as she was right now. "It's going to be better with you. Deeper. As deep as I can go."

"Then do it." His voice went raspy. "Just do it."

She took her sweet time, lapping at the oil glistening on his thighs. "You taste like dessert." The strawberry stuff was yummy.

"Allison, *please*."

The begging had begun, just as she'd hoped it would. But she waited another beat before she used her mouth to drive him mad. While she took him to euphoric heights, she looked up at him, glad to see that he was watching.

Rand praised her, telling her how incredible she was, how mesmerized he was by her deep, deep throat. He cupped her chin and moved his hips to the rhythm she'd set.

She planned to keep going, to bring him to fruition, but his desire took another turn. He told her to stop, insisting that he wanted to be inside her.

She considered testing his limits, but he wouldn't let her. He dragged her up off her knees, making her as hot for him as he was for her. She fitted him with a condom and straddled his lap. He pulled her onto the bed, and with their bodies bathed in oil, they made voracious love.

He came quickly, fiercely, and so did Allison, replete with satisfaction. But she felt a bit dizzy, too, as if her heart was never going to stop spinning.

Needing to stay close to him, she cuddled in his arms and put her head on his chest. He stroked a hand down her spine, and she closed her eyes, allowing him to lull her to sleep.


On Sunday afternoon, just two days after the fundraiser, Allison and Rand hosted a barbecue. Their guests included Ted and Sharon Marks, Ted's mother, Mavis, and Rand's granny, Lottie.

The menu consisted of grilled salmon, a fresh green salad, soda bread and champ, the latter being a traditional Irish dish made with spring onions, butter, milk and mashed potatoes. Soda bread was common in Ireland, too. For dessert, they would have a light and frothy lemon pudding.

While the men drank Texas-brewed beer and fired up the grill, Mavis and Lottie chatted in the dining room, and Allison and Sharon worked side by side in the kitchen.

Allison checked on the bread, but it wasn't quite ready yet. In the old days, it used to be baked over hot coals in a covered skillet. She was making it the modern way, of course, using the oven. Earlier she'd taught Sharon how to make the champ, sharing that recipe with her.

At the moment, Sharon was in charge of the salad, creating a colorful masterpiece out of the vegetables she'd diced. She stood tall and slim in a casual blouse and ankle-cuffed linen slacks, her short blond hair perfectly coiffed. She took impeccable care of herself, wearing her fiftysomething years well.

Allison had fixed herself up, too, using the Clarity skin care products and cosmetics Selena had given her. She liked how being glamorous made her feel. She didn't want her makeover to be a onetime thing.

"It's interesting how Mavis and Lottie live in the same condominium complex and didn't even know each other until today," Sharon said, peering in the direction of the elderly women. "But it's a big place, so I can see where their paths might not have crossed."

"They certainly seem to be getting along well." Allison thought it was nice that Ted's widowed mother and Rand's never-married granny were becoming instant friends. Although Mavis was about ten years younger than Lottie, they were both former socialites living quiet lives now.

Allison checked on the bread again. This time, she removed it from the oven and placed it on the stove top to cool.

"That smells marvelous." Sharon sniffed the air. "I loved the hearty food in Ireland. I loved everything about it."

"I'm so glad you enjoyed your trip." Allison appreciated Sharon's enthusiasm. "Rand has never been there."

"Really? He needs to see where you come from. He needs to experience it."

"We plan on renewing our vows in Kenmare next year." The lie rolled off Allison's tongue before she could take it back. And now that she'd said it, she was forced to expound. "The second ceremony will be held in the church where I was baptized."

"Oh, how lovely. You and Rand make a fascinating couple." Sharon lowered her voice. "Ted is impressed with the influence you've had on Rand. He's so different now that he's with you." Her tone returned to normal, as if she realized there wasn't any reason to whisper. They were the only two people within earshot. "It sounds like your family raised you well. I'll bet they're just the nicest people."

"Thank you. That's such a kind thing to say." The compliments made Allison feel warm and homey, even if her influence on Rand wasn't what it appeared to be. "My parents would be thrilled about how much you love Ireland. If you and Ted ever go back, I'll put you in touch with them. They love having company at the farm."

"That would be wonderful." Sharon completed the salad, topping it with shredded cheese. "Hey, here's an idea! You can invite us to your wedding ceremony in Kenmare. It'll be a great excuse for us to return to Ireland, and we can meet your family and see the farm then."

"That's a brilliant idea." Allison embellished the lie. But what else could she do? Telling the truth wasn't an option. "A destination wedding like that will take some planning, so I should probably start compiling the guest list now." To include no one, she thought, a lump rising to her throat. By next year, she and Rand would be long-since divorced.

When it was time to eat, they sat outside, enjoying the weather. During the meal, Rand and Ted talked sports. Both men were golfers with similar handicaps.

"Kenmare has a famous old golf course," Allison said, joining the conversation. Since the gated community where Rand lived was a golfer's haven, she wanted everyone to know that her hometown had a golf club, too.

Ted jumped in and excitedly said, "I golfed there." He proceeded to tell Rand it was one of most scenic courses he'd ever had the pleasure of playing, with its breathtaking views of the Irish countryside.

Suddenly Allison wished that she and Rand really would be going to Ireland together next year. But her wish made no sense. What were they supposed to do while they were there? Hang out as a divorced couple?

After the afternoon wound down, everyone went home except for Rand's grandmother. She wanted to stay and visit a bit longer. Instead of returning to the patio, they gathered in the living room, sipping mint-flavored iced tea and eating second helpings of dessert. Allison and Rand sat side by side on the sofa, while his granny took a wingback chair.

Lottie was an elegant sight to behold, with her snow-white hair, fragile skin and deep blue eyes. Pinned to the lapel of her blouse was a red garnet brooch. It looked like an antique piece, probably purchased from the same jeweler who'd provided Allison's engagement and wedding rings.

They chatted about inconsequential things, until Lottie said to Allison, "I'm aware that my short-term memory is failing. I know that I'm being treated for it. But it's strange because I can't really tell how bad it is. When you're the one it's happening to, you don't remember that you're being forgetful."

"I can only imagine how difficult that must be," Allison replied. "To have other people reminding you of what you're supposed to remember."

Lottie dipped into her pudding, stirring it with her spoon. "At my age, I'm lucky I still have all of my other faculties. But you know what? I remember my past. I remember when Rand's mother died. She was my only child, and I loved her dearly. I remember raising Rand and Trey and how much joy they gave me." She quietly added, "And I remember the feeling of being in love."

Allison's heart thudded in her chest, and she glanced at Rand to get his reaction. He met her gaze, then returned his attention to his grandmother, letting her speak her emotional piece.

Lottie continued by saying, "His name was Eduardo Ruiz, and he was the love of my life and the father of my child. But I knew it would never work between us. That he was incapable of returning my love. I used to think that Rand had inherited Eduardo's restless spirit. That he was just like him. But he isn't." Lottie spoke directly to him. "You wouldn't have married Allison if you were like him. You wouldn't have fallen in love with her."

Rand closed his eyes, as if he was summoning the courage to reaffirm his deception. When he opened them, he said, "You're right, Grandma. I'm not who I used to be. My wife changed me."

Lottie quickly replied, "Then you should tell her about your grandfather. The entire story. She's part of our family now, and she should know how deeply it affected you when you first learned about him. You should show her the pictures I gave you of him, too." She said to Allison, "The resemblance between them is uncanny."

"I'm looking forward to hearing more about him and seeing his pictures," Allison replied, curious to make the comparison herself. "Rand already mentioned him briefly to me. He was cautious about saying too much because he was protecting your privacy."

Lottie sighed. "I've always kept Eduardo close to my heart. He was a secret I preferred not to share, except with my grandsons. I probably wouldn't have even told them if Rand hadn't bore such a strong likeness to him." After a light pause, she sighed again. "Eduardo was wrong for me. But Rand isn't wrong for you. Just seeing the two of you, so much in love, fills me with gladness."

Allison's chest went tight. She sensed Rand's discomfort, too. But as usual, they carried on their charade, behaving like the newlyweds they were supposed to be. He even reached for her hand, threading his fingers through hers.

"You're living my dream," Lottie said. "You and Rand."

No, they weren't, Allison thought. But she smiled as if they were, holding much too tightly to Rand's hand. Earlier, she'd gotten sidetracked by a second wedding ceremony in Ireland that wasn't going to happen, and now Rand's granny was pulling her into the fray, too.

Making Allison wonder how it would feel to fall in love with Rand for real.

At bedtime, Allison tried not to fret about her wayward thoughts. She was a romantic, after all, an aspiring novelist with a curious imagination. She was bound to have weak moments. But the fact that she'd actually entertained the notion of loving her husband presented a fear she hadn't intended to face.

Rand emerged from the bathroom. He'd already brushed his teeth and stripped down to his underwear, but he'd yet to get into bed with her. They were in his suite, amid his belongings. He hadn't invited her to move into his room, and she didn't expect him to. Lovers or not, they still had separate accommodations.

"Are you all right?" he asked. "You seem preoccupied."

"I'm fine." If she had another bout of weakness, she would simply will it away. Surely she was strong enough to do that.

He gave her an uncertain look. "Are you sure?"

Instead of insisting on how dandy she was, she turned the conversation around on him. "You seem distracted, too. You haven't even told me about your grandfather yet."

"I was waiting until you were settled in for the night."

"Then I'm ready now." After the emotional day she'd had, she was as settled as she was going to be.

"I'll go get Eduardo's pictures." He proceeded to his walk-in closet and returned with a small wooden keepsake box.

He joined her in bed, opened the box and showed her a head-and-shoulders photograph of a man dressed in an intricately embellished gold jacket, like that of a matador.

"Oh, my goodness." She studied the image. "Your resemblance to him *is* uncanny." There were differences, of course. Eduardo had brown eyes instead of green. He was also leaner than Rand, with cheekbones that arched higher and sharper. He wore his hair slicked straight back and was clean shaven. Beard stubble wasn't a trend in the 1950s, which she presumed was the era of the picture. But overall, they bore strikingly similar features, with the same straight noses, flared nostrils, dark eyebrows, sexy mouths and strong jawbones. "You told me before that he was really famous in his country. A bullfighter, I presume?" Based on his ceremonial clothes, she figured that was an accurate guess.

"He was from Spain, and he was legendary in his field. Not only for his performance in the ring, but because of his brash behavior in public, too. Eduardo was an illegitimate descendant of a Spanish duke, who was the half brother of a long-ago king."

She widened her eyes. "That's quite a legacy."

"In theory, it was. Except by then, Spain was being ruled by a military dictator with no ties to Eduardo's ancestors. Of course, his illegitimate connection to royalty wouldn't have awarded him that status even if they were still in power. But he liked to flaunt his lineage anyway, especially to the current regime."

"What a brave thing to do." She doubted that the dictator in charge appreciated being called out by a daring young matador.

"Everything about him seemed larger than life. He even died in a dramatic way, getting gorged by a bull and dying in the ring, with a crowd of people watching."

"That's horrible." She couldn't fathom seeing something like that. "How old was he when he died?"

"Around my age. It happened about ten years after his affair with my grandmother. They were both in their twenties when they had their fling." Rand removed another photo from the box. "Here's a snapshot of them together."

She took the picture and held it up to the light. "Your granny was beautiful." Lottie had been a leggy brunette back then, with smooth, fair skin and a bewitching smile. "She could've been a movie star. They made a stunning couple. They look really good together."

"He looked good with lots of women. He was a renowned playboy. You heard what Grandma said about him being the wrong man for her. She knew better than to try to pin him down."

Although Allison was compelled to know more, she tried not to think about the parallels between his grandparents and her relationship with Rand. "How did they meet?"

"She was on an extended holiday in Europe, traveling by herself and learning about other cultures. On her second day in Spain, she attended one of his bullfights. It's customary for people to toss flowers and gifts into the ring, and she tossed a bouquet of red roses at his feet. She was seated very close, and he noticed her in the stands and bowed to her. That's not something a matador is supposed to do. Or it wasn't in those days. I don't know about now. They weren't supposed to look around or show their fans favor. But Eduardo had become notorious for choosing his lovers that way."

Allison envisioned the scenario in her mind, the power of Eduardo's effect on the women he took to his bed. "And that's how their affair began?"

Rand nodded. "He introduced himself to her after the fight, and she spent the rest of that summer with him at his estate. She didn't speak Spanish, but he spoke fluent English, so there wasn't a language barrier. He was proficient in French, too."

"It sounds like he valued his education."

"He definitely did. He was impressed with my grandmother's alma mater in the States. Her beauty and intelligence fascinated him. He was devoted to her during the time they were together. She said that he doted on her. But he never stayed with anyone longer than a few months. That's pretty much my record, too." He took the photo of his grandparents and set it aside. "Eduardo was a wealthy man. Even when Spain was suffering economically, he managed to rise to the top. He enjoyed being a celebrity and thumbing his nose at authority."

She mulled over Rand's character, and Eduardo's, too. "Sort of like the way you thumbed your nose at Texas society to get back at your dad? I can see why Lottie thought that you inherited Eduardo's restless spirit."

"It bothers me that she thinks I've changed. I know I shouldn't be upset by it. The whole idea was to clean up my image and fool everyone into believing that we're a committed couple." A hard frown creased Rand's forehead. "But I'm still the same man I was before, and this ruse of ours isn't going to change me."

Allison didn't want to think too deeply about Rand's unchanged ways, so she focused on his grandfather instead. "I'll bet Eduardo would have married Lottie if he'd known about the baby." She wanted to believe the best of Eduardo.

"I agree. He probably would've. Wild as he was, he was still raised in a traditional family. But that was a factor in why my grandmother didn't tell him she was pregnant. She didn't want him marrying her out of duty and resenting her for it. She didn't want a husband who would be mourning his freedom."

She couldn't help herself from saying, "But maybe it wouldn't have been that way. Maybe he would have fallen in love with her."

Rand scowled. "What are you doing, Allison? Trying to rewrite my grandfather's story and make him into one of your book heroes?"

"It's better than the way it turned out, with your granny raising a daughter all by herself and Eduardo dying so young."

"I'm sorry that he was killed the way he was, but he

knew the risks he was taking. To be honest, I don't believe in bullfighting. I think it's a brutal practice."

She didn't approve of the tradition, either, but Eduardo's passing still made her sad. "Maybe he would have quit his profession if he'd married Lottie. He obviously had plenty of money to start over in the States. Between the two of them, they could've had a nice, safe life here in Texas."

Rand blew out a breath. "Do you honestly think Eduardo would still be alive if he and my grandmother had stayed together?"

"I'd like to think it could've happened." She wanted to reunite Lottie with the man she'd loved, if only in a make-believe way. It was certainly safer than daydreaming about herself and Rand.

He adjusted his weight on the bed. "You really are a hopeless romantic."

"I always said that I was." Denouncing that side of her personality would be futile.

He toyed with the strap on her nightgown, lowering it, letting it drop below her shoulder. "You look different now, with the way you changed your makeup and hair. But you're still the same person deep inside."

"Yes, I'm still the same me." The same woman who believed in happily-ever-after, who was supposed to find her true husband someday. But it was impossible to think about her future, about marrying someone else, when she was here with Rand.

"Let's see if you taste as sweet as you always have." He kissed her, soft and slow.

She returned his affection, eager to breathe him into her pores. There was no time to think, to be rational; all she could do was react. Once they were naked, their bodies entwined, he looked into her eyes. She tried to glance away, but she couldn't. He was holding her captive, making her want him even more. But as enticing as he was, she knew how important it was to keep her heart intact.

So even when he was inside of her, so close and deep that she could barely distinguish her heartbeat from his, she kept fighting her feelings.

Every silky, sexy moment of the way.

# Ten

The following day, Allison continued to manage her feelings, reminding herself that her marriage to Rand wasn't meant to last. That he wasn't her true husband. That she wasn't destined to spend the rest of her life with him.

But she would miss him terribly when it was over. He was fast becoming the person she felt closest to in this world, a dear friend, a passionate lover, a kind and caring confidant, everything she always dreamed a real husband should be. But that didn't mean she could allow herself to love him. She simply had to stay strong and stop her romantic notions from taking over. Rand made it clear that he was still the same uncommitted man he'd always been.

Luckily, other things were falling into place that she didn't have to worry about. The social media feedback about her makeover was positive, and she was busy researching and writing the featured articles in her current contracts.

She sat at the dining room table, a soothing breeze coming in from a set of etched glass doors, and tapped away on her laptop. It was one of her favorite spots in the house. The pool was visible from her vantage point, the water glistening like a blue lagoon.

Rand was at the office, but she'd received a text from him, saying that he would be home shortly. He had some great news to share, except he wanted to wait to tell her in person. He also told her not to fix anything for dinner. Instead, they would go out tonight to celebrate.

For now, she snacked on corn chips and salsa. Allison had a habit of eating at her computer, and sometimes she made a mess. But she was trying not to do that today. She shoved the chips into her mouth as quickly as she scooped them into the salsa bowl, keeping her laptop out of the line of fire.

About fifteen minutes later, Rand entered the house. She heard the familiar sound of his footsteps. She turned around in her chair, preparing to greet him.

He approached her, looking like the handsome young CEO that he was. His blue-striped, classic-cut suit fit him to perfection. His megawatt smile was perfect, too. This wonderful man she wasn't allowing herself to love.

Determined to keep things light, she stood and teasingly said, "Hey, sugar. How was your day?" using a really bad Texas accent. But at least she had on the right clothes to fit her voice. She was wearing her one-and-only pair of cowboy boots.

He laughed. "Seriously? You're poking fun at the way I talk, and you won't let me say 'top of the morning' to you? How is that fair?"

She moved closer to him, keeping the silly banter going. "Then go ahead and say it."

"I would, but it's not morning." He swept her into his arms, bending her backward for a steamy kiss.

Mercy, she thought. Morning, noon or night, she savored the feel of him. He ended the kiss, righted their postures and let her go. Still spellbound, she gazed into the glittering greenness of his eyes.

"You taste spicy," he said.

And he tasted like heaven on earth. "It's the peppers in the salsa I ate. You know how I like to snack." She dusted her hands on her jeans, just in case she had salt from the chips on them.

He removed his jacket and draped it over the back of the chair she'd been using. "Do you want to hear my news?"

"Yes, of course." She was interested to know what they would be celebrating tonight.

He grinned broadly. "I met with Ted today and acquired the Brisbane account. I brought his company in as a new client."

"Congratulations!" She'd never seen him so boyish and smiley. She considered flinging her arms around him, but his kiss had already knocked her for a loop.

He loosened his tie. "It wouldn't have happened without you. You're my good luck charm."

She definitely felt a part of it, with how friendly they'd both become with Sharon and Ted. "I was glad to help."

"Now all we have to do is get you your green card, and our final mission will be accomplished."

A final mission that would end in divorce, she thought, with no more kisses, no more hugs, no more husband and wife.

If only things could be different, if only…

"So what are you in the mood to eat?" he asked. "Where should we go?"

Trying to clear her head, she made an instant decision. "Mexican food and margaritas sounds good."

"Really? After the chips and spicy salsa you just munched on?"

She nodded. "That's what got me in the mood for it."

"There's a really great Tex-Mex place in town. Will that do?"

"Sure." She didn't care if it was Tex-Mex or traditional Mexican cuisine. She just needed to go out and have a good time, to be as upbeat as possible.

He smiled once again. Not as boyishly as before, but still a little crookedly. "I'll change into something casual, and we can head out."

She nodded and smiled, too. "No hurry. I have to go to my room to get my purse." Just as she reached for her smartphone, so she could take it upstairs and put it in her purse, the device rang. It was on the table, next to her laptop.

Rand said, "You can let it go to voice mail and deal with it later."

"Let me check to see who it is first. It could be my agent with a mega book deal." She was joking, naturally. But someday, she intended to get that call. She glanced at the name on the screen. "It's my brother. I should probably take it." Rhys rarely called her.

She answered with a goofy "Howdy," using her ridiculous Texas accent on him.

"Allison? Is that you?" He sounded worried.

"Yes, it's me." She turned serious. His reaction to her joke was alarming. Normally Rhys had a good sense of humor. Or with her, he typically did. "Is something wrong?"

"Granny had a stroke. We don't know if she's going to recover. We don't—"

"Oh, dear God." Her knees nearly buckled, the fear of losing her grandmother flooding her like a storm. "I'll be there as soon as I can." Allison wasn't supposed to return to Ireland, not while her green card interview was pending, but this would be considered an emergency. She needed to go home.

Her brother replied, "I'll keep in touch. Be safe and let me know when you'll arrive."

"I will. I'll talk to you later." She had to figure out her traveling plans. She turned toward Rand. He'd been watching her with a concerned expression.

"What happened?" he asked.

"It's Granny. *Maimeó*," she said, using the Irish term, before she burst into tears.

Rand used his private jet to take Allison and himself to Ireland. He wasn't going to let her go alone—he wanted to be with her, to support her, to help her through this difficult time. Once he freed up his schedule, he contacted the USCIS to let them know that Allison needed to return to her homeland for a family illness. The two of them both breathed a sigh of relief when she was granted permission to leave the States.

They arrived at Kerry Airport and rented a car. Allison's grandmother was in a nearby hospital. The town of Kenmare, which was located in Kerry County, was a bit farther. But for now, they were headed directly to the hospital.

While Rand drove, Allison kept in constant touch with her family. She'd texted them from the plane, too. So far, the status of her grandmother's condition hadn't changed. She was still in critical condition.

Allison looked tired and worried and frazzled, more vulnerable than he'd ever seen her. He would be in a state of fear, too, if it was Lottie who'd fallen ill.

"This isn't how I envisioned your first trip to Ireland," Allison said to him, "if you ever came here at all."

"This isn't something I could've imagined, either." Not with someone in her family being in jeopardy. As far as Rand knew, her grandmother, Fiona, was seventy-eight years old and had been in excellent health up until now. No doubt Allison's grandfather, Cormac, was a nervous wreck. He and Fiona had been married for over fifty years. Rand couldn't fathom losing someone who'd been in your life that long. He prayed silently that Fiona recovered. Allison had prayed openly on the plane, using Celtic rosary beads that her grandma had given her when she was a child.

The hospital, a series of white brick-and-glass buildings, was only fifteen minutes away. Rand parked, and they rushed inside and got directions to the unit where her grandma was. He held Allison's hand as they dashed down sterile hallways.

The family was gathered around Fiona's bed. Cormac sat beside his wife, keeping a loving vigil. Amid the starched white sheets, Fiona appeared small and weak, with her cap of matted white hair, pale complexion and IVs taped to her arms.

Allison's distraught parents, Sheila and Angus, took turns hugging their daughter. They hugged Rand, too. When Rhys approached them, Allison put her head on her brother's shoulder. He was a solid wall of a man, as big and strong as could be, with short, medium brown hair and light brown eyes. After he comforted his sister, he shook Rand's hand and thanked him for coming.

Allison approached the bed and stood next to her

grandfather's chair. Rand held back and watched the scene unfold.

Sheila came over to him and said, "Allison's granny is getting the best care possible. She was treated immediately, and her doctor told us how important that is. But I think having Allison here is going to be the best medicine of all."

He glanced at Fiona. She definitely seemed aware that her beloved granddaughter was by her side now. But there still wasn't anything any of them could do, except continue to pray as they'd been doing all long.

By the next day Fiona's condition was upgraded to stable, and if her progress continued the way it was, she would be transferred to a rehabilitation center in the area. For now, she still had some residual effects from the stroke. But overall, she was doing much better. To Rand, it felt like nothing short of a miracle, and on this picturesque afternoon while everyone else was visiting Fiona, he was at the farm with Allison's brother.

Typically, July was the driest month in Kenmare with mild temperatures, although it could turn cool and damp without warning. Either way, Rhys had put Rand to work on the farm. Rhys claimed that he was shorthanded and needed extra help, but Rand suspected that he was being "tested" to see how he measured up.

Cartwright Farms owned hundreds of sheep and baby lambs. Just this morning, Rhys had taught Rand how to shear sheep—with a pair of hand shears. Most farmers used machines these days, but the Cartwrights still did it the old, traditional way. They thought machines took off too much wool, also leaving the sheep too cold afterward. Sheep could be shorn in all seasons, depending on the location and the conditions. Here, it was a summer activity.

As hard as the work was, Rand was invigorated by it. Although he'd always enjoyed being outdoors, he'd never known anything quite like this. It felt good being part of something so real, something that didn't involve taking selfies and promoting himself online. The influence of Allison's homeland was putting Rand in an authentic state of mind. Would he feel this way once he returned to Texas, too? Would he start living a more private life? He'd already gotten a little weirded out on the night of the fund-raiser about sharing pictures of Allison. He'd actually wanted to keep her to himself.

Before hc taxed his mind too deeply about that, he returned his attention to the farm. At the moment, he and Rhys were taking a break, away from the barn where they'd shorn the first group of sheep.

Rhys stood near a fence rail. A black-and-white border collie, a National Champion Sheepdog finalist, sat loyally at his feet. Beyond man and dog were acres and acres of lush green valleys, surrounded by natural brush, low hills and high mountains.

Rand said, "If my father could see me now, he would accuse me of just playing in the dirt. He didn't think I was good for anything."

"I'm rather surprised myself," Rhys replied. "I didn't expect you to take to this so easily. But you do look as if you've been rolling around in the dirt."

"Maybe because I have?" The first few sheep Rand had tried to shear had knocked him on his butt. "There are tons of ranches where I come from, and some of my closest friends are renowned horse breeders and cattlemen, but I was raised in a luxurious mansion that my grandmother used to own."

"Then you're doing all right for a spoiled rich boy."

Rhys chuckled, flashing what could only be described as a lethal smile.

"Gee, thanks." Rand swigged his water.

Silent, Rhys rubbed his hand across his jaw. He had the kind of beard scruff that made him look tough, not trendy. But as rugged as he was, he was a savvy businessman, too. His London-based company, Cartwright News and Media, was highly successful.

"Have you always taunted Allison's beaus?" Rand asked. "Or were you just reserving it for me?"

"I've done far worse to some of the lads she dated. But she isn't dating you." Rhys squinted at him. "If you weren't already married to her, I would probably be hounding you about your intentions, making sure they were honorable."

Rand's guilt reared its head. *Honorable* wasn't a word that applied to the reasons he'd married Allison. Sure, he'd accompanied her to Ireland to see her ailing grandmother, but that didn't change the dynamics of their phony marriage.

"She seems happy with you," Rhys added.

Now the big Irishman was being brotherly, heightening Rand's guilt. Allison deserved better; all of the Cartwrights did. Rand wasn't the man her family thought he was. His divorce to Allison was imminent. But even as the thought crossed his mind, a sense of loneliness came over him. He was getting used to being her husband.

Her *fraudulent* husband, he reminded himself. He didn't know the first thing about being a loyal partner, and he never would. It simply wasn't in his DNA. The grandfather he favored was a party boy, and even Rand's own father, with his high-and-mighty attitude, had been a terrible husband—and not just to Rand's mother. His dad had been married four times in total, with each of his screwed-up marriages ending in divorce.

"When Allison gets back, you two should go into town," Rhys said, cutting into Rand's troubled thoughts. "With everything else that's been going on you haven't gotten the chance to see the sights. She can show you the church where your convalidation is going to take place next year. That's going to be a major event around here. So you might as well start gearing up for it now."

The last thing Rand wanted was to visit the site where his marriage to Allison was supposed to be blessed. To keep his anxiety in check, he made a joke. "Maybe you and I ought to go out for a pint of Guinness instead."

Thankfully, Rhys laughed. "I'll take you pub hopping another time. For today, you should go to Holy Cross. You and Allison can light a candle for Granny while you're there."

"Then that'll be the plan." Rand certainly couldn't refuse. Even if he was no longer a churchgoer, he still believed in the power of prayer. But pretending to her family that he and Allison were going to renew their vows in a sacred ceremony was another matter.

"Come on." Rhys gestured in the direction of the barn. "We've got more work to do before either of us can go anywhere."

Rand nodded, clearing the emotional tension from his mind and returning his focus to the farm.

Later that afternoon, Rand sat across from Allison in a secondhand bookstore that doubled as a vegetarian café and organic produce market, eating biscuits and soup.

He learned that she used to come here often. Writer that she was, she loved being surrounded by used books, immersing herself in the essence of how they looked and felt and smelled. He enjoyed the setting, too. Rand liked everything about Kenmare. The Irish name for it was Neidin, meaning little nest. He thought it fit the town beautifully, with how charmingly it was nestled against the mountains. In addition to its quaint atmosphere, Kenmare was also known for scenic walks, offering short jaunts or long-distance routes, along the peninsulas or through the hills.

"It's almost as if time stands still here," he said. "I've traveled to lots of places, to many countries and continents, but nothing has affected me like this."

"I'm so glad you're here with me." Allison took a sip of her soup. Afterward, she said, "And to think that Rhys has been teaching you to work the farm." She grinned. "Who knew that you'd be so good at it?"

Rand slathered his biscuit with almond butter. "I was trying not to look like a fool in front of him. Your brother is one tough dude."

"And I'm one tough gal." She waved her spoon at him. "Remember how I kicked your arse during our football and rugby match back in Texas?"

He rolled his eyes, but he smiled, too. "How could I forget?" His losing that game had been the start of their affair.

She lowered her spoon. "I can relax now that Granny is getting better. I was so worried about her. I can't even…"

Her words drifted, but he understood what she was trying to convey: the fear, the possibility of losing her grandmother. But everything was going to be okay now.

He reached across the table for her hand, and the tips of their fingers touched.

She asked, "When we leave here, do you want to see the restaurant where I used to work? Not to eat there since we're already eating, but just to have me point it out?"

"Sure." He wanted to become more familiar with her past. But even so, the reminder of the restaurant bothered him. He knew it was where she'd met Rich Lowell, and now Rand was beginning to wonder if he was being as unscrupulous as Rich. Even if he wasn't lying to Allison about his identity or plotting to steal her money, he was conning her family, doing whatever he could to earn their admiration and respect. But his biggest issue was Allison herself. What if he broke her heart when their marriage was over?

She'd promised that she wasn't going to get attached to him, and he'd taken her at her word. But could a hopeless romantic like Allison truly keep a promise like that? Was it only a matter of time before she developed feelings for him that weren't part of their deal? Even now, she was giving him a tender look. A wifely look, he thought.

Well, of course she was, he relented. She was supposed to act like that when they were in public. He was probably giving her goo-goo eyes, too. It was a habit they'd both formed.

But still, there was something about the way she was behaving that gave him pause. It just felt different, somehow.

They finished their soup and biscuits and proceeded to the restaurant where Allison used to work.

"It gets lots of tourist business," she said, as they stood in front of the colorfully painted building.

"It looks like a nice place. But it makes me think of Rich being here with you." He couldn't seem to stop himself from admitting that her affair with Rich had crossed his mind.

"He only came into the restaurant when we were first getting to know each other. Once we started dating, we were careful not to be seen in town together. It's crazy now that I think back on it. I should have known that no good would come of a relationship I was hiding from my family."

"We're hiding things about our relationship from your family, too. And mine and everyone else we know."

"At least neither of us is married to someone else."

Yes, but were the circumstances of their marriage any less deceptive? Rand hardly thought so. "Your brother wants you to show me the church where our second ceremony is supposed to take place."

"He mentioned it to me, as well. But he assumed I would want you to see it." She paused. "I hope you don't mind going there. I agree with him that we should light a candle for Granny."

"I think we should, too." Rand was already prepared to do that.

Since Holy Cross was within walking distance, they continued on foot.

As they approached the building, he stopped to study the Gothic Revival–style architecture, with its gray-and-white stone exterior, pitched slate roofs, corner buttresses and stunning stained glass windows. A large, freestanding Celtic cross was part of the design, too.

"It's a beautiful church," he said, realizing that Allison's family had probably worshipped here for generations. "Do you know when it was consecrated?"

"It was in 1864, but the local land agent didn't want to provide a site for it. In fact, the priest who built it topped the spire with a weather vane rooster. Everyone around here thinks it's because he wanted the rooster to crow over the pernickety agent. The agent's office used to be located in the town square." She gestured in the direction of where the agent had supposedly been crowed upon.

Rand laughed. "Now, that's my kind of priest."

She laughed, as well. "Mine, too." After a breath of serious silence, she asked, "Do you want to go inside now?"

"Not yet." He needed to talk to her first. "Remember when I told you that I hadn't been to church in a really long time? I never explained why I stayed away, and I want to do that now."

She met his gaze. "I'm listening, Rand. You can say whatever feels right."

At this point, he didn't know what felt right, but he started at the beginning. "My grandmother didn't raise me in this faith. Neither did my father. But my mother did. She joined the church after she and Dad got divorced. Mom had me baptized, and I used to like going to mass with her. But after she died, that part of my life ended." He hesitated before he said, "When I was old enough to attend services by myself, I returned to the parish where she used to take me. But it wasn't the same. It just reminded me of my mother's funeral and how painful it had been to lose her. So I stopped going, and I haven't been back since."

"I'm so sorry." She made a soft sound. "Did it help to stay away?"

"No. The pain was still there." He glanced at the arched doorways, leading to the entrance of the church. "I'd like to light a candle for my mother while we're here. I think she would've loved this place."

Allison's eyes went misty. "I'll bet she's watching over us right now."

He let out the breath he was holding, releasing it from his lungs. "I hope so."

They entered the building, and Allison dipped into the holy water, making the sign of the cross in front of her. Rand did, too, with his childhood memories flooding back. Good memories, he thought, of when his mom was alive.

The interior was even more impressive, light and airy with a high marble altar, decorative floors and carved wooden ceilings, rife with angels.

They approached the alcove and lit two candles, one for her grandmother and another one for his mother. After they spent some quiet time in prayer, Rand glanced over at Allison and wondered what renewing their vows here would be like.

A second later, he shook away the thought. One peaceful moment in a big, beautiful Irish church didn't mean that he was meant to stay with Allison. Nor did it make him the kind of husband she needed. If anything, it just solidified the fact that she deserved more than he was capable of giving her.

When they returned to Texas, he was going to do everything within his power to get the green card interview moved up, hastening her opportunity to start a new life.

Without him.

# Eleven

On Allison and Rand's third and final day in Ireland, the weather turned cool and windy. They would be flying back to Texas that evening, but for now they were on a long and winding walk through the hills. For Allison, the trail was wonderfully familiar. She was taking Rand to see her childhood hideaway.

He asked, "How much farther is it?"

"We're getting closer." The location was adjacent to the farm, but still on Cartwright property.

He glanced around. "The scenery is breathtaking. It's wonderful how well your grandmother is doing, too."

Allison nodded. She was extremely grateful for Granny's prognosis. "She certainly likes you." When they visited her this morning, she called him, "A prince from a land called Royal."

"I'll bet she was a flirt in her day."

"Yes, she was." But Ma swooned over him, too. She was even knitting him a sweater with wool from the farm, promising to send it to him. Da, Granda and Rhys were impressed with Rand, as well. He'd passed their inspections with flying colors.

As for Allison, she'd finally given up the fight. She was no longer battling her feelings. Somewhere in the midst of this emotionally charged trip, she'd fallen madly, irreversibly in love with Rand.

But love was a good thing, a beautiful thing, and she refused to regret that it had happened to her. She needed to be hopeful, to work toward keeping the man she loved instead of dwelling on the idea of losing him.

But even with her newfound confidence, she was still afraid, doubt and worry creeping in. He'd told her countless times he couldn't be tamed. That he was the same man he'd always been. Yet now that she'd fallen in love with him, she wanted to believe otherwise. With as wonderful a husband as he was—how could she not think that he'd changed?

Before her brain got too befuddled, she pointed to the final hill they had to cross. "We're almost there. It's just beyond that ridge."

"So what exactly is this hideaway of yours?"

"It's just some lovely old ruins." She didn't want to give him too much detail, not until he saw it for himself. "When I was a girl, I used to think of it as my fort. And when I was a teenager, it's where I used to come to write poems to my fantasy husband."

The wind rustled his hair. "Ah, yes, those secret poems. It's too bad you didn't keep them."

It wouldn't matter if she still had them. She already knew that Rand Gibson had emerged from her fantasies, becoming the man of her heart.

After they trudged over the final hill and he spotted her hideaway, an awed expression appeared on his handsome face. Allison felt that way every time she saw it, particularly at this time of year when it was surrounded by wildflowers.

He said, "I would have used this as my fort, too. It's incredible."

"It's called a beehive hut because of the rounded way it's shaped. No windows, nothing but an opening that serves as a door. But you can see how small the opening is, so it can easily be covered with one larger stone." She explained further, "It's a prehistoric home, a single-family dwelling of sorts. There's a little community of these in another part of Kerry County, where the huts were once attached to each other through interlocking doorways. But on our land, there's just this one."

Rand approached the structure and glided his hands along the exterior. "Look at the way each stone is stacked and how they're angled outward. Was that so the rain could run off it?"

Allison nodded. "Do you want to duck inside?"

"Definitely." He gestured for her to go first. "I'll follow you in."

She warned him by saying, "It's going to be dark in there, except for the bit of light that comes through the opening. But with as small as the hut is, there isn't much to explore inside. Still, I used to carry a battery-operated lantern with me when I came here."

He smiled. "So you could sit and write your poems by the lantern light? I can just see you doing that, all alone in your make-believe world."

Was she tumbling into a make-believe world now, imagining happily-ever-after with him? Focusing on her task, she crawled into the hut.

He joined her, and they sat near the opening. He said,

"I can't fathom living in one of these. But it's a perfect hideaway."

She peered out at the flowers scattered in the grass. "It served me well."

"It's serving us well, too."

He leaned over to kiss her, and she sighed. The child in her had grown up, but the starry-eyed teenager she used to be had never gone away.

"Can I touch you?" he asked.

She knew he meant in a sexual way, doing more than a soft, sweet kiss. "Yes," she breathed. As far as she was concerned, he could touch her for the rest of their lives.

"I'll just use my hands." He lifted her onto his lap, with her sitting with her back to his front. He nuzzled the side of her face and unzipped her jeans.

She closed her eyes, and he worked his right hand past the waistband of her knickers. With his left hand, he unbuttoned the front of her rugged plaid blouse.

He cast an erotic spell, making her nipples peak, causing dampness to pool between her thighs. She leaned back against him, the long-ago poems she'd written twirling in her mind. She'd found her fantasy husband. He'd become real.

He whispered, "I'm never going to forget you, Allison."

She opened her eyes and gazed into a darkened corner of the hut. He sounded as if he were saying goodbye. "We're still together, Rand."

"I know. But I just wanted to tell you how special you are for when we're not together anymore."

She refused to accept his words. "We still have lots of time." Time, she prayed, for her to keep him.

He didn't reply. Instead, he went farther into her knickers.

She grabbed ahold of his blue-jeaned thighs, scratching her nails along the denim. He seemed hell-bent on making her come. But what choice did she have?

She lifted her hips and pressed against his fingers, the sensation of being seduced by him igniting its way to her lovelorn heart. The more he aroused her, the more she wanted, the more she needed. Allison climaxed hard and quick, wrapped in her husband's arms.

Both Allison and Rand slept on the plane, and the next day they were back in Texas and returning to work. She noticed that he seemed pensive, far quieter than his usual self. He was dressed for the office, sipping coffee and gazing out the patio doors.

She stood behind him, with her laptop on the table. She had her articles to write.

He finally turned toward her and said, "We have our green card interview tomorrow."

She staggered as if she'd been shot. "Tomorrow? How is that even possible? It's too soon. It must be a mistake."

"No, it's not. I contacted my friend at the USCIS to see how things were going and if he could push things along even more than he already had."

Allison knew that Rand's friend had gotten her security clearance processed faster and was working toward getting their interview date moved up. But she hadn't envisioned anything this quick. "I figured we were at least a month off." Even that would have been quicker than the usual expected wait time. "How did he manage it?"

"Mostly it was timing and luck. When he checked the books, he discovered that another couple had canceled, so he moved us up the line and arranged for us to take their slot. He faxed me the notification this morning. He sent the original, too, overnight, so it'll arrive first thing in tomorrow's mail."

To her, this was the worst thing that could've happened. Getting her green card sooner meant their marriage would end sooner. How could she try to hold on to Rand if they weren't married anymore? "We can't take that appointment. We're not ready."

"I disagree. I think we're totally ready. With everything we've been through, we know each other exceptionally well."

She argued her case. "I think we need more time to prepare."

"Our marriage seems real, Allison. We've fooled everyone around us, and we're going to fool the officer who interviews us, too. We've got nothing to worry about."

"I'm scared." Of living the rest of her life without him, she thought, of losing him.

"It'll be okay." He set his coffee on the table and came over to her. Behind him, the rising sun seeped through the glass doors, casting a graceful gold glow. "We can do this."

She blew out a shaky breath. She was a bundle of nerves. "What time is the appointment tomorrow?"

"Ten o'clock. If the officer approves us, he or she will stamp your passport. The stamp acts as a green card and will last thirty days, until your actual green card arrives in the mail."

"You just said *if* the officer approves us."

"I was just repeating what the notification said," he told her. "But even if they don't approve us on the spot, they probably wouldn't deny us outright, either. They'd take more time to review our case, and if they still aren't satisfied, they'd schedule us for another interview with their fraud unit."

"That sounds daunting."

"Mostly they'll be looking for inconsistencies in our stories. But we can work up some makeshift questions tonight and test each other. It might help you relax."

"Thank you. I'd like that." The outcome of the interview was out of their control. They could only do their best. But either way, she still loved Rand the way a wife should. In her heart, their marriage was genuine. She just needed to convince him that they should stay together.

He said, "It helps that we speak the same language, are around the same age and share the same spiritual beliefs. We have all of that in our favor. Our chemistry should help us, too, how obvious our attraction to each other is."

She nodded. "You're right. No one could deny that."

"Are you less scared now?"

Of the interview, yes. Of their marriage ending, no. But she said, "I'm feeling better about it."

"Good." He smoothed a strand of her hair, tucking it behind her ear.

She noticed that his tie was skewed, so she reached out to straighten it for him. Then she realized how easily they did those types of things for each other, how natural it was for them.

She lifted her gaze. "Will you kiss me?" He always kissed her before he left for work, but she wanted to be extra certain that he did it this morning.

"Of course." He slipped his arms around her waist, brought her body next to his and slanted his mouth over hers.

She savored the warmth between them and returned his kiss, as deeply and romantically as the situation would allow. She couldn't lure him off to bed. With their trip to Ireland, he'd already missed too much work as it was.

After they separated, she said, "Thank you again for helping me through my family crisis."

"I'm glad I got to meet them in person. They're such wonderful people. I hate that we're deceiving them, though. It's even worse now that I got so close to them. I hate how we're deceiving my grandmother, too. But at least my brother can say 'I told you so' to me after you and I part ways."

"I don't want to talk about that. It's not a good thing to think about so close to our interview." Nor did she feel guilty about their deception anymore. Now that her love for him had turned real, she wasn't lying to anyone.

Except for Rand, she thought miserably. Sooner or later she would have to tell him the truth. She would have to admit that she loved him. But for now, she kept quiet.

Keeping her heart all bottled up.

The following morning, Allison and Rand arrived at the local USCIS office thirty minutes early and waited in a small lobby for their names to be called. He was in business attire, and she wore a conservatively stylish skirt ensemble. She'd done her hair and makeup with an elegant touch, befitting a woman of her new social standing. Rand was a well-known millionaire. She couldn't come to the interview looking like a farm girl. But she wished that a casual top and blue jeans would have been acceptable. Being so stiff and formal was making her antsy.

They brought a packet of required documents with them, along with anything else they could think of that helped prove the validity of their marriage and the closeness of their relationship. Rand was prepared to show the interviewer his social media accounts, as well as the gossip blogs that had featured AliRan. By now, Rand was being referred to as a former playboy and no one was suggesting anymore that Allison should run from him. She couldn't agree more.

Last night they'd spent hours quizzing each other with probable questions. They'd scored 100 percent on their makeshift tests and could only hope they did as well in the real interview.

Rand's USCIS friend wouldn't be present. Nor had he advised them in any way. All he'd done was help speed up the process. As it turned out, he didn't even work in this office. When Allison asked Rand more about him this morning, she discovered that he was an executive at the main location in Washington, DC, and was an old fraternity brother of Rand's.

Allison hadn't even gone to university. Would their interviewer think that was a red flag?

She dismissed the thought. Their levels of education didn't make them an unsuitable match. Nothing did, in her opinion. She wanted to be Rand's wife forever.

Finally, their names were called and they were directed to a windowless room down the hall, where the interview began.

The immigrant official, a middle-aged woman named Maria Martinez, interviewed them together and separately. She didn't take her position lightly. She videotaped each session and asked scores of questions. As intense as it was, Allison could tell the interview was based on more than just questions and answers. Officer Martinez analyzed their body language, too.

When it was over, she stamped Allison's passport. Their marriage was deemed bona fide, their application approved.

Once they were free to leave, they left the building and proceeded to Rand's Porsche.

He said, "I'd never been so nervous in all my life. That was way harder than I thought it was going to be, especially when she separated us."

"That part concerned me, too." But they'd obviously done everything right.

He opened her car door. "Do you want to stop for a celebratory lunch? Maybe the Tex-Mex and margaritas we never got from before?"

Allison shook her head. "I'd rather just go home. I'm not very hungry right now." She still had to figure out how to stop the divorce.

"Then I can wait, too." He got behind the wheel.

She glanced over at him. "We're still going to need to be careful over these next thirty days."

He fired up the engine. "What do you mean?"

"We can't do anything to raise suspicion. We're going to have to keep living together."

"I wasn't planning on doing anything drastic."

She relaxed a little. That gave her thirty days to win him over. Thirty days of doing what? she asked herself. Of living the same lie, of pretending nothing had changed?

No, she thought. *No.* If she was going win Rand over, then she had to tell to him how she felt. She had to admit that she loved him. She didn't want the next thirty days to be based on anything except the truth.

Allison made up her mind to do it today, just as soon as they got home. She couldn't embark on an important discussion while they were riding in the car. She needed to be in a soothing environment, where there wouldn't be any distractions.

"Do you want to change into some comfy clothes and sit on the patio when we get home?" she asked. "I could use some fresh air."

"Sure. That sounds nice. Then we can go to lunch later."

She nodded, even if food was the last thing on her mind. For now, all Alison could think about was exposing her heart.

To the man who'd become her everything.

# Twelve

"Why are you looking at me like that?" Rand asked Allison, as they settled onto the patio. Now that they were outside, she was behaving strangely.

She stammered, "I just…there's just…something I need to tell you."

He prodded her to say whatever was on her mind. "What is it? What's going on?"

"I love you, Rand." Her voice went horribly, terribly scratchy. "I fell in love with you."

Good God, he thought. His worst fear had just come true, and he couldn't seem to respond. He couldn't do anything but sit there, white knuckling the arms of his chair.

"I'm sorry if this is freaking you out," she said.

Oh, yeah. He was freaked out, all right. He glanced past her and caught sight of her fairy gardens on the other side of the patio. If he could ask the fairies to undo the spell she was under, he would. But he knew that wouldn't work.

Rand returned his gaze to hers. He needed to convince her of the mistake she was making by loving him, persuading her to see him for who he really was. "When we were in Ireland, I sensed that you were getting too attached to me. I even started comparing myself to Rich, wondering if I was as bad as he was for preying on your feelings."

She moved her chair closer to his. "You're nothing like him. You're kind and decent and heroic."

"I'm far from heroic." And he didn't feel very kind and decent, either. "I'm not the guy in the book you're going to write. You can't turn me into him."

"But what if you're already becoming him on your own?"

"You're just being idealistic." He was the wrong man for her, the wrong husband, and he knew better than to prolong the agony.

"I tried not to fall for you." She fidgeted with the hem of her buttery-yellow T-shirt, pulling at a loose thread. "So help me I did. I've been fighting my feelings for you since the night you told me about your grandfather."

"The same night you tried to rewrite my grandparents' story and give them a happy ending? Real life doesn't work that way, Allison. You can't erase the past for them, and you can't conjure up a future for you and me, either." He revealed his truth to her. "When we were in the church in Ireland, I had a wavering moment of wondering what staying with you would be like, of renewing our vows there. But I knew it wasn't meant to be. I knew you'd be better off without me."

"So you're making this big noble sacrifice by letting me go? Wouldn't it be easier to just try to make it work?"

"I don't know how to do that. I wasn't raised like you. I wasn't taught how to be a loving, caring partner. I didn't have a family who set that sort of example. My mother loved my father and look what happened to her. He divorced her and two years later, she got sick and died."

She blew out a sigh. "We're not your parents, Rand."

"All right, then what about my grandparents? At least Lottie was smart enough to walk away from Eduardo. She knew that loving a playboy like him was a mistake. And you should know the same thing about me."

"But you're not the playboy type anymore," she insisted.

"Says who? The gossip blogs? We duped them, Allison. We duped everyone. And now you're buying into the fiction we created, too."

"Maybe you're the one who can't see reality from make-believe," she said. "Maybe you're not the wilding you always thought you were. Maybe deep down, there's always been a loving, caring partner clamoring to get out."

Frustrated with her romance-stricken ways, he dragged a hand through his hair. "You don't know what you're talking about."

"I know how thoughtful you were from the beginning, agreeing to ask for my father's blessing to marry me. How many playboys would do that? And how many would insist that he wanted to make the ring he gave his wife mean something? Or be eager about seeing her in her wedding dress? You've done things from the start that identified you in ways neither of us even considered at the time."

"And now they're a big deal? Now that you love me?" he demanded.

"Everything that's ever happened between us matters now. You could have let me go to Ireland alone. You didn't have to take that trip with me. You didn't have to get close to my family or light candles with me. And you especially didn't have to wonder what renewing our vows would be like. Do you know how major it was for you to be having those sorts of thoughts?"

"And do you know how major it was for me to decide against it?" he retorted. "That was a defining moment for me. The moment I knew I had to get our marriage to end sooner. That's why I called my friend from the USCIS and prodded him to keep hurrying things along."

She flinched. "You wanted to be rid of me?"

"I wanted to stop this from happening." He made a grand gesture, referring to her feelings for him. "I don't know how to accept your love. I don't know what to do with it." He searched her wounded gaze, wishing he could kiss and hold her and be the man she wanted him to be. "I'm so sorry. The last thing I ever wanted to do was hurt you."

Her voice hitched. "So there's no chance for us?"

"Between a marriage-minded woman like you and a confirmed bachelor like me? Not that I can see."

She squeezed her eyes shut, and suddenly he wanted to reel his "confirmed bachelor" remark back, to say that he didn't mean it. That he wanted to spend the rest of his life with her. But he was scared of making that kind of commitment. Terrified, he thought, of falling in love with her, too.

Allison opened her eyes, and they stared awkwardly at each other, pain and discomfort zigzagging between them. She glanced away, and he suspected that she was suppressing the urge to cry, trying to seem stronger than she was.

"I'm so sorry," he said again. "I'm so damned sorry."

"You don't have to keep apologizing. You never promised me that we were going to stay together. I just wanted to believe it was possible."

But it wasn't, he thought. In his screwed-up family, love never panned out. So why would it be any different for him? Allison deserved someone who understood love, who wasn't afraid of it. When Rand was on the farm and immersed in her homeland, he'd gotten caught up in the idea of it being real, of it feeling authentic. But this was getting way more real than he'd bargained for. He didn't like having emotions he couldn't escape from.

Allison stood and held on to the back of her chair. "I'm going to pack an overnight bag and head off to my apartment in Dallas. After that, I'll make plans to get the rest of my belongings and return to Ireland."

He started. "You're going to go home? And give up your green card?"

She tightened her hold on the chair. "Staying in America doesn't make sense anymore."

Hating himself for being such a miserable coward, Rand got to his feet. He hadn't just broken her heart; he'd crushed her lifelong dream of living in the States, too. He'd taken her natural sweetness, her innocence, all of the qualities he'd chosen for her to become his wife and mangled them to bits.

"I can drive you to your apartment," he said, trying to stop her from going off alone.

She shook her head. "I'd rather that you didn't. I'd also prefer that you weren't here when I come back for the rest of my things. I'll let you know what day it'll be."

"So we're never going to see each other again?"

"I think it would be easier if we make a clean break." She moved forward as if she were going to hug him goodbye, but then she pulled back, protecting herself from getting too close. "Be well, Rand. Be happy."

"You, too." He went numb inside, feeling as if a part of him was dying. The part she loved, he thought. The husband she so desperately wanted him to be.

He stayed in the yard while she packed her overnight bag and arranged for an Uber. After she was gone, he returned to his big empty house.

Missing her already.

Allison entered her apartment feeling horribly alone and trying not to cry. If she broke down in a puddle of tears, she feared the pain would only get worse. Already she hurt so badly, her bones ached from it.

She'd meant everything she'd said to Rand about what a wonderful husband he'd turned out to be, about how attentive he'd been to her. But he'd spurned her belief in him.

She didn't want to go back to Ireland, but she didn't know what else to do. Living in Texas would never be the same, not without Rand.

She sank onto her sofa and curled up into a ball. Every moment they'd spent together was turning like a pinwheel in her mind. She couldn't envision her life without him.

If he could just see himself through her eyes, he would know that she was right, that they were meant to be together.

Allison was still going to write her novel and make the hero a man like Rand. Except in the book, he was going to fall desperately in love with the heroine. He was going to believe in her, in himself, in them as a couple.

Her fantasy Rand. Her dream husband.

The tears she'd been banking began to fall—hard, sobbing, racking tears, burning their way down her cheeks.

She got the maddening urge to call Rand, to hear his voice, but she didn't do it. She stayed on the sofa, crying for what she'd lost.

When the sogginess became too much, she went into the bathroom to get some tissues. She blew her nose until it was dry and chafed. Then, catching her tormented reflection in the mirror, she splashed water onto her face.

From there, she returned to the main room and found her way onto the patio, needing a breath of air.

She'd told Rand that she was going to arrange to get the rest of her belongings. But she wasn't going take the fairy gardens back to Ireland with her. She was going to leave them at Rand's house, so the tiny sprites could watch over him.

A gift to the man she loved.

If only the fairies could have swept her and Rand into a supernatural realm for all eternity. At least then they would still be together, frozen in time and married forever.

Rand couldn't stay home by himself. He was about ready to climb the walls, so he shot his brother a text and asked if he could stop by.

When he arrived, Trey was waiting for him in the garage and tinkering around on his workbench. He took one look at Rand and handed him a longneck from a nearby mini fridge.

Rand twisted the cap and took a swig. But he quickly set it aside. A cold beer wasn't going to help. Nothing would.

"What's going on?" his brother asked. "What's wrong?"

Rand got right to the crux of it. "Allison left me. She went back to Dallas and soon she'll be going back to Ireland." He waited a beat before he added, "I screwed up my marriage, just like you said I would. I hurt her, bro. I broke her heart."

Trey frowned at him, a scowl of instant disapproval. But that was what Rand needed. It was part of the reason he came here. He wanted his brother to confirm his crappy character.

"What did you do, exactly? How did you hurt her?"

Rand gave him a condensed version. "After we got the approval for her green card today, she told me how wonderful I was, and I told her I wasn't cut out to be her husband."

Trey leaned against the workbench, grilling him, asking another probing question. "And why did you do that?"

"Because she thinks I'm better than I am. Because if we stay together, I'll never be able to live up to her expectations."

"But according to her, it sounds as if you already are."

Rand blinked. "Since when did you become so supportive of my marriage? You're the one who told me from the beginning that I wasn't husband material."

"Yeah, but I must have been wrong. I mean, look at you. You're missing your wife so much, you can hardly see straight."

"Of course I miss her, but that isn't the point."

Trey made a confused face. "So what is the point? That she thinks you're the greatest guy on earth? Isn't that how it's supposed to be?"

"Yeah, but it's complicated." Rand couldn't blow the whistle on his phony marriage. He and Allison had agreed to keep that secret to their graves.

"You still love her, don't you? Because when you first came here to say that you were getting married, you kept saying how much you loved her."

Once again, Rand couldn't admit that he'd lied. But

it didn't matter anyway. By now, there was no denying it. He knew that he loved Allison as passionately as she loved him. If he didn't, he wouldn't be feeling as if his heart had been ripped clean out of his chest. "Yes, I love her." He paused to come to grips with his admission, with accepting it. "I totally do."

Trey went silent, but so did Rand. His pulse was beating a mile a minute.

A few seconds later, Trey said, "You need to fix this."

"You're right, I do." He needed to figure things out. "Thanks for listening, for being here for me, but I should go."

"Don't mess it up any more than you already have."

"Yeah, I know." Rand needed to get his shit together. But damn, he'd never been in love before, either.

Their visit ended, and Rand drove straight to Dallas. He stopped at a park in Allison's neighborhood, just to keep himself close to her.

He exited the car and walked along the grass. When he came to a duck pond, he watched the birds float along the water. They looked so peaceful, content with where they belonged.

But Rand wasn't. He'd never been so lonely.

He thought about how amazing it was to have a wife who believed in him, who loved him, who felt safe and warm in his arms. Crazy thing was, she made him feel that way, too, even when he was too damn stubborn to realize it.

But he wasn't too hardheaded to know it now.

Love wasn't something to be feared and neither was commitment. They were gifts life had to offer, and so was the sanctity of marriage.

Allison had been perfect for him all along: sweet and funny and spunky, loving, sexy and supportive. Everything a man should cherish. She was his dream girl, the living, breathing fantasy he didn't even know he had. And now he wanted to settle down with her, to give her his heart, to raise a family, to be the husband she needed. But would she forgive him for the pain he'd caused her? Would she allow him to retract the hurtful things he'd said to her?

God, but he hoped so.

When the doorbell chimed, Allison ignored it. It could be someone selling something, she supposed. Or it could be the lady next door searching for her cat. On occasion, the friendly old feline jumped over the fence and slept on Allison's patio furniture. But she hadn't seen the cat today, and she couldn't bear to see anyone else, either.

She wasn't even supposed to be here herself. If she hadn't told Rand that she loved him, she would still be at his house with him. But that wouldn't have solved anything. She just would have been living a lie.

The doorbell chimed again. But once again, she didn't answer it. She needed to be alone in her misery. Not that anyone, aside from Rand, knew she was miserable.

What if it was him at the door? What if he was here?

To do what? she asked herself. Rehash the same conversation they'd had earlier, with him apologizing for not being able to return her feelings? As much as she loved him, she couldn't bear to go through that again.

Still, she took a chance and peered through the peephole. Sakes alive, but it was him.

Forcing herself to be brave, she undid the latch and opened the door. They stared at each other, gazes locked.

"Look what I've done to you," he said.

She assumed he meant her ragged appearance. He

looked disheveled, too, but nothing marred his handsomeness, at least not to her.

She defended her person. "I just had a good cry, that's all." A horrible, life-will-never-be-the-same breakdown, she thought.

She gestured for him to come inside, and they stared at each other all over again. She hated how much smaller her apartment seemed, dwarfed by his big, broad-shouldered body. He was achingly close to her.

Too, too close.

"I'm so sorry," he said, reaching out to touch her cheek. "I'm so sorry I hurt you."

She flinched and stepped away from him, his apology drumming in her ears. "Please don't do that."

"Am I too late?" A fearful expression clouded his eyes. "Have you stopped loving me?" He thumped a hand against his heart. "Because I love you, Allison."

She went dizzy, her mind spinning in all sorts of directions. Was this really happening? Had he really said that? "You love me?"

"Yes." He closed the gap between them, taking both of her hands in his. "It scared me at first, thinking that I might be falling in love with you. But I'm not afraid anymore. I want to share my life with you, to have kids with you, to do everything real married people do."

"This feels like a dream." But it wasn't. The man she loved, the man who loved her, wasn't a figment of her imagination. The hands that held hers were strong and solid, flesh and bone.

"Will you marry me a second time? Will you return to Ireland with me next year on our anniversary and have the ceremony your family wants us to have?"

She nodded. "I'd marry you a million times more."

She fell into his arms, and they held each other. He

kissed her, his mouth warm and tender against her own. Nothing had ever tasted so good or seemed so right.

After they separated and she caught her breath, he asked, "Do you have a piece of paper and a pen I can use?"

"Yes, of course. But what for?"

"I want to write something down for you."

She couldn't begin to guess what he was up to, but she would soon find out. She went over to her stationery drawer and retrieved a felt-tip pen and a small lined sheet of paper, tearing it from a notepad. "Will these do?"

"They're perfect."

He put pen to paper. But it only took him a matter of seconds. He folded the note and gave it to her.

She eagerly opened it. Along with today's date and his signature, the letters *IOU* were written on it. "I don't understand. What do you owe me?"

"I'm going to write you a poem, like the ones you used to write to your fantasy husband. I can't guarantee how long it'll take me or how good it'll be. I'm not much of a writer. But I want us to have a tangible connection to that time in your life, and that'll be my way of doing it."

Allison could have melted like a teenager at his feet. No doubt about it, he was the hero she'd dreamed about since she was a girl. He absolutely, positively was.

"I need you," she said. Here and now and naked beside her, she thought. "Will you lie down with me? Will you hold me and touch me?"

He took her hand in his. "You know I will. I need you just as much."

She led him to her bed, and they removed their clothes. The tears she'd cried were gone now. In their place were warmth and happiness.

They turned down the covers and slid beneath them.

She luxuriated in the masculine beauty of his body, in the familiarity of it. He whispered in her ear, telling her that he loved her, and hearing him say those three little words thrilled her to the marrow of her bones. She repeated them to him and felt the same wondrous thrill of saying them.

There was no actual penetration. But they made it work anyway, pleasuring each other with hands and mouths and being wildly creative. She didn't have a supply of condoms at her apartment. He hadn't brought protection with him, either. But he had love on his mind when he'd arrived at her door, not sex.

She adored him even more for that. There was nothing sexier than a man who was thinking about love. Nothing more perfect than knowing you were part of his soul.

Hours later Allison went home with Rand, marveling at his determination to share his life with her. He opened the safe in his bedroom and tore up the prenuptial agreement she'd signed, tossing it in the air and making confetti out of it.

She smiled at his boyish enthusiasm, the shredded document fluttering around them. "You're being crazy."

"Yeah, but it's a good kind of crazy." He returned her playful smile. "I want everything I have to belong to you, with no barriers between us. Speaking of which, we need to get rid of the doors between our rooms and make this one big master suite."

Allison nodded her approval. There was nothing better than being happily married, than knowing her joy in Texas was just beginning. "I think I'd like to try my hand at driving the American way, too."

He swung her into his arms. "You can do anything you want."

She squealed as he spun her around, and when his stomach growled, they both laughed. "Maybe I better fix us something to eat."

"That's probably a good idea. I haven't had anything since breakfast. I doubt you have, either."

"I was too emotional to eat. But I'm famished now. How does chicken and dumplings sound?"

"That works for me. I can help, if you want. You can teach me to cook."

"Sure. That'll be fun." She envisioned him years from now, with their children toddling around. "Then you can cook for me on Mother's Day, you and our adorable, green-eyed kids."

"Yeah, but how funny would it be if they ended up with blue or brown eyes?"

"That's a possibility. We both have blue and brown eyes in our family histories." She rocked in his arms. "Our life together is going to be amazing."

"It already is." He released his hold on her, and they went downstairs to the kitchen to start the meal.

Just as she prepared to gather the ingredients, his cell rang. She got an immediate sense of foreboding. "The last time we got interrupted by a phone call, it was bad news."

"Hopefully this is something good." He checked the screen. "It's Will."

She held her breath. Was there information about Rich or did they have an update on Megan's brother Jason?

Allison stood back while Rand talked to Will. Since she could only hear one side of the conversation, she tried not to jump to any conclusions. She waited for Rand to tell her what was going on.

After the call ended, he came over to her and said, "The test results from the ashes came in. They don't belong to Rich. He wasn't the person who died in the plane crash."

Her chest went tight. "Then who did?"

"The authorities don't know. All they know is that the ashes are male human remains."

"So Rich faked his own death? And put someone else's ashes in his place?"

"That's the assumption. But wherever that bastard is, he better never come anywhere near you again. If he does, I'll kill him myself."

"I appreciate you wanting to protect me, but I'll be fine." Allison assured her husband not to worry. "There's no reason for Rich to ever try to see me again. He took my money and that's all he ever really wanted from me."

Rand blew out a breath. "I just hope they catch him."

"Me, too." Rich was a sociopath who needed to be stopped, a rotten-to-the-core man Allison would just as soon forget ever existed. "Did Will mention Jason? Is there any word from him?"

He shook his head. "Jason still hasn't returned Will's calls. Megan hasn't heard from her brother, either. And neither has Jason's daughter, at least not since he first sent her those sporadic emails. It's disturbing, though, how closely Jason appears to be tied to this since he's the one who mailed the urn to Megan to begin with, saying that the ashes belonged to Will."

Allison had never met Jason. But she prayed that he hadn't aligned himself with Rich. She could only imagine how heartbreaking that would be to Will and Megan and the rest of Jason's family. Or worse yet, if he'd come into harm's way. "So there wasn't any positive news?"

"Actually, there was." Rand graced her with a smile. "Will's brother got married yesterday."

"Jesse and Jillian had their wedding? I heard they were engaged." She'd even thought about them on the night of the TCC fund-raiser.

"They tied the knot at the Ace in the Hole. It was an intimate family wedding. Jillian's little daughter, Mackenzie, was the flower girl. Will said she looked cute as a button."

"I'll bet she did." Mackenzie was the toddler Rich had fathered, the same child Jesse Navarro had claimed as his own when he'd fallen in love with the girl's mother. "They're going to make a wonderful family."

"Just like us."

Rand kissed her, and Allison closed her eyes, savoring the moment. Even with the bad things that had happened in Royal, good things were unfolding, too, she thought, as he deepened the kiss and made her sigh.

Very good things.

* * * * *

# LONE STAR
# LOVERS

## JESSICA LEMMON

For Grandma Edie.

Thank you for putting that first Harlequin
book in my hands. I wish you were here
so I could put this one in yours.

# One

Texas in the springtime was a sight to behold. The Dallas sunshine warmed the patio of Hip Stir, where Penelope Brand sat across from her most recent client. Blue cloudless skies stretched over the glass-and-steel city buildings, practically begging the city-dwellers to take a deep breath. Given that nearly every table was full, it appeared that most of downtown had obeyed.

Pen adjusted her sunglasses before carefully lifting her filled-to-the-brim café au lait. The mug's contents wobbled but she made that first sip to her lips rather than to her lap. Which was a relief since Pen always wore white. Today she'd chosen her favorite white jacket with black silk piping over a vibrant pink cami. Her pants were white to match, slim-fitting and ended in a pair of black five-inch stilettos.

White was her power color. Pen's clients came to her for crisis control—sometimes for a completely fresh start. As their public relations maven, a crisp, clean do-over had become Pen's specialty.

She'd started her business in the Midwest. Until last year, the Chicago elite had trusted her with their bank accounts, their marriages and their hard-won reputations. When her own reputation took a header, Pen was forced to regroup. That unfortunate circumstance was rapidly gaining ground as her "past." The woman sitting across from her now had laid the foundation for Penelope's future.

"I can't thank you enough." Stefanie Ferguson shook her head, tossing her dark blond ponytail to the side. "Though I suppose I should thank my stupid brother for the introduction." She lifted her espresso and rolled her eyes.

Pen smothered a smile. Stefanie's *stupid brother* was none other than the well-loved mayor of Dallas, and he'd called on Penelope's services to help his younger sister out of a mess that could mar his reputation.

Stef didn't share her brother's reverent love for politics and being careful in the public eye. She flew by the seat of her skinny jeans, the most recent flight landing her in the arms of one of the mayor's most critical opponents, Blake Eastwood.

Blake's development company wanted to break ground for a new civic center that Mayor Ferguson opposed. Critics argued that the mayor was biased, given the civic center was to be built near his family's oil wells, but the mayor's supporters argued the unneeded new-build would be a waste of city funds.

Either way, the photograph of Stefanie exiting a hotel, her arm wrapped around Blake's while they both wore wrinkled clothing and sexually satisfied smiles, had caused some unwanted media attention.

The mayor had hired Brand Consulting to smooth out the wrinkles of what could have turned into a PR nightmare. Penelope had done her job and done it well. One week after the snafu, and the media had already moved on to gossiping about someone else.

All in a day's work.

"You're coming to the party tonight, right?" Stef asked.

"I'm looking forward to you being there so I have a girl to talk to."

Stef was younger than Pen by four years, but Pen could easily become close friends with her. Stef was smart, savvy and, while she was a tad too honest for her brother's taste, Pen welcomed that sort of frankness. Too bad a friendship with Stefanie broke Pen's most recently adopted rule: never become personally involved with a client.

That included an intimate friendship with the blonde across from her.

A pang of regret faded and faded fast as Pen remembered why she'd had to ink the rule in the first place. Her ex in Chicago had tanked her reputation, cashed her checks and forced her to journey to her own fresh start.

"I wouldn't miss it," Pen answered with a smile. Because yes, she wasn't going to become besties with Stefanie Ferguson, but neither would she turn down a coveted invitation to the mayor's birthday party.

Those who gained entry to the mayor's annual soiree, held at his private gated mansion, were the envy of the city. Pen had worked with billionaires, local celebrities and sports stars in her professional past, but she'd never worked directly with a civil servant. Attending the most sought-after party of the year was as good as a gold star on her résumé.

Pen picked up the tab for her client and said her goodbyes to Stefanie before walking two blocks back to her office.

Thank God for the mayor's troublemaking sister.

Stepping in at the pleasure of Mayor Chase Ferguson might have been the best decision Pen had made since moving to Dallas. Her heart thudded heavily against her breastbone as she thought about what this could mean for her growing PR firm—and for her future as an entrepreneur. There were going to be many, *many* people at this party who would eventually require her services. The world of politics teemed with scandal.

After finishing her work for the day, she locked the glass door on her tenth-floor suite and drew the blinds. In her private bathroom, Pen spritzed on a dash of floral perfume and brushed her teeth, swapping out her suit for the white dress she'd chosen to wear to the mayor's party. She'd brought it with her to work since her apartment was on the other side of town and the mayor's mansion was closer to her office.

She smoothed her palms down the skirt and checked the back view in the full-length mirror on the door. *Not bad at all.* After way too much vacillating this morning, she'd opted for hair down versus hair up. Soft waves fell around her shoulders and the color of her pale blue eyes popped beneath a veil of black-mascaraed lashes and smoky, silver-blue shadow.

The dress was doing her several favors, hugging her hips and her derriere in a way that wasn't inappropriate, but showcased her daily efforts at the gym.

*I couldn't let you leave without pointing out how well you wear that dress.*

Shivers tracked down her arms and she rubbed away the gooseflesh as the silken voice from two weeks ago wound around her brain.

Pen had moved to Dallas thinking she'd sworn off men forever, but after nearly a year of working nonstop to rebuild her business, she'd admitted she was lonely. She'd been at a swanky jazz club enjoying her martini when yet another man had approached to try his luck.

This one had been a tall, muscled, delicious male specimen with a confident walk and a paralyzing green stare that held her fastened in place. He'd introduced himself as "Just Zach," and then asked to sit. She'd surprised herself by saying yes.

Over a drink, she learned they'd crossed paths once before—at a party in Chicago. They knew the same billionaire family who owned Crane Hotels, though she'd never imagined running into Zach again anywhere other than Chicago.

She also never imagined she'd ask him to come home with her…but she did. When one drink led to another, Penelope let him lead her out of the club.

What a night it'd been.

His kisses had seared, branding her his for those stolen few hours. Hotter than his mouth were the acres of golden muscles, and she'd reveled in smoothing her palms over his bulging pecs and the bumps of his abs. Zach had a great ass, a better smile, and when he left in the morning, he'd even kissed her goodbye.

*Stay in bed and recover, Penelope Brand.*

A dimple had punctuated one of his cheeks, and her laugh had eased into a soft hum as she'd watched Zach's silhouetted masculine form dress in the sunlight pressing through her white bedroom curtains.

*Sigh.*

It had been the perfect night, curing her of her loneliness and adding a much-needed spring in her step. Pen had felt like she could take over the damn world. Amazing what a few earth-shattering orgasms could do for a girl's morale.

She was still smiling at that memory of "Just Zach" from Chicago when she climbed behind the wheel of her Audi and started toward her destination. One night with Zach had been fun, but Pen wasn't foolish enough to believe it could have been more. As the daughter of entrepreneurs, success had been ingrained in Pen's mind from an early age. She'd taken her eye off the prize in Chicago and look what'd happened.

Never again.

At the gates of the mayor's mansion, Pen presented the shiny black invitation, personalized with her name in an elegant silver script, and smiled down at the slender silver bangle on her left wrist. It had been included with her invitation. Dangling from the bracelet was a letter *F*, and she'd bet her new shoes that the diamond set in the charm was a real one. Every first-time attendee received a gift from the mayor.

The security guard waved her through and she smiled in triumph. She was *in*. The world of politics was ripe with men and women who might need to hire her firm in the future, and she would make sure every guest knew her name by the end of the evening.

Pen passed her car keys to the valet and walked the cobblestone path to the mayor's mansion. The grounds were elegant, lined with tall, slender shrubberies and short, boxed hedges. Fragrant, colorful flowers were in full bloom thanks to an early spring. Looming oaks that'd been there since the Ferguson family earned their first dollar in Dallas, ushered her in.

Inside, she checked her wrap and tucked her clutch under her arm. When her turn came, an attendant walked her to the mayor for a proper introduction.

Standing before the mayor, was it any wonder the man had earned the hearts of the majority of Dallas's female voters? Chase Ferguson was tall, his dark hair pushed this way and that as if it couldn't be tamed, but the angle of his clean-shaven jaw and the lines on his dark suit showed control where it counted.

"Ms. Brand." Hazel eyes lowered to a respectable survey of her person before Chase offered a hand. She shook it and he released her to signal to a nearby waiter. "Stefanie is around here somewhere," he said of his younger sister. He leaned in. "And thanks to you, on her best behavior."

The mayor straightened as a waiter approached with a tray of champagne.

"Drink?" Chase's Texas accent had all but vanished beneath a perfected veneer, but Pen could hear the slightest drawl when he lowered his voice. "You'll get to meet my brother tonight."

She was embarrassed she didn't know a thing about another Ferguson sibling. She'd only been in Texas for a year, and between juggling her new business, moving into her apartment and handling crises for the Dallas elite, she hadn't climbed the Ferguson family tree any higher than Chase and Stefanie.

"Perfect timing," Chase said, his eyes going over her shoulder to welcome a new arrival.

"Hey, hey, big brother."

Now *that* was a drawl.

The back of her neck prickled. She recognized the voice instantly. It sent warmth pooling in her belly and lower. It stood her nipples on end. The Texas accent over her shoulder was a tad thicker than Chase's, but not as lazy as it'd been two weeks ago. Not like it was when she'd invited him home and he'd leaned close, his lips brushing the shell of her ear.

*Lead the way, gorgeous.*

Squaring her shoulders, Pen prayed Zach had the shortest memory ever, and turned to make his acquaintance.

*Correction: re-acquaintance.*

She was floored by broad shoulders outlined by a sharp black tux, longish dark blond hair smoothed away from his handsome face and the greenest eyes she'd ever seen. Zach had been gorgeous the first time she'd laid eyes on him, but his current look suited the air of control and power swirling around him.

A primal, hidden part of her wanted to lean into his solid form and rest in his capable, strong arms again. As tempting as reaching out to him was, she wouldn't. She'd had her night with him. She was in the process of assembling a solid bedrock for her fragile, rebuilt business and she refused to let her world fall apart because of a sexy man with a dimple.

A dimple that was notably missing since he was gaping at her with shock. His poker face needed work.

"I'll be damned," Zach muttered. "I didn't expect to see you here."

"That makes two of us," Pen said, and then she polished off half her champagne in one long drink.

# Two

Zach schooled his expression—albeit a bit late.

Penelope Brand wore a curve-hugging white dress like the night he'd seen her at the club. He'd been there with a friend who had long since left with a woman. Zach hadn't been looking to hook up until he spotted Pen's upswept blond hair and the elegant line from her neck to her bare shoulders.

Seeing her hair down tonight dropkicked him two weeks into the past. Her apartment. The moment he'd tugged on the clip holding her hair back and let those luscious locks down. The way he'd speared his fingers into those silken strands, before kicking her door closed and carrying her to her bedroom.

He'd sampled her mouth before depositing her onto her bed and sampling every other part of her.

And he did mean *every* part.

They hadn't discussed rules, but each had known the score—he wouldn't call and she wouldn't want him to—so they'd made the most of that night. She'd tasted like every debased teenage fantasy he'd ever had, and she'd delivered. He'd left that morning with a smile on his face that matched hers.

When he'd stepped into the shower at home that morning, he'd experienced a brief pinch of regret that he wouldn't see her again.

Though, hell, maybe he *would* see her again given lightning had already stricken them twice. He hadn't wanted to let her get away that night at the bar—not without testing the attraction between them.

He felt a similar pull now.

"If you'll excuse me." His brother Chase moved off, arm extended to shake the palm of a round-bellied man who ruled half of Texas. As one-third owner of Ferguson Oil, it was Zach's job to know the powerful players in his brother's life—in the entire state—but this man was unfamiliar.

"Just Zach," Pen snapped, drawing his attention. Her blue eyes ignited. "I thought you were a contractor in Chicago."

"I used to be."

"And now you're the mayor's brother?"

"I've always been the mayor's brother," he told her with a sideways smile.

He'd also always been an oil tycoon. A brief stint of going out on his own in Chicago hadn't changed his parentage or his inheritance. When Zach had received a call from his mother letting him know his father, Rand Ferguson, had suffered a heart attack, Zach had left Chicago and never looked back.

He wasn't the black sheep—had never resented working for the family business. He'd simply wanted to do his own thing for a while. He had, and now he was back, and yeah, he was pretty damn good at being the head honcho of Ferguson Oil. It also let his mother breathe a sigh of relief to have Zach in charge.

Penelope's face pinched. "Are you adopted or something?"

He chuckled. Not the first time he'd heard that. "Actually, Chase and I are twins."

"Really?" Her nose scrunched. It was cute.

"No."

She pursed her lips and damn if he didn't want to experience their sweetness all over again. He hadn't dated much over the past year, but the way Penelope smiled at him had towed him in. He hadn't recognized her at first—the briefest of meetings at a Crane Hotel function three years ago hadn't cemented her in his mind—but there was a pull there he couldn't deny.

Pen finished her champagne and rested the flute on a passing waiter's tray. With straight shoulders and the lift of one fair eyebrow, she faced Zach again. "You didn't divulge your family status when I met you on Saturday."

"You didn't divulge yours."

Her eyes coasted over his tuxedo, obviously trying to square the man before her with the slacks and button-down he'd worn to the club.

"It's still me." He gave her a grin, one that popped his dimple. He pointed at it while she frowned. "You liked this a few weeks ago." He gestured to himself generally as he leaned in to murmur, "You liked a lot of this a few weeks ago."

*Miffed* wasn't a good enough word for the expression that crossed her pretty face. The attraction was still there, the lure that had existed as they came together that night in her bed twice—no, wait, *three times*.

Zach decided he'd end tonight with her in his bed. They'd been good together, and while he wasn't one to make a habit of two-night stands, he'd make an exception for Penelope Brand.

Because *damn*.

"I'll escort you to the dining room. You can sit with me."
He offered his arm.

Pen sighed, the action lifting her breasts and softening
her features. Zach's grin widened.

*So close.*

She qualified with, "Fine. But only because there are a
lot of people here I would like to meet. This is a business
function for me, so I'd appreciate—"

The words died on Penelope's lips when a female shriek
rose on the air. "Where is he? Where is that son of a bitch
who owes me money?"

The crowd gasped and Pen's hand tightened on his forearm.

Zach turned in the direction of the outburst to find a
rail-thin redhead in a long black dress waving a rolled-
slash-wadded stack of paper in her hand. Her brown eyes
snapped around the room, and her upper lip curled in a way
that made him wonder how he'd ever found her attractive.

Granted she wasn't foaming at the mouth when they'd
exchanged their vows.

*"You."* Her eyes landed on him as the security guards
positioned around the house rushed toward her. Zach held
up a hand to stop them. He'd try and talk Yvonne down
from whatever crazy idea she'd birthed before they caused
a bigger scene.

"V," he said, hoping to gain ground with the nickname
he'd coined the night they met. A night soaked in tequila.
"You're at my brother's birthday party. You have my attention. Is there something I can help you with?"

A big, bald security guy with an ugly scar down one
cheek stepped closer to Yvonne, his mitts poised to drag
her out the second Zach gave the signal.

"Write me a check for a million dollars and I'll be on
my way." Yvonne cocked her head and waved the crum-

pled stack of papers in front of her. "Or else I'll tear up our annulment."

Tearing it up wouldn't make it go away. What was her angle?

"Marrying you entitled me to at least half your fortune, Zachary Ferguson."

It was laughable that she thought a million was *half*.

Penelope's hand slipped from his forearm and Zach reached over and put it back.

"Ex-wife," he corrected for Penelope's—hell, for everyone's—benefit. "And no, it doesn't."

"I'm going to make your life miserable, Zachary Ferguson. You just wait."

"Too late." He gave a subtle nod to the beefcake guard who circled Yvonne's upper arm in his firm grip as he warned her against fighting him.

To her credit, she didn't struggle. But neither did she go willingly. Yvonne's eyes sliced over to Penelope. "Who is this? Are you *cheating* on me?"

Here they went again. Yvonne had asked that question so many times in the two days they were married, Zach would swear she'd gone to bed sane and woken crazy.

He'd had the good sense to get out of the marriage, which was more than he could say for the sense he'd had going in. The details were fuzzy: Vegas, Elvis, the Chapel of Love, etcetera, etcetera… Getting married had seemed fun at the time, but spontaneity had its downfalls. Within twenty-four hours Yvonne had grown horns and a forked tongue.

"Make it two million dollars," Yvonne hissed, illustrating his point. The guard tugged her back a step, looking inconvenienced when she fought him.

Zach had money—plenty of it—but relinquishing it to the crazed redhead wasn't going to make her go away. If anything, she'd be back for more later.

"Get her out of here," Zach said smoothly, putting his hand over Pen's. "She's upsetting my fiancée."

"Your what?" Yvonne asked at the same time Penelope stiffened at his side.

"Penelope Brand, my fiancée. Yvonne, uh…" What was her maiden name? "Yvonne, my ex-wife." Yvonne's eyes burned with anger—flames Zach was only too happy to fan. "Penelope and I are engaged to be married. It's real, unlike what you and I had. You can contact my lawyers with any further questions."

Yvonne shrieked like the eels from *The Princess Bride* as security dragged her away.

Another security detail, this one slimmer but no less mean-looking, stepped in front of Zach.

"How the hell did she get in here?"

His eyes dipped to his shoes in chagrin before meeting Zach's angry expression again. "We'll call the police department, sir."

"No, don't. She's exuberant, but harmless." He took a breath. Who wanted to deal with the paperwork?

"Very well." Security Guy Number Two followed in the path of the beefy guy.

Chase took his place, using his extra two inches of height to scowl down at Zach. "Let me get this straight," his brother said in that exaggerated calm way he had about him. "You're engaged…and married?"

"*Was* married."

"You didn't tell me you were married."

"Well, it only lasted forty-four hours."

"And you—" Chase's hawk-like gaze snapped away from Zach to lock on Penelope "—didn't tell me you were engaged to my brother."

"I—" Pen started.

"It's not true." Zach couldn't bullshit a bullshitter, and

his brother was in politics, so he was overqualified. "I wanted to refocus Yvonne's attention."

He would come clean with Chase, even though he'd been left out of the loop where Stefanie was concerned. Zach had known Stef was having some issues but he didn't realize his brother had called in the cavalry in the form of Penelope's PR services.

"You succeeded," Chase said. He smiled amiably at Penelope. "Looks like you've secured your next client, Ms. Brand. I trust you can clean up my brother's mess."

A few truncated sounds that might have been Pen struggling for breath came from her throat, but she reined in her simmering argument to say, "Yes. Of course."

"Excellent." Chase lifted his voice to address the guests milling around the bar. "If everyone would find your seats in the dining room, dinner will be served shortly." He turned his attention back to Zach and Penelope. "I assume you two would prefer to sit together."

Zach simply smiled as he looked down at a wide-eyed Penelope. This evening had fun written all over it. "I wouldn't allow my fiancée to sit with anyone else."

# Three

Penelope strolled into the oversize ballroom on Zach's arm. The mansion boasted enough round tables and slipcovered chairs to seat the mayor's one-hundred-plus guests. Similar to a wedding, there was a head table for the guests of honor. In this case those guests were Mayor Chase Ferguson, Stefanie Ferguson, Zach and the recent addition of Penelope.

The rectangular table was set apart from the others and dotted with votive candles and low vases with flower arrangements.

A few staff members from the mayor's office were also seated at the head table. A plucky, talkative woman named Barb, Roger, who looked and acted the part of secret service, and a scowling, large-framed man named Emmett Keaton.

Emmett, who had been introduced as the mayor's "friend and confidant," had short, cropped hair, a healthy dash of stubble on his face and eyed Stefanie with disdain the entire time he ate his pear and Gorgonzola salad. Stefanie had glared at him from her spot across the table before rolling her eyes and drinking down her white wine.

Clearly there was no love lost between those two.

Penelope wasn't surprised. Stefanie's recent scrape had drawn attention to the Ferguson family—and not the good kind. It would make sense that she wasn't favored among the mayor's staff.

Speaking of scrapes, Pen now had another to deal with in the form of Zach's ex-wife. Pen didn't know what shocked her more—that Zach had married the unhinged woman, or that he'd been married at all. It might be a tie.

Zach wasn't the marrying type. He was the one-night-stand type. Or so Pen had thought.

Slicing into the sun-dried-tomato-crusted rack of lamb on her plate, she kept her voice low and asked Zach the million-dollar question.

"Were you married when we slept together two weeks ago?"

His jaw paused midchew before he continued, smiling with his mouth shut, and then swallowed down the bite. He swept his tongue over his teeth and took a drink of water before responding. Pen didn't mind the delay. The lamb was spectacular. She sliced off another petite bite, this time plunging it into the ramekin of balsamic dipping sauce first.

"No," he finally said.

She patted her lips with her napkin. "When did it happen?"

"Last New Year's Eve." He glanced around the table, but no one was paying them any attention. Barb was chattering to Stefanie, and Emmett and Chase were having a low conversation of their own. Roger wasn't at the table any longer. When had he left? He was sneaky, but then—secret service, so it made sense.

"In Vegas," Zach finished.

Pen laughed, drawing Emmett's and Chase's attention before they returned to their conversation. "Cliché, Zach."

"Yeah, as was the annulment."

"And the need for our betrothal?"

Zach shrugged muscular, tux-covered shoulders. "You helped Stef. You're a good ally to have."

"You could have introduced me as an adviser. As anyone."

He stabbed a bite of meat with his fork and waved it as he said, "Fiancée had a nice ring to it."

"Very funny." Fiancée. Ring. At least his personality was the same as the night she'd invited him home with her. He'd been cheeky then, too.

She smiled, glued her eyes to his and enjoyed the sizzling heat in the scant space between them for the next three heartbeats. Then she focused on her food again.

Once the dinner dishes were cleared, dessert appeared in the form of a dark chocolate tart, a single, perfect raspberry interrupting a decadent white-chocolate drizzle.

"Speech time," Zach prompted his brother.

"Go get 'em, Tiger," Stefanie said, clearly teasing him.

Chase stood and buttoned his suit jacket, then glided to the podium. From her side of the table, Pen wouldn't have to so much as turn her head to watch. Unlike everyone else who had swiveled in their chairs.

Chase had great presence. Elegant. Regal. He talked and the world quieted to listen. She remembered the first time she'd seen him on television and thought—

A gasp stole her throat when warm fingers landed on her knee.

*Zach.*

Barb looked over her shoulder and offered a wide smile. Pen gave the other woman a tight nod as she reached beneath the table and removed Zach's wandering hand.

Pen cleared her throat and refocused on Chase's speech when Zach's fingers returned. This time she managed to stifle the surprised bleat in her throat. She slanted a glare to her right where he lounged, elbow resting on the arm of his chair, his fingers pressed to his lips and his eyes narrowed as if hanging on to every word his brother said.

With the fingers of Zach's other hand swirling circles on the inside of her knee, Pen couldn't concentrate on a single word of the speech. A quick glance around confirmed that no one could see what was happening beneath the tablecloth.

She shifted in her seat, but before she could crush his fingers between her kneecaps, he gripped her leg with a tight hold. She swallowed down a ball of thick lust as he pushed her legs apart.

Pen flattened her hands on the tablecloth as Zach's hand traveled from her knee and climbed the inside of her thigh. She closed her eyes, visions of the night they'd spent together flashing on the screen of her mind.

His firm, insistent kisses on her jaw, her neck and lower.

The deep timbre of his laugh when she'd struggled with his belt.

He'd ended up stripping for her while she sat on her bed and watched every tantalizing second.

She was snapped to the present when Zach's fingertips dug into the soft skin of her thigh, and without warning, brushed her silk panties. Pen fisted one hand on the tablecloth, dragging her dessert plate to the edge of the table. Her glass of red gave a dangerous wobble.

She held her breath when he touched her intimately again, the scrap of silk going damp against his pressing fingers. When he pulled her panties aside and brushed bare skin, Pen bit down on her bottom lip to contain a whimper.

Then the mayor's voice crashed into her psyche.

"To Penelope and my brother, Zach. Many congratulations on your engagement."

She jerked ramrod straight to find every set of eyes in the room on her and glasses raised.

"Cheers," Chase said into the microphone.

Stiff as a cadaver, Pen managed a frozen smile. Conversely, Zach moved like a sunbathing cat, lazily tossing his napkin on the table before taking Pen's napkin from her lap and standing.

He offered his hand and a smirk, and Pen prayed that the flush of her cheeks would be taken for embarrassment at the attention.

Placing her palm in his, she surreptitiously tugged her skirt down and stood with him to accept the room's applause.

Smooth as butter, Zach pushed her dessert plate from its perch at the edge of the table, handed Pen her wineglass and lifted his own.

Then, they drank to their engagement.

"I like this." Zach touched the *F* dangling from Pen's bracelet with his thumb. "Makes me feel possessive."

Her hand in his, Pen swayed to the music.

He liked her hand in his. He liked her laugh and the sweet scent of her perfume tickling his senses. He liked the way she smoothly handled Barb's question about a missing engagement ring.

*Where is your diamond ring, darling?*

*Oh, we didn't want to upstage the mayor on his big day.*

Pen was the right partner to choose for this particular snafu. She was a woman at the top of her game. Touching her under the table and listening as her breaths shortened and tightened was a bonus.

"What are you grinning about?" she asked him now.

"I think you know."

She hummed, not confirming or denying. Like he said, top of her game.

He turned her to the beat of the music, pressing his palm flat on her back and drawing her closer. She came rather than resist him, which he liked a whole hell of a lot.

"It's kind of your brother to give first-time guests such decadent gifts," she commented, redirecting his attention back to the bracelet. She waggled their joined hands so the pendant moved against her pale skin.

"You think *that's* what this is for?" Zach joked as he clucked his tongue. "You don't know the underground Chase Ferguson birthday secret."

Her eyes widened slightly and he didn't say more. Finally, she broke. "Are you going to tell me or not?"

"Depends." He leaned in, his whisper conspiratorial. "Are you into multiple sex partners?"

"Zach!" she quietly scolded. A second later her lips parted in a laugh that warmed the very center of his chest. She took her hand from his shoulder to playfully shove his chest. If he wasn't mistaken, she lingered a bit over his pectoral before resting her hand on his shoulder once again. "You're impossible."

He hovered just over her lips, testing her. "You're wearing the first letter of my last name, Pen. That means you're mine."

Blue eyes turned up to his and for a second he thought she might give him the gift of saying, *Show me to your room.* She hadn't been the least bit shy the night she'd invited him home with her.

Instead those blues rolled skyward and she hedged with, "Caveman."

But she'd given him an inch not arguing that she was his.

"What *really* happens next?" she asked. The crowd was thinning. Only a few couples danced, while others ringed the bar or sat with their coffees at the cleared tables.

"Things wind down. Cigars are smoked. Bourbon poured. Stef and I have rooms here so we usually stay the night."

"Well, make sure you tell me when it's the proper time to

leave. I don't want to overstay my welcome on my maiden voyage to the mayor's birthday party."

"How about you don't leave?"

She'd been looking around the room, but now snapped her attention back to him. "What?"

"You heard me. Don't leave. Stay in my room. With me." He pulled her closer, resting his cheek on hers as he spoke into the delicate shell of her ear. "Spend the night in my bed, Penelope. You won't regret it."

Her hand tightened in his. "I—I can't. It's…inappropriate."

He pulled his face away from hers to find she looked as flustered as she sounded. Her eyes bounced from his face to his chest. Her steps faltered.

Zach dropped the pretense of dancing, and cradled her gorgeous face in both hands. "It's not only appropriate. It's expected. To this room of people, you're my future wife. I would never let my fiancée drive home alone this late."

A small smile found her face. "My God. You really are a caveman."

"Aw, honey," he said with a wink as he laced his fingers with hers. "But I'm your caveman."

Her silken laughter as he led them to the bar was a good sign she'd join him upstairs when the night wound to a close. Zach wasn't ready to draw the curtain on their evening yet, but he was anticipating getting her alone again. He'd give her the best night of her life.

Well, assuming the last night they'd spent together could be topped.

It was a challenge he embraced.

# Four

"We're turning in. Happy birthday." Zach offered his brother a hand and Chase shook it, which Penelope found charming though formal. She wondered if those two had ever wrestled or punched each other in the face when growing up, and then figured they probably had. It wasn't hard to imagine rough and tumble boys beneath their polished exteriors.

"Penelope, make yourself at home," Chase told her. "My staff will get you whatever you need."

"*I'll* get her what she needs," Zach said, taking her hand in his. "She's my fiancée."

At his offered wink, Pen let herself smile. Zach was a lot of things—more than she knew before she learned he was Chase Ferguson's brother—but among his top qualities, Zach was *fun*. Now that Pen had taken him on, she was breaking her cardinal rule of not sleeping with a client. She'd break it this time—if only for him. He made rule-breaking downright delicious. He focused her attention on the present. Which was the exact reason she'd invited him home that night at the club.

An inkling of warning that her ex had cost her every-thing vibrated at the back of her skull, but the champagne bubbles swimming in her tummy drowned it out.

Her situation with Zach was totally different. The fake fiancée act was a ruse, true, but she couldn't see a rea-son not to take advantage of another night with him. He'd been working that angle since he touched her under the table tonight.

Hand in hand they passed by Stefanie, who pushed her lip into an exaggerated pout. "I can't believe you didn't tell me you were engaged to this idiot." Stef shot a thumb toward Zach.

"Your secret-keeping skills are dubious," he grumbled.

They'd opted not to share the truth with Stefanie—Chase's idea. He thought it was better if she was in the dark like everyone else.

"You have a lot of secrets lately." Stef eyed Zach, her mouth pulling at the corners.

"So do you," he said. "I had no idea you were working with my beautiful fiancée on a cover-up."

"It wasn't a cover-up," Pen interjected before these two sniped away her good mood. "We simply rerouted the pub-lic's attention."

"Thank you for that." Stefanie gripped Pen's arm and squeezed. "In all seriousness, I'm happy for you two."

"Thanks, sis," Zach said as a wave of guilt crashed over Penelope. She didn't mind contorting public opinion but lying to Zach's sister felt…wrong.

"I'm not staying here tonight," Stef told them. "I have a date with another of my brother's mortal enemies."

Zach's shoulders went rigid, a wave of heat emanating from his form.

"Just kidding!" Stef's grin was wide. She bid them good-night and Pen stroked her hand up Zach's tuxedo jacket to soothe him.

"Down, boy."

His eyes snapped over to her, the heat there transforming from anger to lust—which was even more sinister.

*"Boy?"* Zach startled Pen by bending at the knees to lift her into his arms. The few guests left milling about reacted with gasps or soft laughs. Pen, eyes wide, held on to him, her fingers entwining in the thick blond hair at the back of his neck.

"Sounds like you need a reminder from the *man* who shared your bed a few weeks back."

His confident smile, strong arms and twinkling green eyes consumed her. She bit down on her lip and remembered all too well the details of that night. Nevertheless, she said, "I could, now that you mention it."

A smile spread his full lips.

Fake fiancée or not, for her, the attraction part of their relationship was very real. Penelope was going to take advantage of every exciting, promising part of it.

She barely had a moment to take in her surroundings when Zach's muscular chest was flush with her back. He swept her hair off her neck and put his lips over her pounding pulse.

"I don't have an overnight bag," she breathed, tilting her head to give him better access.

His tongue covered her earlobe before he tugged with his teeth. Goose bumps rose on her skin and she reached up to palm the back of his head.

His mouth was as intoxicating as any liquor, but a thousand times more potent.

"I'll at least need—" a gasp stole her words as his hand coasted from her waist to the sides of her breasts, teasing her "—a toothbrush," she finished.

He replied to her complaint by sliding warm fingers over

her bare back, then snicking the zipper of her dress down over her backside.

"Gorgeous. Damn, Pen. I love your ass."

"Likewise." She managed a breathy laugh and turned in his arms. The way he looked at her made her feel gorgeous. Like she was the only one he wanted in this world.

His fingers pushed into her hair and he cupped the back of her neck, pegging her with a serious green stare. "Tell me the truth."

"About?" She raised her eyebrows in curiosity.

"Have you thought of me in the past few weeks?"

"Yes."

Zach's palm warmed her neck and shifted upward until he cradled the back of her skull. He dipped his head but didn't kiss her, continuing his interrogation.

"Tell me what you thought about, Penelope Brand." His dimple dented one cheek when he offered a lopsided smile. "In graphic detail."

It was a smile she couldn't help returning. Her hands fisting the material of his shirt, she yanked it from his pants and stroked her hands along his hot, golden skin.

"You first," she whispered a hairsbreadth away from his lips.

She'd meant to be cute, but Zach's smile vanished. His other hand went to her back and, pressing her until her breasts flattened against his chest, he answered her.

"Every morning since I walked out of your apartment, I wake up hard and ready. The woman in my head missing her clothes has blond hair, pale blue eyes and your name."

His pupils dilated, the black darkening his surrounding green irises. "Your turn."

She remembered lots of things. The way he moved over her, the way he filled her, consumed her, during their lovemaking. But mostly the way he laughed and made her life fun for that slice of time.

He made her forget her obligations or the fact that she'd once let a man trample over her business and her good sense. Zach made her feel beautiful and cherished and hot. Really freaking hot.

"I remember," she started, tugging at his black leather belt, "your face when you came." She unfastened his pants and slipped her hand inside, gliding her palm along the thick ridge of his erection.

Zach's nostrils flared, his hands rerouting to her hips and digging in for purchase.

"You looked a lot like you do right now." She massaged his manhood, tipping her chin to swipe her tongue along his bottom lip. That lip tasted like she remembered—warm and firm and laced with desire. "In control but in danger of losing it."

She'd meant to spur him on. He didn't disappoint.

He reached for the skirt of her dress and peeled it past her hips and stomach and over her head. He tossed it inside out to the floor.

"I'm in no danger of losing control, Ms. Brand," Zach informed her, his lazy Texas drawl intensifying. "But you are."

Her white lace bra was the next article of clothing to get the heave-ho. He disarmed the strap so quickly that in a blink both her breasts were bare, her nipples standing up, begging for his attention.

Attention they got.

Zach's arms looped her back and Pen had to move both hands to his shoulders when he dropped his mouth to sample a breast. His tongue swirled and suckled and she let her head fall back, losing herself in the moment. That was what he did to her—made her live in the right now and not beyond.

Who could resist?

He backed her across the room and she went, turning to

take in the bed they were about to make very good use of. The regal four-poster frame reached for the ceiling above a pile of gold-and-maroon bedding and pillows fit for royalty.

Thighs against hers, Zach walked her two steps until her butt collided with the mattress. She sat, eyes tipped to his. He stood looking down at her, shirt untucked, pants open, eyes aflame.

"Damn, I don't know what to do first."

"I do." Pen reached for his cock again but Zach snatched her hand.

"Not that." His smirk was confident when he hooked his fingers into her panties and swept them off her legs. At her ankles, he paused, watching her as he tossed one of her tall shoes over his shoulder, then the other. The scrap of silk went next. With a tip of his chin, he said, "Scoot."

She did, naked and so excited she wondered if he could see the shake in her arms as she settled herself on the middle of the bed.

He unbuttoned his tuxedo shirt, his eyes taking inventory of her like she was his next meal. Shirt discarded, he pushed his pants and briefs to his ankles, kicking off his shoes and socks in the process.

Penelope had to struggle not to drool.

Zach's lean, muscular chest was as mouthwatering as in her memory, the scant bit of chest hair whirling around two flat brown nipples. His erection jutted proudly between slim hips, which gave way to thick thighs. She realized she'd become lost staring at his body and quickly jerked her attention to his face.

Didn't help.

His body was to die for, but the real panty-melter was the dimple indenting one cheek when he smiled. His jaw was firm and strong, at odds with the playful twinkle in his eyes. Some might say his hair was in need of a trim, but Pen preferred the longish style. Especially when he braced himself over her and a thick lock fell rakishly over his forehead.

One knee depressed the mattress, then another. Her mouth dropped open when he lowered his head to her stomach and swiped her belly button with the tip of his tongue.

Flames licked her core. This was the treat she'd enjoyed most with him, and when he dragged his tongue an inch lower on her tummy, a high-pitched gasp betrayed her.

"That's what I like to hear." He hoisted a brow as he pulled her knees apart and settled between her thighs. "Be as loud as you want. No one stays in this part of the house, but if they do, I want them to know exactly why you agreed to marry me."

"Your money?" Pen teased to break the thick band of sexual tension strangling her.

"Oh, you'll pay for that." He didn't offer another teasing lick, but buried his face between her thighs and doled out the promised punishment.

She took every lash she was owed, her fists mangling the duvet, her head thrashing on the pillows that one by one met their final resting places on the floor.

He wrung an orgasm from her without trying, and two more when he stepped up his game.

Panting, delirious with pleasure, Pen lazily opened her eyelids when he began climbing her body. Zach's lips coasted over her ribs, breasts and to her neck where he bit her earlobe.

"Still on the pill?" His heated breath coated her ear.

"Yes." She gripped his biceps, anticipation wriggling within. She wanted him. Now. Hell, five minutes ago.

He positioned his hips over hers, his erection pressing into her pelvis and so very close to home.

"Have you been with anyone since our night together?"

The question pulled her out of the moment and she frowned ever so briefly.

"I haven't, Pen," he told her, sincerity on his face. "Unless you count my hand and a few showers where I tried to erase the memory of you."

He'd...thought about her. He was telling the truth.

Firm lips coasted over hers and a whisper of breath coated her mouth when he asked for her answer again.

"Have you?"

"No," she answered.

She was rewarded with the roll of Zach's hips and the feel of him sliding deep, overtaking her, filling her like she remembered.

His low groan reverberated against her breasts as she clung to his back, their bodies sealed by a thin layer of sweat.

He uttered a harsh curse that sounded a lot like a compliment before pushing his fingers into her hair and focusing his eyes on hers.

"You're mine, Pen."

Her eyes went to the bracelet sliding up her wrist when she looped her arms at his neck. The letter *F* dangling there like a brand.

"Say it," he demanded, claiming her with another deep thrust.

"I'm yours."

Another thrust had her pulse thrumming anew between her legs.

"Whose?" he growled, picking up the pace. All of her overheated. She knew what he was asking. Knew what he wanted. Pen threw her head back and gave him the answer he'd earned.

"Yours."

"Say my name, beautiful."

She did, on a shout. "Zach!"

The slide of his body against hers, the feel of his breath in her ear, the heat of his mouth on hers took her to new heights.

On another cry, she came again, and one more thrust brought forth his release. Sobering from her own tumble down Mount Orgasm, Pen watched Zach's face contort into pleats of pleasure. The way his eyes squeezed closed, his lips peeled back from his teeth while his powerful body shook.

The almost surprised expression and awestruck wonder in his eyes.

He watched her for the space of a few heartbeats and then a familiar smile crested his handsome face.

She returned it, equally awestruck. Equally pleased.

# Five

The morning after the party, Zach woke in the guest bedroom next to Pen, in the bed they'd all but destroyed the previous night. The comforter and blankets were on the floor, the remaining sheets twisted and pulled from three corners, revealing the naked mattress.

He was also naked and sporting the morning wood he'd bragged to Penelope about, but this time instead of him taking the problem in hand, she was willing to alleviate it for him.

She slid down his body and he watched her pretty blond head bob over his thighs, eliciting so much pleasure, he thought he might never recover.

He did, though.

Enough to make love to her again and talk her into a shared shower en suite. Soaping Pen's body could become his new favorite pastime.

Dressed in the white, albeit wrinkled, dress from last night, she looked like a woman who'd been claimed. Zach liked that look on her a hell of a lot. He liked learning she hadn't been with anyone since him more. Not only because he hadn't moved on from her yet, but also because that meant they could have sex without a condom, which was his other favorite pastime with her.

He took her hand and walked with her down the staircase. His brother was dressed in a suit, and it wouldn't surprise Zach to learn that he was working—even on a Saturday. Zach had pulled on a pair of pressed trousers and a button-down, but Chase had gone full-on jacket and tie.

His brother took in Zach and Pen as they entered the foyer, pausing with his cell phone in hand to smirk knowingly.

"Good morning, Zach. Penelope."

"Mayor," she said, chin held high.

Zach admired the hell out of her for that. In last night's clothes, her hair sexily rumpled and cheeks pink from their steamy shower this morning, Pen didn't care what Chase thought about her sleeping with his only brother.

"I have a meeting in thirty minutes," Chase informed Zach, his gaze returning to his phone. "Legislature for…"

He trailed off as he ran his thumb along the screen. His expression blanked, accentuating his pallor.

"Chase?" Zach asked, alarm rising within. "Is there a problem?"

Chase blinked and offered a tight smile. "An old friend." He gestured with the phone. "Haven't thought of her in a long time."

Her? Chase had a few *hers* in his past, but there was one more noteworthy than the others. But it couldn't be…

Zach wasn't going to find out anytime soon. Chase exited his house and climbed into the back seat of a town car idling out front.

"Sounds mysterious," Pen commented at Zach's side, curiosity outlining her pursed lips. Without digging deeper, she leaned in for a kiss and he gladly obliged. "I'm going to go. Thanks for…everything."

"Don't tell me you work today, too?"

She paused at the door and looked over her shoulder. "Your ex-wife situation isn't going to go away on its own."

Zach looped her arm in his. "I'll walk you out."

The valet had moved Pen's car next to his in the cobblestone drive. Her white Audi sat gleaming next to his black Porsche. He opened her car door but before he closed her inside, stole another kiss for the road.

"You'll be hearing from me, Mr. Ferguson."

"I'll be expecting a full report, Ms. Brand."

She looked sleepy and adorable, as well she should after he'd kept her up all night. He opened his mouth to add that he was in no hurry for her to wrap things up with Yvonne, but instead he backed away and watched as she drove off.

A week later Zach was sitting in his office, Penelope on the other side of his desk. She'd come to Ferguson Oil to discuss the details of the Yvonne Tsunami, which was swallowing up way too much of his time.

The arrangement was far from the way he wanted to spend time with Pen. For starters, she was way too clothed for his taste, and secondly, his brother was brooding in the corner, arms folded over his suit.

Zach stood in frustration the moment Pen stopped talking.

"I won't do it," he said, his words clipped.

"Hear her out," Chase advised from his position near the window. Dallas's cityscape shone outside in the sunny day, several buildings dwarfed from Zach's top-floor vantage.

"I heard her out," Zach told his meddling brother. He softened his voice with Pen, but kept a position of strength when he leaned over his desk to address her where she sat in his guest chair. "I'm not giving Yvonne any money."

"Zach…" Her pink mouth parted to argue and he cut her off.

"No." His desk phone chirped and he pushed a button. "Yes, Sam?"

His male assistant rattled off the name of an investor who was waiting on the line.

"Zach will call him back," Chase called loud enough to be heard.

"Yes, sir." Sam clicked off.

Zach sent his brother a death glare. Chase was unperturbed. He was in one of the highest ranks of government. A wilting glare from his younger brother wasn't going to rankle him anytime soon.

"Listen." Penelope stood, eye level with Zach since he was still looming over the desk. Her pale blue eyes locked with his and she softened her voice. "Yvonne has threatened to make more noise about your marriage. This could not only harm your newly minted position as Ferguson Oil's CEO, but also put a dent in the mayor's approval rating."

Zach fought a growl. Chase's mayoral reputation had been overshadowing everything for the past decade. God, how Zach hated politics. Unfortunately, he loved his brother, so he had a feeling this wouldn't be the last time he did something he didn't want to do for Chase's career.

"It's a relatively small amount of money to ensure her silence," Pen continued. "The world knows you were married, but I wouldn't put it past her to make up a few unbecoming stories and share them on social media. I've seen exes go public with false facts before." Her eyebrows lifted in determination.

"And if she goes against the agreement?" Chase asked, stepping into their tight circle.

"She'll have to pay Zach ten times the amount we're paying for her silence."

Chase and Zach exchanged glances.

"Short of that," Pen said, folding her arms to mirror

Chase. "Zach could get ahold of a time machine and steer clear of the Chapel of Love last New Year's Eve."

"I don't like it," Zach told both of them.

"You don't have to like it. You just have to do it." Pen's voice was tender, reminding him of the gentle way she moaned when he was in bed with her three days ago. When he'd struck the pretend fiancée agreement with her, he'd hoped they'd share a bed more often than once a week. She'd been doing a good job of avoiding him on that front.

"Zach." Chase's voice crashed into Zach's fantasy about the blonde in front of him.

"Fine," he said between his teeth. "Now get out."

Chase let the command roll off him. "I have a lunch with important people. Penelope. Thank you."

"Anytime, Mr. Mayor." When he was gone, the door shut behind him, Zach breached the few inches separating him and Pen, tugged her by the nape of the neck and kissed her mouth. She hummed, her eyelids drooping in satisfaction.

"Where have you been hiding?" He thumbed her bottom lip when she pulled back too soon.

"I've been working. On your problems and a few others."

"None are my sister's I take it?"

"No." She shouldered her purse and tucked away her cell phone. "None are Stefanie's. She's been on her best behavior."

"Have dinner with me," he said as she pivoted on one high, high heel.

Pen peeked over her shoulder and Zach allowed his gaze to trickle down her fitted white jacket and short white skirt. Her platinum-blond hair was in a ponytail at the back of her head, the smooth length of it brushing her shoulder when she turned her head.

"I'm... I have to check my schedule."

"You have to make an appearance with me. Especially if we're going to approach Yvonne with a deal." Yvonne believed Zach and Pen were engaged. Everyone who'd attended his brother's party believed they were engaged.

"Okay. Dinner."

He pulled his shoulders back, proud to get a yes out of the evasive woman in front of him. His eyes dipped to the cleavage dividing the neckline of a sapphire blue shirt.

"And after dinner, you can come home with me."

She opened her mouth, maybe to protest, but smiled in spite of herself. He tucked two fingers into her shirt and pulled her closer, brushing her perky breasts.

"I'll make you breakfast in the morning," he told her. "And afterward, I'll make you something to eat."

She rolled her eyes but a soft chuckle escaped her. It was a yes if he'd ever heard one.

"I'll pick you up at your place at seven."

"I have to work late."

Zach was already back at his desk. "No. You don't. Seven o'clock."

He punched a button and summoned Sam. "Make reservations at One Eighty for myself and Ms. Brand for seven this evening."

"One Eighty?" Pen's brow rose. Was she impressed? He hoped so.

"Have you been?"

"Once. With a client who shall remain nameless."

"A male client?" he asked before he could stop himself.

Her Cheshire cat smile held. "Wouldn't you like to know?"

"Seven," he reiterated.

"Seven." She walked out of his office and Zach watched her go, looking forward to viewing her over candlelight the next time they saw each other. His phone beeped and Sam announced that the investor had called back.

Zach picked up the phone, but by the time he lifted his head, Pen was gone, his office door whispering shut.

# Six

One Eighty was named for its half-circle shape. The restaurant hovered over Dallas, on the eighty-eighth floor of one of the city's most shimmering skyscrapers.

Outside the smudgeless windows, deep blue skies were losing their light and the moon was making its nightly appearance.

Pen had stopped working at five, unusual for her, but then so were billionaire dinner dates that were personal rather than solely business.

"How are your prawns?" Zach, fork and knife in hand, leaned over his steak dinner to ask.

"Delightful. How is your strip?"

"Fantastic."

They shared a grin over the low candlelight, and a ping of awareness that started in Pen's stomach radiated out until it created a bubble around her and Zach.

Along with that ping of awareness came a lower, subtler thrum of warning.

She liked him. A lot.

Their chemistry was off the charts in bed, but also out of it.

She could've easily dismissed him as a playboy—a charmer who knew what to say to get a woman out of her clothes. Admittedly, Zach had done just that. But along with getting her out of her clothes, he'd also made a point to keep her in his life.

After what went down with her ex-boyfriend, Cliff, in Chicago—where she'd quite literally been bamboozled by a smooth-talking charmer—she should be wary of Zach.

But she wasn't wary.

Maybe it was because she'd gotten to know his brother, the mayor, and Stefanie, his sister. Maybe it was because of the way Zach had asked her to dinner when he full well could have invited her to his place.

She'd have said yes either way.

Did he know that?

She sliced into her shrimp dinner—buttery, garlicky, lemony heaven. "I contacted Yvonne today and let her know you were willing to talk about—"

"Penelope."

Fork hovering over her plate, she hazarded a glance at her date. Zach didn't look perturbed as much as patient.

"Sorry," she said. "I want to get this over with."

His eyes narrowed, eyelashes a shade darker than his hair obliterating his gorgeous green stare. "With Yvonne, yes. You and I? Not so much."

When she'd called him a caveman at the mayor's party, she hadn't been far off the mark. But she saw no reason to argue the point. The fact was she would wrap up the issue with Zach's ex-wife and then they'd have no reason to see each other. She'd make her services available for Chase or for their party-loving sister, but Pen and Zach had an expiration date.

*So why are you here?*

Excellent question.

"Did you pack a bag like I asked?" Zach lifted his wineglass, which was as foreign as the black shirt and black suit combo. She'd been so sure at that jazz club that she'd run into a blue-collar guy moonlighting in slacks. Now that she'd seen him in tuxes and suits, her brain scrambled to make sense of it.

He'd seemed safer when he was a contractor. Before she learned of his bank account or his heritage.

Nevertheless…

"I packed a change of clothes, yes." She took a dainty sip from her own wineglass. While she wasn't sure how to define what she and Zach had or to know how long they had access to it, she wasn't going to miss the opportunity to fill her head and heart full of sexy, vivid memories that would last if not a lifetime, at least a few years.

"Good. I want to show you my place. I think you'll like it," He took another bite of his steak, but not before dragging it through his mashed potatoes. A steak and potatoes guy. She shook her head as she tried to merge the two versions of Zach she thought she knew.

"Why did you leave Chicago? You seemed…at home there."

"I like the city. I liked the work more," he said. "But my family needed me, so I came home."

"Do you mean Stefanie?" She could imagine the youngest Ferguson sibling asking for his help.

"No. She leans on Chase." His smile took on a slightly sad quality. In a firmer voice, he added, "My father's heart attack required surgery and a long recovery. He was under strict orders not to return as acting CEO of Ferguson Oil."

"Doctors," Pen said with a roll of her eyes.

"Worse. My mother." Half of Zach's mouth pulled to one side in good humor, his dimple shadowing his stubbled cheek. She liked him a touch unkempt. "Once Dad was benched, that left me to work for the family business.

Chase is obviously busy and Stef is obviously uninterested. She'll grow out of it."

Pen couldn't imagine Stef giving up her life as a socialite heiress to go into the oil business, but she kept that thought to herself.

"What about you?" Zach asked, turning the tables on her. She'd seen that possibility coming and had already decided she wouldn't deflect. She'd been eager to leave her life behind in Chicago, but face it—the internet was alive and well. If Zach typed her name into Google, he'd learn about her association with Cliff.

Still, she inhaled deeply before telling him the sordid, slightly embarrassing tale.

"Ever heard of the phrase 'the plumber's pipes are always leaking'?"

"The cobbler's children have no shoes?"

"Same idea." She laughed, already feeling better about confessing. She sobered quickly. "I had a PR problem I couldn't spin."

Zach's eyebrows lowered. He didn't know.

"Cliff Goodman started out as a client. He hired me to repair his business's reputation when he was accused of dishonest practices." She'd believed him at the time—the research she'd done on him pointed to his upstanding reputation. "Once the issue was handled, he and I started dating and then—" she lifted her wine and ripped off the Band-Aid "—he became involved in my public relations business."

Her date's face darkened. Pen looked away from his intense stare. Diners quietly chatted at their tables, points of candlelight dotting the dimly lit room, mimicking the city lights outside the windows. The blue sky had gone black.

"Long story short, he went from involved to over-involved. I found out he'd been meeting with my clients in my place, cashing their checks and never following through. He left the city with a lot of my money after destroying my hard-won reputation. I didn't want to leave Chicago, but I didn't want to stay, either."

"Why Dallas?"

"A college friend of mine started an organic cosmetic company. She lives here and needed help maintaining her pure reputation in the face of a nasty divorce. So she hired me."

"And you stayed."

"I did."

They shared a silent moment. Pen wondered if he was thinking what she was thinking—that had it not been for her friend Miranda's phone call, Pen and Zach may never have seen each other again.

"It's a beautiful city." Pen swallowed some more wine, smoothly changing the subject.

"You're beautiful in it."

See? When he said things like that, she forgot all about her past and her rules and her personal struggles.

She forgot everything—including her promise to herself about not letting a client get too close. Especially a male client.

The waiter approached after they'd finished their plates.

"Madame, sir," the older man greeted, hands clasped in front of him. "Might I interest you in our fine dessert selections, or perhaps a glass of port wine or coffee?"

"No," Zach answered for them. "We'll pay and be on our way. My compliments to the chef."

"Such a gentleman," Pen teased.

"I grew up right." He leaned over the table and then, tossing the idea of his humble upbringing on its ear, took her hand and murmured, "I'm making you my dessert, tonight."

"Your post-dessert dessert." Zach's hand appeared from behind Pen, a glass of port wine in his grip. "It's a tawny, which I prefer. That bit of vanilla goes a long way."

She accepted the miniature wineglass and a kiss to her cheek. Zach rounded the enormous brown leather couch wearing nothing at all, another miniature glass dwarfed in his large hand.

Pen wasn't wearing anything, either, but had curled up in a blanket she'd found tossed over his ottoman. A blanket she now opened to include Zach. He accepted, cradling one of her breasts and delivering a tender kiss to the side of her mouth.

They'd stepped foot in his expansive apartment and stripped off each other's clothes in record time. She hadn't so much as seen the bedroom yet, though she did make a quick stop to the bathroom. Zach's apartment was a manly array of exposed brick, lights suspended from long, metal rods, his furniture deep browns and grays. The overall vibe was more industrial than rustic, yet had warmth that mirrored the owner himself.

She sipped the super-sweet wine, savoring the vanilla notes that Zach mentioned and quirking her lips at the way her dress had been haphazardly tossed over a chair along with Zach's discarded suit. Their shoes made a line from the foyer to the living room, the first articles of clothing they'd kicked off.

"You have a really nice apartment."

"Thanks."

"No billionaire mansion for you?"

"Nah, that's Chase's style."

"What about Stef? Does she tend toward high-rise apartment or sprawling mansion with horses and twenty-two bathrooms?"

"See, you think you're being cute, but my parents' house has twenty-two bathrooms."

"I know." She sipped her wine and peered over the tiny rim at Zach. "I looked them up and their house was in *Architectural Digest*. It's incredible."

"It's ridiculous. But my mother likes to redecorate. With thirty-seven thousand square feet, she's never at a loss for a room to have painted or altered to her ever-changing preferences."

Zach leaned back on the sofa, his arm draped around Pen. She snuggled closer and he adjusted the blanket to cover them both.

"Do you get along with them? Or are you the classically overlooked middle child?"

A low laugh that might have been confirmation bobbed his throat. "I get along with them. I joke about my mother's frivolity, but she's a great mother. My dad became sick and her world stopped on a dime."

"How is he now?"

"Good. Misses his bacon and sausage."

"And strip steaks?" she teased.

"It's Dallas, sweetheart. Men eat steak."

"Right. Heaven forbid you do something as effeminate as not eat a cow." She grinned, liking the way she could volley back at him. He was one of the easiest people she'd ever been around.

He moved in on her again and the kiss lasted a little longer than either of them intended. "Glad you packed a bag, Penelope Brand."

Her heart kicked into overdrive when Zach set aside his wine and took her wineglass from her hand. His insistent kisses peppered down her throat and collarbone. When he reached her stomach, his hand flattened on the space between her breasts and he pushed her to her back.

Then he lifted one of her legs onto his shoulder and made her dessert.

Again.

# Seven

"Tell me everything," Miranda's bubbly voice, on speakerphone, filled Pen's office.

Pen had called her friend to thank her for the generous basket she was now digging through. She pulled out a tube of lipstick and spun it to examine the lush red color.

"I love this lipstick. 'Red Rum,'" she read off the bottom of the tube with a laugh. Sassy. That was Miranda.

"It's long-wearing, not tested on animals and one hundred percent organic. Now, if you don't tell me everything about the man you've been having sex with for the last month, I'm going to come to your office with torture implements."

She laughed at her friend's colorful description. Pen had casually mentioned Zach and that she'd been seeing him.

"It was supposed to be one night, and then we had a two-week gap." She lifted the basket from her desk and put it on the couch. She was *so* giving herself a makeover later. "But when I saw him again at the mayor's party, well… I couldn't help starting up with him again."

"And you ended up engaged! It's a fairy tale. It's a fantasy!"

It was a load of crap, but Pen had to keep up the facade with everyone.

"Yes, I was very surprised." That, at least, was the truth.

"I'll bet. Zachary Ferguson is one yummy prospect if you don't mind my saying. And he must be a real catch for you to have leaped in with both feet so soon."

"Yes," Pen said, unable to trot out any more false explanations.

"Listen, doll, I have to go. We're working on the spring line and I have an appointment."

"Thank you again for the gift."

"You bet. I expect a wedding invitation."

Pen opened her mouth to make an empty promise, but Miranda clicked off. With a sigh, she cleaned a few pieces of crinkled pink paper that had been used as packing in her gift basket from her planner pages.

May's schedule wasn't as full as she'd like it to be, but she had a few phone calls to return. She turned to her weekly page and checked off the line item that read "call Miranda," eyes skimming past the list of messages she'd written down to return on Monday but hadn't gotten the chance. And here it was Friday already.

Halfway to dialing a number for Maude Braxton, Pen's eyes landed on a tiny red heart beneath Monday's date, and she frowned.

She'd been on birth control pills since she was a teenager because of erratic periods, and since she'd been on birth control pills, her cycle was correct down to the minute.

She hastily flipped back to April, located the red heart, and counted the days to today.

She was five days late.

Five. Days.

"Oh, my God." Her stomach tightened, her mind racing. Could she be…? No. No way. She was on the pill. And even if her trusted form of birth control failed her, she was in her early thirties. At her age it was normal for things to go haywire. There could be a perfectly good explanation. Stress. It could totally be stress. But when she flipped back to April and saw the name of a jazz club scheduled for eight p.m., another *perfectly good explanation* came to mind.

This one an even better explanation for a missed period.

Numbly, she stood from her desk and pulled her purse out from behind the basket overflowing with tubes of lipsticks, moisturizers and eye shadow palettes. So much for giving herself a makeover.

Pen was off to buy a pregnancy test.

Penelope's wine sat untouched in front of her, but she couldn't bring herself to say no and raise Zach's suspicions. Even though telling him he was going to be the father of their unborn child was the very reason she was sitting here with him. She'd successfully avoided him all weekend, which wasn't easy. It took a lot of circumventing on her part, but she had to wrap her head around the unfathomable truth.

Despite being on the pill the entire time she and Zach were together, that night after the jazz club, one of his swimmers had reached its goal.

"I have a charity dinner on Friday. Come with me." He sat on one corner of the wrap couch rather than in the middle next to her, and for once she was grateful for the space. "Chase and several of the Dallas brass who attended his party will be there. Good networking opportunity. Plus, now that we've wrapped up everything with Yvonne, it's best that we're seen together."

"Right." Pen somehow managed the one-word response despite her heart being lodged in her esophagus. He was right. It made sense to continue seeing him. If they mysteriously ended their engagement right when Yvonne had agreed to keep her trap shut, no one would believe it was real. Which might not matter except that Chase had announced to one and all that his brother was going to be married. She didn't want to be responsible for making Dallas's trustworthy mayor into a liar. If that wasn't enough public attention, there was the business world wagging their tongues about Ferguson Oil's youngest CEO taking a wife. Soon they'd have to amend their announcement to add that Zach had impregnated his bride-to-be…who the public would later learn wasn't going to be his wife at all.

God. This was a nightmare.

Maybe she didn't have to tell him today. Hope sparked fresh in her chest. She had a good four weeks before her baby bump made itself known. Why not avoid him until then? And the paparazzi and public functions… She could become a hermit.

If she folded up the shingle on her PR business.

*Sigh.* That wasn't a realistic plan at all.

The only certainty was that she was keeping the baby. Her pregnancy was unexpected, yes, but Penelope believed deep in her soul that life unfolded in the order it did for a reason. If fate decided she was to be a mother, then she'd accept. It was as simple, and terrifying, as that.

Zach drank from his beer glass and eyed Pen's untouched wine. There was no way to avoid him for an extended period of time. He was a force—he was in her life. She had to do the mature thing and tell him the damn truth.

She filtered through her muddy mind until she located the speech she'd practiced in her office's bathroom mirror five times before she came here tonight. It was short, sweet and to the point.

"I'm pregnant."

Zach's limbs were stiff and unmoving, the blood sloshing against his eardrums making Pen's voice sound a mile away.

"I found out Friday night and I couldn't tell you over the weekend until I decided what to do. So here I am." Pen fastened her gaze on the wineglass. The wine she couldn't drink because she was *pregnant with his child*.

He focused on the beer glass in his hand for an exaggerated beat before managing, "What do you mean?"

His tone was as flat as the firm line of his pretend fiancée's unsmiling mouth. Pale blue eyes rested on his as if she was as shell-shocked as him. Only she couldn't be, because she'd been processing for three days and he'd had three seconds.

"I mean I'm having the baby—*your* baby. Keeping this a secret from you was never an option."

*Hell, no, it's not*, came the immediate thought.

He hadn't sat around and contemplated fatherhood, but now that he knew it was a reality, the surety of being involved rang tuning-fork true in the pit of his gut.

"The due date is December, right before Christmas." She shared it like she was talking about some other couple who was suddenly expecting a bundle of joy. For as distant as he felt from this announcement, she might as well be talking about someone else.

He set his beer aside and stood, unable to sit any longer. His measured steps were more of a stalk, but he reined in his energy to face the woman on his couch. Penelope had radically changed his future—his entire family's future—in a few short weeks.

Wait. Weeks? He did some quick math.

"It's been a little over two weeks since my brother's party. How the hell could you know you're pregnant already?"

Her porcelain skin went pink. "It's been *four* weeks, Zach, since you and I had sex the first time."

The first time?

*Ah, hell.*

He nodded to himself as reality reared its head. That was the clincher about math—the answer wasn't up for debate.

The jazz club. The night he'd explored her up and down and up again. The night he thought would be the last he saw of her.

He pulled a hand down his face, pausing with it over his mouth for a moment. His shock was a palpable entity swirling the room, his thoughts ranging from excitement to horror to wanting to accuse her of attempting to take his money like his ex-wife.

But this was Penelope he was talking about. Even if he didn't trust her—and he did—there was the significant matter of her not knowing he had that many zeroes in his bank account the night he took her back to her place.

"I have a plan," she said.

"A plan." Mind racing, his vision blurred as his thoughts circled the track again.

"I'm a public relations superhero, Zach. I have a plan." She patted the cushion next to her. He sat, but not next to her, and lifted his beer to take a hearty gulp. Hell, he might drink Pen's wine, too.

"It's simple. Over the next two weeks, you and I will be seen together less and less until we aren't seen together at all. We'll share a press release that you and I will not be raising the child together. We could even go with a story that we were friends and I wanted a child and you didn't and—"

"No." Zach's voice was thunderous, bouncing off the high ceilings and echoing around the room.

Pen's mouth was frozen midspeech for a second before she said, "I don't expect you to take on a baby. You're a CEO with a budding career. What we had—"

"Have."

Her slim eyebrows rose. "Pardon?"

"What we *have*. Present tense."

"What we *have* is a month-long, on-and-off sexual relationship."

"Until five minutes ago, that was true." She might have alarmed him with unexpected news, but his brain was now sliding into operation mode.

"I didn't mean for this to happen."

"That makes two of us."

"I came here to reassure you that I'm not coming after your money." She stood suddenly. He stood with her. She thrust her chin out, pride gleaming in her slitted eyes. "Plenty of working mothers manage to raise a child alone. I certainly don't need your wealth to do it."

"This isn't a challenge," Zach said, his voice firm. "I don't doubt you're capable of doing whatever you damn well set your mind to, but know this." With his thumb and forefinger, he tipped her chin up. "My child growing in your belly isn't insignificant to me. I'm not walking away."

*From you or our baby.*

None of the determination slipped from her gaze but tenderness joined it. "I'd never deny you the right to see or support your child, Zach. I was suggesting that I get out of the way."

"Whose way are you in, Penelope?"

She didn't say it but he could feel the word *yours* in the tense air between them.

He dipped his face and captured her lips, sliding his tongue into her mouth and claiming her as his yet again. She wouldn't be eschewing herself from his presence anytime soon.

*In fact...*

He bent and scooped her into his arms never breaking their lip-lock as he made a path for the bedroom. He was going to see to it that she didn't get any farther away than his apartment.

Baby or no, he'd staked a claim on the blonde in his arms long before her surprise announcement.

And now she'd given him another reason to convince her to stay.

# Eight

Penelope wasn't aware the charity dinner Zach invited her to would be at his parents' home. Until they pulled into the long driveway, fountains flanking either side, the grass mowed into an artistic crisscross pattern.

The house was gargantuan. She hadn't been joking about seeing it online, but one couldn't fathom thirty-seven thousand square feet until looking right at it. The place was like its own city.

"Wow," she murmured, gripping her wrap and clutch. "This is impressive."

From beside her in the back of the limo, Zach emitted a noncommittal grunt.

"Did you grow up in this house?"

"No. They bought this place about seven or eight years ago. We grew up in a big house, but not this big."

The driver pulled to a stop and an attendant in a fine tuxedo opened the limo door for her. She accepted his offered hand, stepped out and transferred that hand to Zach.

"You've done this before," he commented. His tux was like the one he'd worn to Chase's birthday party, but he'd chosen an all-black ensemble: shirt and bowtie included. The darkness made his golden skin, bright green eyes and hair in need of a trim stand out in tantalizing contrast.

"Keep looking at me like that," he murmured into her hair, "and I'll have to show you to one of the many private bedrooms."

She should scold him but couldn't. Finding a bedroom sounded, well…lovely.

The charity function was being held in the house's ballroom on the far east side—or as Pen liked to think of it, "left." They joined the well-dressed throngs clicking through the marble hallways and stopping to admire what had to be million-dollar-plus paintings and sculptures dotting the long corridor.

"Pretentious, right?" Zach muttered, earning a gasp from an older woman whose gray curls were piled on top of her head.

Pen swallowed the laugh pushing against her throat. If that older woman knew who Zach was would she be more or less offended?

It wasn't until they entered the ballroom where the silent auction was underway that the butterflies in Pen's tummy took flight. Right at the same moment her date said…

"There's my mom."

His mom. As in *a mom*. As in what Penelope would soon be—or was now, depending on when one started counting. She might start hyperventilating.

"Before I forget…" Zach stepped in her line of vision, taking it up with his fine attire and gorgeous self. "This is for you."

He reached into his pocket and light winked off a small metal object—okay, *now* she was going to hyperventilate.

He slid the band onto the third finger of Pen's left hand, a massive square-cut diamond in the center of an army of smaller diamonds. She…gaped. The ring was stunningly beautiful, and would likely require stronger biceps in order to hold her arm up while wearing it.

"Zach." Her gasp was muted, and then vanished altogether, when he lifted her knuckles and placed a kiss on them and the ring.

"Can't look engaged without the ring, now, can you?" His dimple made a brief appearance.

"I suppose not."

"Let's say hello." He offered his right arm and Pen looped her left hand around his elbow, trying hard not to stare at the blinding facets winking up at her.

"Eleanor Ferguson," he said when he reached his mother. "I have someone I'd like you to meet."

Eleanor turned, her martini balanced between manicured pink nails and a few stunning rings of her own, all diamond-encrusted and throwing off nearly as much light as Penelope's. Her blond hair was coiffed and stylish with warm honey highlights.

"Penelope, I presume."

Pen nodded.

"Please, call me Elle. It's wonderful to meet the woman who stole Zach's heart." There was nothing disingenuous about her smile, but Pen still felt as if the woman's reaction was a touch insincere.

"Heavens, Zach. Renaldo did well." Elle lifted Pen's left hand and examined the engagement ring. "Renaldo is our family jeweler. He's the best." She slid the pad of her thumb over the diamonds. "Perfect fit, too. A little wiggle room is always nice in case you eat too much salt."

*Or if I'm pregnant with your grandchild.*

"Where's Dad?"

"Hors d'oeuvres." Elle rolled eyes that were a muted shade of Zach's envious greens. "Since his heart attack, I make him eat healthy, but the very moment he's out of my sight, he's elbow deep in sausage canapés."

Elle waved over an extremely tall, white-haired man who was patting his lips with a napkin. Zach's father didn't look like a man who'd suffered a heart attack. He walked with a lazy swagger, his tuxedo fitted over his lean body. His hair tickled his collar, in need of a trim like his son's. His gray eyes narrowed on Penelope as he approached.

"Hey, son."

"Penelope Brand, this is my father, Rand, but everyone calls him Rider."

"Pretty girls like you can call me whatever you please," Rider said in a deep baritone before he kissed her hand. Then he held her hand out at arm's length. "Congratulations on your engagement to Zach. Looks like he chose better the second time around."

"Rand! Honestly," Elle scolded, clucking her tongue. "It's lovely to meet you, Penelope. Zach, your brother was looking for you earlier. If you see him, do ask him to bring his date by to say hello. He's being quite rude."

Zach's parents linked arms and walked away and Penelope let out the breath going stale in her lungs.

"They're intense," she said.

"Are they?" Zach looked after them and then turned to face Penelope. "My mother's favorite phrase is *quite rude* by the way, so don't let that alarm you."

Still, the woman made Pen's shoulders crawl under her ears.

"What can I get you to drink?"

"Anything clear and sparkling." Sadly. She could use a glass of champagne.

"Club soda?"

"With a lime." What the hell. Might as well go crazy.

"Perfect timing. Stef!" Zach lifted his voice to be heard and a few heads turned in their direction. It was clear that he was comfortable in the stuffy crowd. Pen already wanted to slip outside for some fresh air.

"Hey, kids." Stefanie approached in a fuchsia dress, her dark blond hair wound into a fancy twist. She smiled over her martini. "Penelope, you have to try these. The gin is the best I've ever had."

"Pen's not drinking this evening. Hang out here for a moment with her while I get her a club soda."

"Club soda?" Stef asked, but her words bounced off Zach's retreating back.

"I haven't been feeling well today." It was the truth. Pen woke with morning sickness that kept her in bed an extra hour. She nibbled on saltine crackers while checking her email on her phone. She'd yet to throw up as a result of morning sickness, but she'd become increasingly grateful that her private office had an attached bathroom.

"You don't look the least bit pale, so that's a plus." Stefanie's assessing gaze trickled over her, and Pen worried for a moment the younger woman might see right through her facade.

"I hear your oldest brother has a date," Pen said, successfully rerouting Stef's gaze.

Stef's eyes swept the room. "He does. I met her. She's a stiff like he is."

Pen saw them then, a slight woman with dark hair whose arm was linked with Chase's. He was talking to his parents now, so there was no need to pass on Elle's observation that he was being *quite rude*.

"Did you bid on anything?" Pen asked Stef.

"The spa package." She pointed to one corner and then to a painting to the right. "And that horrible artwork."

A chuckle erupted out of Pen before she could help it.

"I like you, Penelope." Stef's sincerity was obvious. The woman didn't say things she didn't mean. Pen knew that much. "If anyone is going to enter this family, I'm glad it's you. Zach hasn't always had the best taste."

"Oh?" Pen stepped closer, curious about Zach's dating habits. "Let me guess. Complete playboy."

"He has a good heart, but most women never access it. As for Yvonne and that Vegas wedding thing… What the hell?"

"It is curious that he tied the knot with her." The thin redhead seemed better suited for anyone other than Zach Ferguson.

"He said getting married sounded fun," Stef said. "But that's pretty much his prescription for life, isn't it? If it sounds like a good time, why not attempt?"

Penelope's stomach sank. This time she did palm her torso as a bout of queasiness overtook her.

What Stef said was true—and Pen had seen it in action. Zach introduced her as his fiancée the evening of Chase's birthday party because it sounded fun. They slept together that first night—and several nights thereafter because it was fun. Pen fell in line with that thinking because being around Zach made her embrace the fun. His world was shimmering and enticing, and she'd wanted some of that for herself.

Only that *fun* had turned into a baby due at the end of this year. That *fun* had become a human being, half Zach, half Pen. A baby wasn't something you "attempted" because it sounded fun. There'd be no walking away if their son or daughter suddenly lost his or her luster. At least not for her. While she was definitely ill-equipped for motherhood, she was willing to live and learn. Her own mother had set a stellar example and, like her, Pen planned on rocking the business world as well as a breast pump. It'd take some practice and she was sure there would be moments where she had no idea what she was doing, but she'd manage.

What about Zach, though? Would her fake fiancé turn his back on their child if he or she suddenly didn't fit into his *fun* lifestyle? Did Pen make a mistake letting him talk her into staying?

"Pen? You don't look so good." Stef's hand rested on Penelope's shoulder as the world swam in and out.

Pen's cheeks heated, her head spun and she rocked on her high heels. She swept her blurring vision over to Zach, who approached with a drink in each hand.

The last thing she remembered was him dropping both glasses to rush over as her world was swallowed in black.

# Nine

Zach's concerned expression was the first sight Pen saw when she opened her eyes.

She reached for her forehead, where a damp weight sat, and pulled away a black washcloth.

He took it from her. "Stef, rewet this for me?"

His sister jumped to help, returning in a few seconds with a much cooler cloth. Zach pressed it to Pen's forehead again.

"No more high heels," he told her, a muscle flinching in his cheek.

"Leave her alone." Stef entered her range of vision again, this time with a water bottle. "Sip this, Pen."

Zach helped her sit up some and then Pen drank from the water bottle, her head much clearer than before. She'd been relocated to an enormous sitting room with settees and low coffee tables and several groupings of chairs. She looked down to find she was resting on a dove-gray chaise longue.

"You passed out. Did you eat today?" That was Zach, his voice low and angry, but his innate tenderness outlined every word.

"I ate a little," Pen mumbled, sitting up and putting her feet on the floor—her bare feet. "Where are my shoes?"

"I'll carry you to the limo. You're not putting those things on again." His mouth pulled down at the corners.

"Yes, I am. I can wear high heels as well as I can flats. Better, in fact."

"It's second nature after a while," Stef concurred. Then to Pen, she added, "He's being overly concerned."

"We need to check with the doctor." He stood from his kneeling position on the floor in front of her and sat on the edge of the lounger. "To make sure nothing's wrong."

"She's light-headed! There's nothing wrong." Stef rolled her eyes and took a bite out of what appeared to be a ham sandwich.

Pen's mouth watered. She literally licked her lips.

"Want half?" Stefanie offered a plate with the other half of her sandwich. "There was too much fancy food out there so I went to the kitchen and made a ham and cheese on white bread like a real American."

"I can get you anything you like from the caterer, Pen. You don't have to—" Zach started to argue.

"If you don't mind." She reached past him for the plate and Stef handed it over. Pen took one bite, then another, and in no time the half sandwich was demolished. "Thank you so much."

Zach took the plate. "Better?"

Pen slugged back the rest of the water and let out a satisfied *Mmm*. "Much better."

"Guess we forgot the eating for two part, didn't we?" He pushed a lock of hair away from her face before his eyes went wide at his faux pas.

"Oh my God! You guys are *pregnant*?" Stef stood from her seat on top of the coffee table, the remainder of her sandwich still in one hand. "I'm so excited! I'm going to be an aunt!"

"Stef," Zach growled. "We haven't told anyone yet."

His sister promptly returned her derrière to the coffee table and pressed her lips closed. She mimed zipping her lips but when she looked back to Pen, she air clapped.

"I'm going to take you home." Zach stood. "*My* home, where you'll be staying." He leveled Pen with an impatient glare before leaving the sitting room.

"Bossy." Stef polished off her sandwich and dusted her hands on her skirt like she was wearing jeans instead of Carolina Herrera.

"What does he mean 'where I'll be staying?'" she asked herself, but Stef answered.

"While you were unconscious, Zach said he was going to ask you to move in with him." Stef turned to study the doorway he'd disappeared through. "I guess that was his way of asking."

"You're overreacting," Penelope told Zach as he moved from the couch to the kitchen on Monday morning. She'd spent Saturday night at his house, and Sunday, too, but this was ridiculous. She was itching to go home. Despite him having stopped by her apartment to gather a few changes of clothes—and shoes—she was ready to sleep in her own bed. And, as of Monday morning, ready to work in her own office.

He returned to the living room with a steaming mug, a string and tag dangling from the edge.

"The doctor said plenty of fluids and that peppermint tea would help as long as you don't drink it too often." He placed the mug in front of her on the couch where he'd arranged a remote, a few paperback novels, magazines and a plate of cheese and crackers.

A doctor made a house call Saturday afternoon and told her everything seemed fine, though he'd like her to come in soon for an ultrasound. He did take her blood for a workup, so she was glad to have that unpleasantness over with.

Zach threw a blanket over her legs and Pen tossed it off with a laugh.

"It's nearly June, Zach. I don't need a blanket. I don't have the flu. I have morning sickness. I'm not going to sit here when I have work to do."

"Yes, you are."

"No. I'm not."

She stood and he took a step toward her. The room canted to one side and she gripped his biceps, willing her feet to keep her upright. Strong hands wrapped around her arms and when she looked sheepishly up at her caretaker, his eyes were filled with concern.

"Pen."

"Fine. I'll rest. But only for today. And I'm going to return emails, then maybe a few phone calls."

Sensing he'd lost the battle, Zach didn't argue. But then Penelope did make a show of sipping her tea and eating a cracker—no cheese yet; her stomach couldn't handle it.

"The doctor also said the nausea will subside. You won't feel like this every day." Zach, her new nursemaid, delivered a paper napkin to her next. She knew everything the doctor had said. She'd been there. But Zach was making her his top priority, and that was really...nice.

"Thank you." In all sincerity, she should be thanking him. He was overbearing and a worrywart, but he was also looking out for her. For a woman who'd been on her own since she started staying home alone at age eleven, Pen wasn't accustomed to someone taking care of her.

"I had lunch and dinner delivered. The meals are prepared and in the fridge. All you have to do is take the lid off and eat them."

When Zach started listing ingredients like "chicken salad on rye" Pen's stomach did a cannonball.

She held out a hand. "Don't say the word chicken or rye." She swallowed thickly. "Or salad."

He lowered to sit next to her on the sofa, cradling her face in his hands. "You're going to be okay here while I go to work?"

"Yes. Go." She gave him a halfhearted shove and he stole a kiss before standing. One more wave goodbye and he left.

She sat back on the couch and flipped on the TV, using the remote. She sipped her tea, kept down the crackers and yes, a few pieces of the mild Swiss cheese, and decided that maybe she could rest for a little while.

With her body being uncooperative, she could use the break.

Zach's mind was a million miles from work and the man currently droning on in front of him at the board meeting. He slid his gaze to his right where Armand jotted notes on his steno pad, and then to his left where Celia pecked notes into her iPad.

His mind was on Penelope and the scare she'd given him the night of the charity function at his parents' house.

He was able to play it off as her not feeling well to everyone except for Stefanie, thanks to his gaffe when he mentioned Penelope eating for two.

Since then, he'd been in productive mode. He'd taken Pen home, called the doctor and scheduled a house visit and made sure she had everything she needed at his place.

His cell phone buzzed and he grabbed on to the interruption like a lifeline. The entire meeting halted as he stood and checked the screen. Stefanie. Good enough for him.

"Continue without me. Celia, if you could email me your notes." With that, he was out the door, lifting his cell phone to his ear. "Zachary Ferguson."

"Oh, so formal. I like it."

"I have to keep up appearances for the suits."

"Aren't you one of them now?" He could hear her smile. "Never say die, Stef. What's up with you?"

"I'm going to plan a bridal shower for your future wife," she answered, bringing him to a halt a few yards from his office door. "And I didn't know, if by the time I threw it, we'd also include the baby shower part. Thoughts?"

Woodenly, he moved to the sanctuary of his office and shut the door behind him. "No showers. We're doing this low-key."

"No low-key. You're a Ferguson and we do things very high-key. Or off-key, if we're talking about Dad's singing. I'm en route to the florist for a consultation for a fund-raiser dinner Mom is throwing, but I thought I'd ask about bridal arrangements while I was there. By the way, when is the wedding date?"

"We don't have a wedding date. No showers."

"Well, you'd better set one because that baby has a due date and I have a feeling he or she will stick to it whether you're married or not."

His face went cold as the blood drained from his cheeks. When he'd become "engaged" to Pen, no part of him believed they'd actually get married. Now that there was a baby on the way, well…he still hadn't planned on marrying her, but he also hadn't considered that everyone would expect them to make things official. Especially with a child who would carry on the Ferguson name.

"Have to run. Ciao!" Stefanie hung up on him and Zach set the cell phone on his calendar and stared dumbly at the month of May.

His sister had a point. Their baby was coming whether or not he set a wedding date. If he and Pen didn't get married, in a few short weeks they'd have to announce a pregnancy and the decision not to wed.

It was archaic to believe they had to marry because

they were expecting, but his parents would expect it. Especially now that they'd learned he'd married Yvonne on a whim.

Except no one knew the real reason for his marriage to Yvonne. It was a challenge in a way—to see if he could do it. Could he get over the past in one fell swoop without years of therapy or repression?

He could, as it turned out. He'd had to drink half the liquor in Nevada, but he'd walked down the aisle, had a spontaneous Vegas honeymoon and then wrapped things up in a matter of days.

All because once upon a time he'd been in love—for real. Yes, he'd been twenty-six, but he knew in his bones that Lonna was the one for him. She was four years older than him and had absolutely consumed every corner of his world.

They dated for a year and on that one-year anniversary when they sat across from each other at a rooftop bar, Zach proposed.

He recited a speech including how much he loved her, how there was no one else for him and how the rest of his life would be spent by her side.

Lonna had an announcement that evening, too. She'd come to break up with him. She'd had a speech prepared—it was about how she couldn't see herself with him past that year, and how she couldn't bring herself to lie to him because she didn't love him.

She'd said she never had.

It was a blow he was sure he'd never recover from. Thank God he'd kept the relationship quiet, only telling his parents and friends that they were "dating." After the breakup, he kept things quieter. He dodged questions, confided in no one and cried in private.

Then he decided he'd been humiliated for the last time, packed up his life and started a new one away from Dallas.

Now he had a decision to make. About a marriage. About a future with Penelope in his life.

No matter what those future plans entailed, one thing was certain: Pen and he might get married, they would have a baby, but Zach refused to allow himself to fall in love.

Not now.

Not ever again.

# Ten

She wasn't sure what happened, but after a few hours of sipping tea and watching mindless daytime television, Penelope abandoned the vicinity of *craptastic* and exited the off-ramp of *amazing*.

She showered at Zach's house, dressed in her favorite pantsuit—white, of course—and slipped her feet into five-inch heels. She arrived at her office building via a town car—the number she'd pilfered from Zach's refrigerator—thanked the driver and stepped onto the downtown sidewalk.

It wasn't officially summer yet, but the Texas sun was hot. Judging by the passing professionals, summer was already here. Men had gone without their jackets, the women wore shorter hemlines and everyone, Pen included, had sunglasses perched on their noses.

She'd returned as many emails and phone calls as she could from her cell phone. She told herself that she was going to the office simply to retrieve her laptop, but now that she was here, she decided to stay. The idea of settling into her cushy desk chair, hands on the keyboard, was too tempting to resist.

Bonus, the embryo incubating in her uterus decided to allow her to keep the contents of her stomach. She'd be smart to take advantage of the reprieve.

Two hours into her routine, her planner boasted several checked-off boxes and lined-through tasks, and Pen's fingers were practically flying over the keys as she crafted an email to a reporter. Reporters and paparazzi were good friends to have when in PR. Even if they were less friends and more acquaintances with benefits.

She sent the email by punching the enter key with a flourish before standing to refill her water bottle. She'd pulled open her office door only a few inches when Zach rounded the corner, paper takeout bag in hand, a scowl on his face.

"Zach, hi!" Rather than fetch herself a much-needed drink, she pulled the door open the rest of the way and ushered him in. "How'd you know where to find me?"

"Tony told me."

The town car driver.

"Right. Well. Welcome to my humble office."

Zach didn't survey her digs, though. He set the paper bag on her desk and glowered down at her. "You're not at my house."

"Correct." She smiled.

"You didn't eat the food I left for you in the refrigerator."

At the mention of food, her stomach roared rather than wilted. That was a good sign—her appetite was back.

"I was going to order from the sandwich cart in the lobby." She'd been so wrapped up in work, she'd forgotten all about eating.

"Now you don't have to."

"Are you under the impression that I'm incapable of feeding myself?" She smiled sweetly.

"Don't be cute." His voice was thick with warning. "It's my responsibility to keep you in good health since this situation is at least half my doing."

"Ha! I'm not a prize pig, Zach. I'm responsible for my-self. And I hope you're not suggesting that you need to en-sure I eat for two because I'm neglecting our baby."

His brows slammed over his nose. "I'm not suggesting anything. I'm *telling* you that parenting, for me, starts here."

Her eyes went to the paper sack. That…was actually kind of sweet. Barbaric and completely chauvinist, but sweet. She hooked a finger on the edge of the bag and peeked inside. "You brought enough for both of us. Are you staying?"

Pen scraped the bottom of her salad bowl with the plastic fork to catch the last bit of honey mustard dressing and cranberry. She hummed while chewing, then opened her beautiful blue eyes and laid them right on Zach. He was glad to see that the color had returned to her face.

"Thank you," she said. "This was delicious."

He raised the plastic container containing the remaining half of his Reuben sandwich, dripping with Thousand Is-land dressing and tart sauerkraut. "Want the rest of mine?"

Her eyes brightened. "Really?"

"Yes, really."

She eagerly accepted the container and wolfed down the rest of his sandwich. As she swiped her mouth with a napkin, he gathered the plastic containers and stuffed them into the paper sack so he could take them to the trash on the way out.

"Nice to have an appetite." She swallowed a few guzzles of water from the bottle he'd refilled for her. "It must kick in late afternoon."

The *bing* of her email inbox sounded again. That had to be the sixth or seventh time since they'd sat down to eat. She rose to check it and he rose with her, curling a hand around her slender wrist.

"It's after five, Pen. Time to clock off."

"Just let me check." She tilted her head, sending her blond hair sliding over breasts that were pushed against the low V-cut of her silky shirt.

Keeping her wrist captive, he lowered his lips to hers.

"No," he whispered, lifting his head to find her wearing a disdainful frown. "Gather your things and I'll drive you home."

"Oh, all right." She shut down her desktop computer and slid her laptop into a bag along with a few other files and her planner. "If you could send my things back to my place, I'd appreciate it. There are a few outfits I'd like to have on hand for this week."

"Home is my place, Penelope." He lifted the sack and her water bottle, holding the door open for her.

"No. I'm going to my house."

"Guess again. Let's go."

"Zach!" She straightened her back and squared her jaw, ready for a fight. He slid a lingering gaze down her body—over the fitted jacket and pants to the shoes he should have thrown out rather than hid in his closet.

He took a step closer to her and she adjusted the bag on her shoulder. "You're wearing the shoes I told you not to." His voice dipped to communicate his displeasure.

"It's a free country." She arched one fair eyebrow.

"You're coming to my house," he reiterated. He couldn't risk her slipping in the shoes or forgetting to eat or no one being there if she felt sick in the morning. He wanted her safe. He wanted her with him. "No more discussion."

"You can't keep me prisoner, you know." She propped a fist on one hip.

Stubborn thing...

Zach dropped the bag and scooped Pen against him, his arm locked at her lower back. He kissed her, his tongue plunging past her lips, pleased when her free hand went from pushing him away to fisting in his shirt and tugging him forward. A thrill pulsed through him when her lips went pliant and her tongue began sparring with his.

When she finally surfaced, he kissed her lips softly once, twice more, and made sure she was steady on her spindly shoes before letting her go.

He then bent and lifted the bag and smirked down at her. Her hair was rumpled, her jacket askance and her lips pink and swollen from his five o'clock shadow.

*His.* Through and through.

"Your place." She said it with an eye roll, and offered a droll, "But only because there's no one at my house who kisses me like that," over her shoulder while they walked to the elevator.

Yeah, he thought she'd see things his way.

"Engaged?" Penelope's mother squawked into the phone.

Penelope'd had a feeling the news would be a surprise. Her mother knew Pen had all but sworn off men since one ran her out of Chicago.

Paula Brand had always been a busy woman. When Penelope was growing up, one indelible fact stood out about her mother: she worked.

Part of Pen's work ethic had come directly from her mother. Yes, her father worked on their co-owned real estate business, but it was Paula whom Penelope had always wanted to grow up and be like.

"I'm getting you the news a little late," Pen said. "There was a bit of a kerfuffle here in Dallas about my being engaged to the mayor's brother." Not that the news would have traveled to Chicago.

"Well, what's he like? Other than being the mayor's brother," her mother said, rustling papers. Paula was most likely sitting at the kitchen table of her latest project. Pen could imagine a paper-strewn surface surrounded by refinished cabinet drawers leaning against every wall, stacks of to-be-installed tile dotting worn linoleum. Paula was usually busy with one house project or the next, but she always made time for her only daughter.

"Well, I actually met him in Chicago in passing a few years back." Hopefully this would foster the notion that she hadn't rushed into anything. "He relocated to Dallas, and when I did, too, I ran into him at…a concert." Concert seemed better than a club. No way was Pen sharing what transpired that evening. Namely: the conception of their son or daughter.

"What does the mayor's brother *do*?" Possibly the most important question her mother could've asked. Vocation in the Brand family was paramount. The answer would please her, Pen was sure.

"He's the CEO of Ferguson Oil."

A drawn out silence, and then, "Impressive." Her mother took a breath and then issued a warning of sorts. "I hope this man has more to him than money. I raised you to support yourself."

Paula, though in a strong marriage with Pen's father, had always encouraged her to be independent. She knew her mother was looking out for her rather than accusing her of chasing a man because of the size of his wallet.

"Funny story. I didn't even know about his monetary status until we became serious. He used to be a contractor. A very good one. He came home to run the family business."

"Even when you try to go blue-collar, you end up with a suit." Paula's tone was filled with mild humor, yet approving. "That sounds like you."

Zach looked as delicious in worn jeans as he did in suits, if memory served. Pen hadn't had much of an opportunity to see him in jeans—though he had worn a pair of low-slung sweats the other night that nearly made her eyes tumble from their sockets. This morning he'd kissed her while she slept, and walked out of the bedroom wearing his running gear. She regretted now not waking up completely to take in the view.

"If you are happy, darling, I'm happy," her mother said. "That's all I want."

"Thanks, Mom." Her support would make the baby bombshell easier to drop in the future.

"As long as this man is ten times the man Cliff was."

Unfortunately, Pen hadn't been able to hide the circumstance that drove her out of Chicago and away from her parents. When she'd decided to relocate to Dallas, she'd told them the truth.

"Zach is one hundred times the man Cliff was." She'd been pacing the living room as she talked on her cell phone, so when she turned on her heel to pace back, she was surprised to find the subject of her conversation already in the room. She bid her mother farewell, and with a promise to check in soon, ended the call.

"I can get used to coming home to high compliments." Zach's words were puffed out between a few labored breaths. "You're up."

"Did you take the stairs?" Not what she wanted to say, but she had to fill the gap of silence that had mostly involved her staring. Zach's black T-shirt was damp with sweat, his biceps pressing the edges of the sleeves, and his strong legs poking out from beneath a pair of gray shorts. Had she ever known a man with a body this incredible? She didn't have to think long to come up with that answer.

*No*. No was the answer.

"I confessed to my mother about the engagement. I figured if she was comfortable with the idea of us getting married, she'll embrace the idea of being a grandmother."

He nodded, taking the information in stride. "Guess we should make that announcement eventually. I'm not sure how long we can hide it."

She dragged her palm over her flat stomach. She wasn't showing yet, but she would be soon enough.

"We could always tell everyone we were waiting until we were positive nothing would go wrong."

"It's our news to share whenever we want, for whatever reasons we decide."

She liked Zach's confidence. She liked sharing this with him. Though unexpected, the baby was their little secret—well, theirs and Stef's.

"I'm going to grab a shower. Join me?" His crooked smile went a long way to convincing her to do just that. Unfortunately...

"I already took one. And I have another phone call to make. Rain check?"

Even sweaty, he was sexy. He strolled over, water bottle in hand, and grinned down at her. The earthy outdoor scent wafting off him didn't deter her in the least—only made her want him more.

"In your case, Penelope, it's always raining."

The delicious lilt of his drawl was enough to bring her to her tiptoes. She placed a kiss on his lips and when he pulled back he dragged his top teeth along his full bottom lip. That move almost made her change her mind.

Almost.

Her mother's words echoed in her mind. Penelope had been raised to support herself.

Sexy baby daddy or no, her workday called.

# Eleven

Serena Fern and Ashton Weaver sat at a round table by the swimming pool, Pen across from them in a matching cushioned wicker chair. She'd met them at Ashton's mansion, per his request, and was as grateful for the peppermint candy he offered as much as the warmth of the summer sun.

These two were currently interviewing for a public relations specialist to handle an incident that happened during a particularly wild party where Serena, who was engaged to Michael Guff, her manager, was photographed sliding lips with her fellow actor, Ashton.

And who could blame her? Serena and Ashton were in their early twenties and Michael was pushing forty.

In their matching aviator sunglasses, Serena and Ashton looked very much like a couple. Especially since they held hands on the tabletop next to three sweating glasses of lemonade.

"We want to go public," Ashton declared. "She doesn't love Michael."

Serena's smile was sweet—hopeful. She liked that Ashton claimed her; Pen could tell that much.

"You *are* public," Pen informed them. "You're public in a big way." TMZ had plastered those photos all over the internet. There was nothing demure about Serena in her string bikini in this very pool and Ashton's tongue visible as she clung to his neck. The engagement was off, but Serena said Michael hadn't dropped her as a client yet. Because he was smart. He knew Serena was at the top of her game, and wasn't about to let his cash cow go. So to speak.

"I don't want to be the bad guy here. I look like I cheated." Serena's full pout appeared. She was gorgeous, if not a petite little thing.

"You *did* cheat," Pen reminded her. Her clients came to her for the truth and she wasn't holding back. "The good news is, most of the public will see this as predatory. Michael knows what he's doing. He wooed you with his professionalism and expertise. We'll perpetuate the story that he was marrying you for a cut of your money. A few timely interviews and tweets, and then you and Ashton can go public. For now, you can be seen together, but no kissing. No hand-holding. Go out and have coffee—better yet, with your scripts like you're rehearsing. In a few weeks you can snog in public all you like."

Serena grinned. Ashton didn't.

"What about Michael?"

Pen smiled. And here came the part where the young actors hired her.

"I'd recommend Serena firing him."

Ashton grinned. Serena gasped.

"Can I...do that?" she asked.

"Not only can you do that, you should. I know a couple of wonderful agents who could recommend someone reputable for your career."

"And then we could stop sneaking around and pretending it was an accident." Serena grasped Ashton's hands with both of hers and then, the two most adorable people ever embraced and kissed in a way that made Pen uncomfortable.

Job acquired, Pen left Ashton's mansion and those two to their inevitable lovemaking. Serena's words wound around her brain as Pen climbed into her car. *Sneaking around*.

While Pen and Zach weren't exactly sneaking, it irked her that she didn't have a blueprint for their situation. This was what she did for a living—she should be able to draw up a concise plan.

Which would be…what?

She thought back to Chicago, to Reese and Merina Crane's marriage of convenience, and how it turned into love despite starting as a farce.

Is that what Pen was hoping would happen with her and Zach? Because that was…silly.

What they had was an engagement that had started out as a distraction for Zach's PR issue. What they currently had was an entanglement that couldn't be resolved by a few tweets and sound bites.

What they had was a budding family and Pen needed to decide how, exactly, to move forward while preserving the Ferguson family's good name.

She drove to her apartment, deep in thought about what that plan would look like. How she and Zach would maintain a friendship throughout raising their child. When the best time would be to announce the dissolving of their engagement.

Probably the wisest move was to announce the baby on the heels of them not being engaged—that way everyone would be too excited about the baby to focus on the breakup.

Sigh.

Maybe she should hire a PR person to handle her case.

From where she sat, everything looked muddy.

At her apartment, she pulled into the lot. Without a private garage like Zach had, she didn't have much choice but to park her car in the elements. As luxurious as his apartment and amenities were, she couldn't stay there forever. She had to start thinking about where to put the baby— and considering that her apartment was a compact one-bedroom, one-bath, that meant she would have to consider moving.

Perhaps that was the first order of business.

She stepped from her car and turned for the property manager's office directly across from her building. As luck would have it, Jenny was heading her way.

"Ms. Brand." Her cropped blond hair blew in the summer breeze. She wore a fitted pencil skirt and a button-down shirt over a pair of sensible pumps. "Great timing. I was coming to give you this."

"Oh?" Pen pushed her hair behind her ear and accepted the paper Jenny offered. "What is it?"

"Your lease has been terminated. Congratulations on your engagement!" Jenny squeezed Pen's upper arm. "I hate to see you go, but I'm thrilled you've found love. Zach told me it was a surprise—his wedding gift to you. *Ohmygoshisthatthering?*" She snatched Pen's left hand and admired the diamond resting there, before rerouting her hand to her chest. Pen swore the other woman was tearing up. "You have until the end of the month to clear your things. No hurry, but honestly, I wouldn't hesitate moving in with a man who gives you a rock like this one!"

Before she could respond to…well, any of it, Jenny waved and said something about returning to her desk. Pen watched her go, the paper in her hand blowing and folding in half. She straightened it and read over the words Paid In Full as her temper skyrocketed.

Yes, she'd been contemplating moving from her one-bedroom into a larger place, but she wasn't planning on moving in with Zach.

She lifted her cell phone and punched in his number. When he answered in his office-y voice, she let him have it.

"I'm homeless." She wrestled her keys from her bag and marched inside her building.

"You're far from homeless," came his easy response.

"I'm not moving into your apartment, Zach."

"No. You're not."

She blinked as she pushed the button on the elevator for her floor. "Pardon?"

"I'm looking at a house right now. There's not enough room for a baby at my place." His voice sounded distant when he spoke to someone other than her. "I'll take it."

"Zach?"

"Gotta go, gorgeous. I have paperwork to deal with."

*"Zach."*

But one glance at her cell phone and she could see he'd already ended the call.

Zach tried Pen's phone number again only to be greeted by voice mail. He tapped the screen on the dashboard to end the call and pulled off the highway, changing direction to drive to her apartment. If she wasn't there, he'd try her office, and if she wasn't *there*, he'd see her at his apartment tonight.

When he'd gone to her place of residence to pick up a few things for her a week ago, he'd nearly had an aneurysm. The apartment building was in need of more than paint and TLC, and the area wasn't the safest. He'd decided then and there to keep her close by. Safe. Now that she was having his baby, there was no need for her to struggle.

He didn't want their child growing up worried about his or her safety.

From what he could tell, Pen dumped all her money into her office. He understood why. With a job like hers, working with business and celebrity elite, she needed to look the part.

He drove through the parking lot but there was no sign of Pen's car. He'd try her office next. He hit the screen on his dashboard to call her cell again, knowing it was futile.

But then her voice surprised him.

"I'm trying to be mad at you."

He couldn't help smiling. Not because she was mad at him but because hearing her voice lined with anger meant she was safe. She was okay.

"Where are you?"

"Why? Planning on coming by and buying me out of whatever building I'm in? What if I'm shopping?"

"A shopping center is well within my pay grade."

Her silence let him know his joke didn't fly.

"I want to know where you are so I can show you our new house."

"Zach."

"We also need to talk about our plans and what we're sharing when. I'm not going to dodge questions when they start rolling in, regardless of my brother's political career or Ferguson Oil's reputation. I'm not going to hide you or what we're doing."

"I agree. We need a plan." Her voice was wooden, but he'd take the agreement. "I don't want that, either."

"All right, then. Where are you? I'll take you to dinner."

"I'm at your apartment. Throwing your clothes out the window." Her voice was petulant, but he could guess she was kidding.

"I guess I have to buy that shopping center after all."

More silence.

"Pen."

"Come home. We'll talk then."

The way she said *home*, with ownership, and invited him to join her, snagged his chest.

"I was serious about dinner," he said as he sat back in his seat and accelerated.

"You bet your sweet ass you are," Pen snapped. "I'll see you soon."

Another grin. Damn, he liked her feisty.

He liked her, period.

At home he found Penelope dressed down in a tight pair of form-fitting pants and a baggy tee. Her hair was in a ponytail and she was on the floor, eyes closed, hands resting on her knees.

"Yoga?" he guessed, setting his cell phone and briefcase on the kitchen counter.

"I'm meditating so I don't kill you," she said without opening her eyes. Then she did, and pegged him with a pair of pale blues that never failed to make him smile. She had a pull on him—a physical one, sure, but there was a deeper connection there. Because of the baby? Yes, that was definitely part of it, but that wasn't all. "How was your day, dear?"

"Hectic. I bought a house."

"I heard." Her mouth flattened. She reached behind her and lifted a sheet of paper, waving it in the air for him. "I lost mine."

"I wanted it to be a surprise."

She stood from her mat and slapped the paper against his chest. "I was surprised."

He palmed the paper and followed her into the kitchen. She swallowed a few drinks of water before gesturing to the paper he still held. "Flip it over."

Her handwriting took up the entire backside of the page.

"'PR Plan for Zachary Ferguson and Penelope Brand,'" he read.

"I drafted our plan."

Under their names were dates and bulletpoints for items

like "announce end of engagement" and "be seen shopping for baby" and "press release."

"This is…interesting." He couldn't come up with another word for it.

"This is the way we're doing it."

"I don't see a line item for moving into my house."

"Sorry. I'm going to be living apart from you before that happens." She waggled her hand where the engagement ring sat. "The breakup and all."

"I don't see why we have to break up." He felt his brow furrow while hers lifted.

"Because this isn't real. I've orchestrated engagements before. I've even dealt with unplanned pregnancies. Couples don't usually argue with my sound and reliable suggestion to announce a split." She bit her lip. "Mostly."

*Mostly.*

He wondered if that meant some of the couples she'd walked through the valley of the shadow of matrimony fell in love for real and unraveled her precious plans. That wasn't their case, but he could see the discomfort in her expression.

He set the paper aside and walked toward her until she plastered her back against the fridge and lifted her chin to take him in. There wasn't anything quite like her delicate features contrasted with all that strength and sass. She was a drug.

His palm on her stomach, he crowded her until his body was pressed against hers. "*This*. Is real."

"I know," she said just above a whisper. "But the engagement isn't."

"There's no reason to dismantle it yet. We could say we're waiting to marry until after you have the baby."

She gave him a slow nod, her eyes averting. "Is that what you want?"

Yes. Because he knew what he didn't want. He didn't

want her to leave. He didn't want to miss a single moment of the pregnancy. That was only one of the reasons he wanted her to move in. He wanted to watch over her, but he also wanted to be with her.

"How about this for a proposal?" he asked, pleased when she turned her head, and her lips were dangerously close to his. "Move into my house. Have my baby. Wear this ring."

"And then what?"

"We have time to decide the *what*, Penelope." He palmed her soft cheek and ran his thumb over her bottom lip. "In the meantime, I want you in my house. In my bed. In my world."

"You don't have to—"

"Let me. Allow yourself to let me. You don't have to have a rigid plan for your own life, Pen. Live on the edge." He gave her a lazy grin. "It's fun here."

She licked her lips and before she could argue, he covered them with a kiss. Deflecting? Possibly. Where they were concerned, there was one surefire way to get them back on track and that was in the bedroom.

"You promised me dinner," she breathed, but her fists clung to him.

He was aware of the time, more aware of her pending hunger than his hardening manhood. "Are you hungry?"

"Starving." Her eyebrows bent in the sincerest apology. "How about after dinner?"

"You have to ask?" He shook his head, still marveling over how off-kilter this woman could throw him. "Dinner. Get changed."

Her beaming smile made him almost as happy as having her underneath him. She bounced out of the kitchen and down the hallway and Zach took another look at the paper in front of him.

He grabbed a pen from a nearby drawer and drew a line through "announce end of engagement."

# Twelve

Having billions of dollars made moving much easier.

When Pen moved, she'd hired movers and packed every one of her belongings, plus loaded many of the boxes into her own car, for the traverse to Dallas from Chicago.

When Zach moved, he made one phone call to an assistant to gather Penelope's belongings from her apartment, and another to an interior designer to decorate his new home.

Two weeks had passed since the move from her apartment. His buying her out of her lease was heavy-handed, but she could admit it made sense in the short-term. Everyone would assume it was the natural next step after hearing about the pregnancy. Plus, Zach would need more room for the baby whether Pen lived with him or not.

He'd purchased a beautiful home just outside the city, with six bedrooms and six bathrooms and a sprawling yard. A low stone wall ran the perimeter of the property, and the front featured a gate, not unlike Chase's mansion.

The house was far more approachable than a mansion, however, with a wide front porch and white columns, and, thanks to a savvy interior decorator, a pair of rockers on the porch overlooking the front yard and curved driveway.

That was where she and Zach sat tonight.

She'd finished up at work and he'd met her at home for dinner—a dinner cooked by a chef he'd hired to monitor her feedings, or so she'd joked. Now they sat, a mug of peppermint tea for her, and a cold beer for him, rocking back and forth on the porch.

"This is really beautiful, Zach."

He turned his head and smiled. Tonight he wore jeans and a T-shirt, looking the part of laid-back country boy. Even the recent trim of his hair couldn't dash the relaxed line of his long body. He pushed, one knee crooked, the other leg straight out, and rocked again, finishing his bottle of beer before setting it on the wooden porch.

"Glad you like it."

She tapped her mug with her fingernails and thought. The PR plan for them had been drawn up. She'd typed it neatly, presented it to him and he'd made changes—some she'd agreed to, others she hadn't.

*Maintain engagement (to be revisited after the baby is born)*

*Shopping for the baby (covered by the press)*

*Press release confirming baby Ferguson*

"We should talk," she said.

Zach's hands gripped the arms of the rocker and he slowly turned to face her. His eyebrows were down, his mouth flat.

"It's not bad!" she assured him with a soft laugh.

"Do me the favor of never saying those three words to me again?" He visibly relaxed some, sucking in a deep breath.

There had to be a story behind his request, but she wasn't going into that now.

"It's time to tell our families." She placed her hand over

her tummy. She'd always had a slim waist, but the bump was showing enough that people would start talking. "I can't hide this much longer. And I'd like to tell them before we're seen at the store."

"That'd be best, yes." His ease returned, along with his smile.

"How about this weekend? We can stop by your parents' house before going to Love & Tumble." The upscale boutique selling children's clothing was bordering pretentious, but for the press release, they needed the attention. What better store to emerge from carrying several shiny sage-green bags in their hands while kissing? She'd already lined up a photographer and requested the shots.

"And your parents?"

"We can't very well fly to Chicago, now can we?"

"Why not?" He shrugged. "It's a two-hour flight."

"On your private jet?" She snorted. This amount of convenience was all so…hard to get used to.

"I don't own one, but I can charter a plane." He leaned on one arm, coming closer to her chair. "Your parents might want to meet me."

She nodded, her fantasy world ripping at the seams. Once her parents met him, once he was on her stomping grounds, would the fantasy bubble burst? She'd been sheltered, in a way. Living in this safe existence with work and Zach. Sequestered from reality while she juggled nausea, fatigue and doctor's appointments.

"I'll book it for Friday. We can grab a hotel."

A dry laugh chafed her throat. "My parents would die if we booked a hotel. They would insist we stay with them."

"We can stay with them."

She watched him for a solid beat, wondering who this man was, really. Was he the billionaire who moved them into a regal house with the snap of his fingers? Or the family guy kicked back on a rocking chair? Could he be both?

"Friday," she repeated, still unsure.

He grabbed his empty beer bottle, stood from the rocker and bent to kiss her. "But we're still having sex at your parents' house, whether they like it or not."

She pressed a hand to her cheek as he walked inside, waiting until he'd gone to react. Despite her worries about Friday—when reality met fantasy—Zach's comment made her laugh.

"How perfect that you both made it here for Fourth of July weekend!" Paula Brand grinned as she piled raw seasoned steaks and chicken breasts onto a platter.

Penelope's father, Louis, came in from the back and accepted the platter, slicing Zach in two with a curt nod.

Zach was accustomed to suspicious reactions from fathers of the women he'd dated—he'd met a few. Mothers loved him but the dads were harder to win over. Zach took a healthy slug from his beer bottle. He just had to come up with the how.

He'd played down the "Dallas billionaire" bit, sliding into his clothing from his Chicago days. A comfortable and approachable pair of jeans paired with a gray T-shirt.

Penelope opted for a billowy summer dress, cut to disguise the roundness of her belly starting to make itself known. She was leaning against the counter, a carbon copy of her mother, with an hourglass figure and blond hair. Paula's blond was a paler shade, her stature shorter, but she was as womanly and beautiful as her daughter.

A vision of Pen at that age, standing over a sink while Zach flipped through the mail hit him square in the solar plexus. His next breath was a struggle, but he managed.

"Zach, honey?"

He blinked out of his fortune-seeing stupor to find Paula's brows lifted in question.

"Another beer?"

"Oh. Sure. Yeah. Thanks."

Pen raised an eyebrow in his direction but moved to the fridge on his behalf. When she handed over the bottle, she smiled up at him, her eyes sparkling and skin glowing.

It seemed no matter how he tried to cordon off this situation as one he could control, she continually kicked down barriers and knocked him off center.

The real kicker? He didn't mind it a bit.

"Pen tells me you were a contractor when you lived here," Paula said as Zach took a swig of his fresh beer. "What do you think of this place?"

Paula and Louis bought and sold real estate for a living, so their current digs was a three-bed, two-bath fixer-upper north of Chicago.

"Good bones," he said, happy to turn his attention to the surrounding rooms. They'd obviously moved in here while they did the work. The house was clean, but there were various projects started in the kitchen, one of the bedrooms, and the half-bath downstairs had been gutted.

"We bought it for a steal." Paula washed the cutting board and her hands. "Foreclosure. We're hoping to double our profit. Louis insists on rebuilding the back deck, but I wanted to tear it down."

"The deck is a good feature." Zach walked to the back door. Louis manned the grill, his stout, muscular body stiff. The deck was worn and splintered, and a pile of fresh wood was lying under a tarp in the backyard.

Maybe after they told Pen's parents about the baby, and Louis *didn't* murder him and bury his body in the backyard, Zach and Pen's father would have a topic in common.

Zach knew how to build a deck.

Pen didn't miss the wind in the windy city, that was for sure. She'd wrestled her hair into a ponytail and was forced to hold her paper plate down with one hand while she ate her chicken sandwich to keep it from blowing away.

Her parents' temporary deck, strewn with Craftsman tools, made her feel right at home. She remembered many occasions where she'd sidestepped piles of wood or stacks of tile in whatever house they were currently working on. After she moved out, they'd started moving into the homes they were flipping. She was glad they'd waited because as much as the nomadic lifestyle appealed to her hardworking family, Pen liked to be in one place. It was what had made leaving Chicago so difficult.

Her mother peppered Zach with questions about his family and his job, which he handled with ease as he sawed into his second steak. Pen's father did a good job of shoving food in his mouth whenever her mom tried to include him in the conversation, so that all he had to do was nod or shake his head in response.

Pen pushed her sandwich aside, focusing on the potato salad on her plate. She waited for a lull in the conversation and when it came she reached under the picnic table and grabbed Zach's knee. He jerked his attention toward her, gave her a subtle nod and put down his cutlery.

"Mr. and Mrs. Brand," he started, and Pen's stomach flopped. She hoped her dinner stayed down.

Paula looked up, eyebrows aloft and Louis did his impersonation of Sam the Eagle from *The Muppets*. Seriously. If his eyebrows were any lower they'd be his mustache.

"Pen and I have an ulterior motive for visiting this weekend, other than showing off the engagement ring."

Miraculously, her father managed to lower his eyebrows farther.

"We're excited to tell you that—" Zach put an arm around Pen and hugged her close, looking down into her eyes when he made the announcement "—we're expecting a baby in December." He faced her parents first, then

Pen followed suit, in time to witness their twin expressions of shock.

"I beg your pardon?" That was her mom, who, knife and fork in hand over her plate, sat statue-still while the wind whipped her hair.

"We're pregnant, Mom. You and Dad are going to be grandparents."

"Oh, my. I'm…" Her mouth froze open until finally, *finally*, that gape turned into a wide smile. "I'm so happy!" She was off her chair so fast to wrap her arms around Pen's neck that Louis had to slap his hand down on her plate to keep it from blowing off the table.

Paula returned to her seat, chattering about due dates and how she'd have to apply for a credit card that offered frequent flier miles so she could visit Dallas on a regular basis.

"No need, Mrs. Brand," Zach said smoothly. "We'll fly you down."

At the kind offer, Louis stood with his plate and climbed over the picnic bench's seat. He grunted once, then stormed into the house, letting the screen door bang behind him.

That went about like Pen had expected.

# Thirteen

"They're okay." Paula was peeking out of the kitchen window overlooking the deck.

"You mean Dad isn't strangling Zach or freezing him out completely?"

"Nope." Paula returned to the living room with two mugs of tea. "They're measuring."

"Measuring…do I want to ask what?"

"The deck, sweetheart." Paula handed over a mug.

"Oh, that."

Her mother sat on the dilapidated couch next to her, placing a comforting hand on Pen's knee. "This seems very sudden."

"Three months is one quarter of the year. It's not that sudden." Pen held her tea close to her lips. She hadn't meant to sound so defensive.

"Three months is how long you've been pregnant. When did you meet him?"

"I told you. When I lived here. That's been years ago." Pen lifted her thumbnail and nibbled. Her mother's serious expression remained. "Yes. Okay, it was sudden."

"But you're in love."

Thank goodness her mother didn't put a question mark at the end of that sentence. Pen didn't like to lie. She smiled instead. No, she and Zach weren't in love. What they had wasn't ever supposed to be about love. She couldn't deny she felt close to him—and that she liked him a whole lot.

When she thought of her baby, a worrisome thought niggled its way forward. Would her son or daughter grow up thinking love was a fairy tale?

*No*, she decided in an instant.

Pen would show her child love, and Zach would, too. Romantic love was avoidable. She thought back through her past boyfriends and wasn't sure she'd ever been in love herself. There'd always been an obstacle, an excuse she'd found to keep from getting in too deep.

Maybe because she'd arranged many false marriages and engagements for publicity and had become the ultimate skeptic. Or maybe the idea of giving in and being some-one's all meant she'd be at risk to lose it all.

With a child on the way, she couldn't afford to be selfish.

A pair of low male laughs carried on the Chicago wind and into the living room and Penelope and Paula exchanged glances.

"Are they…?" Pen started.

Paula blinked, then smiled. "I think they are."

Zach and Pen's baby would know love—so much of it, he or she would never want for more.

But as she made that empty assurance to herself Pen wondered if she could settle for the same.

Louis not only liked to talk about houses and building, he was also a Dallas Cowboys fan.

Go fucking figure.

Zach ended up at the picnic table drinking beers and yapping with Pen's father until well after midnight.

"I should go up," Louis said. He cast a glance at an upstairs window. "Paula waits for me."

How...nice. Zach's parents got along fine, but he didn't remember his mother ever waiting on his dad, or his dad cutting anything short to go to her.

Louis stood and Zach stood with him. "Thanks for letting us stay."

"Paula insisted on always having a guest room for Pen since she moved to Dallas. We lost her to Texas a year before we're losing her to you." Louis's words held no venom, and actually sounded kind of sad. "You'll see when that baby is born. Just how much you'll do for it. Just how protective you'll become."

Zach could imagine. He'd already been that way with Penelope. He met Louis's eyes and confessed just that.

"I'm like that about your daughter. She'll never want for anything. Our child wasn't the reason we became engaged." His ex-wife was, but Zach sure as hell wasn't sharing that. "But the baby definitely gave us a good reason to stay that way."

Louis nodded slowly, obviously trying to accept the fact that his baby girl had gotten engaged and impregnated by some billionaire cowboy. Damn if Zach could understand Pen's father's position when he imagined having a daughter of his own.

With a slap to Zach's shoulder, Louis echoed his fear. "God help you if you have a girl."

Zach shut the door to the guest bedroom after brushing his teeth, stepping lightly across the real wood floors that were scarred and in need of a good wax. Paula had mentioned as much when she'd shown them to their room before looking to Zach to check if he'd be appalled by staying in such squalor. Her words, said on a tight laugh.

He'd assured her he could sleep anywhere, and though he'd kept it to himself, he'd also considered that he *would* sleep anywhere as long as Penelope was by his side.

He climbed into the double bed, a tight fit, the mattress sagging in the center. Pen let out a soft hum and wiggled under the blankets. Wrapping his arm around her middle, he tugged her close and buried his nose in her hair.

When he'd met her years ago in Chicago at a party, he'd been in full-on playboy mode. He'd set his Dallas drawl to full-tilt and laid on the charm, promising not to get into any trouble lest Pen's PR firm would have to step in and straighten him out. He hadn't seen her after that, so running into her at a swanky club in Texas had taken him by surprise.

He wasn't a man who believed in fate, kismet or meant-to-be, but as he allowed his fingers to drape over his fiancée's abdomen, he wondered if he wasn't seeing this for what it was.

A second chance.

But as the thought hit him, so did the palpable fear of screwing it up. Of being in a position to lose not only the woman beside him but also access to their child.

Zach hadn't thought about fatherhood. Hadn't thought about it even when he'd asked Lonna to marry him. But the moment Pen announced her pregnancy an overwhelming feeling of right swept over him.

It wasn't just the baby. It wasn't just that he was in his thirties and it was past time for him to consider starting a family. It wasn't that he'd crafted a fake engagement to distract from the real issue at hand.

The game-changer was Penelope Brand.

She murmured in her sleep—or her half sleep, as it were—and he kissed her shoulder. He'd promised to claim her in this very bed, parents' house or no, believing their sexual chemistry would rival the need for sleep and trump the need to be quiet with her parents down the hall.

Now, though…

She rolled in his direction, her eyes opening briefly then shutting again. The moonlight streamed through the window, highlighting her fair hair and kissing her curved cheekbone.

He'd claim her in a different way tonight.

He scooted in the springy bed to give her room. Her body was going through the rigorous toils of crafting a baby—their baby—and she needed all the sleep she could get.

He couldn't give her everything, but that, he could.

The flight home from Chicago was quick, and soon enough Zach and Pen were changing from their comfy flight clothes into slightly more formalwear for visiting the Ferguson house.

One set of parents down, one to go.

She'd let Zach choose the nature of the venue, which he'd scheduled for cocktail hour. She'd argued about building their visit around alcohol since she wouldn't be having any but he'd assured her she didn't have to worry.

At a little after seven Saturday evening, Pen settled onto the settee across from the chaise longue in the sitting room at the Ferguson mansion.

Elle was perched formally on the edge of a high-backed chair, Rider settled into the one next to it. A female member of the house staff walked in with a tray holding four martinis with speared olives in each elegant glass.

Zach accepted his glass, but held up a hand when the younger woman bent to give Penelope her drink. "My fiancée is expecting, so she'll need something nonalcoholic.

Club soda with a lime, okay?" He pegged Pen with a play-ful look while she struggled not to swallow her tongue.

Evidently, breaking the news to his parents wasn't going to be a slow build.

Rider accepted his drink, Elle hers, and Pen offered a shaky smile in response. Elle's right eyebrow was curved so high on her forehead, it'd been lost in her hair.

No one said a word until Pen had a club soda in hand. Elle went first.

"And here we thought you'd come to tell us that your engagement was a sham to distract from your ex-wife."

"Eleanor, for the love of—" Rider let out an exasperated huff and swallowed a mouthful of his martini.

"You're only allowed one of those, don't forget. Savor it."

Pen stiffened, but the comforting weight of Zach's arm was around her back in an instant.

"We're due in December. We wanted to tell you in per-son before you found out from someone else."

Elle pursed her already pursed lips, her cool green stare assessing and, from Pen's vantage point, not all that ap-proving.

"I think it's great," Rider said with a huge smile. Pen latched on to the man's sentiment like a lifeline. "We al-ready wrote you a check." He reached into the pocket of his slacks and came out with a folded paper. "It's for the wed-ding, but now I suppose you can include it with preparing for our first grandchild."

He let out a hearty laugh and embraced Elle's hand. "Better than croaking of a heart attack before I get to meet my grandkids, eh, Elle?"

"I suppose that's true." She narrowed her eyes again and Pen shifted in her seat. "What interested you most in my son, Ms. Brand? His money or his DNA?"

Next to her, Zach went on alert, but Pen stayed his re-tort by touching his arm.

"I can understand how this information comes as a shock to you, but there's no need to be rude, Mrs. Ferguson. I'm neither a gold digger nor a woman who expected to get pregnant. Trust me when I tell you that you don't want to know the part of your son that most interests me. I simply saw someone I liked." She paused to take in Zach, whose mouth flinched like he might be fighting a proud smile. "And had to have him."

She snapped her attention back to Elle, who'd dropped her jaw. Likely no one dared speak to the Oil Queen of Dallas the way Pen had, but the older woman had started it.

"Mom."

Elle turned her stunned reaction to Zach.

"We're not asking your permission, or for your approval. But I expect you to be much more gracious when the baby is here. He or she will be the first-born grandchild in the family."

Elle drank down her martini in hearty gulps, then retrieved the spare martini left behind when Pen refused it and gulped that one, too.

Rider, his good humor intact, let out a crack of laughter. "Guess she'll be having my second one, then."

# Fourteen

"Pen, hang on."

The moment they'd exited Zach's parents' house, Pen marched down the driveway, fists at her sides.

"Wait." Zach caught her easily, snagging her biceps with a gentle hand and spinning her to face him. He was grinning and she glared at the dimple rather than admire it. Nothing about this evening had been funny.

"They hate me."

"No, they don't."

"Your mother hates me."

"No, she doesn't. She's just…in shock. Not everyone is going to take this news as well as we did."

"I didn't take it well. I avoided you for three days and drafted nine PR plans before I decided I couldn't make one until I told the father of my child I was having his baby!"

Zach's emerald eyes darkened when he tugged her closer, his grip tight but tender. She'd been battling fatigue, nausea and dizziness for weeks, but now it seemed the worst was behind her. The sexual tension that existed between them returned.

"You handling Eleanor Ferguson was quite possibly the sexiest moment I've ever witnessed."

Some of the fire went out of her. "Ever?"

His grin widened. "No. Not ever. Why don't I take you home and we can try for a new sexiest moment ever?"

"It's been a while."

"I know."

"You haven't complained." He'd been damn near angelic.

"I know."

She took a few steps closer in heels he hadn't bitched about tonight. Her shoes were a battle he'd allowed her to win. She fingered his collar and slipped her other hand down his buttoned shirt and over his black slacks.

A low grunt came from his throat when she pressed her lips to his, continuing her intimate massage down below. A few firm strokes and soon that part of him was much bigger than before.

He deepened their kiss, hands coming around to cup her ass. Every firm inch of him was flush against her and her hormones perked up.

"Zach." The breathy lilt of her voice was one she'd forgotten she'd possessed. "How about we take the car out in the yard and see if I can't break the sexiest moment record here."

"In the car?" His voice took on a husky quality and she laughed.

"Don't tell me you've never had a girl go down on you in a car."

"Not a girl as classy as you are," he all but growled.

"Good." She put a teasing kiss on the center of his mouth. "I love being first."

He wasn't wearing a tie, so she settled for dragging him to his car by the shirtsleeve. Zach followed, wide steps allowing for the part of him currently cheering the most for Pen's bold offer.

She liked that she had the power to affect him. It made her feel as if she could do anything. It made her feel like the woman she'd been before Cliff strangled her business into submission.

Zach put the car in gear and drove them behind the house and to the back of the grounds where trimmed trees and perfectly clipped grass met elegantly arranged flowers and shrubberies that were works of art.

"Your mom's going to freak about the landscaping when she sees the tire treads."

"First." Zach turned off the car and rolled the windows down. "That's the last time you mention my mom tonight. Second. I can't think of a second because my brains have relocated to my crotch."

"Hmm." Pen stifled her laughter to take advantage of the very sexy scene this created. Bucket leather seats, windows down, a warm Texas breeze heating the interior of the car and covering her neck in a light sheet of sweat where her hair fell. "I'm going to have to get a closer look to confirm."

Nothing felt better than turning him on. He wore lust so baldly—the flare of his nostrils, the widening of his pupils.

She undid his belt and released the clasp on his slacks. He was hard and ready, and when she slipped the waistband of his boxers past his erection, she licked her lips.

"You're doing that on purpose."

"Well. Yes." She rolled her eyes and he crushed another kiss onto her lips before she pulled away and lowered her head. She took him on her tongue, guiding his length deep into her mouth. His legs went rigid, knees locking as she continued working him over. His utterances were a mixture of swear words, reverent callouts to the Almighty, and incoherent groans. Just when she was starting to enjoy herself, he tugged her up and pressed another kiss onto her lips.

"Don't you dare move."

He jerked his pants over his hips and came around to

her side of the car, pulling the door open and offering his hand like a prince helping her from a carriage. Except his pants were sagging open, his erection outlined by the tails of his untucked, wrinkled white shirt.

"No laughing," he warned.

She didn't laugh, and when the heels of her shoes sank into the soft earth, she kicked them off. Zach maneuvered them to a particularly soft patch of grass surrounded by bushes.

He hoisted her dress over her head, tossed her bra aside and gently lowered her to the ground. He kissed her nipples, leaving them to pucker in the breeze while he unbuttoned his shirt and whipped it off his shoulders. Pants around his thighs, he didn't bother taking them off, and she couldn't think of a single reason he should.

She peeled her thong down her legs, ready for him and grateful to avoid another delay.

He slipped inside her, dropping his forehead to hers and letting out what might be a shudder. She tilted her hips and closed her eyes, head tossed back to appreciate the way she felt whenever he was inside her.

Full.

No.

*Whole*.

Her eyes flew open to meet his and he started moving again. Slowly, fluidly. Pumping in and out at a rhythm he set and she easily matched. Never had sex felt this intimate before Zach—before now. She reminded herself that her rounding belly and raging hormones were responsible for a plethora of emotions she hadn't experienced before.

Until he said, "You've never been more beautiful than you are now."

She pressed her fingertips to his mouth and he gave them a playful nip.

"You're saying that," she breathed as she braced for another sensual slide, "because you have to."

"I'm saying that—" another harsh breath from him blew her hair from her forehead "—because it's the truth."

She pushed on his chest. "On your back, cowboy."

His pause was momentary, but a second later he cupped her head and hip and, keeping them joined, shifted so that he was on his back instead.

"Impressive move with your pants around your knees." She smiled down at him.

"Thank ya, ma'am."

She rolled her eyes as he tipped a pretend cowboy hat, but his good humor erased when she pushed his chest to leverage herself up, and sank down on him again.

A hiss of air came from between his teeth, but he didn't close his eyes. No, he kept them right on her as she moved. His hands covered her breasts, his hips rising to meet hers.

And when her orgasm all but shattered her, Zach caught her against him, holding her hair from her face as he kissed her. He tilted his hips while she held on to the moving earth and then he came inside her.

The only sounds in the garden were crickets humming, the distant bark of a dog and Zach's father's shout on the air.

"Seriously?" The Zen of Penelope's orgasm washed away as her eyes went wide, her hands covering her breasts.

He let out a laugh. She speared him with a murderous glare before looking over her shoulder. He'd driven them deep into the gardens at the side of the house, so all his old man had seen—or could currently see—was the black blob of Zach's car.

And he and Pen were safely hidden on one side of it.

He sat up, keeping their connection as a tremor ran down his spine. Damn, he could have used a few more minutes to Zen out with her. Cradling her face, he gave her a swift kiss. Unfortunately, timing was of the essence before Rider called the cops.

"Get dressed," Zach told Pen. "I'll handle this."

Not since he was sixteen had he been caught with his pants around his ankles, and he wasn't starting today. He yanked them up, buckling his belt and pushing a hand through his hair.

He snatched his shirt off the ground and turned to find Pen, grass in her hair, roll her tiny scrap of a pair of panties up those long, golden legs.

He lifted her dress off the ground and handed it to her, noticing the grass stain a microsecond before she did. She merely shook her head and pulled it on, tugging it down and wadding the bra in her hand while Zach stepped into his shoes.

He spared one last glance the second his dad turned on the floodlight, enough to see her grow a little more irked, and in the process, a whole lot more beautiful.

Who knew that could happen?

"Zach?" his dad bellowed.

"It's me!" he called back. "Don't shoot!" He was only half kidding. From what he could see, Rider wasn't carrying a shotgun, but one could never be too careful.

So much for his parents never using this part of the house. He'd been sure this side was left to the staff or only opened up for parties.

His father strolled into the yard. Zach approached while he finished buttoning his white collared shirt.

"What in Sam hell are you doing?" Rider asked, his voice filled with mirth. "Trying to give me another heart attack? Because if your mother knew you were out here having sex in the petunias, she'd make sure I had one."

Rider turned to look over his shoulder but only briefly. They both knew Eleanor was in her bath by now with the TV on and a magazine in hand.

"I don't think those were petunias," Zach said in response.

"You two have your own place and you're carrying on like teenagers." His father sent a look over to the car where Pen sat in the front seat, elbow on the window, one hand hiding her face. "She knows I know that's her, right?"

"Yeah. She does." His own gaze lingered there a moment before he bid his dad adieu. "I'll pay to repair the lawn."

"You know I don't give a shit about that." Rider chuckled. "Get your girl home. Continue what you started indoors."

Zach's back straightened on his walk to the car, his swagger taking over. He was proud that this woman was with him. And that she'd offered to do dastardly things outside with him. Pen embodied the motto "work hard, play hard." He liked that a hell of a lot.

Zach reached the car and Rider called out, "'Night, Penny!" His loud boom of a guffaw heard as clear as day.

When Zach sank into his leather seat, Pen watched him for a solid thirty seconds. Fine by him. It gave him a moment to rebutton his shirt since he'd done it wrong on the walk over to his dad. He adjusted his seat belt and started the car, aware of her watching him the entire time.

"What?"

"Now your mom definitely hates me."

"She has no idea. Dad won't tell her." He reversed the car and drove through the grass.

Pen went stone silent.

Zach grasped her chin and turned her to face him, his car idling at the gate of his parents' gargantuan home. "I would never let her hate you. Give her time."

Pen's blue eyes softened with worry.

"I mean it. Give her a little time and she'll love you as much as my dad does."

He pulled out of the driveway and onto the street, the

words he'd said wending around his brain. He'd meant them. Everyone loved Penelope—her clients, his siblings, his dad.

*Do you?* came the unplanned thought.

But that kind of love was different—he'd learned long ago that loving with his full heart wasn't rewarded. He wouldn't make that mistake again.

He drove home, arm leaning on his open window and the summer air blowing his hair.

Some thoughts were best left unexplored.

# Fifteen

"Have your assistant return everything but this." Pen held up a tiny pair of shoes. "I can't part with these even though they're hysterically overpriced. The rest of it I can shop for online." She stood over the boutique baby clothes spread on Zach's king-size bed, her hands on her hips. There was a line in the center of her brows communicating her worry.

"Why?" He slid out of his suit jacket and hung it in his closet.

"Because a growing baby doesn't need extravagant—" she gestured to the stacks of gender-neutral clothing "—everything."

She'd set up the visit to the baby boutique for Saturday afternoon, and then they did something he'd never pictured himself doing. They shopped for their future son or daughter.

He'd purchased the clothing, shoes and toys that he and Pen carried out in the boutique's signature shiny bags, but he didn't stop there. He'd also snapped several pictures of furniture with his iPhone and sent them to his interior designer. Like right now, Pen had loved it but protested the inflated price tag.

"No one *needs* extravagant everything," Zach commented, unbuttoning his shirt. Pen paused, a yellow stuffed elephant rattle in her hand, and watched. He liked the way she looked at him—like he was her next meal. "Come take your clothes off."

"There's an invitation," she said with a laugh.

She tossed the elephant aside and came to him in the closet. Her eyes were sleepy despite it being hours before bedtime. After a shopping excursion and a late lunch, she looked beat. Not that it hindered her beauty at all.

Holding herself steady on the closet's interior wall, she slipped off one high-heeled shoe and then the other.

"Ah, so much better."

He'd lectured her nonstop about the damn shoes. It hadn't done any good.

"Just so we're clear," he said, shrugging off his shirt and tossing it into a hamper, "our child is entitled to have as many extravagant things as we see fit."

Her eyes roamed over his bare chest and he sucked in a breath to expand it farther. She smiled and gave him a playful shove.

"That's what I'd like to avoid. An *entitled* child." She turned and lifted her hair and he pulled down the delicate zipper holding her dress closed. "I want our son or daughter to be loved and know that 'stuff' doesn't matter."

Zach ran his fingers down her exposed back, pausing at her bra strap. "This, too?"

She eyed him over her shoulder, a spark of want in her eyes mingling with the fatigue. As tempting as it was to seduce her, he'd digress.

"I'm going to work at home for a bit. Why not grab a nap?"

She slipped out of her dress, revealing smooth skin

and a softly rounding belly. His chest flooded with possessiveness.

She covered her stomach and her brows bent.

He moved her hand and gave her a smile. "I like watching the changes in your body."

She cocked her head as if to challenge him. "You mean my growing girth?"

"You're making a human being. That takes up some real estate." It was a miracle in every sense of the word. "It's okay to take a break."

"I'll relax, but I want to keep my eye on the internet for our inevitable online debut."

The photographer had shown up like Pen arranged, snapping pictures of them inside the store through the windows as well as from across the street when they left the baby boutique.

"Right. The blogger."

"Not just any blogger." She hung her white dress and pulled on a pair of stretchy pale-pink pants.

He wanted to dispute the long white shirt covering her, until he realized he could see the shape of her nipples and the swell of her heavy breasts outlined by the thin fabric.

"The Dallas Duchess," Pen stated with a gesture that sent her breasts jiggling.

He pulled on a T-shirt and jeans and slipped into a pair of tennis shoes. "And she's important, I gather."

"Mmm-hmm. She keeps an eye on the Dallas movers and shakers. She'll have our photo up by this afternoon or tomorrow morning. I made sure of it."

That rogue twinkle in Pen's eye lit whenever she talked about her work. Whether she was digging a pair of canoodling actors out of a steaming pile of drama or arranging Zach's internet debut. He couldn't resist capturing some of that fire for himself. Not while she stood this close to him.

He wrapped an arm around her back and lowered his lips to hers, pressing her breasts to his chest as he made out with her long and slow. She tracked her fingers along his abs, and his belly clenched. He let out a low growl as she dropped from her toes and smiled up at him. He wanted her. Badly.

"You don't have to work right away, do you?" she asked with the quirk of one eyebrow.

"Hell, no," he answered, and then hoisted her in his arms and carried her the short distance to the bed.

She and Zach had played their roles while shopping earlier today. They'd kissed and hugged and smiled. She'd coached him this morning en route to the store, and he'd grumbled about the preparation, arguing that he wasn't that good of an actor.

Yet this afternoon, there he was, heat in his eyes and firmness in his kiss. But that wasn't all acting, now, was it? He'd been looking at her with heated eyes and owning her with his kisses since they'd re-met. And their going to bed together when they returned home was definitely par for course.

Mercy. She wondered how much of the sex she could blame on the hormones.

She finished packing the baby clothes and toys into the shopping bags for returning later. She was serious about not wanting an entitled child.

What she hadn't told him was that she'd also started thinking about the massive income gap between hers and Zach's annual earnings. Obviously, that'd always been a factor, but today especially, as she thought about providing for her son or daughter, she realized that half the child's time would be spent at Zach's house where everything would be provided in abundance. The other half? Spent with her where she'd earn a decent living, yes, and her child would never do without the necessities, but a two hundred dollar jumper wouldn't be hanging in the closet.

She shoved thoughts of the future aside and focused on the task in front of her. An email from the Dallas Duchess herself. The duchess confirmed that the blog would go live tomorrow.

So that was that.

Penelope and Zach would be making their announcement publicly soon after, confirming that yes, they were expecting. Being that Zach was both CEO of Ferguson Oil and the mayor's brother, the story was news to anyone looking for gossip. The Fergusons weren't royal family status, but neither were they ignored. Their staggering good looks paired with their billionaire incomes made the two brothers and sister popular in this city.

"Way to pick a baby daddy," Pen joked aloud. But she didn't feel an ounce of regret for going to bed with Zach—or moving in with him. Like Cinderella, her fairy tale would soon come to an end.

She glanced around the living room—masculine browns and earth tones like his apartment with a touch of hominess in shades of blue—and admitted she liked nesting here, even if it wasn't permanent. There would be time to ready her apartment—to *acquire* an apartment. In the meantime, she would be treated like a queen.

She scraped her bottom lip with her teeth as she turned over the shallow thoughts. Pen wasn't accustomed to being dependent on anyone but herself. Her mother had raised her to be her own godmother, not the princess flailing about wearing only one glass slipper.

Once upon a time Pen had been involved with a client who had offered to "take care of everything" and look how that'd ended up. She'd vowed never to let her guard down again—yet here she was, breaking her rules for Zach.

Had she traded her pluck for comfort? Was she shallow? Or, was Zach different? Was what they had something she'd never truly experienced—the beginning of a trusting relationship that might lead to that elusive beast: love?

Surely not.

Pen had looked forward to the day she'd moved away from home. She'd excelled at running her own life. So well, in fact, she'd begun advising others how to run theirs and charging them for it.

Right now she was simply being practical. Her affinity for Zach—the doting as well as the sex—was temporary. Soon, she'd have a child to raise. A baby to nurse. And still have her business to run. She wouldn't have time for frivolous relationships any more than she'd have time for a mani-pedi on a Sunday afternoon.

They were sacrifices she was willing to make. And with Zach in the picture, it wasn't as if she'd be doing it alone. She'd have help. Albeit not living under this same roof, because that was impractical. But they'd have shared custody…

The sentence trailed to a muted end and her head spun.

Zach *would* share custody, wouldn't he? He wouldn't try and take her child from her? Of course he wouldn't. Unless…he dated someone else in the future. Maybe things would get serious and the woman would want to play a bigger role in their child's life.

Pen's eyebrows snapped together. She didn't want their child raised by another woman. And what if that other woman ended up like Yvonne, with no scruples and a money-grubbing attitude? Zach hadn't only dated Yvonne, he'd *married* her.

"Whoa. You okay?" Zach stepped into the living room, casual attire doing nothing to dash the air of power surrounding him. Power and money. "You look…not okay."

She could imagine. If her face revealed any of her

thoughts about a future custody battle, she must resemble a gladiator readying for a fight. Pen launched into a conversation without any preempting whatsoever.

"I wanted to talk to you about custody of our baby." The words were as thick as wet sand, but she got them out.

He frowned as he came deeper into the living room and sat next to her on the couch. She set aside her phone.

"We'll share it. Obviously," she stated.

"When the time comes." His eyelids narrowed. "Your home is here, Pen. I'm in no hurry to have you gone."

"But eventually, I'll leave."

"Maybe. Maybe not."

"Zach." He'd been saying that a lot and she'd gone along, but what happened when her carriage turned into a pumpkin? "Eventually. I'll leave. I hope you won't fight me for full custody of our child."

"I'm not going to fight you for anything involving our child." He tipped his head toward the bags of clothing she'd set by the front door. "Except you keeping the purchases we made at the boutique."

"It's too much."

"Penelope." He placed his hand on her neck, his thumb sliding along her jaw as he met her eyes with his potent green stare. "I'm having a child, too. Buying for our baby, taking care of you, are the only ways I know how to participate. Let me."

His eyebrows lifted into an earnest expression and she closed her eyes. Maybe she was too emotional about…well, everything. Shaking her head, she said, "I'm sorry. I'm worrying about everything."

"Worry about one thing. What you want for dinner. And then tell me and I'll either make it or have it delivered." He stood from the couch, bending and placing a kiss on her forehead. She watched him walk out of the room, his sure, strong steps and presence making every hectic thought in her tired brain calmer.

She might not be in love with the father of her baby, but she could admit that the biggest part she'd miss about the princess treatment was going to be Zach himself.

# Sixteen

Zach had adapted to his role as CEO of Ferguson Oil easily, sliding into the slot left for him by his father like he was meant to be there all along. Kind of made him wonder if he'd been avoiding his destiny when he left for Chicago.

Which kind of made him wonder if no matter what direction he ran, he would've still ended up right back here in this very position: father-to-be of a baby boy or girl.

The night he took Penelope home from the jazz club, he'd never considered that they might someday share a child. Shortsighted? A bit. Sex equaled babies for lots of couples. But he'd been in the habit of chasing his physical desires rather than worrying about outcomes.

He rubbed eyes that were crossing to center. When he reopened them, the spreadsheet on his computer screen blurred. He redirected his gaze to the wall clock to see it was past five; another day had gotten away from him.

His assistant patched through a call. "Mr. Ferguson, it's the mayor on line three."

"It's Zach, and my brother's name is Chase," he reminded Sam, who insisted on the formality.

"Yes, sir," Sam replied. "Will you be taking the mayor's call?"

Zach shook his head at the futility and answered the line.

"Chase," he said into the phone. "What's up?"

"Were you planning on telling me about my niece or nephew?" came his brother's terse question.

Zach's eyes sank closed as he pressed his fingers into his eyelids. "Shit, Chase. I meant to tell you."

What an oversight.

"You mean before my press conference where a reporter asked if *I* was expecting a baby because you and Penelope were spotted baby shopping over the weekend? Yeah. You should've told me."

There was a twist neither Zach nor Pen had seen coming.

"The press assumed it was you who was having a baby?"

"Me and the woman on my arm at the charity event at our parents' house. She's a financial adviser and I offered to show her around." Zach could tell by his brother's grumbling that he was serious about the woman being an acquaintance. The mayor wasn't into spur of the moment or temporary relationships. For Chase, every woman on his arm had a purpose, a reason for being there.

"That photo of us was supposed to pad our public announcement of the pregnancy, not start a rumor mill about you."

He grunted at the irony. Chase was the star of the Ferguson show no matter what happened to any of them.

"Stefanie already knew." Chase's tone was clipped.

"Not on purpose. I let it slip and swore her to secrecy."

"Mom and Dad. They know. *She* had to tell me." Before Zach could make an excuse about how it'd been a busy week, his brother added, "What the hell are you doing?"

Zach straightened his back, on alert. "What's that supposed to mean?"

"Your engagement with Penelope Brand is fake. Or *was*

anyway. Has that changed?" His brother believed that relationships had beginnings and endings that were mapped out ahead of time. But Zach didn't have to think that way. He wasn't the one who'd put his balls in the public sling.

"Not that I have to explain anything to you," Zach told his brother, "but Pen was pregnant the night of your birthday party. We just didn't know it at the time."

Chase uttered a curse under his breath. "Are you planning on making it a real engagement to go along with your real future child?"

"What if I do?"

"Then I suggest you consider how long you want to keep this up."

Off his chair, Zach felt his blood pressure rise. "Come again?"

"You're not the only one involved, Zach. You'll have a child soon and you can't marry Pen because it sounds *fun*. The stakes are sky-high."

"I know that." Zach's words gritted from between his clenched teeth. "I can handle my own life. You're just worried how my actions will affect your precious career."

"Wrong. I'm reminding you because I've seen the two of you together. You're behaving like a couple. A *real* one. Has that sunk in for you yet?"

He thought it had. Until Chase pointed out he'd noticed a difference. Zach dated casually, sure, but he felt like his brother was referring to a relationship in Zach's past—way in his past. One in particular that hadn't ended well.

"I'm handling it," Zach repeated rather than broach the topic of Lonna.

"Let's start over." Chase blew out a heavy breath. "What I should've said, rather than dispense a big brother lecture, was that I'm excited for you. For our family. The first baby is a big deal."

"You're jealous you didn't get there first." Zach allowed a sideways smile when his brother chuckled.

"Yeah, you win."

But Chase's words settled in the center of Zach's chest. A baby *was* a big deal. So was an engagement. And Penelope living in his house.

"I'm taking this seriously." Zach felt the urge to clarify. After a pause, Chase spoke.

"How is she?"

"Healthy. Gorgeous. Stubborn." *Impossible*, he mentally added. "Returned every bit of the baby clothes we purchased because they were too expensive."

"You call that stubborn? I call it practical."

"Stubborn," Zach reiterated.

"Almost as stubborn as you." Chase wasn't wrong. "Way to pick 'em, brother. How about you?"

"How about me what?" He closed the spreadsheet and powered down the computer.

"How are you?"

"I'm good. I'm fine."

Chase waited, not buying the blow-off.

Zach sat back down and rested his forehead on his hand. Then he confessed something to Chase he hadn't told anyone. "I'm trying not to screw everything up for my child."

"You'll figure it out. You're not a screw-up, Zach. You try everything once, and that's not a bad thing. I'm the careful planner, and knowing what I know of Penelope, I'm guessing she's a careful planner, too."

"The *carefulest*."

"You'll find your way. You don't know how to fail. You stay on the balls of your feet and roll with the punches better than anyone I've ever known."

The vote of confidence from the man he admired most, second to Dad, meant the world to Zach. His throat thick with emotion, he couldn't even manage a muttered "Thanks." Zach wasn't the get-choked-up kind, but *damn*.

"When do you find out if I'm having a niece or a nephew?"

He smiled at his brother's use of the monikers again—if he wasn't mistaken, Chase was looking forward to being an uncle.

"Next week." Zach swept his eyes to his desk calendar to confirm.

"Tell me *first* this time."

"We'll see. Stefanie has already mentioned some gender reveal something-or-another."

Chase's reaction was a mumbled curse followed by, "Of course she did."

Zach ended the call with his brother as a quick knock came from Sam who ushered in Mara, his bubbly and completely kick-ass CFO.

"Zach." Her eyes sparkled with interest. Not in him personally—he'd never before met someone so happily married—but like she knew something he didn't. "Here are the reports you asked for."

She handed them over and then stood smiling at him. He studied her with a frown for a moment, then decided to give it up. She knew. It was evident in every jittering line of her body.

"We can't officially announce it yet, so I appreciate your discretion."

Mara clapped her hands and let out a discreet "Yay!" To his shock, she rounded the desk and gave him a quick side hug.

"I'm so thrilled for you both! When Vic and I had our baby it was exciting and scary and amazing. You're going to do great. And Penelope is so gorgeous—you'll have the prettiest baby in the world! Second to mine, of course."

Okay, that made him smile.

Mara skipped away. As she pulled the door shut, she gave him a wink in the diminishing gap and said in a stage whisper, "I won't breathe a word to anyone."

"Thanks, Mara."

She shut the door behind her and he glanced at his desk calendar where he'd jotted Pen's ultrasound with the shorthand *ult* in case of wandering eyes.

Chase was right. Zach would slide seamlessly into the role of father as well as he'd slid into CEO at Ferguson Oil. And if he had a hiccup or two along the way, Pen would be there to bail him out—planner that she was.

Smile on his face, he relaxed in his chair.

They had this.

A blur of elegance from outside the wall of her glass office windows caught Penelope's eye. She blinked once, then twice to make sure what she was seeing wasn't a mirage.

Nope.

It was Zach's mother, all right.

Pen beckoned her in and rounded her desk. "Elle. This is a surprise."

Especially since she didn't know how Elle knew where she worked. Pen's mind went to their last interaction. Elle reacted poorly to the news of the pregnancy and then Pen and Zach had sex in the woman's flower beds.

*Real classy, Pen.*

Elle clutched a large camel-colored handbag and gestured to the white leather couch. "May I sit?"

"Yes, please. I was just wrapping up." Pen sat with her, pretty sure the fluttering in her stomach wasn't her baby but nerves instead. Maybe a bit of both.

"How are you feeling?"

"Lately, much better than before."

"I'm so glad for you! When I was pregnant with Stefanie, I remember the worst morning sickness and bloating." Elle waved a hand dismissively. "If I had that with Chase and Zach, I've blocked it because all I remember is how painful the birth was." Elle let out a soft laugh and then a look of chagrin colored her features. "I didn't mean to alarm you. What a thing to say."

"It's fine, really." Pen meant it. "Believe it or not, I've heard a thing or two about childbirth being painful."

A gap in the conversation settled in the room like a third party. Pen filtered through her brain for a topic to fill the dead air. Luckily, Elle filled it for her.

"I came by to apologize for my poor reaction when you came to tell us about your bundle of joy."

"Thank you. We sprung it on you, so it's understandable."

"No. It's not. Rider's mother wanted to throttle us when she found out I was pregnant with Chase before the wedding." Elle rolled her eyes, and it wasn't hard to imagine what she'd looked like as a much younger woman railing against her future in-laws. "I've made a few mistakes with my children when it comes to their relationships. Being a matriarch is a tough business."

Pen's eyebrows climbed her forehead.

"Oh, you think the men are in charge in our family?" Elle picked at an invisible piece of lint on her skirt and smoothed her hand over the material. "We let them think that. You're a strong woman. You're an amazing addition to this family."

Guiltily, Pen looked at her lap. She felt like she was lying by letting Elle believe Pen and Zach were really together, but there was no way to unravel the lie without causing damage to everyone.

"I'm about to overstep my boundaries," Elle said next.

Pen lifted her head to meet eyes with the older woman.

"Do you know about Lonna?"

The name didn't bring forth the barest whisper of familiarity. "I don't think so."

"I don't know that Zach knows *I* know how in-deep he was with her. But I'm his mother. I knew."

Pen was dancing in dangerous territory. Part of her wanted to ask Elle about the woman from Zach's past, and another part of her felt loyalty to her fake fiancé. In the end, her curiosity won.

"Who was she?"

"They dated when Zach was in his midtwenties. She was a few years older than him and there was always something I didn't like about her. Her strength wasn't so much strength as fierce independence. Independence she cherished over our son's heart.

"Zach would sooner die than admit to us that she broke his heart, but I could tell. He was different after her. After they split, he withdrew. Then he moved to Chicago and we swore we'd never see him again."

That was why he moved to Chicago? *Away* from a woman? Rather than chasing a dream? Did that make a difference?

Yes, Pen realized.

She'd run from Chicago because of a business endeavor—because she'd needed to reform her reputation. Not because she couldn't bear to be in the same state as an ex.

"My point of telling you this isn't to worry you, Penelope." Elle placed her hand gently over Pen's, making Pen wonder if the worry showed on her brow. "My point is to let you know that I'd started believing he'd never commit to another woman. Not seriously." Elle sneered, but still managed to look elegant doing it. "We all know that Yvonne debacle was a blip of rash stupidity."

"Let's hope," Pen blurted.

"I know my son. I'm right. But here you are, and Penelope, believe me when I tell you that Zach has finally given his heart to someone. To you. He wouldn't get engaged again so soon unless he meant it."

Pen's smile was as brittle as burned paper. *Or unless he wanted to get out of hot water with his raving lunatic of an ex-wife.*

"You're going to be an amazing mother, Penelope, and you'll have a dedicated husband and father at your side. Trust me when I tell you that."

Pen blinked her eyes against forming tears and when her vision cleared, Elle was reaching into her handbag and bringing out a blue-and-white crocheted blanket.

"This was Zach's when he was a baby. His great-grandmother Edna made it for him." She handed over the soft pile of yarn, a few frayed ends tied into knots. "He'll kill me if I tell you this, but what the hell." Elle cupped her mouth with one hand and stage-whispered, "He slept with it until he was eleven."

Pen laughed and lost the battle with a few tears that streaked down her cheeks. She swiped at them quickly, and then held the blanket in both hands.

Her baby would someday be a grown man or woman and have a history—a history with two parents who pretended to be in love. A history that had to be history.

The more distance she put between this baby's birth and her living with and pretending with Zach, the better. She wasn't being fair to anyone. Not Zach's siblings or parents, or her own parents, or especially her child.

Lying was going to have a ripple effect on her baby's life and she couldn't allow that. As kind as it was for Elle to stop by and apologize and declare her son's love for Pen, there was one fact that remained unchallenged.

Zach and Pen, while they liked each other just fine,

weren't in love. They didn't share their plans for a long future, or discuss grandmothers or past heartbreaks.

They shared plans and a schedule. They shared a bed. And those things did not a love story make.

# Seventeen

Pen blew out a breath, lying on a table in the doctor's office and not feeling the least little bit relaxed. Today she and Zach would learn if they were having a son or a daughter and the anticipation was almost too much to handle.

She hadn't told Zach that his mother had stopped by to chat. Reason being, she wasn't sure how to broach the topic. The Lonna Story was his story to tell, and frankly, that he hadn't told her was…well, *telling*. Pen and Zach were in deep together. They were engaged—kinda—expecting a baby and he'd pretty much decreed that she wasn't moving out.

Yet when it came to divulging his personal past, he was silent. Which could only mean one thing. Zach had been hurt and quite possibly wasn't over the mysterious Lonna.

"How are you doing, Ms. Brand?" The doctor stepped into the room. Dr. Cho was young and beautiful, her silken black hair tied back at the base of her neck. Her kind, almond-shaped eyes swept to Zach and she nodded in greeting.

Zach promised Pen that Dr. Cho was the best in Dallas.

He'd insisted on the very best care and Pen hadn't argued. She might not relish the idea of piles of outrageous baby clothing, but she agreed that the best care for their child was the *only* care.

"I'm nervous," Pen admitted.

"Nothing to be nervous about." Dr. Cho squirted clear goo onto a flat plastic ultrasound paddle and warned it'd be cold. "How about you, Dad?"

Pen's eyes clashed with Zach's and he held her gaze while he said, "Doing just fine."

"Good."

Cold, definitely, but the shock of the chill faded as Pen searched the image on screen for her baby. And there it was. A whooshing sound of the heartbeat and what actually resembled a human being.

Incredible.

Tears pricked the corners of her eyes but accompanied a resilient smile. Zach breathed a "Wow" next to her, his gaze glued to the screen, his mouth ajar.

It was a miracle.

An unexpected, unrelenting miracle.

After a few minutes and measurements, Dr. Cho asked if they'd like to know the sex.

"Yes," Pen and Zach answered eagerly—both on the same page. This little gem had given them enough surprises.

Pen held her breath and wondered if Zach did the same. Then Dr. Cho told them the sex of their baby.

"It's incredible, isn't it?" Zach said on the ride home from the doctor's office. Hearing the heartbeat had been one thing, but seeing their child on the screen and knowing a little Ferguson would soon be entering their lives was unbelievable.

Pen was lying back against the headrest, the A/C cranked

up so high her hair blew in the air coming from the vent. August in Texas was hell. But Zach didn't mind the heat or the fact that he had to lift his voice to talk over the vent forcing out cool air. He was on cloud nine.

In spite of today's announcement ruining a particular surprise.

He pulled into the garage of his new house and rounded the car to open Pen's door for her. She wore a long white dress and heels, but her shoes were lower heeled than her normal nine-to-five wear. His favorite part of the dress was the wispy material that slitted up both sides showing peeks of her smooth calves when she walked as well as the off-the-shoulder straps that showcased not only a gorgeous collarbone but also cleavage that was going for the World's Record for holding Zach's undivided attention.

Inside he gave her the bad news. "I had a surprise planned, and now it's not as good of a surprise unless you want to leave the house for a day or two so I can fix it."

She slanted her head and narrowed one eye, her smile playful. "What'd you do?"

He shook his head in chagrin, but found his smile wasn't going anywhere, either. "You're gonna laugh."

"Now I have to know."

Here went nothing. Time to own it.

He led her through the house and upstairs to the baby's room. His designer had come in and furnished the room with a crib and dresser and changing table—the same furniture that Pen had pointed out at Love & Tumble. The style was what he preferred: clean, simple, warm. No pastels or frilly anything. His designer had insisted on beige with white crown molding running along the center of the wall, which he at first protested. She'd argued it was "the perfect blank palette ready for a splash of color" for when they found out the sex. When he'd first showed Pen, she loved it. Zach turned the knob, gave Pen one last lift of his eyebrows and pushed the door wide.

He was right about the laughing.

His surprise? Decking their child's room floor to ceiling in Dallas Cowboys paraphernalia.

"You were awfully certain we were having a boy," Pen said with a giggle as she stepped into the room.

"I was." And then the ultrasound proved him wrong. He shook his head but he didn't have a single ounce of regret about the outcome.

A daughter with Pen's gorgeous blue eyes? He'd take it. He'd have to scare off testosterone-infused boys once she was a teen, but he'd worry about that later. This was Texas. He had a shotgun.

"Zach." Pen searched the room, her eyes landing on framed posters of the players, a mobile featuring footballs and cowboy hats, and on the shelf, a signed football in a case. He'd gone all out. The mother of his child faced him.

Fingers shoved in his front pockets, he explained with a shrug. "Maybe she's a Cowboys fan."

"Clearly you're one."

"Honey, I'm in Dallas. I'm a Cowboys fan." He took a look around for himself. He was pretty damn proud of the cool stuff he'd picked out. "We can tone it down a little."

"A little?" She lifted a blanket thrown over the crib that resembled a football field—green with the yardage marked in white. "Really?"

"I wanted to surprise you. You're surprised. Mission accomplished."

"Yeah. I'm surprised, all right." She rested her hand on the crib and palmed her belly, not yet as big as it would be. He felt a firm tug in his chest. "I'm grateful that it's a girl after your mother told me how big you two boys were."

"When did she tell you that?" She hadn't mentioned talking with his mother.

"Last week. She stopped by my office."

A pair of chairs flanked a side table with a lamp and, yes, a Cowboys lampshade, and Pen sat in one and beckoned for him to sit in the other one.

She opened the side table drawer as he sat, coming out with his crocheted baby blanket he hadn't seen in decades.

"She dropped this off for our daughter."

"It's blue." He took it, then gestured around the room. "Matches the theme."

"She apologized for her reaction. I know she wanted to smooth things over. She wasn't proud of herself. I didn't hold it against her, though."

"No, you wouldn't," he said. "You take issues on. You don't push them off on others." And just so Pen didn't think he meant it any other way, he amended, "That's a compliment."

"I know it is." She inhaled and held her breath for a few seconds and that tug in his chest turned uncomfortable. What else did his mother say when she stopped by?

"Is there more?"

Pen released the breath she'd been holding. "Elle said... Well, she brought up a woman named Lonna. Then she told me she never thought you'd fall in love again."

His shoulders stiffened. He kneaded the super-soft blanket in his hands, avoiding looking at Pen. His mother knew about Lonna, of course, but what gave her the right to barge in on his fiancée and offer her opinion on his heart, for God's sake?

"I bring it up because your mom thinks we're in love."

That lifted his head. He watched her carefully. "She doesn't know anything about Lonna." The edge in his voice forced him from his seated position. He dropped the baby blanket on the chair and paced to the door.

"Did you love her? For real?"

Anger stopped him in his tracks. As if he was only capable of "unreal" relationships? His eyes went to the stairs leading to the front door, but he didn't run away from problems any longer. He ran toward them. He ran back to Texas, ran headfirst into a Vegas wedding to prove to himself he was "fine" and ran straight to Pen when she delivered news most men would've run *from*.

He faced Pen, leaned on the jamb and shoved his fingers back into his pockets. She lifted her hand to push a lock of hair from her face, and the diamond ring he'd slipped onto her finger glinted in the sunlight streaming in through the Cowboys-blue curtains.

Zach was a lot of things but he wasn't a liar. So, he told Pen the truth. "Yes."

She took the news well, simply nodding. But she wasn't done.

"Did you go to Chicago because she broke up with you?"

In part, but he saw no reason to explain himself. "Yes."

Pen took that news well, too, but had one final question for him. "Are you over her?"

That question required no hesitation. "Yes."

If he wasn't mistaken, that was a relieved breath Pen just blew out. "Your mother believes we're in love, Zach. She thinks this is our happily-ever-after and I couldn't correct her."

"You and my mother had quite the conversation."

"I didn't know she was going to go into all of that. And I honestly wouldn't ask you to clarify any of this if it wasn't for what lies before us."

That statement settled into the room like an elephant.

"Which is what?" She kept making decisions and telling him last. He didn't like it.

"When we announce the sex of the baby at our surprise shower, we should also announce that we won't be getting married. Hear me out." She held a hand in front of her as if to silence him, probably because he'd filled his chest full of air to protest how they didn't have to do anything. Before she said more, he managed to blow out one question in an infuriated tone.

"What surprise shower?"

"I'm guessing that's why your sister asked me to clear a spot on my calendar in two weeks for a 'cake-tasting appointment.'" Pen used air quotes. "It sounded very... suspicious. Plus, she asked that we tell no one the sex of the baby—not even her."

"The gender reveal," he mumbled. "She'd mentioned she wanted to host one and then never said another word." He'd hoped she would forget about it. He should've known better.

Zach swiped a hand over his forehead, frustrated. Why the hell was everyone arranging parties around him, talking about him like he was a backdrop? Like he was a store mannequin. He was the one who arranged his life. It was *his* life, dammit.

"Before you blow up, let me finish."

He gave her the most patient glare he could manage, aware of the heat warming his face.

"We thank everyone for the gifts. And we hold hands—I'll take this off first—" she waggled her ring finger "—and then we'll let everyone know that while we'll be living separate lives we are very much going to raise our daughter together. Everyone will be so overjoyed to learn that we're having a girl that I'm betting they won't even focus on the fact that we're announcing a breakup."

"We're not breaking up."

"Zach." She stood, her hand protectively over her middle. "We're not in love. You can't believe our sex-soaked relationship isn't going to fall apart. There's nothing holding us together except our attraction for each other. What about when that fades?"

"What if it doesn't?" He saw no reason to put a head-stone on what they had. Not yet. They had time.

"Come on. We've both been in relationships. Did the infatuation stage last forever?"

He ground his back teeth together. "We're not breaking up. Wear the ring on Sunday. We're not doing this."

"You can't run from this forever."

"I'm not running from anything." To illustrate his point, he stepped deeper into the room and stood in front of her. "I'm here, right in front of you. And that's where I'm staying until I decide. Not you. Not my mother. Not my family. Not the duchess of fucking Dallas. *Me*."

# Eighteen

Pen smoothed cocoa butter over her stomach, determined to avoid stretch marks at any cost. She'd read that moisturizing helped, and she'd started her nightly routine almost right after she found out she was pregnant.

As she ran her hand over her rounding belly, she considered the warring feelings inside her.

Frustration with Zach. Frustration with herself. Amusement for how he'd decorated the room for a son. Admiration at the way he was determined to be a good father. And the biggest: so much love for her unborn baby, she was ready to burst with it.

If she was being honest with herself, that love was inching closer and closer to Zach himself. Encircling him and swallowing him up in it. But she couldn't confuse her love for their daughter for romantic love with him. They weren't the same.

When she'd asked him about Lonna, he'd confirmed one of Pen's biggest fears. Falling in love meant you could lose it all. And for all of Zachary Ferguson's bliss-chasing, he'd drawn a very distinct boundary around true love.

Romantic love had no place in his plans. Not any longer. Not since Lonna.

It was unfair.

Unfair because for the first time in her life, Pen feared she was starting to fall in love…with a man incapable of loving her back.

"Hey," came a soft rumble from the doorway.

Pen spun the lid on the lotion and set it on her nightstand. "Hey."

Zach's hooded eyes and sideways smile had replaced his flattened mouth and ruddy complexion. After their conversation in the baby's room, he'd mumbled something about working and shut himself in his office. She hadn't seen him since.

They weren't fighting. Not really. They just had very different views of the way things were.

For Penelope, she needed to leave before she fell for him and couldn't pull away as easily. For Zach, there was no hurry because falling for her wasn't a remote possibility.

Perhaps acknowledging that was what hurt most.

"I overreacted," he said, walking into the room. "Did you eat?"

"All I do is eat." She gave him a tired smile. "Did you?"

"Just ate a sandwich."

"Dinner at nine-thirty."

"Bachelor," he explained.

Her heart squeezed at the word. That was the problem. Even with his pregnant fiancée in the house, Zach still considered himself single.

His eyes searched the room before landing on her again. "I don't want you to move out. I don't want to miss anything."

She had to close herself off from the sincerity in his voice. There was a bigger picture—the baby girl residing in her growing belly.

"You won't miss anything," she promised. "My stomach is going to get larger, my ankles more swollen, my temper more out of control. It might even get as bad as yours."

He shook his head in agreement. "I'm sorry about that."

He sat on the bed and lifted the delicate edge of her short cotton nightie, skimming the lace hemline up to expose her thighs. When one large, warm hand landed on her skin, she found it suddenly hard to breathe.

This was such a bad idea. Sealing her tumultuous feelings with sex wouldn't bring her closer to a resolution but take her further from it.

"How tired are you?" His green eyes sought hers.

Who was she fooling? Could she really convince herself she wasn't in love with him? Not when he looked at her the way he looked at her now. Not when he was watching the monitor at Dr. Cho's office with rapt attention and pride. And not when he touched her—especially when he touched her.

Zach claimed her as his that night in the mayor's mansion. She thought then it'd been about sex and physical love, but now she realized that claim was staked deep in her heart and soul. And the proof of it was incubating in her womb.

"Not too tired," she whispered, her eyes glazing over with staunch acceptance. She'd rather have him than not—even if it drove another stake into her lovesick heart.

He leaned forward to place a kiss on her bared shoulder. His tongue flicked under the strap, then dragged up her neck, giving her all of his attention like no other woman in his past or present who'd commanded it.

Warmth flooded her tummy, the flutter between her legs having everything to do with a million jettisoning hormones. She buried her lovelorn emotions into a deep, dark corner of her being and focused on the present. Focused on giving in to her physical needs—and riding Zach like the cowboy she once thought he was.

Her nightie was gone in a whisper as he lifted it over her head and tossed it to the floor. He smoothed his hand along her swollen belly, moving to her breasts next.

Lying back, she closed her eyes as his amazing mouth skated over one nipple then the other. The sensations assaulting her brought an end to the warring emotions in her chest and the thoughts littering her brain. And when his hands moved between her thighs and stroked, every ounce of her attention went there. Nothing felt as natural, as all-consuming, as making love with Zachary Ferguson.

His lips were at home on her body—*anywhere* on her body. Every inch of her belonged to him.

She reached for his T-shirt, tugging at it weakly. "Off."

"Yes, ma'am." There was the drawl she loved so much. He whipped off his shirt to reveal his chest and once again, breathing became difficult. Was it any wonder she let herself indulge in what she thought would only be one night with him? Was it any wonder she indulged now?

She took a page from Zach's book and released her worries of responsibility and the future, letting go like dandelion fluff on a thick summer's breeze. She focused on his physicality instead.

His broad shoulders, round like he spent the day hauling hay bales instead of sliding a mouse across his desk. His biceps, straining as he shoved his jeans to his knees. Thick thighs, covered in coarse, dark-blond hair and leading down to sturdy feet. All of him was gorgeous. And for the moment, hers.

"You keep looking at me like that, Penelope Brand, and I'm not going to last a minute." His green eyes sparked in challenge. His dimple dented his cheek as he shucked his boxers.

She embraced the idea of behaving like an out-of-control teenager. Pen had always been drawn to stability...until she'd moved to Dallas. Until she'd laid eyes on Zach. He made her embrace the moment. Made her live in right now.

His hot skin came in contact with hers and she could've sworn she felt sparks dance on her skin. He stripped her panties down her legs and once she was naked, pressed every part of himself against her.

She moaned. He was perfect.

He was hers. In a superficial, temporary sense, but nonetheless *hers*.

"Remember to pretend to be surprised," Penelope told Zach as they stepped up to the entryway of the hotel. At the top floor stood the Regal Room, their destination. A popular choice for parties of the upscale variety. She'd never been, but knew about it, and had recommended it for some of her more elite clients in Dallas.

"Should I add clutching my heart for effect?" Zach leaned over to ask, his voice low. Then pressed the button for the elevator.

"That might be poor form since Rider will be there."

"Oh, right." But his smirk hinted that he'd already figured that out.

This was the way things had been in the two weeks since their argument that ended in bed. They'd ended up in bed several times since and each interaction was like the last. Penelope fell deeper in love with him, and Zach maintained his position as kind, caring father of her child.

It should be enough. She wanted to be the woman for whom it would be enough. Where his loyalty and limited offerings would be substantial for as long as they lasted.

But they weren't.

It was the wrong time to broach the topic, but she'd been unable to summon the bravery to do it before. Now or never, as the saying went. So while the elevator zipped them to their destination, she blurted, "I'm going to announce that the wedding is on hold when I announce that we're having a daughter."

His steely glare matched the hardness of his jaw. "Penelope."

"I'm not asking permission." She lifted her chin. It was past time she pulled the plug on the relationship that was rapidly eating away at her heart.

"This isn't—" he started, but the elevator doors swished open at that moment.

They stepped out of the elevator and were greeted by a sea of smiling faces, very few of which she recognized.

Collectively, a shout rose in the room. "Congratulations!"

The "surprise" baby shower wasn't pink and blue or even green and yellow. The palette was a sophisticated blend of white and gold, right down to the confetti now littering the floor. Balloons tied with gold-and-black ribbon were suspended from the main table, which boasted flutes of champagne and an array of tapas displayed on elegant platters.

The banner draping the back of the room was white with gold metallic cursive lettering reading, "It's a baby!"

A few flashes from cameras snapped as Stefanie broke off from the crowd and enveloped Pen into a warm hug. Pen held on a beat longer than she expected. Ending the engagement with Zach also would mean distancing herself from his family, and she was going to miss Stef when she left.

"We're very surprised," Pen said, including Zach, who stood at her side like a wall. She quirked an eyebrow at him and his mouth pulled into a tight smile for the benefit of their guests. Yes, probably her timing wasn't the best on telling him her plans.

Stef hugged her brother next. "I know you hate surprises, Zach, but try to lighten up."

"I'll try," came his gruff response.

"So, I lied about this being a cake-tasting," Stefanie said, gesturing to a round table off to the side, "but we do have cake."

Chase, Elle and Rider emerged from the crowd next to deliver hugs and welcomes. Elle, in particular, was notably excited.

"Granddaughter or grandson?" she asked Pen conspiratorially. "One blink for a girl, two for a boy."

"No! Absolutely not." Stefanie positioned herself between her mother and Penelope. "Nine o'clock is the announcement, and not a moment before."

"Nine o'clock," Pen said, her own smile faltering. A quick glance to Zach confirmed that his was gone completely. "Uh, Stefanie, this room is amazing. The party, the food. Everything looks incredible."

She had to focus on her appreciation for what Stef had done, and pray that she could somehow dismantle the engagement and announce that she was expecting a girl without ruining the vibe of the party, or undoing Stef's hard work. She hoped Stef would understand and forgive her.

Stefanie put a hand on her hip and gestured like a model on *The Price is Right*. "I did it myself. I mean, yeah, okay, I had a team helping, but the ideas came out of my brain."

"Well, it's incredible," Pen said, meaning it. "If I need a party of any kind in the future, I'm coming to you."

"Sparkling grape juice." Stef plucked a flute from a waiter's tray. "I put little purple ribbons on the nonalcoholic drinks for you." Pen accepted her bubbly drink, a lump settling in her throat. She forced it down and called up her party smile again.

"Come see what else I have planned." Stef wrapped her arm around Pen's and led her away. Pen gladly took the reprieve—anything to keep Zach from bringing up the conversation she'd railroaded him with in the elevator.

He was easy to avoid over the next two hours given that

Stef had filled the evening with games—albeit sophisticated ones.

"We're adults," Stef had said with committed seriousness. "I'm not melting chocolate bars in diapers, or asking guests to guess your belly width with lengths of toilet paper."

"Thank you for that." As sisters went, Zach hit the jackpot. Pen ignored the feeling of melancholy that swept over her. No matter where Pen and Zach ended up, Stef would always be their daughter's aunt. Pen would hold on to that.

Dessert was a selection of miniature cakes or cupcakes, and cake pops on sticks, all decorated in white fondant with edible gold sprinkles. Pen sampled the sweets, and drank down another sparkling grape juice as she played coy about her baby's sex. She'd lost count of how many times she'd told someone "Sorry. The announcement is at nine."

About twenty minutes before the evening's most anticipated hour, she found an opening and slipped away from the crowd. Zach and Chase were speaking to their grandparents' friends and since Pen had already spoken with Rudy and Ana, she knew their conversation could last well past the time Pen and Zach were to take the mic.

August in Illinois was hot, but nothing like Texas hot. There wasn't much fresh air to be had on the balcony, but it was private, and she desperately needed a break from the fake smiles. Her cheeks were starting to ache.

Sweltering heat, even this late in the day, blanketed her bare shoulders. Hot, yes, but quiet. She rested her hands on the railing and looked out at the city beyond. Of all the goals for a fresh start she'd made when she left Chicago, none of them had involved a giant engagement ring on her finger, a billionaire fiancé and a baby due by Christmas.

The phrase "Man plans and God laughs" flitted through her brain, but she could admit she was laughing with Him. True, she hadn't planned any of this, but she was also so incredibly grateful to be pregnant—something she likely never would've planned.

Her eyes tracked to the windows and she spotted Zach, dark slacks accentuating his height, button-down pale blue shirt unable to hide his muscular build.

Her heart did what it'd been doing for a few weeks now, and gave an almost painful squeeze. She'd fallen for him. Head over heels. Ass over teakettle. Hook, line and sinker.

No matter how hard she tried to compartmentalize her feelings from the relationship, they managed to glob together into one four-letter word.

Love.

Whenever he walked into a room, she lit up. She sank into him whenever he pulled her close for a kiss, like she could fuse her very being with his. But all of this oneness and overwhelming feeling of rightness wasn't shared by her betrothed.

Zach offered support, loyalty and means but not love. Love for his daughter? Most definitely. But for Pen, his caring stopped at friendship, and some days before that. Since she'd learned about his ex, Lonna, it was like she could visibly spot each and every boundary line he drew. Those boundaries were intentional—whether he was aware he was doing it or not.

He took care of her, provided for her every need and was adamant about not missing a moment of his daughter's life. Zach made love to Penelope with a single-minded focus on her pleasure, and if she were a fresh-faced twentysomething, she might mistake his actions for love.

But as a thirtysomething who'd been around the proverbial block a few times, she knew better.

He gave and gave and gave…everything but his heart. That part of his anatomy was walled off so solidly, she hadn't managed to breach the outer layer. And if she noticed the distance between them—her besotted, and him casually comfortable—so would his family, eventually. And so would their daughter.

Pen had made a lot of decisions recently—big, sweeping life decisions—and the number-one decision she'd made was to put her daughter first.

She would sacrifice anything—her job, her home, her very lifestyle—to give her daughter what she needed. She'd even sacrifice what she had with Zach. And that was saying something as it was the first time she'd truly been in love.

In the quiet, dark corners of her mind lay a flickering hope that Zach might come around. That he might open up and learn to love her. The optimist in her thought he might, but the realist in her couldn't risk what it meant if he never did.

She wasn't waiting around for him to decide to love her. Not with their daughter watching. And that was why she also couldn't let the engagement continue. Sure, there'd be a stir of interest and a touch of gossip, but she could spin their interest toward their daughter. She was the reason for the relationship anyway. Most of it.

*Some of it*, Pen sadly corrected.

Regardless, percentages didn't matter. Penelope didn't want her love for Zach to grow bitter and stale after years of not being returned. More important, she didn't want her daughter to witness her mother's feelings for her father crumbling into dust.

Their daughter would have a mother and a father who cared about one another, who respected one another. Who loved her with all their hearts. And that was going to have to be enough. For all of them.

Zach must've escaped the clutches of his grandparents' friends, because he now stood at the balcony door with Chase. They were talking, looking very much like brothers with the same strong lines of their backs and hands buried in pants pockets.

Zach chose that moment to look over and catch her eye. He didn't smile, but held her gaze with a smoldering one of his own. His longish hair was tickling the collar of his shirt, his full mouth flinching in displeasure.

As magnanimous as she'd sounded in her own ears moments ago, Pen's heart throbbed with the need to satisfy her own desires rather than her daughter's.

She only wished loving Zach satisfied both.

# Nineteen

Zach took in Pen on the balcony, observing her as he had when he'd first laid eyes on her. A white lace dress hugged every inch of her, from exquisite breasts to shapely hips. The graceful line of her neck led to pale blue eyes that could stop a man dead in his tracks—and full lips that had stopped his heart for at least one beat on several occasions.

Now, knowing her the way he did, he still appreciated her physical attributes, but what he mostly saw was beauty. Beauty in a dress that showed off what women at the party kept referring to as her "baby bump." Beauty, decadently outlined in white lace, snatching away first place from the breathtaking sunset behind her.

Beauty that was all woman.

That was all his.

*Was.* That word punched him in the solar plexus so hard, the room around him seemed to cant. He'd been possessive over her since the beginning, not wanting to let her go.

And now she was going.

Pen played with a few strands of her hair that had come

down from an elegant twist at the back of her neck, her other hand resting on the railing. Her red shoes had tall, spindly heels, in spite of how many times he'd asked her not to wear them.

Throughout the evening, his flared temper had died down. His thoughts, while meeting guests who were his parents' friends more than his, kept returning to Penelope and his unborn child. His future.

Not only his future.

*Theirs.*

He envisioned his daughter's birthdays. Holidays. Family vacations.

As he'd glimpsed each fractured bit, he realized it was an impermanent, if not impossible, future.

Because Penelope was backing away from him.

There was no escaping how much she'd infiltrated his life in a short period of time. Zach barely recognized himself from the man who'd smoothly followed her back to her apartment for what was supposed to be a hell of a one-night stand.

And tonight it was ending.

Pen turned and caught his gaze, only to face the city lights once again. Over his shoulder, Chase spoke, and Zach wrenched his attention away from her.

"You've done it, haven't you?" Chase asked, expression serious.

Zach threw back his champagne and wished it was beer. He had a good idea of what his brother was referring to, but damned if he was about to guess.

"The pretending has become real."

"The pretending," Zach said, relinquishing his empty glass to a nearby table, "is about to come to an end." At Chase's frown, Zach explained in a low voice so no one could overhear. "The engagement is over."

"Why?"

"Why?" Zach practically spat the word. "Weren't you the one advising me not to get in too deep because I thought this would be 'fun'?"

"Yes."

Their silent standoff ended with Chase explaining.

"It's become clear to me that she means a lot more than a good time to you. So again, I ask, why?"

Zach blinked, his brother's stern visage blurring as Stef's voice crackled over the speakers in the room.

"Five minutes until we learn whether I have a niece or a nephew!"

The crowd clapped, and there were a few titters of excitement.

"If you don't know, you'd better figure it out in five minutes," Chase recommended. Zach followed his brother's gaze to Penelope and the world wasn't just canting but *swimming*.

"If you were going to succumb to a woman—" Chase nodded his head in greeting when Pen turned to look at them "—that'd be the one to lie down for."

"I've tried," Zach mumbled through numb lips. She was the one ending it. He was the one who wanted to keep her close.

"Try harder." One more cocky tilt of his lips and Chase was gone.

Rather than make another excuse that he had tried, Zach considered that maybe he hadn't. That maybe a fake engagement wasn't enough for the woman who spelled out future with a capital *F*.

*Like the* F *dangling from the bracelet on her wrist.*

*His.* Pen was still his. She needed to know that the engagement he'd thrown out as a distraction had become real for him. That was what Chase had meant when he'd told Zach to try harder.

Decisively, and damn that felt better than uncertainty,

Zach slid the balcony door aside and stepped out into the heated air with his fiancée.

"Is it time?" Her tone was neutral, her body held in check. She was ready to unravel everything at that microphone, and Zach had about two minutes to stop her from doing it.

"We have to talk."

Her fair eyebrows lifted. "Didn't I get in trouble for saying something similar to you before?"

He didn't break stride, reaching her in a few steps and cradling her elbow. The deep hues of a purple-and-pink sky had given way to ink-blue.

"We have to talk about the announcement," he said, throat tight, sweat beading on his forehead, and *not* from the summer temperatures. He wasn't at the mercy of his nerves—not ever. Not when he proposed to Lonna years ago, or when he proposed to his ex-wife in Vegas, but now that he was faced with proposing to Penelope, there was no other word for it.

He was nervous.

Not only did he have no idea if she'd say yes, but he was almost positive she'd say no.

He needed her not to say no.

Not just for him. For herself—for their daughter. For all of them.

"Penelope Brand." He cleared his throat, the seriousness in his tone causing her lips to softly part. He lifted her left hand and thumbed the engagement ring he'd placed there on a whim. Or some kind of mental dare. Now that he knew her inside and out, and knowing she'd bear his first child, he knew better.

It might have started out as a whim, but now? He meant it.

"I know what we have started out as fake, but over the past several months, having you at my side, being with you day in and day out… The announcement that you were pregnant, learning we're expecting a daughter…" He trailed off, the magnitude of what they'd shared stealing his breath. "The reality is, Penelope—" he locked his gaze on her startled one "—this isn't fake. Not anymore."

"Zach…"

"Let me finish."

His eyebrows closed over his nose in concentration as the second hand rapidly ticked away precious minutes. Quickly, he reordered his thoughts. Now to deliver them in the most genuine, efficient way possible.

"We're good together," he told her. "Not only in the bedroom. As a unit. We're learning our way, and I probably have further to go than you do, but we're committed to the same important goal. Raising our child surrounded by so much love she'll never want for anything."

Pen's eyes filled and she blinked. In her expression, Zach saw hope—hope that gave him the courage to continue.

"I love our daughter with a fierceness I didn't know was possible. I care about you, Penelope. I don't want to end what we have because your PR timeline says we should."

Her expression blanked. He couldn't tell if she was shocked or in agreement, or if she felt equal measures of both.

He thumbed her diamond engagement ring so that it was centered on her finger. Then he looked her dead in the eye and forced past his constricting throat, "Will you marry me? For real this time."

In the space of one heartbeat, then two, Pen only stared. Then her lips firmed, tears streaked down her cheeks and she tugged her hand away from his.

Pen swiped her tears away almost angrily as the city melted in her watery vision. She sucked in a gulp of air, calling upon her very strong constitution for assistance. Her heart was cracked when she'd arrived.

Zach had just shattered it.

He moved to comfort her instantly, his wide, warm hands on her hips, strong chest flanking her back.

"Pen. I know how this sounds. I know you think it's too late…"

But that wasn't it. This wasn't about timing.

*I love our daughter. I care about you.*

He couldn't have been any clearer about the division of his feelings—about the clearly marked boundary lines—during his proposal.

She'd believed when he'd started his speech that miraculously, she'd broken through. That during the course of this party, Zach had seen the light.

*I love our daughter. I care about you.*

His was a marriage proposal of convenience the first time, and now it was one of merged interests. It hadn't come from his heart and soul. A long time ago she'd convinced herself she didn't need romantic love. But now that she was looking at Zach, her heart twisting like a wrung-out cloth, she was certain about two things.

One, she loved him, and two, she refused to enter a marriage where Zach was only half in.

He might never leave her, cheat on her, or abandon her, but he also wouldn't ever love her the way she deserved to be loved.

And she *deserved* love.

He stood behind her, his breath on her ear when he bent forward. "I know I'm springing this on you, but this is the best plan. We can have each other, have our daughter, have our lives together."

She closed her eyes against the surge of longing in her chest. There was a part of her, and it wasn't small, that wanted to turn in the circle of his arms and say *yes*. Give in to the idea that Zach might someday love her the way she loved him.

But that was a fairy tale. Her life wasn't glass slippers and godmothers. It was pumpkins and practicality.

She turned and faced him, shoulders back, chin tipped to take in his handsome face, and spoke in her most practical voice. "We can't be this selfish because we like to have sex, Zach."

His head jerked on his neck like she'd slapped him instead of spoken.

"What the hell's that supposed to mean?" he bit out.

"It means exactly what I said. We have a child to think about."

"A child who needs both of her parents around," he said, his voice escalating, "not one at a time at prearranged intervals."

"Our child needs parents who love her and love each other. If we can't fulfill both of those bare minimums, then we have nothing more to talk about."

"Marriage isn't good enough for you?" Zach's cheeks reddened. "Marriage *and* sex isn't good enough for you?" His voice was measured and low, but anger outlined every word.

"Is it good enough for you?"

"Marriage and sex and you? Damn straight it's good enough. What more do you want from me, Penelope?"

She parted her lips to tell him there was so, *so* much more to want. So much more to marriage apart from sex and sharing a house. She and Zach could be so much more than parents. What about when their daughter was raised and out of the house? What about Penelope's *own* life beyond being a mother? What about that deep, committed love she'd seen in her parents' lives? Didn't he want that?

"The original agreement was to untangle these knots *before* our baby was born. And that's what we're doing."

She started for the balcony door, but Zach caught her upper arm and tugged her back.

In his face, she saw a plethora of emotion. Pain. Fear. Anger. Hope.

As per his usual, he went with his standby: demanding.

"I can't let you do that. I'm far from done exploring what we have. Sharing what we've built."

She shook out of his grip. "What we *have* is built on a lie and an accident!"

The moment she lifted her voice to shout the accusation, his eyes slid over her shoulder and the sound of low, casual chatter filtered out onto the balcony.

Reason being, Stefanie Ferguson stood at the threshold to the balcony, door open wide. Her eyes welled with unshed tears, betrayal radiating off her strong, petite form.

"Stefanie," Pen started, but Stef steeled her spine and looked, not to Penelope, but to Zach for answers.

"Is that true?" Stef asked him.

Behind her, onlookers peered out, eyebrows raised, mouths forming *O*s of curiosity. Stef shut the door behind her and stepped onto the patio, crossing her arms over her midsection.

"What lie?" she asked.

"Stef," Pen tried again, but the younger woman stood in front of her brother. Zach, who'd released Pen the moment Stefanie appeared, shoved his hands into his pockets.

"Penelope and I are discussing something very important. Go inside and we'll be in soon."

"Tell me what lie and I'll leave you to it," Stef said.

"I said—"

"The engagement isn't real," Pen blurted. Zach's jaw clenched and he shot Pen a look showcasing both his outrage and feelings of betrayal. Well, too bad. She felt betrayed, too.

Pen took her eyes off him to comfort her almost-future-sister-in-law, who looked thoroughly heartbroken.

"Zach made up the engagement when Yvonne interrupted Chase's birthday party," Pen said softly. "He needed a distraction."

"And you agreed." Stef's voice was steel, similar to the tone her brother had used many times before.

"I agreed to help him, yes." Pen thrust her chin forward. She hadn't done anything wrong.

"And the pregnancy?" Mortification colored Stef's features as she swept her eyes to Pen's belly. "Is it real?"

"Yes." Pen let out a gusty sigh. "God. Yes, Stefanie. I'd never lie about that. I was pregnant the night of Chase's birthday party, but didn't know it."

Stef's sigh of relief was short-lived. "You lied to me." She swung her gaze from Pen to include Zach. "Both of you."

"It started out as a lie to distract from Yvonne, yes," Zach said. "But things between Pen and me have developed since then." He fastened his eyes on Penelope, but spoke to his sister. "I proposed to Pen right before you walked out here."

The warm breeze lifted Stefanie's bangs from her forehead. She tightened her arms around her middle and shook her head.

"I don't think your proposal went over well." Stef backed to the door. "I came out here to tell you we're ready for the announcement about the baby…" Inside a sea of curious faces studied the scene beyond the wide windows. Pen and Zach and Stef must look like a dramatic silent movie from their guests' vantage point. "Now it seems you owe your guests an explanation.

"Tell them the truth, Zach," Stef said. "It's the least you could've done for me." She pulled open the door but before she went inside, skewered Pen with, "I expected it from him. Not from you."

Once she was inside, Chase pushed out the door next and angled his head at his brother.

"Excuse me." Penelope bumped past Chase's suited arm and darted through the crowd. Zach called her name, but when she peeked over her shoulder, Chase was blocking the door and giving advice she knew Zach didn't want to hear.

"Let her go."

# Twenty

Zach muscled past his brother. Or tried anyway. Chase, despite his suit and community standing, pushed *back*.

He banded an arm around Zach, which might look like he was consoling his younger brother, but felt more like he was attempting to crush Zach's ribs until they audibly snapped.

Through his teeth, Chase said, "Hold it together," as he shut the door to the balcony behind them. "We're outside having a brotherly chat."

Chase released him and pulled his shoulders back and Zach mirrored his stance. Inside family and friends dashed concerned looks to the balcony and then in the direction Penelope had left.

"You have thirty seconds. I'm not going to stand out here when I should be going after her."

"Stefanie went after her. Didn't you see?" Chase replied calmly. Years of experience in the public eye had made him adept at handling a crisis situation with ease. "If Pen wanted to talk to you, she'd still be standing on this balcony. Everyone inside is waiting for an announcement. Granted, they got one, but it wasn't the one they were expecting."

Zach thrust his hand into his hair. Of course it hadn't been what they were expecting. Pen's reaction to his proposal hadn't been what *he* was expecting.

"Your options," Chase continued, "are to either leave and let the gossip begin. Or stay and offer a generic explanation."

"Like what?"

"If it were me? I'd apologize with no more explanation than a 'my fault.'" Chase demonstrated with his hands in surrender pose.

"*My* fault," Zach growled. "*My fault?* It's my fault for asking Penelope to marry me? For asking the woman carrying my baby to stay with me the rest of our lives?"

"Lower your voice."

"You're as bad as the rest of them, Chase. I don't give a fuck about public opinion or what anyone in that room needs."

"Yes, that's clear." Chase reprimanded in an irritatingly calm tone. "You only care about one person. *You*."

That was it. He'd had it. Had it with trying to do the right thing and being crucified for it.

"You know what?" Zach shouldered by Chase and gripped the handle to the door. "Tell them whatever the hell you want."

"Penelope! Wait."

Pen paused on the sidewalk, surprised that Stefanie had followed her down. Stef had been clear upstairs that she didn't appreciate being left in the dark.

"Where are you going?" the younger woman called as she clipped to a stop next to Pen.

"You were right in there. You deserved to know. I'm sorry I didn't tell you. I couldn't."

"You should be. I'm mad at you and my idiot brother for keeping a secret this huge from me. I kept your pregnancy to myself! I could've kept this quiet, too." Stefanie stepped closer, kindness in her eyes. "But no matter how mad I am, I'd still give you a ride home."

Pen folded her arms over her middle, the reality of her situation settling in. She didn't have a home…only the home she shared with Zach. "I don't want to go home."

Not tonight. Maybe never again. This was as good of a break as any. Her leaving had always been inevitable. From the first time she spotted Zach in Chicago, to the jazz club, to the morning he kissed her goodbye, some part of her knew that holding on to him would be like trying to hold on to the wind.

Maybe getting it over with would allow her to heal quickly.

She hoped.

"I won't ask you to choose between me and your brother," Pen told Stef, because she refused to be unfair.

"I'm not *choosing.*" Stefanie dug through her clutch. "I'm helping out a friend. If that makes Zach mad, so be it."

Stefanie approached the valet with her ticket. "We're in a hurry."

"Yes, ma'am," the valet replied with a hat-tip. Then he ran—yes, *ran*—to get the car.

Sadly, not fast enough.

This time when Penelope heard her name, it was Zach. He slowed his jog when he was close, brow pinched and fists bunched.

"I'm taking her home with me," Stefanie stated.

"No, you're not."

Stef turned on him. "Yes. I am."

"Pen." In his eyes, Penelope saw the plea. A dab of pain that hadn't been there before. But she couldn't open up again, not after what it took to get to this point.

"I have nothing more to discuss, Zach," Pen announced sadly. "You offered me everything and nothing at the same time."

His mouth froze open for a moment before clacking shut. Baring his teeth, he said, "I offered you everything I could."

She swallowed past a thick throat as the valet pulled Stef's car to the curb. Through a watery, sad smile, she nodded. "I know. And it's not enough."

Zach, arms folded, watched one of the movers walk the last of Penelope's boxes downstairs before loading the box into a moving truck.

He wasn't one for admitting defeat, but with Penelope standing in the hallway, notebook in hand as she checked off a list, it was clear they were over.

"What about the baby stuff?" the other mover asked, pointing to the room behind Zach.

Pen turned, her white summer dress rounded at the front, her heeled sandals reasonably high for a change.

"Yes," Zach answered at the same time Penelope said, "No."

Their gazes clashed, and in her pale blue eyes, he saw both challenge and loss. Or maybe he felt it.

"Take it," he told her.

"You'll need it," she said with a head-shake.

"I can buy more." He could replace every single thing in this house with a phone call, save one. The blonde across from him on the landing.

He'd tried contacting her for the past few days, but after the one night she slept at Stef's, he hadn't been able to reach her. Even Pen's office had been dark when he stopped by.

Then, this morning she'd texted him to ask if he'd be home. Foolishly, he'd believed she was coming by to reconcile. Instead, she'd shown up driving ahead of a moving truck.

So this was it.

She'd made up her mind. She was leaving.

"I can buy more, too, Zach. I have time before she's born. And anyway, I'm not sure how much of the furniture I can fit in my apartment."

His chest tightened as his eyes dipped to Pen's stomach. He was losing…everything. And it flat-out pissed him off.

"Are we going to talk about this?" he all but shouted. A mover leaned on the wall outside the bedroom door to watch. Oh, hell no. Zach curled his lip when he addressed him. "Get the hell out of my house."

He went, ambling down the stairs, and bitching to his friend who stood on the porch. But both men stayed outside.

Zach turned back to Pen. "Well?"

"Well, what? There's nothing to talk about." She gestured with her notebook. "I've decided. Luckily, my landlady loves me and ushered me into the first available two-bedroom she had."

"You had the space you needed here." He widened his arms to encompass the massive house he now lived in alone.

"I never asked for this," she replied. He wished she would've yelled. Her maintaining her composure made him wonder if she cared about him at all.

"There are arrangements to be made," he growled, hating the loss of control, the feeling of spinning out of it. "Decisions about our daughter."

"Yes." She flipped to the back of the notebook, tore out a sheet of paper and handed it to him. "They've been made. Consider this a proposal. We can define the particulars later."

Penelope the Planner had an answer for everything. He folded his arms rather than take the sheet of paper.

"Why are you doing this really?" he asked.

"Because." She sighed. "As much as you claim to know

what you want—" she tucked the paper back into her notebook "—you deserve better than an arranged marriage with a child as the prize."

Her smile was sad when she finished with, "And so do I."

Stepping close to him, she placed her hand on his chest, went up on her toes and placed a brief kiss on the corner of his mouth. Too brief. When he moved to hold her, she backed away.

"We'll be okay," she promised. Her eyes went to the baby's room. "Keep the furniture. You'll need it for when she visits."

Pen walked downstairs, calling out to the movers, "We're done here, guys. I'll follow in my car."

Zach's screen door shut with a bang behind her as car and truck engines turned over and pulled out of the driveway. He lowered to the top step upstairs, elbows on his knees and listened to the quiet of the house.

There was defeat in the silence.

Zachary Ferguson didn't do defeat.

He stood, in that instant deciding he'd do whatever it took to win Penelope back. To make her understand what she was walking away from. To make crystal clear that the best path for their future was a future with him in it.

He had a few billion in the bank.

Surely he could come up with something.

# Twenty-One

Pen's mother sprayed the dusting cloth with Pledge and wiped the rungs of a wooden crib. Paula and Louis had driven to Texas, claiming the road trip would do them good. They'd arrived the day after the movers left everything behind and Pen had been so glad to see them, she could've cried.

In fact, she had.

"It was yours when you were a baby," her mother said as she polished the crib. "I honestly didn't remember that we had it. Your father cleaned out the storage unit and there it was."

"Thank you, Mom."

Paula Brand abandoned her work and scooped Pen into a hug with just the right amount of pressure. Pen would have cried more if there were any tears left.

"Are you going to tell me the real reason behind you walking out on your billionaire fiancé?" Her mom held her at arm's length and waited.

Pen's lips compressed as she considered doing just that. She was willing to tell her mother a partial truth, but she couldn't bear confessing that the engagement was never real. Especially since, for Pen, her love for Zach was *very* real.

"When Zach proposed—" *both times* "—he did it out of obligation rather than love. I couldn't settle for less than his whole heart." Speaking of heart, hers gave a mournful wail. Walking out on him instead of accepting half measures was harder than she'd like to believe.

She'd been comfortable with him. She had a home, combined parenting, and yes, the money was a source of comfort, as well. But she wasn't the type of woman to let comfort and stability rule her world. If she were, she never would've left Chicago.

Hand resting on her swollen stomach, Pen thanked God that she had left Chicago. That she carried this baby in her belly and that, for all the heartache Zach had caused her, she'd finally experienced love.

"I'm sorry, sweetheart." Paula shook her head and let out an exasperated sigh. "I wish I could share a story so I could relate, but the truth is I was lucky to find your father when I was young."

Penelope's parents were high school sweethearts who married and built a business and had a baby because they were ready. Not because, in the midst of finding companionship, the birth control hadn't worked. But she didn't begrudge them their happiness.

"I'm glad you can't relate," she told her mother with a smile.

"Regardless, life is not without its struggles." Paula palmed her daughter's cheeks and returned her smile.

"I'll be fine. I've picked myself up and dusted myself off more times than I can count." Pen felt like bawling, but she was going to have to buck up. She wanted her daughter to be as proud of her as Pen was of her own mother.

Pen had done the unthinkable—she'd fallen for a guy

who was unwilling to share his heart. His world, his money, yes. But not his heart. And in the end, that was all she'd wanted.

"I have something for you." Paula went to her purse and came out with an envelope. A very flat envelope. "We had an unexpected windfall after that last house flip—"

"Mom, no." Pen backed away like her mother held a live spider by the leg rather than an envelope by the corner.

"Your dad and I want you to have this. We're going to be grandparents. We want to start our spoiling early." She shook the envelope. "I mean it."

Pen accepted it with a murmured "Thank you."

Paula rubbed her hands together. "I can't wait to go shopping for this baby!"

Pen thought of the Love & Tumble boutique, of the photographer she'd hired and the Dallas Duchess blog. She'd avoided much of the handling of her own potential PR nightmare for the last week-plus. She didn't care about her reputation—none of it was career-altering—but there were elements to handle that affected the Fergusons.

The mayor.

Stefanie.

Zach.

Penelope resolved to handle them as soon as possible.

"I don't know what to say," Pen said, holding the envelope in both hands. Blank on the outside, and who knew how much money on the inside. It didn't matter. What mattered was that her parents were supportive of her decision to raise her child apart from Zach, and that they loved her no matter what.

Anything beyond that involved items on Pen's own to-do list. Items like shared custody and drop-offs. Announcing the sex of the baby as well as confirming the breakup for the public.

"I'm going to run to work, if that's okay?" She phrased

it like a question but knew her mother's response before she gave it.

"That a girl." Paula smiled proudly.

In her downtown office, Pen sat at her desk and jotted a quick list of phone calls to make, pausing to mourn the space. She'd have to abandon her office to work at home. Start having meetings in coffee shops and her clients' offices again. She could no longer afford both Brand Consulting's shingle and her daughter.

Hand on her tummy, she closed her eyes and reminded herself of what was important.

Then she picked up her desk phone and called the mayor of Dallas.

Chase showed up in Zach's office five minutes before five o'clock, a shadow of the same hour decorating his jaw.

"You look like shit," Zach offered. "Rough day?"

Chase held his gaze but didn't cop to the status of his day, instead returning, "I'd talk. You look like your rough days had friends who came by to beat the hell out of you at night."

"Wonder why that is." Zach blinked tired eyes. He hadn't been sleeping well. Or eating well. Or thinking well, either. Suffering from a breakup would do that. And he did mean *suffering*.

"Penelope called me this afternoon," Chase said.

That snapped Zach awake. "You? Why?"

"She let me know she was announcing your amicable breakup via a blogger. Duchess something. Pen asked me to pass it on. In person."

"That was bold." No one told the mayor of Dallas what to do. "And you agreed."

"I came to tell you that and one more thing."

"Which is?" Zach asked as he typed in the URL for the Dallas Duchess. No news about himself was on the front page, but an ad for Love & Tumble caught his eye and snagged his heart.

"Penelope misses you."

Zach tore his eyes from the screen. "Did she say that?"

"She didn't have to. She sounded...sad." Chase's eyes skated over Zach's rumpled shirt. "I wonder if she looks as bad as you do. I doubt it. She's a helluva lot prettier."

No arguing that finer point.

"I can't go by your gut, Chase." But even as he said it, Zach's mind was turning. He'd been racking his brain all week for ways to win her back.

His eyes on the blog in front of him, he considered a new possibility. Maybe he could out-PR the PR maven.

"I'm not giving up," Zach told his brother.

"It's hard to know when to give up and when to dig in." Chase's tone was contemplative. He sucked in a breath and expelled such a personal comment, Zach stared at him in shock. "Like when Mimi and I unraveled. Mom and Dad were right. She wasn't a good fit for a political partner, but at the time, I struggled. I didn't know my future. I didn't know if I'd actually make it to mayor when she left. But I knew if I did, I'd be better off without her."

Despite Chase's assuredness as he recited the tale of the decay of his past relationship, Zach had been there when it happened. He remembered his older brother's state when he lost Mimi. He'd been devastated for months. Then again, devastation on Chase looked different than it did on other people. Chase had dug his heels in and honed his focus on world domination.

He'd fallen just short of the world, but he'd landed Dallas. Zach wasn't sure if his stiff-lipped older brother was a good template with which to map out his own future or not.

"The point is you need to figure out what you want your life to look like in five, ten, twenty years," Chase said. "What role does Penelope play? She's the mother of your child, but is marrying her really what's best for you? Or is the best thing for you to back away from her and let the future fall into place?"

As Chase spoke, Zach rose from his chair.

"Are you kidding me right now? This is the advice you're offering? You don't know what Pen and I were like together. When she was in my house. In my *life*." When she was settled across from him in a restaurant, laughing over her wine. Or in the doctor's office, with tears of joy shining in her eyes. Or when she'd moved out of his house with such resolve, that Zach questioned whether or not he'd imagined her every reaction beforehand.

"Simple question," Chase said in his typical ubercalm state. "She misses you. Do you miss her?"

More than anyone knew.

"Yes."

"Do you love her?" Since the inflection and volume of Chase's voice hadn't changed even a little, Zach had to let that question settle into the pit of his gut.

His churning, uncertain, fear-filled gut.

"There's your answer," Chase said. "Let her go, Zach. Love, even when it's real and lasting, isn't a sure thing. But when it's not there, you're betting on a loss. The longer you let a loveless relationship go on, the bigger that loss is."

On that note, Chase gave him a curt nod and left the office.

# Twenty-Two

Pen stepped into her building and the woman positioned at the front desk waved her over. "This came for you, Ms. Brand."

Oh, no. Not again.

Penelope pasted a smile on her face and accepted a padded envelope…and then another one.

"One more," the woman said, handing over a small box. She eyed Pen's rounded tummy. "I can carry these up if it's too much for you."

"No, I have them." The packages were awkward, especially while juggling her purse and working the elevator, but they weren't heavy.

Upstairs she dropped everything on a chair in her living room and stared at the packages in contemplation.

The return address was Love & Tumble. She'd received packages from there every day—several of them. So far, they'd been the items she'd had Zach's assistant return to the store right after they'd purchased them. Zach had tried to talk her into keeping them but of course, she hadn't. Now, one by one, or in this case *three by three*, those same items they'd returned had been showing up on her doorstep.

She opened the envelopes. One held a onesie, the other a baby blanket. The smaller box required scissors to cut the tape, so Penelope took the box to the countertop and grabbed her kitchen shears.

Inside the box, wrapped in Love & Tumble's signature shimmer-green tissue paper, was a pair of shoes. But not just any pair of shoes. Blinged out, faux fur, rhinestone encrusted high-top tennies for a girl.

Pen batted her lashes, fighting tears. This wasn't something she'd purchased prior. She and Zach had looked at this pair in the store and she'd mentioned if she had a girl, she'd *never* buy her six-hundred-dollar shoes. He'd argued that if they learned they were having a girl, those would be the *first* pair he'd buy her.

And he had.

A tear streaked Pen's cheek as she thumbed the tiny soles. Zach had been trying to buy back her affection since she left with the movers. He was being very sweet. Very thoughtful.

As the father of her child, she couldn't have picked a better man to love her baby more.

But he still didn't love *her*.

She hated how right she'd been in saying no to his proposal. He'd proposed to keep their budding family together, which was honorable, and for some women might have been enough. Still, when she imagined Zach or her marrying other people, Pen's heart ached with loss.

A swift knock at the door jolted her out of her thoughts. One glance at the clock reminded her what she already knew. This morning Stefanie had texted to ask if she could swing by tonight. Pen had texted back yes, then phoned the front desk telling them to send her up when she arrived.

She swiped the hollows of her eyes and shook off her

somber attitude, then rushed to open the door. Stef stood at the entry, her bright smile fading as soon as she got one look at Pen.

"Oh, my gosh. What happened now?" Zach's sister pushed her way into the apartment, her hands wrapping around Pen's shoulders.

Rather than explain, Pen gestured around the apartment. At the pile of boxes she'd been meaning to break down for recycling. At another pile of their contents: baby clothes and toys and blankets, taking up the length of the sofa. She lost her battle holding back tears. "Your brother mails me gifts every day."

"That jerk," Stefanie said.

Pen let out a startled laugh, but Stef didn't laugh with her.

"Has he come to see you?"

Pen shook her head. "No, but I wouldn't want him to."

"Has he called you?"

Pen shook her head again.

"Texted?" Stef asked, her voice small.

Pen confirmed with another head shake.

Stef clucked her tongue and proffered an envelope. "This came for you, and Zach handed it to me when I barged in on him at the office."

Pen took the envelope. Her name was on the front in fanciful calligraphy, addressed to the house Zach had purchased.

"How…is he?" Pen hated herself for asking, but she couldn't not ask.

"Stressed. He looks tired. Heartbroken. About like you do." At Pen's wan smile, Stef tapped the envelope. "Expensive card stock. What do you think it is?"

Pen flipped over the envelope where there was a return address in black block letters, but no name.

"Not sure." Pen tore open the back and pulled out a

sturdy white square with a vellum overlay. In gold lettering, two names stood out. Ashton Weaver and Serena Fern. "It's a wedding invitation."

Stef snatched it back and read the invite. "The actors?"

"Yep."

"Wow. I don't get starstruck often, but *wow*."

"They'll probably make it." Pen, shoulders rounded in defeat, trudged to the couch, shoved the baby stuff aside and collapsed onto a cushion. "And then I'll have to go to their twenty-fifth anniversary party knowing that two unlikely souls made it at the same time my engagement ended."

She pulled a pillow onto her lap and squeezed. Stef made room for herself and joined Pen on the couch. Pen had decided not to wallow. She'd decided to move on and pick up the pieces and focus on being the best mom *ever*. Her wounded heart had delayed those plans.

"I didn't mean to," Pen admitted around a sob.

"You didn't mean to what?" Stef's voice softened. She rubbed Pen's back and Pen realized abruptly how badly she'd needed a girlfriend to confide in. Stefanie was the exact wrong person to lean on. As Zach's sister, she shouldn't be forced to choose sides.

And yet, when Pen opened her mouth to say "Never mind," she said, "I fell in love with your stupid brother," instead.

"Chase?"

Pen let out a surprised bleat. Stef smirked.

"Chase is *stupid*. Zach is the *idiot*." But Stef's smile was one of concern when she continued rubbing Pen's back. "You love Zach. You're having my niece. He proposed. What's the problem?"

"Oh, you know. Just that he doesn't love me." Pen swiped her cheeks and sniffed. "He loves the idea of a family and us being together. We're super-compatible in bed." She sniffed. "Sorry if that's too much information," she mumbled when Stef wrinkled her nose in disgust.

"I'm trying to absorb it. I am." Stef sighed. "How can he not love you? *I* love you." After a brief pause, she added, "Do you want to marry me?"

Pen let out a watery laugh. "I'll be fine. No, I'll be great. It's hormones, you know? And there have been a lot of big changes lately. I'm sure it'll all shake out."

Pen gave Stef a reassuring nod, but when Zach's sister nodded back, it was obvious the youngest Ferguson was placating her. Pen could take the placation. What she couldn't take another second of were the tears of regret.

"Enough of that." Pen slapped her hands to her thighs. "Do you want to help me take the tags off my daughter's clothes and sort them for the laundry?"

Stef's face brightened. "That, I can gladly do." With a quick clap of her hands, she leaped off the couch, baby clothes in hand.

Laundry was a lot better than wallowing.

The baby clothes weren't working.

Zach sent package after package from Love & Tumble, and had yet to hear anything from Penelope. He'd have to move on to something else.

Something *bigger*.

He'd fill her apartment with flowers. Hire a skywriter. Buy an island…

He didn't own an island yet.

iPad on his lap, he typed *islands for sale* into the search engine as a red sports car growled to a stop at the front of his house. Yeah, *the house*. He'd sworn he'd move back into his bachelor-pad apartment, but after Pen put the final nail in the coffin of their *us* status, leaving felt like giving up.

He wasn't about to give up.

His sister stepped out of the car into morning sunshine and Zach met her at the door.

"You're up early."

A large pair of sunglasses suggested she was out late. She propped them on top of her head as she came into the house, but her eyes were clear and alert.

"I was up late," she confirmed, "but pregnant ladies don't drink, so Penelope and I indulged in cookies and tea instead." She shrugged her mouth. "Not a bad way to spend a Friday night, actually."

She was at Penelope's apartment?

"How is she?" he asked without hesitation.

"Funny, she asked the same question about you." Stefanie offered a Ferguson-family smirk. "Do you have coffee?"

"I'm working my way through a pot now." He followed Stefanie into the kitchen where she poured herself a mug and offered him a refill. He set the iPad aside and retrieved his mug. When he walked back into the kitchen, Stef was frowning down at the tablet.

"You are not going to buy an island."

"Why not?" He refilled his mug.

"Are you moving there?"

"No." Although if Pen kept ignoring him, an island would be the ideal place to live. "Maybe. I don't know. I was going to buy it for Penelope."

Stefanie scowled. "Seriously, Zach."

"Seriously, Stef." He opened his mouth to argue until it belatedly occurred to him that his sister was a woman.

He didn't have a lot of women at his disposal. He had yet to poll a woman about how to move forward with *Mission: Get Pen Back*. And God knew Chase hadn't been a lot of help.

"Is skywriting a better idea?"

"Man. This is bad." Stef gave him a pitying shake of her head.

"I can buy out every flower shop downtown. Hell, I can *buy* every flower shop downtown. Is that…a better idea?" He palmed the back of his neck and leaned a hip on the counter. He was completely out of his element. "She didn't respond to the baby clothes."

"I'm not sure this is a situation you can buy yourself out of, Zach. If you didn't have billions in the bank, what would you do?"

He drank his coffee. Partially to buy time and partially because the caffeine might help him think.

"If you couldn't *name a planet* after her, what would you do?"

"A planet. Hand me that iPad."

Stef narrowed her eyes in warning.

"I'm kidding. I feel like you're dancing around a point."

"Why are you doing all of this?"

"I'm winning her back." *Duh.* Wasn't that obvious? "We're good together and as soon as I can get her to stop ignoring the truth…"

"Which is?"

He blinked at his sister. What the hell was that supposed to mean?

"Why are you good together, Zach?" she pressed.

He frowned. "What do you mean *why*?"

"How do you feel about her?"

He let out an uncomfortable laugh and pushed away from the counter. "How do I feel… That's obvious, isn't it? I want her around. I want to raise our daughter together."

Stefanie sat down at the breakfast bar and pilfered a cookie from an open bag. "Why?" she asked around a bite.

"Pen's fun. She gets me." And in the bedroom? Forget it. There wasn't a high enough rating for how explosive they were when they came together.

"What else?" Stef cocked her head.

"I…miss her." That hurt to admit.

"And?"

"And what?" He put down his mug before he sloshed hot coffee on his arm. Flattening both hands on the bar, he bent to look his sister in the eyes. "Spell it out."

"Sorry." Stef polished off her cookie and dusted her hands together, not the least bit sorry. "Can't. This is heart stuff not head stuff, and Lord only knows what you're feeling in there. Do you have feelings?"

She pretended to study the ceiling as she contemplatively chewed.

"I have too many feelings. I'm drowning in feelings! Can't you see that? I'm willing to turn over my entire life. To get married!"

"You were married to a crazy person last year. Why is Pen different?"

"That was…" He swallowed thickly, on the verge of admitting the truth for the first time ever. "That was a test."

"A test *marriage*?"

"A test to make sure I could marry and it could mean nothing." Damn. He hadn't meant to be *that* honest.

"So marrying Pen would be nothing?" his sister asked gently.

"Marrying Pen would mean everything." That same jittery fear he felt when he spoke to Chase about her returned, spreading through his chest like wildfire.

Stef waited for him to say more. Could he? Could he admit what was quaking in his gut? What was making his head spin?

"She's…the mother of my child," he started. Lamely. "There's more."

Chin propped in hand, Stef waited.

"She's…" He closed his eyes and then reopened them. Screw it. The truth was obvious to Stef, so he might as well tell her what she already knew. "I'm in love with her."

Stef burst off the stool and thrust both arms into the air. "Yesssss!" She strangled him with a hug.

He smiled against her hair, and embraced his sister. His chest filled to the brim with a feeling of *right*. That ball-zinging surety that had been eluding him—or maybe he'd been denying it for some time now.

He just as quickly deflated.

The sad reality was that he was in love with Penelope and she wanted nothing to do with him.

"She'll never come back to you if you keep showering her with gifts. You have to make a big statement," Stef said. "And trust me, I want her back almost as much as you do." Stef was on the move, her hand lashed around Zach's wrist. "There has to be some clue in this house as to how to go about getting her back."

"She took everything that was hers out of this house," he said as he allowed Stef to drag him room to room. He followed her up the stairs where she made the same sad assessment he had for days in a row.

There was no sign of Penelope here.

Other than the baby's room, it was like she hadn't been here at all.

Stef turned from the Dallas Cowboys decorations Zach hadn't bothered taking down. He'd meant to, but again, that felt like giving up.

He expected his sister to shrug and state that he was a lost cause, but instead a slow grin spread across her lips.

She grabbed his arm and gave him a shake. "I figured it out. I know how you can win her back."

# Twenty-Three

Now that the other bedroom in her apartment housed a crib and a changing table, and Pen had let her office go, she'd taken to working from the sofa. She spread her planner, cell phone and laptop on the coffee table: command central. It was perfect, really, since she was only a few yards away from the coffeepot she couldn't wait to utilize again, and the bathroom.

Okay, so it wasn't perfect.

She missed her office. She needed a designated space. Once her daughter was born, she'd be home fulltime—Pen had almost convinced herself that working from home was the best-case scenario.

Until she went mad from being housebound. Then she'd have to…she didn't know what.

At least she'd landed a new account on Monday. Bridget Baxter, a chirpy, adorable blonde had requested Pen meet her for coffee. Bridget had been referred by Serena, and had a little PR problem of her own. Pen learned that Bridget, who co-managed the Dallas Cowboys, had had a one-night stand with one of the players. She was worried he'd ruin her reputation with the team, and she didn't want to lose her high-up position. Bridget explained she'd worked hard to prove she was qualified.

Pen could *so* relate to having her reputation ruined by a man. She could also understand how Bridget had blindly followed her heart and had wound up at a destination she hadn't foreseen. Pen didn't hesitate accepting the job.

A job that smacked of her recently annihilated relationship, but also gave her something better to focus on than attempting to heal her heart, which had a million tiny lacerations.

Or maybe she was being dramatic.

The reminder for Bridget's appointment popped up on the laptop screen. Pen needed to leave soon if she expected to arrive at the stadium on time.

She'd given a lot of thought to Bridget's situation. How to best utilize the media, if at all. The more she turned it over, the angrier she became. Why was it up to Bridget to save her job? The guy she slept with certainly wasn't in danger of being ousted from the team because he slept with an executive.

It was all so unfair.

*Life* was unfair.

The team was practicing today, which was why Bridget wanted to meet there. That was where her former beau would be, and she wanted to pull him in on the conversation if needed.

After winding around a bunch of corridors and walking into the wrong office, Pen stopped a coach-looking guy wearing a cap and holding a clipboard, and asked for her client.

"Bridget Baxter?" he repeated, regarding Pen like she'd sprouted a horn.

"We have an appointment."

"She's practicing on the field." He shook his head. "You can follow me if you want."

She followed, her head held high. If Bridget was getting this much disrespect from the coach, Pen could imagine the uphill climb she'd have if everyone found out Bridget had slept with a guy on the team.

Determination propelled her steps out into the sticky weather where teammates and cheerleaders dotted the field.

This kind of unfairness wouldn't stand. Pen would make sure Bridget saw justice. She scanned the crowd for the tiny blonde. Ho boy. There were a *sea* of blondes in cheerleader uniforms and not a single pencil skirt in the mix.

Then one of the blondes separated from the crowd and shot Pen a wide grin.

Bridget.

Wearing a cheerleader uniform.

*What?*

"She's here!" Bridget shouted. In a blur of blue and silver, the cheerleaders formed a line on the field. The guys didn't stop practice, but a few of them looked at her and smiled.

Bridget bopped over to stand in front of Pen. "Sorry for the subversion. It was his plan. But I did have fun playing a corporate mogul." With a wink and a buoyant giggle, Bridget ran back to her girls.

"Whose plan?" Pen asked, confused.

"Give me a Z!" Bridget called out, and the cheerleaders echoed with, "Z!" What followed was an *A*, a *C*, and an *H*.

With each letter, Pen felt her knees weaken.

"What's that spell?" Bridget called. In answer, the cheerleaders parted, pom-poms swishing, and a tall, blond man wearing a tuxedo emerged.

Zach's hair had been recently trimmed, and his sexy dimple was in full force. Talk about input overload. The sun, the cheering, the crash of football players in the back-

ground, and in the center of it all, the very man she'd been
trying to put in her rearview mirror.

"Penelope Brand," he said, looking confident and cool,
and…different from before. There was sureness in each
step he took toward her. Certainty in the way he dismissed
the cheerleaders with a "Thanks, ladies."

"What are you doing?" Her voice was cautious for a
very good reason. If he'd gone through this trouble, it was
because he was making a gesture of some sort. One that
didn't involve sending the UPS truck to her building every
single day.

And if he asked her again to share his life with him, she
didn't trust herself to tell him no. If nothing had changed
in his heart, then she couldn't allow anything to change
in hers.

He lifted her hand, the hand where her engagement ring
used to sit. She'd left it on Zach's dresser the day she went
with the movers to the house. She couldn't bear to look at
it on her hand when she knew the truth behind it.

That the love she felt for Zach had ultimately not been
returned.

It'd all been a ruse.

"A long time ago," he said, "I made a rule to never get
hurt again."

Oh, my God, he was doing this…right here. Right now.

"Zach, please."

"You asked about Lonna. Do you want to hear the rest
or not?"

She swallowed around a lump forming in her throat, curiosity and hope—so much hope it made her head spin—
at a peak.

She nodded. He dipped his chin and continued.

"After I proposed to Lonna and she told me in no uncertain terms that she couldn't take me seriously, I swore I'd
never fall in love again. Avoiding love was the only path-

way to happiness. The only path to a fulfilled life. Or so I thought. Then I met you."

She couldn't look away from his earnest green eyes—from the sincerity in them.

"I love our daughter, Penelope, but you have to understand something." He gave her fingers a gentle squeeze. "I love her because of how much I love you."

Pen froze, eyes wide, mouth slightly ajar. Did she hear him right? She shook her head, refusing to hope. Refusing to believe.

"You're…you're… That's not true," she finished on a whisper.

"I'm not attached physically to our baby girl the way you are, Pen," he stated. "The *only* way I could feel this much love and devotion for her is because I felt it for you first. I've been in denial about this for a long time. Since the moment I proposed at my brother's birthday party."

She blinked.

"Even then, I knew." He tugged her close, locking an arm around her lower back. Between them, her swollen belly pressed against his torso.

"I love you, Penelope Brand. I'm sorry I bullied you into everything. Staying when you didn't want to stay. Moving in with me when you didn't want to give up your place. Proposing without confessing how I felt about you. It was a childish way to get what I wanted—you—without putting my heart on the line. I take it all back. I don't want you to marry me."

He didn't? She blinked, confused. That wasn't where she saw this speech headed.

*"Unless,"* he added with a cocky smile, "you love me, too." He lifted one thick eyebrow and when she didn't respond right away, some of that certainty bled from his expression.

He wasn't sure how she felt.

Because she'd never told him.

She'd been as guilty as he was about not sharing. She'd never given him the chance to know how she felt about him. So she'd tell him now.

"I love you so much I can't imagine my life without you." She curled her hand around one of his. "And believe me, I've been trying."

His grin was cunning, wicked with intent and promises to come. "In that case…"

He rested his teeth on his bottom lip and let out a sharp whistle. Behind him, in a flurry of movement, the cheerleaders reformed a line and held up giant white cards with letters that spelled *Marry Me?*

Zach made a circling motion with his finger and a cute redheaded cheerleader at the end flipped her card—a question mark—so that it was an exclamation point instead.

Zach faced Pen, who dropped her purse on the ground at her feet, wrapped her arms around his neck and pushed to her toes.

He sealed her mouth with his.

Behind them, cheers and whistles, and low male hollers of approval, lifted on the air as Pen allowed herself to sink into Zach's embrace.

Into the promise of his words, especially the three that meant more than anything.

He loved her.

As much as she loved him.

# Epilogue

"Penelope told me she hated me," Zach announced. "Over and over."

His father, sister and brother regarded him in shocked concern. His mother, on the other hand, stood from her seat in the waiting room and let out a loud chuckle.

"Women who give birth always say that. Remember, Rider?"

"Three times," his father confirmed, standing next to his wife. "Three times I went through the birthing process at her side and she hated me every time." He pointed at Chase. "Mostly with you, though. Since you were first."

Chase and Stefanie stood from their chairs, Stef ribbing him about how it was no surprise he was the cause of the most strife of the three of them.

Zach's smile emerged—so big, it hurt his face. It'd been a relatively fast labor, but a long night. "Ready to meet her?"

Stef and his mom shrieked happy sounds, and his father and brother didn't hold back their widest grins. Zach shook his head at their attire. "I hate that she is meeting you all dressed like this, though."

"Ugly sweaters are tradition!" Stef argued, her glowing-nose-reindeer sweater one for the books.

He led his family into the room, and a collective gasp lifted on the air when they spotted the pink-wrapped bundle resting on Penelope's chest.

Pen's eyes were drooped, her hair tangled. Her own ugly sweater tossed aside on a chair with the rest of her clothing in favor of the hospital gown she now wore. She was the most beautiful sight Zach had ever seen.

Well. Second to his daughter.

"What's her name?" Elle cooed as she scooped her granddaughter into her arms. "Can you finally tell us?"

"Olivia Edna," Penelope announced with a smile. "After my grandmother, and Zach's."

His father and siblings bent over Olivia in his mother's arms. Even when handed off, Zach's daughter slept soundly.

"Your mom and dad are on their way from the airport," Zach told Pen, swiping her hair from her forehead.

Her eyes drooped sleepily, but her smile was everlasting.

He bent and placed a kiss to her forehead. "You did it."

Her pale blue eyes opened and stabbed him in the heart. How had he ever denied loving her when she was his everything?

"*We* did it," she corrected, giving him credit he hadn't earned.

A gurgle came from Olivia and she fussed in Chase's arms. Those years of holding and kissing babies must have paid off, because the mayor of Dallas bounced and shushed her and a moment later, she cooed.

Chase shot his brother a cocky smile.

"I love you," Pen whispered to Zach, reaching for his arm with her hand—a hand that boasted both a wedding band and an engagement ring. They hadn't waited. They hadn't wanted to.

Zach kissed her lips, lingering a moment. "I love you."

She played with the longer hair at his nape, in need of a trim, and whispered two words that made Zach more grateful than he'd ever been in his life.

"Merry Christmas."

Olivia was the perfect gift. Better than every wrapped present they'd left piled in his parents' living room to rush Penelope to the hospital. Better than the moment Zach spotted Penelope in the jazz club and wondered if she'd let him sample her mouth.

Better, he mused, than the moment she vowed to be with him and he with her, until death do they part.

"Uh-oh, she's had it with us," Stef announced, placing Zach's daughter in his arms.

He adjusted her so that she sank comfortably in the crook of his elbow. Looking down at the faint sweep of blond hair, puckered rosebud lips and tiny fisted hands, Zach's heart filled to capacity—who knew there was more room in there?

"Hey, Livvie," he said, his voice choked with emotion. "Merry Christmas to you, too."

* * * * *

# LET'S TALK
## Romance

For exclusive extracts, competitions
and special offers, find us online:

f facebook.com/millsandboon

⊚ @millsandboonuk

🐦 @millsandboon

Or get in touch on 0844 844 1351*

For all the latest titles coming soon, visit
millsandboon.co.uk/nextmonth

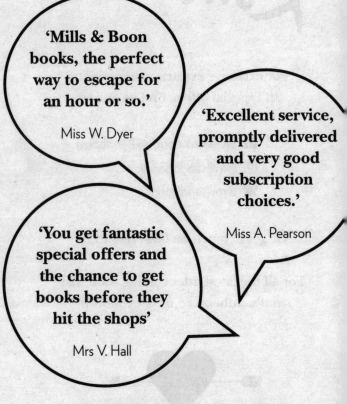